101
AVENUE
HENRI-MARTIN

Also by Régine Deforges

THE BLUE BICYCLE

101 AVENUE HENRI-MARTIN

The Blue Bicycle Book Two

Régine Deforges

Translated from the French by Ros Schwartz

W.H. ALLEN · LONDON
1986

First published in France by Editions Ramsay 1983
First published in Great Britain by W.H. Allen 1986

Set by Phoenix Photosetting, Chatham, Kent.
Printed and bound in Great Britain by
Mackays of Chatham Ltd, Chatham, Kent
for the Publishers, W.H. Allen & Co. Plc
44 Hill Street, London W1X 8LB

British Library Cataloguing in Publication Data

Reforges, Régine
  101 Avenue Henri-Martin: the blue bicycle: book two.
  I. Title   II. 101 Avenue Henri-Martin. *English*
  843'.914[F]   PQ2664.D4/
ISBN 0–491–03932–8

To my daughter, Camille

Acknowledgements

The author would like to thank the following for their collaboration, often unknowingly given: Paul Allard, Henri Amouroux, Pierre Becamps, M. R. Bordes, Richard Chapon, Colette, E. H. Cookridge, Jean-Louis Crémieux-Brilhac, Jacques Debû-Bridel, Jacques Delarue, Jacques Delperrié de Bayac, David Diamant, Claude Ducloux, Georgette Elgey, Jacky Fray, Henri Frenay, Jean Galtier-Boissière, Alice Giroud, Richard Grossmann, Jean Guéhenno, Georges Guingouin, Philippe Henriot, Joseph Kessel, Jean Lafourcade, Claude Mauriac, François Mauriac, Henri Michel, Jean Moulin, Robert O. Paxton, Gilles Perrault, Eric Picquet-Wicks, Edouard de Pomiane, le colonel Rémy, Maurice Sachs, Georges Sadoul, Régine Saux, Simone Savariaud, Michel Slitinsky, Lucien Steinberg, Geneviève Thieuleu, Pierre Uteau, Pierre Veilletet, Dominique Venner, Pierre Wiazemsky.

Summary of Book One (The Blue Bicycle)

It was early in the autumn of 1939 and Pierre and Isabelle Delmas were living happily on their wine growing estate in Montillac near Bordeaux with their three daughters, Françoise, Léa and Laure, and Ruth, their faithful governess. Léa was seventeen and very beautiful. She had inherited her father's love of the land and the vineyards where she had grown up in the company of Mathias Fayard, the son of the head storeman. He was her playmate and was secretly in love with her.

On the 1st September 1939, at Roches-Blanches, the estate of the d'Argilat family, friends of the Delmas's, there was a party to celebrate the betrothal of Laurent d'Argilat and his gentle cousin, Camille. Léa's aunts and uncles were there with their children: there was Luc Delmas the lawyer and his children, Philippe, Corinne and Pierre; then there was Adrien Delmas, the Dominican monk who had a reputation for being something of a revolutionary. Léa's admirers Jean and Raoul Lefèvre were at the party too. Léa was the only person who was not in a festive mood on this occasion: she was in love with Laurent and could not bear the idea of his engagement. She met François Tavernier, an elegant, cynical, rather ambiguous character who seemed very sure of himself. Out of spite, Léa became engaged to Camille's brother, Claude d'Argilat. The same day, war broke out and there was a general mobilization.

In despair, Léa attended Camille and Laurent's wedding where she was taken ill. She was treated by the family doctor, Doctor Blanchard. She postponed the date of her wedding but her fiancé was killed at the beginning of the war. Léa went to Paris to stay with her great-aunts, Lisa and Albertine de Montpleynet. There she met Camille and François Tavernier again, for whom she felt a mixture of hatred and attraction. She made the acquaintance of

7

Raphaël Mahl, a homosexual writer, an opportunist and rather disturbing character, and of Sarah Mulstein, a young German Jewish woman who was fleeing from the Nazis.

Laurent left for the Front and Léa promised she would look after Camille, who was pregnant and in poor health. In spite of Camille's delicate condition, she and Léa fled the Occupation and joined the general exodus on the roads. Conditions were hazardous and there were frequent air-raids. Chance had it that the distraught Léa bumped into Mathias Fayard who, for a brief moment, gave her warmth and affection. She also met François Tavernier who initiated her in the pleasures of physical love. The signing of the Armistice made it possible for the two women to reach the Bordeaux region where little Charles was born, with the help of a German officer, Frederic Hanke.

But on the day of their homecoming, they found the household in mourning. Léa's beloved mother Isabelle had been killed in an air-raid. Her father gradually lapsed into insanity, while on the estate, which had been requisitioned by the Germans, a precarious existence beset with hardship and difficulties went on. Léa, Camille and little Charles met Laurent at the home of the Debrays who had been hiding him since his escape from Germany. He was about to go underground. Rifts set in, dividing families and villages: there were the staunch Pétain supporters on the one hand, and, on the other, those who believed in the fight for freedom. Léa instinctively belonged to the latter. Unaware of the danger, she acted as a messenger for the underground fighters. But her sister Françoise was in love with one of the occupying Germans, Lieutenant Kramer. Mathias Fayard maintained a stormy relationship with Léa which was complicated by the fact that his father had his eye on the estate. Spurned by Léa, he volunteered to go and work in Germany.

Exhausted from the responsibilities weighing on her shoulders, Léa returned to Paris to stay with her aunts, Lisa and Albertine de Montpleynet. Her time was divided between carrying messages for the Resistance and being wined and dined in occupied Paris. In the company of François Tavernier, she tried to forget the war for a brief moment at Maxim's, L'Ami Louis' or at the little clandestine restaurant belonging to the Andrieus. She also saw Sarah Mulstein who opened her eyes to what was going on in the concen-

tration camps, and Raphaël Mahl who had become a collaborator of the most despicable type. She satisfied her lust for life in the arms of François Tavernier. But Montillac needed her: she had to cope single-handed with the shortage of money, Fayard's greed, her father's insanity and the threats hanging over the d'Argilat family. In the underground cellars of Toulouse, thanks to Father Adrien Delmas, she met up with Laurent and abandoned herself to him. On her return, she was interrogated by Lieutenant Dohse and Commissioner Poinsot. She was only saved through the intervention of her Uncle Luc. Françoise ran away when her father refused to give his permission for her to marry Lieutenant Kramer. That was the death of Pierre Delmas. Father Adrien, Uncle Luc, Laurent and François Tavernier met briefly for his funeral. After a last embrace, fragrant with the smell of Montillac soil, Léa found herself facing her precarious future alone with Camille, Charles and the aged Ruth.

Prologue

It was during the night of 20th to 21st September 1942 that the weather, which had been very hot until then, changed to cold, wet and windy. The bad weather blew across the Gironde estuary and up the Garonne river.

All that summer, violent storms, sometimes with hail, had been causing concern among the wine growers. It looked as if it was going to be a bad year.

The clock of the Saint-André cathedral struck four.

In their cell in Fort Hâ, Prosper Guillou and his son Jean were awakened by a violent knocking at the door. In the dark they took turns to relieve themselves then sat on their pallets to wait for the light and the beaker of ditchwater that was supposed to be coffee. Jean was thinking of his wife Yvette, interned in the Boudet Barracks. He had heard no word from her since that day in July when the Gestapo had burst into his farmhouse, Les Violettes, in Thors, at five o'clock in the morning. He relived the arrest of his parents and that elderly couple of communist activists, Albert and Elizabeth Dupeyron, who had come to fetch weapons for the clandestine Bordeaux group.

Gabriel Fleureau, a cabinet maker, let out a cry and woke up with a start. It was like that every night, since the interrogation sessions he had been subjected to at the hands of the two brutes from Commissioner Poinsot's Brigade. They had meticulously broken all the fingers on his right hand. He had not spoken. He derived all his courage from the love he felt for Aurore, the young girl who regularly delivered leaflets to Monsieur

11

Cadou's furniture shop on the Quai de la Salinière for him and Berhgua to distribute. He was unaware that his friend had been arrested. He gingerly moved his bruised fingers.

On the neighbouring pallet, René Antoine arose with a groan. He was haunted by the image of little Michel, aged ten, stretching his arms towards him crying: 'Papa!', as he was taken away and imprisoned with his mother, Hélène, in the Boudet Barracks. They must have been denounced for the Germans to be able to discover the cache of weapons hidden at the bottom of his garden in Bègles.

René Castéra agreed with him. His father, his mother and his brother Gabriel had been arrested on the 8th of July and then he had been arrested on the 14th. For two years, the family had been sheltering Jews and members of the underground, and helping the families of those who had been imprisoned. Like René Antoine, he had no news of his family.

In another cell on the ground floor, Albert Dupeyron comforted Camille Perdriau who was only twenty years old. That helped him not to think too much about his young wife Elizabeth who had been arrested at the same time as him.

Alexandre Pateau clenched his fists at the recollection of the brutal treatment of his wife Yvonne in front of little four-year-old Stéphane. They were both members of the Resistance and they had been taken by surprise at their home in Saint-André-du-Cognac. First they had been taken to Cognac and now they were in Fort Hâ.

As for Raymond Bierge, he was wondering who the swine was that had denounced his wife Félicienne and himself for hiding printing equipment in their house. So long as the child's grandmother looks after him properly!

Jean Vignaux, from Langon, was astonished that he could remember the young girl his best friends Raoul and Jean Lefèvre were in love with so clearly, the ravishing Léa Delmas.

12

Last time he had seen her, she had been pedalling along the road leading to Montillac, her hair flying in the wind.

In the cells, the lights went on one by one. The prisoners blinked and slowly got up.
Since the previous evening, they had known.

The wind had been howling all night long, blowing in under the doors and between the loose boards of the camp at Mérignac, bringing in a little fresh air to the men lying on the uncomfortable metal beds which the sagging straw mattresses barely covered. It was five o'clock in the morning. The prisoners were not asleep.

Lucien Valena, from Cognac, was thinking about his three children, especially little Serge, just turned seven, who was too spoiled by his wife Margot. How brutally the Germans had flung him into the truck! Where were they now?

Gabriel Castéra was thinking about his father, Albert, whom he had embraced a few hours earlier, when they had come to fetch him to take him to a hut a little apart from the others. He could not bear the memory of tears running down the old man's cheeks. Luckily, there was René, his elder brother.

Jean Lapeyrade felt his stomach contract when he looked at René de Oliveira and the nameless young boy who had played the mouth organ for part of the night to hide his fear. How young they were! 'Berthe, where are you?'

'Don't bring the child up in a spirit of revenge and hatred,' Franc Sanson had cried out to his wife.

An unusual commotion reigned in the camp. The door was suddenly flung open and Raymond Rabeaux could see the trucks of the Wehrmacht surrounded by dozens of infantrymen in their greyish-green uniforms. He was surprised by the cold damp air. It was still very dark. The hurricane lamps held by the guards were reflected in large puddles of water.

Some Germans were unlimbering a machine gun opposite the door. The mouth organ had stopped. Since the previous day, they had known.

Director Rousseau's assistant, who had been talking to a German officer, started walking towards the barracks.

'Come out when your name is called. Don't keep these gentlemen waiting, hurry up. Espagnet, Jougourd, Castéra, Noutari, Portier, Valina, Chardin, Meiller, Voignet, Eloi . . .'

One by one, the prisoners filed out and, pushed by the soldiers, lined up, turned up the collars of their jackets and pulled down their berets or caps.

'Move, get into the trucks. Jonet, Brouillon, Meunier, Puech, Moulias . . .'

Franc Sanson, with the agility of his twenty-two years, jumped first.

In the camp, a kind of murmur arose. At the windows of each hut the prisoners stood, mysteriously forewarned. One, then two, then ten, then a hundred, then a thousand began to hum the Internationale. A huge rumbling swelled their chests and escaped in the direction of those who were leaving, maintaining their courage and their dignity. The mud, the rain, the barking of the guards and even their fear was obliterated by the magnificent tune, full of hope.

It was 7 o'clock in the morning. The trucks which had left the Boudet Barracks, Fort Hâ and the Mérignac camp were driving along the road to Souges. As the convoy passed, women crossed themselves and men took off their hats. At the entrance to the military camp, the trucks slowed down. Inside, the prisoners were lost in their own thoughts, indifferent to the four soldiers who were pointing guns at them. The trucks jolted down the furrowed track throwing the men against each other.

The trucks stopped. The soldiers drew back the tarpaulin, lowered the ramps and jumped down on to the sand.

'Schnell . . . schnell . . . Aussteigen . . .'[1]

[1] Quick . . . move . . . get down

The prisoners huddled in a corner, staring at each other and mechanically counting. Seventy. There were seventy of them . . . Seventy men who had known they were going to die since the previous day.

Following an attack in Paris on a German officer, Karl Oberg, the head of the SS and of the Police, and Helmuth Knochen had demanded a list of one hundred and twenty hostages from the Vichy government. Forty-six prisoners from the camps of Compiègne and Romainville satisfied the required conditions. Wilhelm Dohse, of the Bordeaux Gestapo, completed the list.

'Gabriel!'
'René!'
The two Castéra brothers fell into each other's arms. They had both so hoped to be the only one to die.
A tubby officer stood in front of the hostages and read something; the sentence, no doubt. It made no difference. Suddenly a young voice rose above the German's, singing the French National Anthem:
'*Allons enfants de la patrie . . .*
le jour de gloire est arrivé . . . contre nous de la tyrannie. . .
l'étendard sanglant est levé . . .'[1]

Tentative at first, the song burst out in the face of the enemy. They did not understand the terrible meaning but knew that these words could turn a meek flock into a horde crying revenge.
'*Entendez-vous dans nos campagnes,*
rugir ces féroces soldats . . .'[2]

Every five yards was a post. There were ten along a bank. Ten men stepped forward and placed themselves of their own

[1] Come, children of the fatherland,
The day of glory has dawned
Against tyranny,
The bloody flag is raised . . .
[2] Can you hear, in our countryside
these fierce soldiers roar . . .

15

accord in front of the posts. They were tied to the posts, they refused to be blindfolded. A trembling elderly priest blessed them. The firing squad took their places. An order rang out . . . the first round was fired . . . as the bullets hit them, the bodies jerked and crumpled . . .

The voices wavered for a split second then continued all the louder that rainy morning.

'*Aux armes, citoyens . . .*'[1]

Seventy times the final blow was dealt.

The bodies of the victims were thrown into a huge grave dug out behind the bank.

The rain stopped. A pale sun shone over the sand quarry. The smell of mushrooms and pine mingled with that of gunpowder. At the foot of the posts, the blood was reflected in puddles of water seeping slowly into the sand.

The soldiers set off again, their mission accomplished. It was nine o'clock in the morning, on the Souges moor, near Bordeaux, on the 21st September 1942.

[1] Citizens, take up your guns . . .

16

Chapter 1

After Pierre Delmas's death, his sister, Bernadette Bouchardeau, had tried to take over the running of the house. She was obviously full of good intentions, but it was also clear that she was completely unable to manage an estate like Montillac.

Sitting at her brother's desk she was scattering papers everywhere, moaning to Camille d'Argilat, who had offered to help her:

'Dear God, what will become of us? I can't make head or tail of these figures. I'll have to ask Fayard, he's the manager of the estate.'

'Why don't you take a rest, madame, I'll see if I can make any sense of them.'

'Thank you, Camille, dear, you're very kind,' she said, moving away from the desk. 'Léa ought to pull herself together,' she added, removing her spectacles. 'I'm suffering as well, but I'm making an effort.'

Camille hid a smile.

'You must be much stronger than she is.'

'I must be,' agreed Bernadette Bouchardeau.

'What a stupid woman,' thought Camille.

'Good night, child. Don't stay up too late.'

The door closed noiselessly behind her. Camille heard her heavy footfall on the stairs, the creaking of the tenth stair, then the sleeping household was silent once more. The stillness was occasionally ruffled as a gust of cold November wind made the walls shudder and the flames in the fireplace flicker. Camille was standing in the centre of the warm room, staring blankly at the fire. Suddenly a log split open and sent a shower of sparks and embers on to the rug. The young woman jumped and rushed to get the tongs to pick up the firebrands. At the same time she threw a piece of dead vine into the hearth and it flared and crackled merrily.

She drew her dressing gown tighter round her and sat down again at Pierre Delmas's desk.

Camille worked long into the night, only raising her head to rub the back of her aching neck.

The clock struck three.

'Are you still up!' exclaimed Léa, coming into the room.

'You are too, so it seems,' replied Camille with an affectionate smile.

'I came to get a book. I can't sleep.'

'Did you take the tablets Doctor Blanchard gave you?'

'Yes, but all they do is make me dozy during the day.'

'Then tell him and he'll give you something else. You must sleep.'

'I wish I could, but at the same time I'm afraid. As soon as I fall asleep, the man from Orléans appears, his face covered in blood. He walks towards me . . . tries to grab me and says: "Why did you kill me, you little bitch, you little whore? Come, my pretty, I'll show you how good it is to make love with a corpse. I bet you love that, don't you? Filth, you love rotting carcasses, you . . ."'

'Stop it!' cried Camille, shaking her by the shoulders. 'Stop it!'

Léa looked completely distraught as she wiped her hand across her brow, took a few steps forward and collapsed on the old leather settee.

'You've no idea . . . it's so awful, especially when he says: "That's enough playing about. Now let's go and find your father: he's waiting for us with his friends, the worms . . ."'

'Shut up . . .'

'". . . and your dear mummy." Then I follow him, calling my mother.' Camille knelt beside her and took her in her arms, cradling her the way she cradled her son, little Charles, when a nightmare sent him running to her bed, screaming.

'There, calm down. Don't think about it. We both killed him. Remember . . . I fired at him first. I thought he was dead.'

18

'True, but it was I, and I alone who killed him.'

'You had no choice. It was him or us. Your Uncle Adrien said that in your shoes, he would have done exactly the same.'

'He only said that to make me feel better. Can you imagine him, a priest, killing anybody?'

'Yes, if he had to.'

'That's what Laurent and François Tavernier said. But I'm sure Adrien is incapable of such a thing.'

'That's enough of that. I've finished sorting out your father's accounts. The situation isn't exactly rosy. I don't understand Fayard's methods at all. If we are careful, we ought to be able to manage.'

'How can we be any more careful?' she exclaimed, getting up. 'We only eat meat once a week as it is, and what meat! If there were fewer of us, we might manage, but . . .'

Camille bowed her head.

'I know we're a burden on you. One day I'll pay you back every penny you've spent on us.'

'Don't be stupid, that's not what I meant!'

'I know,' said Camille sadly.

'Oh, no! Don't look at me like that. I can't say anything in front of you.'

'Forgive me.'

'There's nothing for me to forgive. You do your share of the work . . . and mine as well at the moment.'

Léa drew back the double curtains. The moonlight cast its pale glow on the gravel courtyard while the wind was trying to rip the last leaves off the big linden tree. 'Do you think the war will last much longer?' she asked. 'Everybody seems to think it's natural that the Vichy government should collaborate with Germany . . .'

'No, Léa, not everybody. Look at the people around us. You know at least ten people who are carrying on the struggle . . .'

'What's ten or so compared to the hundreds of thousands who shout every day: "Long live Pétain!"'

'Soon there'll be hundreds of us, then thousands, who say no.'

'I don't think so. All they think about is getting enough to eat and not being cold any more.'

19

'How can you say that? The French are still in a state of shock over the defeat, but their confidence in Pétain is dwindling. Even Fayard was saying to me the other day: "Madame Camille, don't you think the old boy's going a bit too far?", and yet Fayard . . .'

'He wanted to make a fool of you. I know him, he's a crafty old so-and-so. He wants to know what you think so that he can use it later, when he needs to. WORK, FAMILY, and the FATHERLAND really means something to him.'

'To me too, but not the same thing.'

'Be careful. His sole aim is to get his hands on Montillac. He'll stop at nothing. What's more, he's convinced his son Mathias went away because of me.'

'He did, didn't he?'

'It's not true,' cried Léa, angrily. 'Quite the opposite, I tried to stop him. It's not my fault if he didn't want to listen, if he preferred to go to Germany to earn some money, rather than stay and work at Montillac.'

'That's going a bit far, darling. You know very well why he left . . .'

'No!'

'Because he loved you.'

'Well, that's nice! If he loved me, as you say, he should have stayed here and helped me and stopped his father stealing from us.'

'He could also have joined General de Gaulle. But I understand why he left.'

'You're too tolerant.'

'Don't you believe it. I understand because it's a question of love . . . I don't know what I would have done in the same situation as Mathias or Françoise . . . Perhaps I'd have done the same thing.'

'You're talking nonsense. You'd never have let a German knock you up like poor old Françoise.'

'Don't talk about your sister like that.'

'She isn't my sister any more. It's her fault that papa died.'

'That's not true. Doctor Blanchard said his heart had been weak for years, and in spite of your mother's pleas, he always refused to take care of himself.'

'I don't want to know. If she hadn't left, he'd still be alive,' cried Léa, burying her face in her hands, her shoulders racked by sobs.

Camille repressed the urge to comfort her friend. How could Léa be so unaware of other people's feelings?

'That's what makes her so strong,' Laurent always said. 'She can only see the present. She leaps first and asks questions later. Not because she's lacking in intelligence, but through an excess of vitality.'

Léa restrained herself from stamping her foot as she used to do as a child. She turned to Camille.

'Stop looking at me like that. Go to bed, you look terrible.'

'You're right, I'm tired. You ought to get some sleep too. Good night.'

Camille went over to kiss her. Léa remained passive and did not return the kiss. The young woman said nothing as she left the room.

Furious with Camille and with herself, Léa put another piece of dead vine in the fire, took the tartan blanket in which she used to love to wrap her father from a chest in the library, switched off the light and lay down on the divan.

It was not long before the flickering of the flames sent her to sleep.

Since her father's death, Léa had often spent the night in this dearly loved room, the only place where her familiar ghosts did not come and torment her.

Léa was awakened by the cold. 'I must remember to bring my quilt down,' she said to herself. She drew the curtains and had the strange feeling that she was in the clouds, the fog was so thick. But she could sense, behind this shroud, the presence of the sun. 'It's going to be fine,' she thought. She deftly rekindled the fire and stood there for a moment warming herself. Mechanically she counted the chimes as the clock struck the hour. Eleven. Eleven! It was eleven o'clock! Why had they let her sleep so late?

In the vast kitchen hearth, the dry vine shoots made a big blaze whose warm glow lit up the huge room darkened by the fog which would not lift. On the table with its blue oilskin cloth was her empty bowl and a piece of brioche wrapped in her napkin. With a greedy gesture, Léa buried her nose in the sweet-smelling bread. 'Sidonie made this,' she thought. On a corner of the stove was the old blue enamel coffee pot. Léa poured herself a cup of the brew which resembled coffee only in name. Luckily the milk disguised the flavour.

While she ate, she wondered: 'What day is it for us to be eating brioche?' The answer was provided when she looked up and saw the number 11 written large. The 11th of November . . . It was Sidonie's way of celebrating the end of the Great War. Léa smiled a grim smile and shrugged. When would they see the end of this war? It had been going on for more than two years. Today, the 11th of November 1942, France was still divided; there were more and more people who were refusing to go and work in Germany and were taking refuge in the mountains or the forests, forming groups in search of a leader, mostly dependent on the generosity of the villagers, and sometimes on looting. In his area, Laurent d'Argilat was in charge of bringing these rebels together and incorporating them in the Resistance networks that had formed. Laurent . . . she had not seen him since her father's funeral. Once, Camille, his wife, had met him in Toulouse, leaving Léa sick with envy. And what about Tavernier? What on earth had become of him? He could at least have found out how she was. He was her lover after all, wasn't he? Because of him, she had had the biggest scare of her life: thinking she was pregnant. This false alarm had helped her understand her sister Françoise's confusion better. Her baby was due very soon. Françoise had written to Léa begging her to visit her for the birth of her child. Léa, in her grief and hatred, had not replied.

'Camille, Ruth, Léa, Aunt Bernadette,' shouted Laure, coming into the kitchen.

'What's the matter?' asked Léa, getting to her feet.

'Laure, is that you yelling like that?' inquired Ruth, as she too came in. Léa's younger sister was breathless and unable to speak.

Fayard came in through the door leading to the alleyway, followed by his wife.

'Have you heard?'

'Heard what?'

'The Jerries . . .'

'What about the Jerries?' cried Léa.

'They've invaded the unoccupied zone,' said Laure breathlessly.

Léa sank down on to a chair. Opposite her, Camille, who had come in without her noticing, clasped her child who thought it was all a game and began to shout with laughter.

'We heard it on the wireless,' said Fayard.

'On Radio Paris they said the daily indemnity for occupation was five million francs. How on earth are we going to find all that money?' added his wife.

Chapter 2

The Montpleynet sisters' house had changed a lot since Léa's last visit to Paris. The two apartments on the same landing, linked by a communicating door, once so full of life, were now cold and silent. The two sisters and their maid lived in four rooms, the only ones they had some means of heating. The three bedrooms at the end of the corridor and Albertine's entire apartment were locked up, the furniture protected by dust sheets, the windows shuttered and the fireplaces stone cold. The ladies were resigned to being cramped. They nicknamed all the rooms they could not heat 'the cold rooms' and never set foot in them.

'Don't you see that we couldn't leave her on her own, ill, in that hotel, your mother would never have forgiven us,' said Lisa de Montpleynet, wiping her eyes with her damp handkerchief.

'There's no point going on about it, we did our duty as relatives and Christians,' said her sister, Albertine, brusquely.

Standing in her aunts' little Parisian parlour, Léa found it difficult to conceal her anger.

A frantic letter from Albertine – which was most unlike her – had made Léa jump on to the first train for Paris after half a day's delay at the congested station of Saint-Jean-de-Bordeaux. On her arrival at the apartment in the Rue de L'Université, Estelle, the Montpleynet sisters' housekeeper and maid, came to the door wrapped in gaudy shawls and hugged Léa with obvious relief, repeating over and over as if to convince herself it were true, 'At last you're here, Mademoiselle Léa, at last you're here . . .'

'What's going on, Estelle? Where are my aunts? Are they ill?'

24

'Mademoiselle Léa, if only you knew . . .'

'Léa, you're here at last!' exclaimed Lisa, a fur coat flung over her dressing gown.

A little later, Albertine appeared followed by a man carrying a doctor's bag. Her aunt saw him out, saying:

'Goodbye, doctor, we'll see you tomorrow.'

Léa looked at the three women in astonishment.

'Will you please tell me who is ill?'

'Your sister Françoise,' replied Albertine.

This reply left Léa speechless. Then her surprise gave way to anger. Her harsh words made the sensitive Lisa burst into tears.

'Léa, Léa, it's you,' said a feeble voice from behind a door which slowly opened.

In the doorway stood Françoise, her swollen stomach ill-concealed under a blanket.

Albertine rushed over to her.

'What are you doing out of bed? The doctor has strictly forbidden you to get up.'

Paying no heed to her aunt, Françoise walked towards her sister holding out her arms. The blanket slipped off her shoulders revealing her huge stomach, emphasized by her nightdress which was too tight. They fell into each other's arms.

'Oh, Léa! Thank you for coming.'

Léa led her back to her room, which was not much warmer than the little parlour.

As soon as she was lying down, the young woman seized her sister's hand and pressed it to her lips, murmuring:

'You came . . .'

'Calm down, my darling, you'll make yourself ill,' said Albertine, plumping the pillows.

'No, aunt, happiness can't do any harm. Léa, tell me everything. Everything that's been happening at Montillac.'

Two hours later, the sisters were still chatting.

Léa could not bring herself to get out of the cosy warm bed where she had been basking since she had woken up. She could not bear the idea of getting up and dressed in the cold. Ah! To stay in bed and keep nice and warm until winter was over . . . until the war was over . . .

She remembered with surprise how she had enjoyed recalling happy childhood memories the previous evening with Françoise. For a few moments they discovered a bond that they had never felt before. They parted with the feeling that they had found each other, but they had carefully avoided the subject that preoccupied both of them: the birth of the child and Françoise's future.

There was a knock at the door. It was Estelle with the breakfast tray.

'What! Tea, real sugar!' exclaimed Léa sitting up. 'How do you manage it?'

'It's the first time in three months. In your honour! We got it thanks to Madame Mulstein's friend . . . a writer apparently.'

'Raphaël Mahl!?'

'Yes, that's his name. A shifty-looking gentleman. I saw him on the terrace of the Deux Magots café the other day in the company of a young German officer. He had his arm round his waist and was whispering to him. Everybody was looking away in embarrassment.'

Léa found it hard to conceal a smile which the elderly servant would not have understood.

'I told Mesdemoiselles de Montpleynet about it and told them they ought not to entertain this gentleman any more,' Estelle went on, 'but Mademoiselle Lisa told me I had a dirty mind and that Monsieur Mahl was a perfect gentleman and that it was thanks to him we would not starve to death. As for Mademoiselle Albertine, she told me I shouldn't judge by appearances. What do you think, mademoiselle?'

'I don't know Monsieur Mahl very well. But I will advise my aunts to be a little wary of that character.'

'I've put a kettle of boiling water in the bathroom and I've switched on the electric heater. It doesn't give out much heat, but it takes the chill out of the air.'

'Thank you, Estelle, I'd love a bath.'

'A bath! The bathtub hasn't been filled for months. Your

26

aunts go to the public baths once a week.'

'Oh, I'd love to see them. I bet they don't dare get undressed to go in the water.'

'It's not nice to make fun of them, Mademoiselle Léa. Life is very hard here. We're cold and we're hungry. We're frightened as well.'

'What are you frightened of? You're not in any danger.'

'Who knows, mademoiselle? Do you remember the lady on the first floor whom your aunts used to visit for tea from time to time?'

'Madame Lévy?'

'Yes. Well, the Germans came and arrested her. She was ill and they dragged her from her bed and took her away in her nightdress. Mademoiselle Albertine told Monsieur Tavernier . . .'

'Tavernier?'

'They asked him to find out.'

'And . . .?'

'When he came, a few days later, he was very pale and he had a frightening expression.'

'What did he say?'

'That she'd been taken to Drancy and from there to a camp in Germany with a thousand other people, mainly women and children. Since Madame Lévy left, the apartment has been taken over by an actress who lives it up and entertains German officers. They make a dreadful noise. Everybody's too scared of reprisals to complain.'

'When did Monsieur Tavernier last come here?'

'About three weeks ago. It was he who persuaded your aunts to look after Françoise here.'

Léa could feel her heart beating faster. François was looking after her aunts and her sister.

'I'll leave you in peace, mademoiselle, they say there's going to be a delivery of fish in the Rue de Buci at mid-day. I'd better not get there too late otherwise all I'll get is the leftovers.'

Léa had a hasty wash, slipped a black sweater and a jacket on over her blue wool dress, pulled on thick socks and thus attired went into her sister's room.

Françoise was sitting up in bed smiling at Léa. She was wrapped in a pink bed jacket and shawl which brought out the colour in her cheeks. Her hair was carefully done and she looked rested.

'Good morning, did you sleep well?' she asked. 'I haven't slept so well for months. It's thanks to you.'

Léa kissed her without replying.

'I'm glad you're here. I'm going to get better quickly. I don't want to miss the first night of Henri de Montherlant's new play, *La Reine Morte*.'

'When is it?'

'On December 8th at the Comédie Française.'

'December 8th! But that's the day after tomorrow.'

'So? The baby's not due for another month and I feel perfectly fit. Being pregnant isn't an illness. You'll see when it's your turn.'

'I hope that's never.'

'Why? It's so wonderful to carry the child of the man you love.'

Seeing Léa's impassive expression, Françoise realized she had gone too far. She blushed and hung her head. Then, taking her courage in both hands, she looked up and said in a trembling voice:

'I know what you think. I tried to convince myself that I was wrong to love Otto. I wasn't able to. I love everything about him: his kindness, his love of music, his talent, his bravery, and even the fact that he's German. The only thing I wish is that the war would end. You do understand, don't you? Try to understand.'

Léa could not think about the situation calmly and logically. Something deep down inside her rebelled against this love that shocked her. At the same time she could well understand how much Françoise and Otto had in common. If he had not been German, he would have made a charming brother-in-law.

'What are you going to do?' she asked.

'Marry him as soon as he gets back from Berlin and he's obtained permission from his superiors. Promise me you'll come to my wedding. Please, promise me.'

'It all depends when it is. If it's during the grape harvest or in the spring, I won't be able to.'

28

'You'll manage it,' said Françoise, smiling, happy not to
have had a categoric refusal. 'Otto is wonderful, he writes to
me every day, he worries so much about me and the baby. He
left me in the care of Frederic Hanke. You remember him, he
helped deliver Camille.'

'Well, if there's a problem, he can always take over from the
midwife.'

That was said with such spiteful sarcasm that Françoise was
not able to keep back her tears. Léa was ashamed of her
callousness. She might have apologized to her sister if her aunt
had not come in at that moment.

'Léa, you're wanted on the telephone. Françoise, what's
the matter with you?'

'Nothing, aunt, I'm just a little tired.'

'Hello, who's calling?'

'Is that Léa Delmas?'

'Yes, speaking. Who are you?'

'Don't you recognize my voice? Is something wrong with
your ears?'

'No, tell me who you are or I'll hang up.'

'Still as sharp, I see. Come, come, my friend, try a little
harder.'

'I don't want to try any harder and I find this kind of joke
idiotic.'

'Don't hang up! Do you remember the Chapon Fin restaurant, Mandel's cherries, La Petite Gironde, the church of
Sainte-Eulalie, the Rue Saint-Genès . . .?'

'Raphaël!'

'It took you long enough!'

'I'm sorry, but I hate these mysterious telephone calls. How
did you know I was in Paris?'

'I'm always well-informed about my friends. When am I
going to see you?'

'I've no idea. I've only just got here.'

'I'll drop by for tea at five o'clock. Don't go to any trouble,
I'll bring everything with me. Just put the kettle on.'

'But . . .'

'How are your dear aunts, and your charming sister? Give

them my regards. See you later, my dear. I'll be delighted to see you again.'

Raphaël Mahl hung up, leaving Léa dumbfounded. How had he found out? A shudder ran through her as she was overcome by a feeling of uneasiness.

'Don't stand there in the freezing hall, you'll catch cold, my love.'

The sound of Lisa's voice made her jump.

'How long is it since you saw Raphaël Mahl?'

'I don't know, about a fortnight, perhaps.'

'So he's met Françoise then?'

'No, she arrived the day after his visit, and she hasn't been out since she came. But why all these questions?'

'That was Raphaël Mahl on the telephone and I wondered how he knew I was in Paris.'

'It's a coincidence.'

'With someone like him, I don't believe in coincidences.'

Lisa shrugged her shoulders as if to say she did not know what to think.

'Oh! I forgot, he's coming to tea.'

'But we haven't got anything!'

'He said he'd bring everything except the water.'

The parlour clock had just struck five when the doorbell rang. Estelle, who was wearing an immaculate flounced white apron over her usual overall, went to open the door. Raphaël Mahl came in, half hidden beneath a mountain of parcels tied up with ribbon.

'Quickly, Estelle, help me before I drop all these delicacies on the carpet.'

The maid grumpily obliged.

'Raphaël, you look marvellous!'

'Léa!'

They gazed at each other for a long time as if they wanted to drink in every detail at once, then they walked towards each other.

They had absolutely nothing in common – their concepts of life, friendship and of love were so different – but there was an irresistible attraction that drew them to each other as friends.

Of the two, it was Raphaël who asked himself the most questions on what he called 'the part of me that isn't rotten'. He who was a cheat, a liar, a thief, a police informer, a collaborator with the Gestapo, a Jew, an occasional contributor to the right-wing magazines *Je suis partout*, *Gringoire*, *Pilori* and *Nouveaux Temps*. His anti-semitism almost shocked even the eminent directors and writers of these publications who were professional Jew-haters. But he felt like a big brother towards Léa, wanting to protect her from being sullied by life.

'Lovely Léa, how is it you manage to enchant my eyes and my soul each time I see you?'

She laughed that hoarse laugh that aroused men and aggravated other women, and kissed him on both cheeks.

'I'm sure I shouldn't be, but I'm glad to see you again.'

'Why do you say something nice and something that is not at all nice in the same breath? Well, I'm a generous soul, I'll forget the unpleasant bit. You were saying, when I came in, that I was looking marvellous? I'm so elegant, aren't I? But I'm proudest of my shoes. Not bad, what do you think? They cost me a fortune. I had them custom-made at Hermes.'

'Where on earth did you get the money from? Did you rob an old lady, sell your body to a fat pink German officer or did you prostitute a soft-skinned young private?'

'You're not so far from the truth. What can I do, dear friend, a man has to create his own happiness and more often than not money is in short supply. Having worked out that without money, happiness, that is the little happiness I'm likely to experience, would be out of my grasp, I decided to procure myself some. Nothing is easier at the moment. Everything is for sale: bodies and consciences. Depending on the circumstances, I sell one or the other, or both if the purchaser is very generous.'

'You're disgusting.'

'Good is so imperfect that it doesn't interest me. It is a great mistake, my lovely friend, to believe that man is a reasonable creature . . . The ability to think does not confer the ability to be reasonable. I've always been convinced that to gain pleasure from reasonable things remains the principle of mediocrity. One day I must write a *Praise of Mediocrity*. That would cause a stir in the republic of letters. Before I go into details of my masterpiece, allow me to pay my respects to your aunts and sister.'

In Françoise's room, on a round table with an embroidered cloth, the best tea service had been laid out.

'You've looted every single cake shop and confectioner's in Paris!' exclaimed Léa as she came into the room and set eyes on all the plates piled high with chocolates, petits-fours, cakes and candied fruits.

'You don't know how right you are, I had terrible trouble getting all those things: the glacé petits-fours come from Lamoureux in the Rue Saint-Sulpice, the cream ones from Guerbois in the Rue de Sèvres, the chocolate cake is from Bourdaloue, of course, the shortbread is from Galpin in the Rue du Bac, and I bought the rest from Debauve and Gallet in the Rue des Saints-Pères, "by appointment to past kings of France"!'

'We used to go there too, before the war,' sighed Lisa, looking longingly at all the delicacies.

'As for the tea,' Raphaël went on, taking a tin from his pocket, 'it was brought over from Russia for me by one of my friends. It's delicious, strong and scented. Let me know how it tastes.'

'Monsieur Mahl, you're spoiling us. It's very kind of you. How can we thank you for so many good things?'

'By eating them, ladies.'

For a few minutes, the only sound to be heard was that of chewing. Françoise was the first to declare that she could not eat another mouthful, followed soon after by Albertine and Raphaël. Only Lisa and Léa carried on gorging themselves. Their hands went from the table to their mouths with remarkable speed. The aunt and niece were acting like badly brought-up children whose hands and faces covered in cream betrayed their greed. Raphaël's booming laugh made them jump. They looked around anxiously as if they were afraid someone was going to take away the rest of the cakes. 'Aren't you ashamed of yourself, Lisa?' said Albertine with mock severity.

Lisa blushed scarlet and hung her head.

'If we left you to it, you wouldn't even spare a thought for poor Estelle,' continued her sister mercilessly.

'I was hungry. Forgive me. You're right, I'll take her a plateful. Don't be angry with me, it's so delicious,' she said, sounding so pathetic that they all burst out laughing, even Albertine.

It had been dark for a long time when Raphaël Mahl finally took his leave. Léa saw him out.

'I must see you alone. Can we have lunch together tomorrow?'

'I don't know. You frighten me . . . I can't believe you're as bad as you say you are and at the same time a strange feeling of repulsion warns me to be wary of you.'

'Oh! You're so right, my dear. You can never be too careful with me. I believe I've already told you, one only betrays those one loves. As one who is passionately interested in the Holy Scriptures, you won't be surprised to learn that Judas is my favourite character, my brother, my friend, my double. He through whom all evil was to come, he who had no choice so that what was written could be accomplished. He . . . the most intelligent, the intellectual of the group, had to betray the one he genuinely loved. And by that act, for which he was destined by all eternity, Judas the disciple, Judas the traitor was damned until the end of time. It's unjust, don't you think?'

'I've no idea, I've never been particularly interested in Judas.'

'You're wrong. Of the twelve, he's the only interesting one apart from the good John, with his angelic face, Jesus's favourite fairy, his lover,' he specified as Léa looked puzzled. 'For, as you are aware, they were all a bunch of pansies.'

'You're mad.'

'And I'm a pansy.'

'If my aunts could hear you blaspheming like that they'd forbid you to set foot in here again.'

'Then I'll shut up. I love the old ladies' company. They are the only examples of the female species who are bearable. Other than yourself, of course, and my lovely friend, Sarah Mulstein. By the way, have you heard from her? I haven't had any news from her for days and days.'

So that was what he was leading up to . . . Léa shivered, and felt slightly nauseous. She answered quickly and sharply.

'Neither have I.'

'But you're cold. I'm a beast to keep you standing in this freezing hall. Go and warm yourself in your charming sister's room. Do you know her future husband? A man of great culture with a promising future. Such a marriage is most useful in times like these. Will your Dominican uncle bless the union?'

Léa was overcome with fear and loathing.

'My love, your teeth are chattering . . . you've turned quite pale. It's all my fault, I've made you catch a chill. You must have a temperature.'

Concerned, Raphaël grasped her wrist.

'Don't touch me, I'm perfectly all right,' she cried snatching back her hand.

'See you tomorrow, my lovely friend. I'll telephone you towards the end of the morning. Until then, have a good rest, you need it, otherwise your nerves may start playing tricks on you.'

Chapter 3

The following morning, Léa left the apartment very early so that she would not be there when Raphaël Mahl called.

She had spent a very restless night going over Raphaël's words which held a veiled threat to her friends and her family. She absolutely had to warn Sarah Mulstein and her uncle, Adrien Delmas. Not knowing their whereabouts and the fear of making a blunder made her frantically worried. Who would know where Sarah and the Dominican were hiding? François: François Tavernier, of course.

On the day of her father's funeral he had made her memorize an address where she could contact him or leave him a message in an emergency. At the time, she had thought: 'He'll be lucky if he thinks I'm going to come looking for him in Paris,' and had quickly forgotten the address. What had he said? . . . Near the Arc de Triomphe, Avenue . . . Avenue . . . drat, it was on the tip of her tongue. A general or a marshal from the Empire: Hoche, Marceau, Kléber . . . Kléber, that was it: Avenue Kléber, 32, Avenue Kléber. She had got up to write it down for fear she would forget it again and had fallen asleep at once, muttering: I must remember to burn that address tomorrow.

It was a fine but cold day. Léa walked briskly down the Boulevard Raspail towards the junction at Sèvres-Babylone. She was warmly bundled up in the sumptuous mink coat Françoise had lent her. Her hair was hidden under a matching fur hat and on her feet she wore lined boots that were a little on the big side.

There were few other people in the streets and those Léa met were usually poorly dressed. They turned to stare at this elegant young woman who seemed to be scoffing at the restrictions and the cold. Léa was so absorbed rubbing her face against the silky fur, that she was unaware of the contemptuous and hostile looks people were giving her. She paused outside the Gallimard bookshop. The dark haired young man who liked Marcel Aymé's novels was arranging books in the window. Their eyes met, he recognized her and smiled, showing her the book he was holding: the author was Raphaël Mahl. *Gide*, she read in large letters on the cover. This 'encounter' reawoke her feeling of distress. She hastened her step. As she walked past Camille and Laurent's apartment, which they had abandoned in the panic of June 1940, she looked at it with nothing but indifference.

Nazi banners and insignia hung from the façade of the Hotel Lutétia, sinister decorations which were a shock in the bright morning sunlight. On the entrance steps, several people were having a discussion and there were two German officers in the centre. Among them . . . no, it wasn't possible. To find out for certain, Léa crossed the road and made herself walk slowly past the group. No, she was not mistaken. It was François Tavernier all right who seemed to be on the best of terms with the two German officers. Weak at the knees, Léa felt overwhelmed by grief. Tears ran down her cheeks and there was nothing she could do to stop them. That was the ultimate humiliation: crying in front of that bastard and his sinister companions.

'There's a lovely lady who looks as though she's in distress,' said one of the German officers, catching sight of the young girl.

François Tavernier followed his companion's gaze. It wasn't true . . . It was her all right; the only woman he knew who was able to look pretty when she cried.

'Excuse me, gentlemen, it's my young sister, she must have lost her poodle, she gets upset very easily.'

'That's a good one!' said one of the civilians, clapping him on the back. 'Another of your conquests. Congratulations, old chap, you have extremely good taste. What youth. You ought to be ashamed of keeping such a beauty all to yourself. Bring her along to one of our dinner parties.'

'I shall, without fail. Excuse me, gentlemen, I'll see you soon.'

He rushed down the steps, took Léa's arm and led her away.

'Please, act naturally, they're watching us.'

For a few moments, they walked in silence, crossing the Rue du Cherche-Midi and walking up the Rue d'Assas.

'Let me go, I can walk on my own.'

François obeyed.

'Still the same sweet nature. I'm pleased to see that you haven't changed and I note with pleasure that your financial situation seems to have improved. That sumptuous fur coat looks ravishing on you.'

Léa shrugged but did not reply.

'But it's not a coat that's suitable for a nice young lady. Only the wives and mistresses of black market dealers, some actresses and a few tarts kept by Germans dare dress like that.'

Léa blushed and could only find a lame reply and she regretted it at once:

'It's not mine, I borrowed it from my sister.'

There was a hint of a smile on François's face.

'What are you doing in Paris? Why were you crying?'

'What does it matter?'

He stopped, took her arm and made her look at him.

'Don't you know, you silly creature, that everything to do with you matters to me?'

Why did those words soothe her? She gently disengaged herself and carried on walking. They reached the gates of the Luxembourg Gardens.

'Let's go in, we'll be able to talk in peace inside,' he said.

Around the ornamental lake, children in woollen hats and scarves were chasing each other and yelling boisterously, watched by women who stamped their feet and rubbed their hands to keep warm.

'Now, tell me why you're in Paris.'

'Because of my sister Françoise. Her health isn't too good . . .'

'That's to be expected in her condition.'

'It probably is. My aunts were so worried that I jumped on the first train. But I'm not thinking of staying long. As soon as

I'm a long way from Montillac, I'm frightened something will happen.'

'Have you heard from Laurent d'Argilat?'

'No, not since the execution of the hostages at Souges on the 21st September.'

'I saw him not long after that. He could not forgive himself for not being able to save them,' said Tavernier, taking Léa's arm again.

'What could he do?'

'He knew the camp at Mérignac inside out. That's where the Germans took the hostages from.'

'How did he come to know that place?'

'Shortly after your father's funeral, he was arrested in a round-up in the Rue Sainte-Catherine in Bordeaux. His false papers were in order. They interned him at Mérignac for no reason. Three days later, he escaped and brought back a detailed map of the camp as well as several contacts which could be useful. When he learned that seventy people had been selected at random and were to be shot in return for attacks committed in Paris, he tried to organize a rescue operation with Abbot Lasserre and a few comrades from his network. They were to try and intercept the trucks transporting the hostages, overcome the guards and free the prisoners. At the last minute, they received an order not to try anything.'

'Who gave that order?'

'I don't know, London, perhaps.'

'That's ridiculous.'

'In politics, it's often the things that seem ridiculous which have force of law.'

He looked into her eyes and added suddenly:

'I want to kiss you.'

'Not until I know the truth about your relations with your "friends" from the Hotel Lutétia.'

'I can't talk to you about it. Those are things which it is best for you, and for all of us, to know nothing about.'

'It was a shock when I walked past and saw you with them. I was just on my way to find you at that address you gave me.'

'At 32 Avenue Kléber?'

'Yes.'

'Be grateful to my "German friends" as you call them; if it hadn't been for that meeting and our chance encounter, you would have thrown yourself into the lion's jaws. And I'm not sure I would have been able to get you out, in spite of my contacts and the friendship of Otto Abetz.'

'The German Ambassador?'

'Yes, remember, we met at his house and we danced. Have you forgotten our dance?'

They were leaning on the balustrade looking out over the well-kept lawns and the ornamental lake, with their backs to the bandstand. In the winter sunlight, the Senate house, protected by sandbags, looked like a sleeping castle guarded by the black trees whose bare arms reached towards the sky with a movement that was either threatening or pleading. Behind them, a gardener was pushing a wheelbarrow full of carrots, turnips and leeks. The squeaking of the wheel made them look around.

'What's he doing here with all those vegetables?' asked Léa in surprise.

'Didn't you know that the Luxembourg Gardens have been turned into a vegetable garden?'

'It's not a bad idea,' she replied, looking so serious that François burst out laughing.

'No, it's not a bad idea, although I wonder who gets the benefit of all this market gardening. You still haven't told me why you wanted to reach me.'

'I find all this so confusing. Who are you? Are you on the side of the Germans or the French? The friend of Otto Abetz or of Sarah Mulstein?'

'It's still too soon for me to answer you. Just one thing: no harm will ever come to you because of me. You can tell me everything.'

'Have you heard from Sarah?'

'If you know something, tell me. Every second, she's in danger,' he said, taking her hand.

Léa's eyes tried in vain to penetrate the secret in François's eyes. She shivered despite her fur coat.

He drew her to him and covered her frozen face with kisses. Léa felt as if she had been waiting for this moment since the minute she saw him on the steps of the Hotel Lutétia. When their lips finally met, she was suffused with a warm feeling of happiness and her body yielded to her lover's.

'You little animal, you little creature, you haven't changed. How can we live without each other for such a long time?'

That hand which slid under her pullover and took possession of her breasts . . . it was both icy and burning, torturing her erect nipples.

'Philippe! Marianne! Don't look. It's disgusting . . . in front of children! Aren't you ashamed,' shouted a woman wearing a nanny's uniform and pushing a huge pram and scolding two children of four or five.

When they finally noticed her, the faraway look in their eyes and their secret smiles made her hang her head and hasten her step, averting her eyes.

'That lady's right, this place isn't suitable. Let's go and have lunch at my friend Marthe Andrieu's, it's just round the corner from here.'

'Marthe Andrieu?'

'The owner of the clandestine restaurant in the Rue Saint-Jacques.'

At the exit, French policemen in plain clothes asked for their identity papers. A routine check, no doubt. They let them through without questioning them.

'What are they looking for?' asked Léa as they crossed over the Boulevard Saint-Michel.

'Terrorists, Jews, communists, supporters of de Gaulle . . .'

'What do they do with them when they arrest them?'

'It depends on the different police stations, but in general, they prefer to get rid of them. They hand them over to the Gestapo who sometimes torture, sometimes deport and sometimes kill them.'

'If they arrested Sarah, what would they do with her?'

'Last time I saw her, she belonged to a Resistance network that specialized in smuggling Jews into the unoccupied zone.'

'And now?'

'Now I'm more afraid for her than ever. If they find out she

40

belongs to the Resistance, they'll torture her. Knowing her, she'll refuse to talk and she'll die.'

With his head down and his jaw set, François walked faster. Clutching his arm, Léa had to take enormous strides to keep up with him. She could sense how tense her companion was and felt worried.

In front of them, the Panthéon rose up into the sky which looked even more threatening, while gusts of cold wind whipped up the dust in the Rue Soufflot.

A group of girl students, dressed in short skirts, mostly kilts, and fur-lined jackets, with bare heads and legs, and wearing heavy shoes brightened up with cheerfully-coloured angora socks, jostled them, laughing.

'We must find her.'

'Who?'

'Sarah. I'm afraid for her too. Yesterday, Raphaël Mahl came to my aunts' apartment. He asked if I'd heard from her.'

'I don't see any danger in that. Sarah's known him for a long time and you know she's got a soft spot for him.'

'I've got a soft spot for him too. He amuses me and makes me laugh in spite of myself. But now, I feel he's . . . how can I say . . . uncontrolled. That's it: he can no longer control his bad side. I can feel it, you understand. I feel it, I can't explain myself any better than that.'

'Did he not say anything else that frightened you?'

Léa hung her head, feeling helpless at her inability to communicate her fears. She was convinced that because of Raphaël Mahl, something terrible was going to happen to Sarah.

'He asked me if my Uncle Adrien was going to bless Françoise's marriage to . . . to . . .'

François came to her aid:

'. . . to Sturmbannführer Kramer. In different circumstances, this would have been a perfect marriage for your sister. What could be more harmonious than a couple of music lovers! Unfortunately, Major Kramer is not only a Musician but also an SS officer. I can even tell you that he is held in great esteem by his superiors even though they've always suspected that he only volunteered so as not to disappoint his sick father who is a close friend of the SS leader Heinrich Himmler. He is

41

also protected by another friend of his father's the notorious Paul Hausser, who set up the school for SS officers. Thanks to him, Kramer was able to devote several hours a day to music. I was surprised when I found out he was planning to marry your sister. Old Kramer will never consent to it.'

'But what will become of Françoise?'

He was spared having to give an immediate reply as they had arrived at the building in the Rue Saint-Jacques which housed Marthe Andrieu's clandestine restaurant.

As on the previous occasion, they received a warm welcome, but their hostess was red-eyed.

'What's the matter, Marthe? Is it the onions that are making you cry?'

'No, Monsieur François,' she said, wiping her tear-stained cheeks, 'it's because of René.'

'What's the matter with him? He looks all right to me.'

'They want to send him to Germany.'

René came over to them carrying a plate.

'Calm down, mother, the clients will wonder what's going on.'

'I don't care what the clients think. I don't want you to go.'

François Tavernier stood up and took her by the shoulders.

'Come into the kitchen and tell me all about it. Excuse me, Léa.'

'Follow me, mademoiselle, I'll show you to your table,' said René, leading her away.

Sipping a glass of Sauternes, Léa looked around her wondering who these people were who could afford the luxury of eating in such places. Since she had last come, prices had escalated. The men were comfortably dressed, no longer young, with rather pudgy faces. The women were all wearing hats and displayed that unbearable air of smug vanity. Their fur jackets and coats hung over the back of their chairs. Léa realized that with her sister's coat, she looked just like them. She found that hateful. Perhaps she would have left if, at that precise moment, François had not come back looking worried . . .

'Is something the matter?'

42

'You heard, René has got to do compulsory labour in Germany. I advised him to go.'

'Are you being serious?'

'Very serious. If he doesn't turn up, the police will come here and his parents will be in trouble.'

'But are you going to do something for him?'

'I'm going to try, but it's getting more and more difficult. The Germans have asked for two hundred and fifty thousand men this quarter and they want as many for the first quarter of 1943.'

François Tavernier glanced quickly round the room and continued in a low voice:

'Let's change the subject. How is Camille?'

'Fine. She helps me a lot with the running of Montillac.'

'What about Fayard, the manager, is he back in charge? Has he still got his eyes on the estate?'

'He hasn't mentioned it again, but I don't trust him; I've got the feeling that he's watching us all the time. When I ask him if he's heard from Mathias, he gives me a strange look and turns his back on me, grumbling. He hasn't forgiven me for his son's departure for Germany.'

The scrambled eggs and truffles that Marthe brought them were a real treat.

An odd couple walked into the room. He was of medium height and looked cramped in an overcoat with a fur collar, with the buttons wrongly done up. His unworldly air was belied by his hard, beady, intelligent eyes. She was tall and very elegant, wearing a sumptuous panther coat, with a large black velvet turban wound round her head.

Marcel and Marthe rushed over to them and seated them with great consideration. The woman gave an exaggerated nod of her head in thanks and let her fur slip negligently from her shoulders, revealing her impeccable black suit and a necklace made up of several strings of magnificent pearls.

Léa could not take her eyes off this fabulously glittering creature.

'Léa . . . Léa . . .'

'Yes,' she said, tearing herself away from her reverie.

'Don't stare at people like that . . . Marthe!'

The cook, who was walking past their table, stopped.

'Do you want anything else, Monsieur François?'

'Yes, the bill, quickly.'

'But we haven't finished!' exclaimed Léa.

'Is something the matter, Monsieur François?'

'No, my good friend, but I've just remembered, I have an important appointment . . . which may be useful for your son,' he added, lowering his voice when he saw her hurt look.

'Well, in that case . . .' she said, rushing towards the kitchen.

'François, will you please explain what's going on?'

'Too late . . .'

The man who had just arrived had stood up and was making a beeline for François, proffering his hand.

'I was sure it was you, Monsieur Tavernier. Hélène was right. I see that you know the right addresses too. Here's another one for you to add to your address book: mine. I don't want to boast, but mine is the best table in Paris. Every day I entertain twenty or so guests, I hope you will join us. Of course, mademoiselle will be equally as welcome.'

He bowed to Léa who answered with a mere nod.

Marthe put the bill in front of François.

'Are you leaving so soon, my dear Tavernier?'

'An important meeting,' said François, taking some notes from his wallet.

The man fumbled in his inside pocket.

'Here's my card. Make a note of the address: 19 Rue de Presbourg. Anybody who's anybody in Paris these days is a guest of mine . . . You will meet none but the very best people. Come and say hello to my wife before you leave, otherwise she'll never forgive you and you know how vindictive Hélène is.'

'My dear fellow, how could you think for one moment that I would leave without laying my tribute at the feet of the most charming woman in Paris. I'll follow you.'

François Tavernier placed his hand on Léa's arm and said softly:

'Wait for me, I shan't be long.'

Léa grudgingly sat down again.

'Here, eat this while you're waiting,' said Marthe, placing a slice of apple pie in front of her.

Meanwhile, Tavernier was being ridiculously overpolite to that woman. He looked idiotic bowing and smiling like that. Lea could not get over it, he who was usually distant, sarcastic . . . now he was being almost obsequious. Finally he decided to take his leave and remember her existence.

'I see you haven't been wasting time,' he said, pointing at the crumbs of apple pie.

'It was Marthe . . .'

'I'm not criticizing you.'

'That's the last straw! If you could have seen yourself, playing the ladykiller to that old bag . . .'

'Not so loud! You're being very unfair to that lady. Come on.'

In the hall, they came across Marthe and René, trying to comfort his mother.

'René, can I have a word with you for a moment?'

'Of course, Monsieur François.'

They went into the bedroom where René and Jeannette's little boy was sleeping amid the hams, sausages, tins and crates of vegetables piled ceiling high.

'Would you give a message to the people who are in the little room you keep for friends?'

'I put them there because they're friends of yours.'

'You did the right thing. Ask for Monsieur Jacques Martel. A dark haired man with regular features will answer. Tell him that business isn't good. Have you had the door that leads to the servants' stairs repaired and put the big Chinese panel that matches the two screens in front of it?'

'Yes, I did it all myself so nobody would ask any questions.'

'The staircase was blocked off. Have you cleared the exit by the cellars?'

'Everything is in place, even the dust and dirt which I didn't touch. None of the neighbours has noticed a thing.'

'Perfect. Thank you, René. That exit is going to be used for the first time. There are four of them, aren't there?'

'Yes.'

'They should leave at two minute intervals. Go now and make sure that none of your clients sees them. Everybody's safety is at stake. One more thing, be very careful in front of Monsieur Michel and his friends. Don't let him suspect for a second what sometimes goes on here.'

'Don't worry, not even my parents know. Only Jeannette has a idea.'

'Nothing to fear as far as she's concerned. But purely as a precaution, you should send the child away to the country.'

'I've already thought of that. He'll be leaving as soon as possible.'

'Off you go, quickly, René. Don't forget, Jacques Martel must leave second.'

'Anyone would think we were dealing with General de Gaulle himself.'

François Tavernier did not reply but there was a glimmer of secret amusement in his eye . . .

René left the store room first. Then, in turn, François left the room after caressing the head of the sleeping child who was his godson.

While they were waiting in the kitchen, Marthe and Léa cheered themselves up with sugar lumps dipped in plum brandy made by the family who lived in Limogne. Judging by their sparkling eyes, they must have soaked several lumps of sugar in several liqueur glassfuls of brandy.

Tavernier stopped in the doorway.

Léa was talking animatedly of the *scandalous* way Hélène had been making eyes at François.

He went up to her and took her by the arm. Ignoring her protests, he marched her into the hall and out on to the landing.

'Let me go, I want to talk to that woman. Did you notice how brazenly she looked at you? It was embarrassing. She knew perfectly well you had someone with you. What a cheek!'

They had reached the entrance hall, though not without some difficulty. François found it hard to keep a straight face in front of Léa whose hat was askew and whose face looked ravishing as she drunkenly ranted and raved.

46

'My word! You're making a scene! You're jealous!'

'Jealous! Me! Of whom, may I ask? Of what?'

'Of me, it seems.'

'Of you! You're out of your mind! Of you! That's funny! That's wishful thinking . . . you're mixing me up with those women you usually go out with. Jealous! Me! You make me laugh . . .'

Suddenly, he pulled her towards him.

'Shut up before you start making a fool of yourself. We talk too much. What do I care whether you're jealous or not. To be honest, I'd rather you weren't.'

Looking defiant, she swayed from one foot to the other, without trying to get away from him. She ran her tongue over her dry lips. That was like a signal. François's penis stiffened and Léa's stomach pressed up against him.

Their lips met with the hunger of passionate love or that of long abstinence. That was Léa's case. Since the day of her father's funeral, no man, apart from François, had touched her.

She clung to him, panting, punctuating her kisses with little cries. François Tavernier would have made love to her on the spot, against the dirty wall of the entrance hall, the high door of which was fortunately closed. But someone could come in or the customers of the clandestine restaurant could come downstairs any second.

With some difficulty he extricated himself from the young girl's embrace.

'Come on, let's not stay here. Let's go to my place.'

'No, now . . .'

Voices on the stairs brought her to her senses. Without further resistance, she allowed herself to be steered away.

Léa awoke and stretched herself lazily, groaning. She felt wonderful in spite of a throbbing headache. She sat up in the big bed with its crumpled sheets and looked around her, wrapping herself in the vicuña-wool blanket. She gave a little laugh at the mess. What a funny place! It looked like an attic, a cellar or a nomad's tent. Heavy velvet drapes, a beautiful shade of deep red, hung from the rafters, falling round the biggest bed Léa had ever seen. Facing this Sybaritic bed, a huge fire was burning in the vast carved wooden fireplace. In front of the hearth, there was a very beautiful rug on which cushions and clothes were scattered. The flames cast flickering shadows which were caught up in the rafters. The rest of the room was in darkness. The walls of the room faded into the darkness.

'I feel as though I'm suspended in time and space,' she said out loud.

In the silence where the only sound was the crackling of the fire, Léa was surprised by the sound of her own voice which brought her back down to earth.

'So that's what sin must be,' she thought. That idea made her laugh, as her notion of sin was rather vague, and always had been, ever since her childhood, in spite of the catechism which her mother made her recite every day, and her Uncle Adrien's sermons which she used to hear in Bordeaux Cathedral.

'You're so beautiful like that,' said a voice from the shadows.

'François, where are you hiding? I can't see you.'

A lamp with an opalescent green lightshade was switched on. Behind her, sitting at a large desk piled high with books and papers, was François Tavernier. He stood up and came over to the bed. He was wearing a sort of long embroidered robe which emphasized his rough features and made him look like a Mongolian barbarian.

'What are you doing dressed up like that?'

'Oh, Léa! I thought you'd find my decadent outfit sexy. No such luck.'

'Where does it come from? It's beautiful.'

'I brought it back some years ago when I went to Kabul. An Afghan prince gave it to me. It's a ceremonial robe which was once worn by ministers. It's very warm and was made as a protection against the harshest climates. Since the beginning of the war I've been wearing it around the house in the winter.'

'And did you put the hangings round the bed to keep out the cold as well?'

'Yes, as soon as it was finished, I realized that I had reconstructed my favourite childhood universe on an adult scale: my grandparents' dining-room table, which seemed enormous to me at the time, and the red tablecloth which fell to the floor. I used to sit underneath it and imagine I was a Bedouin, a Hun, a warlord or a slave merchant.'

Léa looked at him in such amazement that he burst out laughing.

'Yes, I'm sure you did,' she said, laughing with him. 'But I find it very hard to imagine you as a child.'

'That's another difference between us. I have no difficulty whatsoever in imagining the sort of little girl you were and not so long ago, either. You still are one in many ways.'

He sat down close to her and looked at her with a tenderness in his expression that moved her. Impulsively, she snuggled up to him, rubbing her nose against her lover's neck.

'I love your smell.'

He hugged her tenderly, savouring her first affectionate words which meant as much to him as a declaration of love. In the 'I love your smell' of a sensual woman, he heard the 'I love you' of a woman in love. That is the state he was in. He did not even feel like laughing at himself. Knowing how precarious such a moment was, and knowing how volatile Léa was, he enjoyed that moment of happiness, keeping silent for fear of breaking the spell that bound them.

The telephone rang.

Léa jumped and sat bolt upright crying:

'Oh my God! It's dark! My aunts will be worried.'

'No they won't, I told them you were with me.'

'Oh, did you?' she said, getting up, not bothered by her nakedness. 'Aren't you going to answer it?'

'No, not today, I'm not at home to anybody.'

'It might be important. Please answer it.'

He obeyed the anxiety in Léa's voice. But when he picked up the receiver, there was no longer anybody on the other end.

'Look how pale you are, you mustn't upset yourself so.'

'Yes, you're right, I'm being silly.'

'I'm going to run you a bath. That'll make you feel better.'

'A bath . . .?'

'Yes, it's not often these days that one can invite one's

visitors to have a bath. Don't think it's always like this. I think there's hot water in the tank. Here, you're cold.'

Léa took the cashmere shawl he held out to her.

'Go and sit by the fire, I'll start the bath running and switch on the electric fire.'

When he returned, Léa was sitting clasping her knees. François sat opposite her, leaning against the fireplace surround.

'You wouldn't have a cigarette by any chance?'

He fumbled in one of the pockets of his robe and brought out a very beautiful cigarette case.

'They're English, do you mind?'

Without answering, Léa took a cigarette and lit it on the glowing twig he was holding in the tongs.

'Thank you,' she said, inhaling the smoke with her eyes closed.

He lit one for himself. For a few moments, they smoked in silence.

'Who was that man who came over and spoke to you in Marthe's restaurant?'

François took his time before replying.

'He's an extremely dangerous scoundrel.'

'You seem to be the best of friends.'

'That's how it seems, it's true. I've got no choice, I have to keep company with people like that.'

'I don't understand.'

'It's best if you don't understand. But I can tell you who he is. He's called Mendel Szkolnikoff, or Sekolnikow, a stateless person of Russian origin, from a family of cloth merchants in Riga. He used to supply the Tsar's army, then he became a revolutionary. He left Russia for Germany, then fled to Holland with his family to escape the fate the Nazis reserved for the Jews. Then he turned up in Brussels where he was soon being prosecuted for fraudulent bankruptcy. I'll spare you the details. After a light sentence, he obtained permission to settle in France. He and his wife separated and in 1934, he and his brother set up a cloth merchants company in the rue d'Aboukir. Business wasn't very good, he was prosecuted for fraud. When the war began, he was known in the underworld as

Michel. In 1940, he began to worry, feeling unsafe as a Jew and stateless person, so he became partners with the Chief of Police who was in charge of keeping a watch on him and contacted the German authorities to do business with them. Business took off in November of that year and he soon began to prosper. His new clients were extremely pleased with him . . .'

'Goodness! You're giving me a full report on him.'

'If I'm boring you, I'll . . .'

'No, no, carry on, I'm finding it most instructive.'

'Thanks to his new contacts, he escaped the notice of the Prices Board and the French police, but in May 1941, he received a blow, his company was classed as a Jewish company. He preferred to close it down. That did not prevent him from carrying on his other dealings . . . Come on, your bath's ready.'

Léa stood up and followed him into the bathroom.

She threw off the shawl and immersed herself in the almost scalding hot water.

'Ah! This is wonderful.'

François sat on the edge of the bath tub and continued his story.

'At that time, he met another supplier of the German buyers he dealt with. She was a woman, a German, Elfrieda, known as Hélène, who was married to a Jewish tradesman. This encounter led to an impressive swindling and trafficking enterprise dealing in all sorts of things. They bought anything that was going, potatoes, cloth, medicines, perfume, books, furs, whatever came their way, which they sold to the occupying forces or anyone who could afford to buy. That's how they became one of the main suppliers of the Kriegsmarine. Then, the arrival in Paris of Hauptsturmführer SS Fritz Engelke of the central administration of the SS, enabled the couple to become involved in very big business. The newcomer settled into Rue du Général Appert and Avenue Marceau. Finally the SS had its Purchasing Office and was able in turn to have a share of the pillaging of French goods. Szkolnikoff asked Otto, a character I'll tell you about one day, perhaps, to introduce him to Engelke. After a few initial deals and a few good meals, the two men became friends, or rather their wives, who were both German, became inseparable. That's how Szkolnikoff became the official buyer of the SS. That's the character he is. Interesting, isn't it?'

Léa's eyes were closed. François never tired of looking at her. He thought she was asleep. He stretched out his hand and brushed aside a lock of hair that had fallen over her forehead. She opened her eyes.

'Don't look at me like that, wash me. Do you remember in Orléans, when you washed me during the air-raid?'

'Be quiet.'

'Why? I've often thought of that first time. At first I was furious . . .'

'And now . . .?'

'It depends. Have you got any soap?'

'I'll nobly let you use my last bar of Guerlain soap.'

He opened a drawer and took out the precious bar of soap which he removed from its wrapping.

'Let me smell it. Mmm . . . it smells good. What is it? It's hardly a masculine smell,' she said, holding it out to him.

'No, it isn't. It's Shalimar.'

François rubbed the soap on to a big sponge and began to wash her lovely shoulders.

'No doubt it's one of your beautiful friends' perfumes,' she said, sounding rather more caustic than she had intended.

'Good heavens! You are jealous. I pity your future husband.'

'Be thankful it won't be you.'

'How do you know, my dear?'

'I'd be very surprised. I don't love you enough to marry you.'

It was stupid, but that little bitch was able to hurt him.

'Ouch! Careful, you're scrubbing my skin away . . .'

'Sorry, my mind was elsewhere.'

'Charming! Here I am, in your hands, and your mind's elsewhere.'

She sulked and turned her back to him, immersing herself deeper in the water.

Without worrying about getting wet, he took hold of her, lifted her out of the water, carried her out of the bathroom and dropped her roughly on to the cushions in front of the fire.

'You're crazy, I'll catch my death of cold. Give me a towel.'

Without bothering to reply, François ripped off his heavy robe. Naked, his penis erect, he spread his legs either side of her and towered over her. Léa could not repress a shudder of pleasure. He looked like the brigand she dreamed of meeting round every bend of the forest paths in the Bordeaux region when she was a little girl.

She brought her hand to the hollow between her thighs. François fell to his knees at the sight of her tense little hand, gently unclenched her fingers and placed his lips where her hand had been. Léa arched her back to offer herself up to his probing tongue. Pleasure took her by surprise with a violence that made her shout out and cling to her lover's hair. Almost as if with regret, he raised his head and contemplated with a delight that showed on his face, the shattering result of his caresses. Then he lay down on top of her and gently penetrated her.

They were awakened by the cold. They rushed to snuggle up under the vicuña-wool blanket and fell asleep until the following morning.

Chapter 4

It was a great thrill for Léa to receive post. When a letter arrived in the morning, she would settle herself comfortably in the big armchair in the hall, her legs tucked up under her and, wrapped in shawls, she would open the envelope with the greatest of care and devour the contents . . .

'Dearest Léa,

I'm sitting at the desk in the big parlour that you know so well. We've moved it nearer the fireplace so as to feel the warmth a little. The vines outside are black, the sky is low, it almost looks as if there'll be snow. The estate has been a little sleepy over the last few weeks. Madame Bouchardeau and I have been trying to put the accounts in order but we've had to give up on a lot of points because of lack of information. Fayard has agreed to take everything in hand. We wish you were here.

We were a little worried to hear about Françoise's condition in your last letter. We hope she'll have a lovely baby and that it won't be long before he joins us in this sinister world. There is no present more beautiful, no greater hope than a little child. Charles, who is playing on the rug in front of me, is wonderful. Every day he enchants us with his discoveries, his progress. I'm always talking to him about his father and you so that he won't forget you and gets to know you. Christmas is drawing near. As soon as he's asleep, Ruth and I secretly make toys with wood from the shed and remnants of cloth. What a pity that we can't all be together . . . We've heard from L. We still have no idea where he is but we know that the task he has decided to undertake is progressing and that every day, he is joined by more and more people. He is well.

Write quickly and let us know how Françoise is.

Charles and I send love and kisses.

Camille'

Léa was always a little irritated by Camille's gentleness, by the hope she wanted to maintain at all costs, by her passionate love for her son which seemed mysterious to Léa . . . Laurent was well. She ought to be satisfied with this vague news. She knew that Laurent continued writing his diary, and when he could, he sent extracts to Camille, but it was too risky to pass them on. She had to be content with these snippets and she scoured the newspapers from the south-west which she managed to find in Paris. Behind each act of 'terrorism', she saw Laurent's hand; a bridge was blown up, it was Laurent; a patrol was attacked, it was Laurent; prisoners were freed, again Laurent . . .

She carefully folded the letter, jumped out of the armchair and went into the parlour, humming away to herself.

Du soir au matin
Voir les Fridolins
Moi j'en ai marre
Entendr' leur radio,
Lire leurs sal' journaux
Moi, j'en ai marre.[1]

She switched on the wireless and tried to tune in to the BBC.

'Mademoiselle Léa, don't sing that song, if the neighbours hear you, we'll be in trouble.'

'Be quiet, Estelle, I'm trying to get London.'

'You know it's forbidden.'

'Everything's forbidden these days. We're being suffocated. Quick, I've got it! Call my aunts.'

Estelle left the room grumbling, wrapped in her many

[1] All day long,
seeing the Fritzes
I'm fed up with them
Hearing their radio
Reading their filthy papers
I'm fed up with them

shawls and looking the picture of reproachfulness.

'Today is the 857th day of French Resistance to oppression. Honour and the Fatherland. The French speak to the French.'

But what on earth were Albertine and Lisa doing? They were going to miss the beginning. Eight hundred and fifty-seven days the Resistance had lasted! What was so terrible was that people were getting used to it. You got used to being cold, to queuing for hours for a crust of bread, to only washing once a week, to buying butter and meat on the black market, to meeting Germans in the street, to accepting anything for an extra ration. Of course, from time to time, people rebelled like the women in the Rue de Buci who smashed the window of a grocer's with tins of food. Estelle, who was there, had never been so frightened in her life. 'You should have seen them, those police brutes, hitting those poor women. They took them away by the dozen in Black Marias, some of them with their children clinging to their skirts. Ah! It was a sorry sight. Luckily, I had a friend who lives in the Rue de Seine, and I went and hid at her place. They say one woman was killed and another was sent to Germany. Mademoiselle Léa, do you think things like that are possible?' What could she reply?

'The Soviet Forces are continuing to gain ground in the Southern sector. The retreat of the VIIth Italian Army, which was by no means equipped to confront the harsh Russian winter, has turned into a rout.'

'Well, that's good news,' thought Léa. 'Whatever are they doing? They never miss the broadcast.'

'Oh my God! Oh my God! It's terrible . . .' wailed Lisa, coming into the parlour.

She sank breathlessly into an easy chair which groaned beneath her weight.

'What's the matter?'

Lisa pointed to the door, spluttering:

'Your . . . sister . . .'

'What about my sister?'

'The baby!'

'Here we go again, it always happens to me . . . first Camille and now Françoise. There's no reason why it shouldn't go on . . . I've got a ready-made vocation: mid-wife . . .'

'Switch off the wireless, darling, I've got a headache.'

'Have you called the doctor?'

'He's on his way. Please go and see your sister, she's asking for you.'

Poor Françoise, since the visit of Captain Frederic Hanke, the friend of Otto Kramer, the 'fiancé' as Lisa discreetly called him, she had not stopped crying and fretting. Léa had learned the reasons for her grief from Frederic Hanke: Major Kramer's superiors had refused to give him permission to marry Françoise and, when he had pressed the matter, they had sent him to the Eastern Front. Before leaving, he had managed to slip Frederic a letter for Françoise in which he assured her of his love and asked her to be brave as befits the wife of a soldier and to do nothing that might endanger the life of their child. He also asked his father to intervene and speak to his friend Himmler. Frederic Hanke had not concealed from Léa the fact that Otto's father was also violently opposed to the marriage.

'What will become of Françoise?' she asked.

'Financially, there'll be no problem. I promised Otto I'd make sure the child lacks nothing.'

'That's not what I was talking about. I mean her situation: the child will be registered as "father unknown".'

'I know, but what can we do?'

'Léa, hurry up, your sister's asking for you,' said Albertine, coming into the room.

The stuffy bedroom smelled of sweat and vomit. Françoise, wild-eyed, lay in the dishevelled bed. Léa sat down beside her. What! Was this the sister she used to race to Bellevue, with whom she used to hide in the chapels of the Verdelais shrine, who used to swim with her in the Garonne at Langon; and the wine harvests when they used to pelt each other with bunches of grapes, staining their dresses, the warm Christmas nights when they used to compare presents out of the corner of their eye, always finding the other one's presents more interesting:

and their first grown-up bicycles, blue for her and red for Françoise; and their quarrels . . .

Françoise looked at her with sad eyes that reminded Léa of their father. It was so unbearable that she lowered her own.

'Otto isn't here. If only you knew how frightened I am. He promised he'd be here. Why has he deserted me . . .?'

She was sitting up and was clinging anxiously to Léa.

'Isn't his child more important than his Führer? And yet he told me he doesn't like Hitler. He told me he didn't, so . . . Why isn't he here for the birth of his child?'

'Calm down, it's not his fault. It's the War. He has to obey orders . . .'

'But he told me . . .'

'Don't think about it any more.'

Françoise's cry made Léa jump.

'Don't think about it! How do you expect me to forget that my child won't have a father . . . that the whole family will point to me . . . the unmarried mother . . . the Jerry's mistress . . . the bitch . . . the whore . . .'

'Be quiet. It's a bit late to think of that now. Ah! You're here, doctor.'

'Well now, my dear young lady, is the great moment nearly here?'

Albertine and Lisa followed the doctor into the room. Like a coward, Léa took advantage of the moment to disappear.

In the hall, the telephone was ringing. She answered it.

'Hello, Léa?'

'Yes.'

'It's Raphaël Mahl. I must see you at once.'

'But that's not possible, my sister's in the middle of giving birth.'

'Let Nature get on with it, she'll manage perfectly well without you.'

'Is it urgent?'

'Very.'

'All right then, come over.'

'I can't.'

'Why not?'

'Too dangerous to tell you over the phone. In half an hour,

I'll be at 16 Rue Dauphine. It's a restaurant which doesn't look much from the outside but the three Raymond sisters cook up the most exquisite caramelized salambo. I beg you, please come.'

'I'm on my way.'

She hung up. His fear was contagious.

'Who was it?' asked Lisa, coming out of the parlour.

'A friend. I have to go out.'

'You have to go . . .'

'Yes, let me through, it's important.'

'But . . . what about your sister?'

'She doesn't need me, there are enough people with her. If François Tavernier telephones, tell him I'm at 16 Rue Dauphine in a restaurant with Raphaël Mahl.'

'Raph . . .'

'Yes, don't forget, 16 Rue Dauphine. Don't worry, I'll try to get home early.'

'What will Albertine say?'

'You'll explain to her.'

Léa took the fur-lined boots with wooden soles that she had bought through Raphaël out of the hall cupboard.

'Wear your sister's coat, it'll keep you warm.'

Since François had told her that only certain types of women dared wear fur coats, she had no longer borrowed Françoise's coat. So as not to aggravate her aunt any further, she slipped it on without a word and donned the matching hat.

'Come home quickly,' said her aunt, kissing her.

An icy wind was blowing in the Rue de l'Université. It was madness to go out in such weather. The dark, empty street echoed the clattering of Léa's wooden soles on the frozen cobblestones.

She reached the Rue Dauphine breathless and perspiring from running to throw off imaginary pursuers. No light indicated the whereabouts of the Raymond sisters' restaurant. Léa pushed open a door which had no bell. Was this the place? An appetizing smell of soup provided the answer.

The restaurant was small and poorly lit. A big tabby cat was asleep on the bar to the right of the door; another rubbed up against Léa's legs. A spiral staircase led up to the first floor. A barrel-shaped woman with a sallow complexion and her hair pulled back in a bun, wearing a white apron that was too long for her, was coming towards her.

'Good day, mademoiselle, are you looking for someone?'

'Yes, Monsieur Mahl.'

'Monsieur Mahl isn't here yet, but his table is ready. Would you like to follow me?'

She walked across the room and Léa followed. She seated her at a little table covered with a white cloth, near the kitchen door. Another woman, who resembled the first, came over and asked with an even heavier Auvergne accent than the first:

'Would you like a drink while you're waiting?'

On seeing Léa's hesitation, she added proudly:

'We still have nearly all the aperitifs.'

'Then I'll have a port.'

'That's a good choice, the port is excellent.'

Léa looked around her.

All the tables were taken by a friendly-looking clientele, dressed in dark clothes of good quality. People were speaking in low voices, gesturing discreetly. The Raymond sisters addressed them with that familiarity reserved for regulars. There was a reassuring family atmosphere.

'Here you are, mademoiselle, here's your port.'

'Thank you.'

Léa sipped her drink slowly, feeling vaguely anxious, not daring to think about the possible reasons for Raphaël's lateness.

Each time the kitchen door opened, the sound of someone practising their singing exercises could be heard.

'It's one of their sons who is a student opera singer,' said Raphaël Mahl, who had joined Léa without her noticing. 'A delightful boy.'

'Why are you late? But . . . have you been hurt?'

A little blood was oozing from his forehead and from the corner of his mouth.

'It's nothing, an argument with a little thug,' he said, wiping his face with a bloodstained handkerchief.

One of the sisters caught sight of him.

'Oh! Monsieur Mahl!'

'Be quiet, please! You'll have the whole restaurant looking at me.'

But that did not stop the good woman from bringing a towel and a bowl of warm water.

'It really isn't necessary.'

Under the insistent eye of the restaurant owner, he gave in, moistened the towel and wiped it over his face. Léa watched him with a sort of irritation.

Another sister, unless it was the same one, came to take their order.

'Today, we've got Auvergne hotpot with cabbage, andouillette, blanquette of veal and jugged hare.'

'What would you like, Léa?'

'The hotpot.'

'And what about you, Monsieur Mahl?'

'I'll have the same. Have you still got that Burgundy?'

'Of course.'

'Give me a bottle at cellar temperature.'

'I know, monsieur, I know my clients' preferences. A selection of charcuterie to start with. How does that sound?'

'Fine. Give me a Suze while I'm waiting.'

'Right away, Monsieur Mahl.'

They did not exchange a word until Raphaël's drink arrived.

'Are you finally going to tell me why you brought me here?'

Raphaël remained silent, sipping his aperitif. He looked wan and drawn.

He was looking at her as if he had only just noticed her presence.

'Léa, I'm a disgusting swine.'

'I know that.'

'No, you don't really know. Another Suze,' he ordered to one of the sisters who was passing their table.

'Why did you want to see me?'

'The Gestapo are going to arrest Sarah Mulstein.'

For a second, Léa could not take in what he was saying, then, gradually, a look of horror came over her face while in her mouth she could taste bile.

61

'What have you done? It wasn't you? Tell me it wasn't you!'

Raphaël, playing with his glass, looked like an old child who had been caught out and did not know how to get out of the situation.

'It's not my fault . . . I had no choice . . .'

Léa's disgust slowly turned into horror.

'You had no choice! What do you mean?'

'It's rather a long and complicated business. To cut a long story short, I was arrested by the Gestapo for gold smuggling. They said they'd forget about it if I agreed to collaborate with them and give them information about press and publishing circles . . .'

'Otherwise . . .?'

'They would hand me over to the French police for a few other trifles or they'd send me to join my fellow Jews in a concentration camp.'

'So you preferred to send Sarah!'

'That's not exactly how it happened. At first I told them what rumours were going around at the publishers Editions Gallimard and in cafés frequented by the intellectuals. In exchange, they turned a blind eye to my little venture. You know, at the moment, you can earn a lot of money if you're shrewd . . .'

'. . . and if you're a swine.'

'Don't judge me so hastily.'

'How long have you been working for them?'

'Just over a year . . . on and off. Since the occupation of the unoccupied zone, they've become more demanding. A month ago they sent for me and told me I had to find out who was helping Jews escape to Spain. "It should be easy for you as a Jew to infiltrate one of these networks. Find them, and we'll forget who you are." It was perfectly clear. What else could I do?'

'Run away.'

'Run away? Where? You don't know them, they're a ruthless and admirable race, made to rule the world, while the Jews, as Moses said, are a perverse and lying race . . .'

'And you're the perfect illustration of that.'

'No doubt it's probably my way of being faithful. Very few men have the courage to acknowledge their weaknesses and brave the direst consequences. We are not a great people while greatness comes naturally to the Germans; they understand and admire it effortlessly. That makes a race of heroes. That's how it once was in France . . .'

'I'm not interested in whether the Germans have a sense of greatness or not. As far as I'm concerned, they're enemies who are occupying our country and I dream of the moment when they'll be hounded out of France and everywhere else. Things are going badly for your friends in Russia. You ought to be thinking of changing your allegiance.'

'Not so loud. I'll think about it when the time comes. Meanwhile, they're winning. If it weren't for them, I'd already be in prison.'

'That's where you should be. Let's get back to Sarah. What did you do? I thought you didn't know her address.'

'True, but in the course of my little inquiry, I came across her network. It wasn't hard for me to get in touch with them. I made it known all over the place that I had to get out of France double quick. One day, while I was having lunch, and a pretty awful one it was too, in a little Jewish restaurant in Belleville, a kid came up to me and told me to go to the Select café on the Champs Elysées and ask for Boby. The name vaguely rang a bell. I thought Boby must have been one of the waiters there. I often go to the Select especially on Saturdays at around seven. What a noise! What chaos! What a squawking! You find queens of all ages, plastered in make up, wiggling their behinds, simpering, flirting unashamedly with cute gigolos, haggling over the price of their embraces. The place has such a bad reputation that the occupying forces have been banned from going there. So it's an ideal place to leave messages. The kid gave me a password like: "I went to bed early for years", and I went to the Select where I asked for Boby. Imagine the prettiest creature there ever was: round, plump, with a childlike voice . . .'

'Spare me the details.'

'. . . young, fresh, a perfect jewel! After I had given him the password, he asked me to follow him. We went into the cellar. My heart was in my boots. He seemed satisfied with my answers to his questions. He said that he was only one link in the chain and that he did not know the others. He ordered me to go to Fouquet's bar the following day, wearing a red carnation in my buttonhole and holding a map of Paris. I did as he told me to. There, a very elegant man came up to me and said, after buying me a drink, that a friend of his was expecting us to lunch. We took a cycle-taxi to the Rue de la Tour, where we entered a splendid apartment. Sarah was there. We fell into each other's arms. I was prepared for anything except meeting her. I knew the Gestapo were looking for her, that's even why I asked you if you knew where she was, so that I could warn her . . .'

'I don't understand any more . . .'

'But it's not that difficult. I was quite happy to relay inconsequential gossip to the Germans, but I didn't want to denounce people, at least, not for nothing.'

'I thought that was hard to believe! You are vile!'

'No, I'm not that bad. I was able to tell Sarah everything, so I confessed what I was doing at her place. She didn't seem at all surprised, she really is an extraordinary woman. I was still a bit surprised, though, when she kissed me and said: "Dear Raphaël, you'll never change." We decided that I'd wait forty-eight hours before telling the Germans of my discovery.'

'So everything's all right, she's had time to go into hiding!'

'No! That's what's wrong. The Germans were suspicious and had me followed. They were waiting outside the building. Ah! My good friend, it took all my courage not to take to my heels.'

'Aren't you eating?'

The three Raymond sisters were standing over their table looking reproachful.

'I'm sorry, we were engrossed in conversation.'

'So we can see,' said one of them in a schoolmarmish voice.

'Here, Léa, help yourself.'

'I'm not hungry.'

'Make an effort. You'll arouse their curiosity if you don't

eat and they'll refuse to serve me in the future. I need to be able to come here.'

Raphaël set an example by swallowing two slices of sausage in one mouthful.

'What did the Germans say to you?'

'They asked me the name of the person I had just visited in the apartment.'

'Did you tell them?'

'They caught me off-guard.'

'Poor you.'

'Go on, insult me, it's too easy. What would you have done, in my shoes?'

'Did they go up and arrest Sarah?'

'No, because I told them that in two days time she was to give me a list of the next group of people who wanted to go to Spain.'

'Did they believe you?'

'I got the impression that they did at the time. They made me get into their car and drove me to Boulevard Flandrin. I felt totally reassured when I saw one of my friends, Rudy de Mérode, sitting at the desk. We've done a few good deals together since the beginning of the war. He's a very high-up official.'

'What did he say to you?'

'That his superiors were waiting for proof that I was loyal to them and that they were counting on me to obtain the names of the members of the network within forty-eight hours.'

'So, did you manage to warn Sarah?'

'No. Since yesterday, I've been followed everywhere. I've tried to shake them off without any success. They're the ones who beat me up at the metro station Sèvres-Babylone. That's why I called you and asked you to come here. You've got to go and warn her.'

'But how? The Rue de la Tour is a long way from here.'

'You don't have to go to the Rue de la Tour, but to 31 Rue Guénégaud.'

'I've completely lost track of what you're talking about.'

'Yesterday, she told me she was leaving the Rue de la Tour as it had become dangerous for her comrades and that she was

65

going to disappear for a while. One of her friends, who has emigrated to the United States, left her the keys to her flat. That's where she's been hiding for a month when she gets the feeling she's being followed to the Rue de la Tour.'

'And she told you all that? There's one thing I don't understand. How do I know you haven't given that address to the Germans?'

'You're right, I could have done. I can't quite explain why I didn't. I'm very fond of Sarah, or rather of the memory of certain drinking sessions in certain Montparnasse bars. Remember what Jules Renard said: "There's no such thing as friends, only moments of friendship." That is a perfect description of Sarah and me.'

'Here's the hotpot. Let me know what you think of it,' said one of the Raymond sisters, placing a steaming dish in front of them.

They waited until she had gone back into the kitchen before continuing their conversation.

'Don't move. Two of the men who were following me have just come in. They haven't seen me yet. Get up. Go into the kitchen. At the back there's a door that leads into the courtyard. Cross the yard and go under an arch. There's a second courtyard and, on the right, you'll see an ancient door. Then you come to a corridor and another door which leads into the little Rue de Nevers. Turn right and head towards the embankment then turn left immediately and that's the Rue Guénégaud. Look out for anything suspicious. Walk normally. If you see nobody, go to number 31, go up to the third floor and ring three times. Sarah will open the door. Tell her to leave at once. Good luck.'

Raphaël Mahl did not flinch from looking into Léa's eyes which clearly said: 'Can I trust you?' She stood up, looking perfectly natural, and casually slung her fur coat over her shoulders. She went up to the bar where two men in raincoats stood with their backs to her. She quietly asked one of the sisters:

'Excuse me, where's the toilet?'

Léa did not listen to the reply but headed towards the kitchen. As she walked past the cook and the opera singer, she put her finger to her lips and went out into the courtyard.

In the little restaurant in the Rue Dauphine, everything was calm, the two men had not moved and Raphaël Mahl tucked into the hotpot.

It was very dark in the Rue de Nevers. Huge rats scuttled across Léa's path nearly making her cry out. An icy wind swept the embankment. There was not a sound to be heard, the city seemed completely deserted. Léa was trying to stop her wooden soles from clattering, her fists clenched in her coat pockets, her ears pricked up, fear in the pit of her stomach as she made her way to the Rue Guénégaud.

Suddenly, a car loomed up coming over the Pont-Neuf bridge, with its lights off. It tore along at great speed and turned into the Rue Dauphine. A sudden squeal of brakes. Léa, forgetting Raphaël's instructions, began to run. The car started to reverse.

The car turned into the Rue Guénégaud, passed the young woman who was running and stopped a few yards further up. The door opened and a man got out and blocked her path. Léa screamed. A hand grabbed her shoulder.

'Don't be frightened, it's me. Get into the car.'

Léa meekly obeyed François Tavernier. They drove down the Rue de Seine to the embankment and stopped outside an art gallery on the corner.

'Where were you running to?'

'When I heard your car I was frightened.'

'What were you doing with Mahl?'

'He knows where Sarah is. The Gestapo are after her, I was on my way to warn her.'

'Why wasn't he doing it himself?'

'He was being watched by two men in the restaurant. I went out the back way.'

'I've got a feeling there's something fishy going on. And so have you, otherwise you wouldn't have left me that message.'

'Maybe, but we must try and warn Sarah.'

'Where is she?'

'At 31 Rue Guénégaud.'

'Did Mahl give you that address?'

'Yes.'

'Well, it's in God's hands. Stay here. If anyone comes along, drive off. If I'm not back in twenty minutes, leave.'

'No, I'm coming with you.'

'It's out of the ques . . .'

'Shut up, we're wasting time.'

François put his arms round her. She murmured:

'I'm frightened.'

Then she broke free and started walking towards the Rue Mazarine.

'No, we won't go that way. Let's go up the Rue de Seine and the Rue Jacques-Callot. From there we'll have a direct view of the Rue Guénégaud.'

François took a revolver from his overcoat pocket and turned the cylinder. Léa felt slightly reassured.

They walked quickly in the silence of that winter night. The absence of noise and light made everything feel a little unreal, rather like the calm that precedes a storm. They stopped at the entrance to the old Passage du Pont-Neuf. In front of them, the street and the crossroads were empty. They took a few steps forward . . .

It all happened very quickly. A female shape was hurled into the street. She tottered, regained her balance, took off. Shouts. She was running towards them. A shot rang out. She spun round on herself . . . and slowly crumpled to the ground.

François had difficulty in restraining Léa.

Two men came running up. She raised herself up. The darkness concealed the blood on the pavement. A blow from the butt of the gun. A hand, so white, so slender, was raised in a pathetic gesture of self-protection. François stifled Léa's groans.

Another blow. The hand fell. They lifted the battered body. One took her shoulders, the other her ankles. Her long black hair hung down and swept up a little blood and dust. She was thrown into the back of a van. The glow of a cigarette as they relaxed after their exertions. Car doors slamming again. The sound of an engine revving. Then silence. Nobody moved. Nobody had heard them assassinate a woman.

Chapter 5

The crying of the newborn child broke into Léa's dream.

She and Laurent were walking together on the terrace at Montillac, their arms lovingly entwined. Nothing else existed, the war had wiped out all the obstacles in the way of their love, leaving them with no memories as they stood facing the vast countryside which lay completely silent.

Léa awoke calling out to her mother, her cheeks wet with tears.

In the next room, the baby's crying stopped. Estelle came in carrying her breakfast tray.

'Good morning, Mademoiselle Léa.'

'Good morning, Estelle, what time is it?'

'Nearly ten o'clock. Don't forget we're having a celebration this evening.'

'Celebration?'

'It's New Year's Eve and it's little Pierre's christening. You're his godmother.'

'Little Pierre? It's true, we've got a little Pierre now. How's Françoise this morning?'

'Much better. Yesterday she walked a few paces. I'll leave you because I've got to start making my cake.'

Léa got up and slipped an old dressing gown of Pyrenees wool that had belonged to her father over the jumper she wore on top of her nightdress, and pulled on a pair of woollen socks. She caught sight of her reflection in the wardrobe mirror. Dressed like that, she was not exactly the picture of elegance, but at least she was not too cold. After cleaning her teeth and brushing her hair, she tucked into her breakfast.

Léa bit into the slice of black bread that was as dry as a bone.

Images from her dream started coming back to her and then those awful images from the night Sarah Mulstein was arrested.

François Tavernier did not have too much difficulty in obtaining news of the young woman from Helmut Knochen himself. She had been taken to the Rue des Saussaies to await interrogation. Her wounds, which turned out not to be serious, were dressed. She was kept in solitary confinement and nobody was allowed to see her. Knochen assured him she was being well-treated. No doubt François Tavernier did not seem convinced as the German officer added:

'Since the departure of Danneker, Eichmann's right-hand man, the interrogations of Jewish terrorists have been carried out with less brutality.'

Helmut Knochen had been put in charge of the *Sonderkommando* on his arrival in Paris on the 14th June 1940. This 32-year-old intellectual, son of a humble primary school teacher and a doctor of philosophy, had dreamed of being a professor of letters before joining the official German Press Agency as the head of research into the French, Belgian and Dutch press. He had been a member of the S.A. since 1933. He was a rather tall, thin man, with a prominent brow and dark hair, who rarely smiled. In less than a year, he had managed to infiltrate Parisian high society and had become the darling of the salons thanks to his wit and culture. It was at one of these that Tavernier had met him. Very quickly the two men met again for reasons that were diametrically opposed. Without beating about the bush, Helmut Knochen had told him that he was looking for agents in these circles who would be able to inform on the politicians in the Vichy government, on industrialists and, of course, on the Resistance movement and its leaders. Apparently interested, François Tavernier had met him again and had learned from him the details of how the fearsome Gestapo organization worked throughout French territory. Curiously, he had won Knochen's trust because of the differences between the Gestapo and the German embassy. Tavernier, who was frequently entertained by Otto Abetz, the ambassador, told him what was being said – true and false –

70

about his services, in the corridors and salons of the embassy. He received these bits of gossip with apparent calmness while his rather large mouth creased into a wry lopsided smile.

It was on this young man – who, in the space of a few months, had set up an organization which even the German army feared – that the fate of Sarah Mulstein depended.

'Don't worry, I'll keep an eye on this business myself.'

François had felt very worried, but had not pressed the matter for fear of making this 'business' sound too important and thus arousing Helmut Knochen's suspicions.

Sarah had been at the Rue des Saussaies for ten days.

Someone was knocking at Léa's door.

'Come in.'

It was Françoise, her face radiant and rested, carrying her newborn child.

'Your godson was dying to see you,' she said, holding out the child.

Léa took him, clumsily, but quickly handed him back to his mother.

'He's very sweet but I'm afraid of dropping him. He's so tiny.'

'Not so tiny. He weighed seven pounds at birth. He's the most beautiful baby. Don't you think he looks like his father?'

Her question irritated Léa.

'You know, I haven't really looked at him properly.'

Françoise tensed her shoulders and looked down. She was a touching sight with her baby in her arms.

'I'm sorry,' said Léa, 'I didn't mean to be nasty. Let me get dressed if you want me to be ready for the christening. What time is it again?'

'Three o'clock.'

Léa stood motionless for a second looking at the door that had just closed. Then, with a shrug, she flung her dressing gown on to the bed, took off her socks, fastened a suspender belt and woollen stockings under her nightdress, slipped on a pair of knickers and, shivering, pulled off her jumper and nightdress. She would never get used to this cold!

What would her mother have thought of all this? What

would the wise Isabelle Delmas have done in this situation. Would she have agreed to be godmother to the child of a German soldier simply because the future Christian was her nephew? And Frederic Hanke, as the father's best friend, was to be the godfather . . .

Léa was too shocked by Sarah's arrest to really take in what Françoise was saying when she had asked her to be godmother to her little boy. She would look pretty stupid in the Church of Saint-Thomas d'Aquin, holding a child above the baptismal font in the company of a German officer. She had told François how she wanted to refuse, but he had advised her against it.

They had seen each other almost every day since that tragic night. A night he had spent beside her in her aunts' apartment in the 'cold rooms', unknown to Léa's aunts who were too overwhelmed by the upheaval caused by Françoise giving birth. The birth was fortunately over by the time they returned.

François proved to be the gentlest, most patient and affectionate of friends, helping Léa to almost forget the worrying sides of her life. Every day, she said to herself: I must talk to him about certain things and every day, she was happy just to drag him into her room and snuggle up to him. Without her having to say anything, he had understood that she did not feel like making love but wanted simply to be close to him. She could have stayed like that for hours, absorbing his warmth and his smell, soothed by his regular heartbeat and the reassuring words he whispered. She felt so good, no longer afraid, that she refused to ruin this fragile happiness by asking questions that he would not answer. She had told him, on the day after the tragedy, of the repulsion she now felt for Raphaël Mahl.

'In this particular instance, you're mistaken. Sarah's arrest was nothing to do with him.'

Léa refused to believe him. Since her dinner with him in the restaurant in the Rue Dauphine, she had not heard from him.

Léa, ensconced in the armchair in the hall, was reading a letter from Camille out loud to her aunts who were standing listening.

'Dear Léa,

You can imagine how sorry all of us here are not to be able to attend the christening of Françoise's baby! We were a little disappointed that you didn't tell us much about him in your last letter. Do tell Françoise that we're all thinking of her. I'll write to her tomorrow.

Charles was thrilled with his presents. He wears the jumper that your aunts knitted all the time and won't take it off. Please tell them.

The carpenter has finished repairing the barn door that was in danger of falling off. As soon as we have a little money, it would be a good idea to replace some of the slates, the attic roof is leaking.

It's raining and I haven't heard from L. for ten days now.

Hugs and kisses,

Camille.'

The christening went much better than everybody had anticipated. First of all, the inhabitants of the Rue de l'Université had been pleasantly surprised to see the godfather, Frederic Hanke, arrive in civilian dress, his arms full of presents. When these had been handed out, he took them out to lunch in a little restaurant in the Rue de Verneuil. The meal was enjoyable, almost merry, so kind had their host been. He spoke of Camille d'Argilat and the emotion he had experienced when delivering her child with great feeling. He said how attached he was to Montillac and the area, and that when the war was over, he would like to live there. Was it because he was out of uniform, but Léa felt as if she were seeing him for the first time. She caught herself out thinking that if he had not been a German, she would have added him to the list of her admirers. That made her smile. At half past two, they went back to fetch little Pierre and Estelle. At three o'clock, in the church of Saint-Thomas d'Aquin, the priest said as he dripped the water on the baby's forehead:

'I christen you Pierre, Otto, Frederic, in the name of the Father, the Son and the Holy Ghost.'

François Tavernier arrived at the Rue de l'Université at

about six o'clock and found the whole family standing round the cradle drinking champagne. He had no alternative but to drink to the health of the baby but he refused to take part in the party they planned to celebrate both New Year's Eve and the birth of the child.

Tavernier and Hanke did not know each other. Françoise introduced them. They shook hands. After exchanging a few platitudes, François dragged Léa into her room.

'Can you give me the key to this apartment block and that of the apartment opposite?'

'What for?'

'I might need to come back here in a hurry tonight.'

'Why can't you go home?'

'Because I've got some business in this area. I need a hiding-place close by.'

'You won't tell me why?'

'No . . .'

'You're very irritating, you never tell me anything. You let me imagine the worst possible things about you. How do I know it wasn't you who denounced Sarah Mulstein?'

Her remark was so unexpected that François was numb for a second, then his features tensed and he turned white while his face became distorted with anger. Léa shrank from this change in him but not quickly enough to avoid the biggest slap she had ever received. Reeling from the blow, she tottered and her head hit one of the bedposts. Her nose was bleeding slightly. He was at her side at once. He took her by the arm and squeezed her so hard that she cried out.

'Don't ever say anything like that again, Léa.'

Leaning over her, he was so threatening that she raised her free arm in a gesture of defence. Her childlike reaction made François relax a little.

'I'm doing everything within my power to get Sarah out of the hands of the Gestapo. I will even go so far as trying to help her escape.'

Léa cried:

'When?'

Tavernier looked at her dubiously.

'You really are strange. You make it clear that you don't

74

trust me an inch and you believe me when I talk to you about helping Sarah escape.'

'Because that I do believe you're capable of. Your contacts with the Germans must be of some use.'

'I don't really intend to inform them of this particular business, but rather to call on the members of Sarah's network.'

'Do you know them?'

'Some of them. By the way, we'll be meeting here. Warn your aunts so that they stay in their rooms and don't ask any questions.'

'But why here?'

'This apartment houses the "fiancée" and the child of an officer of the Reich, and the mistress of General von Rippen lives on the first floor. This building is therefore known to the authorities as being inhabited by German sympathisers. Consequently it is under less surveillance.'

'I understand. I can deal with my aunts, but what about Françoise?'

'She mustn't suspect anything. For the sake of all our lives. Are you still determined to help Sarah?'

'More than ever.'

'Fine. Your mission begins tomorrow: you are to find three or four people and deliver a message to them. This is what you will have to do and say.'

For an hour, he made her learn the messages by heart, their codenames, the places and the signs of recognition.

'Don't forget anything. We'll meet here tomorrow evening for you to report back. Have you got a bicycle?'

'Not here, no.'

'I'll see if I can steal one for you. It'll be a New Year's Eve present from me. What colour would you prefer?'

'I don't mind, mine's blue.'

'Blue it is. It's an excellent colour for warding off bad luck. On your blue bicycle, you'll be the messenger of hope.'

'It's funny you should say that, my Uncle Adrien said exactly the same thing.'

'You see, your uncle and I have a lot in common.'

François took her in his arms and pulled her on to the bed.

'Now come and show me you're sorry for thinking I was a traitor.'

'Leave me alone. I've been feeling dead inside since the other evening.'

He was not listening. His lips and hands were trying to reach her. Léa did not struggle but when he kissed her, his lips tasted salt tears.

'Not until you've saved Sarah.'

He got up and smoothed his clothes.

'Will you give me the keys?'

'I'll go and get them.'

'Whatever you do, don't make too much noise,' she said, handing him the keys.

'I'm not sure I'll be back tonight. In the hall you'll find the bicycle and a pass. Tomorrow, don't forget: Trinité is calling comrades Vautrin, Homais, La Rochelle and Bataille to a meeting to make an important decision concerning Simone Mingot on 3rd January at 10 p.m. at 29 Rue de l'Université. You will give each of them half of a first class metro ticket and they will show you the other half. Be very careful, my love, and if there is the slightest hint of anything being wrong, stop at once. Meanwhile, go back to your party. Tomorrow, a new year begins. I very much hope to spend it with you.'

He kissed her tenderly

Léa joined her family, sad at François's departure. Outside, it had begun to snow.

The following day, Léa found a magnificent blue bicycle in the entrance hall with beautiful synthetic leather panniers. As her aunts were surprised that they had not heard the delivery man ring the bell, Léa claimed that it was a present from Father Christmas who had even been thoughtful enough to add tins of chocolate and milk.

The snow had not settled. The weather was fine and cold. Léa announced that she was going to try out her bicycle and would not be back for lunch as she wanted to make the most of the lovely weather. She wrapped up warmly in a pair of trousers and two thick sweaters. She slipped on her lined boots, wound a woollen turban round her hair and, thus

76

attired, put on the warm fur-lined jacket given to her by François. She completed her outfit with thick gloves lined with rabbit fur.

Her sister and aunts wished her an enjoyable ride.

Chapter 6

Paris had never looked so beautiful to Léa as it did that morning. The air was clear and crisp. There was a luminosity that gave the old stonework of the houses along the Quai Voltaire, caressed by a watery sun, a look of fragile cheeriness. The young girl stopped on the Pont Royal bridge to watch the sparkling grey and lustrous bronze waters of the Seine flow towards the Alma, lulling the black barges as they glided on their way. On that morning of the 1st January 1943, looking at that view, which so many lovers in Paris had lingered over, she felt a sense of peace overwhelm her and a forgotten childhood prayer rose to her lips.

'Dear God, I offer thee my day, happy or unhappy, it is thine, for thee, to do as thou will, but make me, as I draw nearer to my eternity, also draw nearer to thee.'

Full of confidence, she climbed back on to her bicycle. The city was so empty that it felt like a ghost town. Not the slightest human sound disturbed the silence. Léa exulted in that solitude, it enabled her to clear her mind and prepare herself for the mission with which François Tavernier had entrusted her. In spite of everything that was incomprehensible in his behaviour, she could not bring herself, whatever she had said, to distrust him. She was convinced that if there was the slightest chance of freeing Sarah, he was the only person capable of bringing it off.

When she reached the Place Sainte-Opportune, Léa padlocked her bicycle to the railings by the metro station and walked towards the Rue de la Ferronerie.

She pushed open the door of a seedy café whose windows were daubed with blue. A cold and sickly smell of damp

78

sawdust, cheap wine, stale tobacco and coffee substitute assailed her. She felt as if she were entering a dull underwater world peopled by creatures with greenish faces. Behind the bar, enshrined amid the dusty empty bottles, was a squat, gleaming wireless set playing a popular tune. The proprietor, a plump man with his sleeves rolled up, his sparse hair dishevelled, his eyes sticky, a burnt out cigarette butt hanging from his lips, and a tangled beard, shouted gruffly:

'There's nothing to drink, alcohol's off today.'

'I'd just like something hot, a cup of coffee, for example.'

'Coffee! Did you all hear that? With a drop of milk, and a few lumps of sugar . . .'

The handful of customers jeered slavishly.

Léa blushed. She had got off to a fine start!

'Because I like your face, I can give you a little hot *Viandox*[1] . . . you are the young lady who has an appointment with half a metro ticket, aren't you?' he whispered rapidly.

Léa stepped back in surprise.

'Don't run away, young lady, these days *Viandox* isn't any worse than anything else.'

As he talked, he placed a large steaming cup in front of her.

'Don't stay here,' he continued in a low voice. 'One of the people you are looking for has been arrested. Here, drink this. Drink it, for goodness sake, people are looking at us.'

Léa put the cup to her mouth. It was scalding hot but not as bad as she had expected. The proprietor burst out laughing.

'You see, it's drinkable. Go to the church of Saint-Eustache, it's mass, nobody will take any notice of you . . . Hello, Monsieur René, what can I serve you to celebrate the new year?'

'The same as usual, a glass of house wine. Happy New Year, mademoiselle, will you drink to the new year with me?'

'But . . .'

'Be careful or I'll get angry, a pretty lady doesn't say no to the great René, does she, Juju?'

'You'd better believe him, mademoiselle, he's yet to find a woman who can resist his charms.'

[1] *Viandox* – a stock cube, similar to Oxo

'Well,' said René, 'you're a real buddy. Has your phone been repaired?'

'Yes, two days ago.'

'Keep the young lady warm for me, I've got to make a phone call. See you in a minute, sweetheart.'

Léa dodged his wandering hand. The ladykiller laughed and shrugged his shoulders.

'You must leave quickly, he works for them. In the church of Saint-Eustache, in the Chapel of the Virgin, there's a man holding *la Petite Gironde*, he'll tell you what to do. You don't owe me anything, it's on the house. Happy New Year, anyway.'

'Happy New Year to you too,' she said pushing open the door with as much composure as she could muster.

How did she unlock her bicycle? How did she find her way through the winding back streets of les Halles and how did she find herself inside the church within a few minutes? Léa did not have the faintest idea.

The church was filled with worshippers, especially women, who were singing fervently while their frozen breath came out of their mouths in little clouds. A prie-dieu was vacant in front of the altar of the Virgin; Léa knelt down, her heart thumping, unable to think.

It was time for communion. Most of the congregation were making their way towards the holy table. A man knelt down near her and put his head between his hands. A newspaper was protruding from his old overcoat pocket.

In a flash, Léa relived that summer evening in Bordeaux when, followed by Superintendent Poinsot's police officers, she had been looking for a refuge. Catching sight of *la Petite Gironde* on the newspaper stall in the Place du Grand Théâtre, she suddenly knew where to turn for help. She looked round. The man was young and wore a beard which did not succeed in making him look any older. He reminded her a little of . . . No, it wasn't possible, she was imagining things . . .

'Léa . . .'

Someone had said her name! Should she turn round? No, it was the man with *la Petite Gironde*! So?

80

'Don't move, I'll leave first. See you at your place, Rue de l'Université.'

'At my place!'

'It's the only place that's more or less safe.'

After he had left, she counted to twenty before she too set off.

Back at the Rue de l'Université, everybody was celebrating the arrival of Jean Lefèvre, Léa's old playmate who, together with his brother Raoul, took the game of being head over heels in love with her very seriously . . .

They fell into each other's arms.

The family was still at the table. A bottle of champagne was opened and they drank to their reunion, the end of the war and the new year. At least twenty minutes went by before they could shut themselves in Léa's room.

'Quickly, we don't have long. I wish it had been someone else and not you,' said Jean, holding her tight.

'Not me, charming. If it had been someone else, we might never have seen each other again.'

'True, but it's dangerous.'

'I know. What must I do next? Must I go to the other appointments?'

'No, absolutely not. After Simone Mingot's arrest . . .'

'Simone Mingot?'

'Yes, that's the name most of us know her by. After her arrest, the members of her network scattered as planned. Each of us in turn had to go and hang round our old letter box. That's where I met Trinité . . .'

'François . . .?'

'He told me he was going to try and get Simone out and asked me if I agreed. I accepted immediately. A young woman was to bring me news on the morning of the 1st January. Everything was fine until I learned, at dawn, of the arrest of a comrade who knew my address. I just had time to get dressed and escape over the rooftops. The Gestapo were already halfway up the stairs. Luckily there was no snow. I had only one thought in my head: warn Trinité. He wasn't at either of the addresses he had given me. I still went to the meeting at the

Rue de la Ferronerie. While I was going up the Boulevard Sébastopol, a cycle-taxi drew level with me.

'"Vautrin!" shouted the passenger.

'"So you're Vautrin?"

'I ignored the interruption.

'". . . carry on cycling as though nothing's happened. Go to you-know-where in the Rue de la Ferronerie and ask the proprietor where the Church of the Trinity is. He'll tell you you're in the wrong part of Paris, that in this area there's Saint-Eustache, Saint-Leu or Saint-Merri. You'll reply: 'Oh! Really, can you tell me the way to Saint-Merri?' The good man will go out on to the pavement with you to show you the way. Very quickly you'll tell him that a beautiful young girl with auburn hair and violet eyes will be coming.'

'"She sounds the spitting image of a friend of mine," I said.

'"It's her."

'I nearly fell off my bicycle. Trinité, for it was him, continued calmly.

'"This isn't the time to hurt yourself. She'll soon be meeting you in the church of Saint-Eustache in front of the chapel of the Virgin. From there go to the Montpleynet sisters' apartment. Is that quite clear?"

'"Yes," I answered, completely dazed.'

The two friends remained silent for a long time.

'What do we do now?' asked Léa.

'We wait until further instructions.'

'Let's go and join the others, it'll look fishy if we spend too long together.'

During their conversation in private, little Pierre's godfather had come to visit his godson's mother, to whom he gave a huge box of chocolates and a letter from Otto Kramer in which he told her he would soon be on leave. This piece of good news made the young woman look radiant.

When she saw Frederic Hanke, Léa turned very pale. There was no way of getting out of it, she had to make the introductions. Clutching Jean's arm, she went up to the German, who was still wearing civilian dress, and, smiling, she held out her hand and said:

'Happy New Year, Frederic. May I introduce a childhood friend of mine who's passing through Paris? Jean Lefèvre. Jean, let me introduce Françoise's son's godfather, Captain Frederic Hanke.'

If Léa had not pinched him, he would have fallen over. White and speechless, he held out a trembling hand. Frederic shook it, apparently noticing nothing unusual.

'Pleased to meet you. I'm delighted to meet a friend of Françoise and Léa's. A Happy New Year to you. Thank you for your good wishes, Léa. I hope this year will be kinder to you than last year.'

'Thank you, Frederic. Jean, would you like some real coffee?'

'Yes,' whispered Jean, not knowing what to do or say.

Captain Hanke, perfectly at ease, came over to him.

'Are you a close neighbour of the Delmas family?'

'Fairly close, yes, my mother's property is in Cadillac.'

'No doubt you help on the estate?'

'Yes.'

'You're lucky to live in such a beautiful region. I hope to see you again when the war is over and our two nations will be one.'

Jean was about to reply when Léa interrupted.

'The captain fell in love with our vineyards while he was staying with us at Montillac.'

At last, Frederic Hanke took his leave.

'I'm sorry I interrupted your lunch but it was the only time I could come and offer my good wishes. I'm on duty again at three o'clock. Françoise, if you need me, you know where you can get hold of me. Goodbye ladies, goodbye Léa, goodbye Monsieur Lefèvre.'

Everybody felt very relieved to see him go.

'Whew, I thought he'd never push off,' cried Léa, collapsing in an armchair. 'Why didn't you come and tell us he was here?'

'I didn't think of it,' said Françoise, looking ashamed, 'I was so happy to hear from Otto.'

'It doesn't matter, children. That young man is truly charming, very well brought-up and a perfect gentleman,' exclaimed Lisa merrily.

'A perfect gentleman! That's what we hear everywhere. "Just think, Madame Dupont, that officer held the door open for me in the metro. What a gentleman! Not like young French people of today, who bump into you without even apologizing. Communists . . . hooligans . . . madame, no wonder we've lost the war . . . it would have been a surprise if we hadn't. Mark my words, madame, when a people turns away from God, it's only right for God to forsake and punish that people . . . we must atone for and denounce those bad French citizens who listen to the radio broadcasts from London and disobey Marshal Pétain, a saint, who has given himself to France to save the country . . ."'

'Stop it, Léa!' cried Françoise.

'". . . Oh, Madame Durand, I couldn't agree with you more. Just think, the other day, I met an old neighbour of mine, a Jewish woman. Well, you won't believe this, she wasn't wearing the yellow star. Believe me, I gave her a piece of my mind and passers-by agreed. Red as a beetroot she was, madame . . ."'

'That's enough!'

'All right, all right, Aunt Albertine. I'm sorry, I agree with all of you: the Germans are perfect gentlemen!'

'Quite right, whatever you may think. You seem to forget that they are the winners and they can do whatever they like with us. Whereas, in spite of all the attacks, they continue to be well-behaved and patient . . .'

'They shoot hostages all over the place, they deport women and children to goodness-knows-where . . .'

'They're terrorists . . .'

'The children?'

'Be quiet, don't talk about children,' said Françoise, bursting into tears.

An embarrassed silence followed the raised voices.

'Come on, Jean, let's go to my room.'

'It's hardly proper,' said Lisa in a prim voice that would have made everybody laugh in different circumstances.

Léa shrugged and left the room, dragging her friend behind her. They had just walked through the door when the doorbell rang.

With racing hearts the two young people looked at each other. Léa quickly pointed to her room. She waited until the door was closed before going to open the front door.

'Thank God! You're here!' said François Tavernier, hugging her to him.

The feeling of relief that surged through her as his arms closed round her was akin to pleasure.

'I was so frightened. When I learned that one of Sarah's companions had given us away, I thought you would be arrested . . . I'd never have forgiven myself . . . Is Lefèvre with you?'

'Yes, why didn't you tell me it was him?'

'Because I only found out at the last minute. Where is he?'

'In my room. Let's go there before Aunt Lisa comes to see who was at the door.'

'Lead the way, but first, give me a kiss.'

For the first time, Léa responded with genuine spontaneity.

In her bedroom, she found Jean sitting on the bed with his head in his hands waiting for her. When he looked up, his eyes were moist.

François stared hard at him.

'Léa, leave us alone.'

When they were alone, he asked:

'Have you any news of other members of the network?'

The young man shook his head.

'You're going to have to leave Paris immediately. Here are your new papers. Your name is Joël Lemaire, born in La Tranche-sur-Mer in the Vendée region, on the 10th October 1920, the son of Jean Lemaire, farmer, and Thérèse Peyon, housewife. You are an only child and your parents died two years ago at Les Sables-d'Olonne, during a storm that capsized the boat they were on at the time. You work as a fisherman in Aiguillon. It's all in here with the rest of the information you'll need. Learn it by heart before you leave and destroy it. You will take the train to Poitiers this evening and from there, you'll find a connection for La Rochelle. Be very careful, inspections are frequent in that zone. When you reach La

Rochelle, try to find a bus for Luchon and l'Aiguillon. On arrival, go to the café Au rendez-vous des marins-pêcheurs. Ask for Jean-Marie from La Vaillante. When you meet him, tell him that the air is fresher there than in the Paris metro. He will answer:

'"That's very true, especially at la Trinite." Do as he tells you. Is that clear?'

'Yes.'

'Good. I'll give you ten minutes to learn all that. Have you any money?'

'Very little.'

'Here's a thousand francs.'

Jean made a gesture of refusal.

'Accept it, it's money that comes from London. Sign this receipt, it's the rule.'

Jean pocketed the money and signed.

'Please sir, may I ask you something?'

'Yes of course, what is it?'

'I don't want Léa to be mixed up in all this.'

The way François Tavernier looked at him made the young man blush.

'Neither do I, but it's a bit late to change things now.'

'I don't think it is. Tell her to go back home.'

'I'll do my best, but she's determined to help our friend . . .'

The door half-opened and Léa was standing there.

'You're taking a long time. Have you finished? Can I come in? François, I don't understand what's going on. What are we going to do for Sarah now?'

Tavernier looked her straight in the eyes without replying. Then, after a long silence, he said in a flat voice:

'Sarah's been tortured.'

Léa hurled herself at François and beat his chest.

'You lied to me! You lied to me!' she shouted. 'You said she was being well looked after . . . that thanks to your good relations with the Jerries she would be treated well . . . and they tortured her! It's your fault . . . I'll never forgive you . . . It's because of you they arrested her . . . You're a swine . . . a swine!'

'Shut up . . . that's enough,' cried Jean, putting his arms round her. 'Let him explain.'

'There's nothing to explain. He works for them. I saw him laughing outside the Hotel Lutétia,' she cried, breaking free.

Pale and drawn, François Tavernier wiped a deep scratch on his face.

'They lied to me. Sarah wasn't taken to Rue des Saussaies but to Avenue Henri-Martin. By the time I found out, it was too late. After her arrest, they took two other members of the network. One of them talked, which explains what has happened.'

'Who told you about Sarah?' asked Jean.

'One of her friends, Raphaël Mahl . . .'

'Raphaël! So you see . . .'

'. . . it was he who denounced her. No, I'm sure it wasn't him. Not that he wouldn't be capable of it, but because he knew that I was protecting Sarah and that I was in a position to have him arrested within the hour.'

'So how did he know that she wasn't at the Rue de Saussaies but at Avenue Henri-Martin?'

'Through an even viler toad than himself, for whom he works from time to time, Frédéric Martin, alias Rudy Mérode or Rudy de Mérode.'

'What did this so-called Rudy say?'

'Do you really want to know?'

'Yes.'

'Mérode laughingly told Mahl how, together with a friend, he had forced a beautiful Jewish woman to have a bath.'

'Have a bath?'

'Yes, that's what they call the torture of the bathtub. Apparently, this new form of torture was invented by a Belgian. With a man, they are content just to plunge his head in a bath or washtub filled with icy water until he almost chokes. They take him out and plunge him in again until he either talks or faints.'

'That's dreadful.'

'As for women . . .'

'Stop!' cried Jean Lefèvre.

François Tavernier looked at the two young people with a mixture of irony and compassion.

'You've thrown yourselves headlong into an adventure of which you can only see the romantic side, but there's the other side, where they torture, kill and rape, where they send children to die in extermination camps. You should have read *Mein Kampf*, young man, in which Chancellor Hitler has already clearly outlined his solution to the Jewish problem. If Léa wants to carry on playing the heroine, she must know what happens to heroines, sometimes, when they're caught. In the case of Sarah, who was aware of the risk she ran, they sent her to the "infirmary" where they "took care" of her injuries. From the Rue des Saussaies, she was taken to Avenue Henri-Martin. First of all, they interrogated her politely, but, as it was time for dinner, they locked her up in a metal cupboard . . . You know, the kind that are used as coat cupboards for the staff in offices and factories, they're too small to stand up in and too narrow to be able to sit down. Dinner lasted three hours. Then they came back, sated, a little tipsy, in the mood for some fun. When they opened the cupboard, they had to help Sarah out, her legs were completely numb and couldn't support her any more. They dragged her to the bathroom . . . She was so weak that they had to help her undress. Mérode, a glass of champagne in his hand, appreciated her beauty with the eye of a connoisseur . . .'

Léa sat down on the bed. François Tavernier pitilessly went on:

'He asked the head of the place, Christian Masuy, to leave them alone for a few minutes. Masuy agreed, laughing and left the room with his assistants. Sarah did not move, a little blood had seeped through her bandages. Rudi caressed her breasts and told her that if she was good, he could intervene on her behalf. Apparently this kind offer made Sarah burst out laughing, which our Don Juan didn't find very amusing because, according to him, he slapped her and slapped her, in vain, because she just carried on laughing. Furious, he called back his comrades and they handcuffed her hands behind her back then took it in turns to rape her. After that, they allowed themselves a short break for a cigarette, then they tied up her

88

feet and they pushed her, trussed up like that, from one to the other and back again, like a ball, shouting:

'"You're going to talk, you bitch." "Are you or aren't you going to talk?" As she didn't say a word, they got bored with playing and Masuy pushed her into the bathtub. The icy water made her cry out for the first time. So as to shut her up, no doubt, Masuy pushed her head under water. Her wound soon made the water red. For two hours, they carried on without mercy. "What guts that woman's got!" Rudy Mérode said to Raphaël Mahl who told me all that with very real emotion. That's what the torture of the bathtub is. And what's more, these gentlemen take such a delight in describing it . . .'

He was quiet for a minute and then went on:

'Léa, look at me, can you imagine me being the accomplice of men like that?'

The intense and distraught expression on her face when she looked at him and her quivering mouth made her look like a little girl of eight who had just witnessed an injustice or an act of gratuitous maliciousness. How the little girl wanted to cuddle up to the very man who was making her cry!

'Léa, answer me. In spite of certain appearances, do you believe that I could be the accomplice of people like that? Do you believe I'm on the same side as those swine?'

She flung herself at him.

To hold her in his arms, to breathe in the fragrance of her hair, of her neck, to feel her salty lips . . . François closed his eyes with bliss.

When he opened them again, his eyes met Jean's which were full of despair. 'Poor kid, he's in love with this insufferable brat too,' he thought. He gently pushed Léa away.

'Tomorrow, Sarah is to be taken back to the Rue des Saussaies. I'll know the time of the transfer some time tonight. We already know the itinerary and three of our members are posted at strategic points.'

'I want to join you,' said Jean.

'No, old chap, your cover's been blown, you're leaving this evening. I'll leave you to say goodbye to Léa. I'm going to pay my respects to your aunts.'

Left alone, the two childhood friends felt uncomfortable.

'I didn't even ask after Raoul. How is he? Where is he?'

'I found out through a mutual friend that he escaped from Germany last summer. We haven't heard from him since.'

'Poor Raoul. The three of us were so happy together. Do you remember when we used to go swimming in the Garonne? Our cycle rides in the hills . . .?'

'You still loved us then. Montillac's changed without you. It's as though the estate is all withdrawn. The windows stay closed. When Ruth and Camille go out, you get the impression they're walking on tip-toes. They seem to spend their lives waiting. Since Mathias left for Germany, Fayard hasn't said a word. From time to time, you catch sight of him among the vines, barking out a few sharp orders. He's become eccentric and started working at night, making his rounds by torchlight. He treats his wife like a dog.'

'What about Laurent?'

'I haven't seen him for ages, but his network is active, one of the most active in the south-west. They're involved in all the major actions. He'd better not get himself nicked, the Germans aren't particularly fond of him. Apparently he comes and kisses his wife and child in broad daylight, without any protection. I would have loved to work with him but Trinité needed me in Paris. Do you remember when we used to get off our bikes in the forest?'

'That seems such a long time ago. I feel so old now. And I'm so frightened. If only you knew how frightened I am.'

'It doesn't show,' he said, drawing her towards him. 'You haven't changed except that you're even more beautiful. The look in your eyes, perhaps . . . Yes, the look in your eyes has changed. It's a little harder, a little more anxious. You should go back to Montillac and drop all this. Wait patiently until the war's over and look after your vineyards.'

'Wait patiently! But you're still living in the nineteenth century, my poor friend. Wait for what? In the meantime, they continue ransacking the country, torturing our friends, pursuing Laurent and Uncle Adrien. If we don't do anything, they'll never leave. I can't wait, I want to live, do you hear me,

90

live, I don't want to see them in our country any more. When they left Montillac, Ruth, Sidonie and I cleaned the place from top to bottom. Ah! If only we could have purified the house with fire! Françoise, who didn't understand, said: "But we've already done the spring cleaning this year . . ." At first, I told myself I had to get used to their presence, it was only natural, we'd lost the war. Too bad for the losers! That sort of thing. Then, gradually, through talking to Camille, listening to the BBC and above all, when I saw that most of our relatives and neighbours were giving in, I was ashamed. And now, when I think of what they're doing to Sarah, I'd like to pick up a gun and go out and fight.'

'That's not a woman's place.'

'You're so old-fashioned. It wouldn't be the first time women have taken part in a war.'

'I wouldn't want anything to happen to you.'

There was a knock on the door. It was Françoise.

'Aunt Albertine sent me to fetch you.'

She left the room without waiting for a reply.

'I must leave. Say goodbye to your aunts for me. Now leave me alone. I've got to learn this information that Trinité gave me by heart.'

'Kiss me and try and send me news from time to time.'

Their kiss took them back to summer 1939 on the terrace at Montillac when their main worry was: 'What shall we do to amuse ourselves today?' They were so wrapped up in their embrace and their memories that they did not hear the door open and François Tavernier come in. He smiled on seeing the young couple entwined. Noiselessly, he left the room.

'I love you, Léa.'

'I know, love me well, I need it.'

'If I know you, you're not short of admirers. Tavernier for one.'

'You're not going to sulk. This is no time for jealousy.'

'You're right. I'm like Raoul, I can't bear to see another man chasing you.'

'You and your brother always were silly,' she said affectionately.

'Goodbye, Léa, take care.'

'Goodbye, Jeannot, you take care too.'

After a last kiss, Léa joined her family. Ten minutes later, Jean Lefèvre left the apartment.

In the little parlour where the family now ate to save on heating, Albertine and Lisa were listening to the personal messages on the BBC from London while they waited for dinner:

'The crab is going to meet the snakes. We say: the crab is going to meet the snakes.'

'I followed the solitary path as if in a dream. We say: I followed the solitary path as if in a dream.'

'Maurice spent a pleasant Christmas with his friend and is thinking of the two mimosas that will flower.'

'I'm glad for him,' said Léa with a big smile.

Chapter 7

Léa was furious. She had not heard from François Tavernier for more than a week. Was Sarah still a prisoner? Had Jean reached the Vendée region safely? Even Raphaël's silence worried her. No longer able to contain her impatience, she decided to go to the Rue des Saussaies.

Her youth, her beauty and her apparent shyness dispelled any suspicion and curiosity on the part of the German officer who received her. 'Sarah Mulstein?' That name rang a bell. Oh! Yes, the Jewish woman they had brought in injured. No, she wasn't there any more. She should go and see if she was at 101 Avenue Henri-Martin; they might be able to give her some information there, otherwise, she should come back and he would see what he could do for her. It was natural to help such a pretty young lady . . . Léa thanked him.

She went outside and unlocked her bicycle, rode down the Avenue de Marigny and turned into the Champs Elysées. At the roundabout, a policeman was perched on a covered platform surrounded by heavy German signposts directing the non-existent traffic: a few bicycles, the odd car and pedestrians huddled up in their flimsy coats as they hurried along. A cold drizzle made the pavement slippery. At the top of the avenue, the Arc de Triomphe rose up, a pathetic symbol in the leaden grey sky. Exhausted, Léa gave up trying to go that way and turned down the Avenue Montaigne. When she reached the Place de l'Alma, the rain started pouring down. She padlocked her bicycle to the railings of the little garden outside the building in Avenue Henri-Martin, under the indifferent gaze of a passer-by. As she went under the arch, she removed her beret, fluffed out her hair and wiped her face and legs with her handkerchief.

She looked around her in surprise. How calm and comfortable everything was; there was no sign of the Germans' presence. This could not be the place where the horrors described by François Tavernier took place. She walked past the caretaker's lodge, and came to a big glass door leading inside the building. Léa stopped, indecisive, in the middle of the marble hall. On her right was a very beautiful staircase of dark wood, its banisters unfurling upwards. It was held up by a caryatid with a haughty expression and prominent breasts, the wood smooth and shiny from being caressed by the hands of countless residents and their visitors. Opposite, a shaft of coloured light from the high stained glass window fell on the finely worked metal gate of the lift. Two long wooden steps with rounded corners led to a double door on which there was a little copper plaque: 'French Finance Department. Purchasing Office.' What did that mean? She believed they had taken Sarah to the ground floor. Those words did sound familiar. François had mentioned the Purchasing Office. But what had he said about it? Tired and chilled to the bone, she sat down on the bottom step and leaned her head against that of the caryatid.

One of the double doors suddenly opened and a man shot out, pushed by invisible hands. The poor creature lost his balance and collapsed on the tiled entrance hall floor. In spite of the dimness, Léa noticed that his hands were tied behind his back and that blood was running down his swollen face, staining the white and gold marble. Almost immediately, two men came out. They were laughing as they buttoned up their coats. The youngest kicked the prostrate body which lay there trembling.

'Come on, you swine, get up. Now you've told us everything, we don't need you any more. We're taking you back to Fresnes prison.'

'But you promised,' said the prisoner getting up.

'Promised what?'

'That you'd leave my wife and daughter in peace.'

'Promises, promises, we never stop making promises here, in fact our boss keeps scolding us.'

'Oh, no!' he howled, causing a wound on his mouth to open up again.

'Come on, get up. The boss isn't convinced you've told us everything.'

The poor wretch dragged himself to the feet of his two jeering torturers.

'I swear I've told you everything, given you everything, all the names, the codes, everything, everything . . .' he sobbed.

'That's enough, our car's waiting. Stop blubbering like a woman, you're making a spectacle of yourself. Men who cry disgust me. Up you get.'

'Get up, you scum,' said the other one, 'you don't expect us to carry a squealer, do you?'

The sobs suddenly stopped. Léa, huddled behind the statue, saw the creature, who had apparently lost all his human dignity, raise himself up, first on to his knees, then on to one leg and then the other. Tottering but upright, horrible, pitiful, his eyes half closed from the blows, his lower lip torn and hanging down, his neck showing strangulation marks, the thumbnails missing from his hands which were still tied behind his back, he walked slowly past his torturers and, stopping in front of the elder one, he spat in his face.

His companion immediately whipped out a gun.

'Forget it, Bernard, he'd be only too pleased if you shot him.'

They escorted him out of the building, punching and kicking him all the way.

Léa was brought down to earth with a bump by the noise of the lift. She leapt up. Just in time. Two elegant young women alighted, laughing. At the same time, two respectable looking men rang the bell of the Purchasing Office. Not one of them had noticed the blood on the floor.

Léa stood rooted to the spot, fascinated.

'I must go,' she thought, unable to make a move, as if she were waiting for something to happen that would explain not what she had just witnessed, but the reason for it. She sensed that she ought not to stay where she was. Nobody knew she was there. She should run away as quickly as she could, otherwise they would catch her and make her undergo the same fate as Sarah and the miserable wretch who had fallen so close to her.

Still motionless, she did not hear the glass door open. When she turned round to leave, a man who was rather too well-dressed, tall and thin with dark, perfectly groomed hair, was dragging nervously on a fat cigar and staring at her with grey-green eyes.

'No doubt you are looking for someone, mademoiselle? Can I help you?'

His tone was polite, but Léa was choked with panic.

'Anyone would think you were frightened of me. Do I look as dreadful as all that?'

She shook her head, trying to collect her wits and think of some story to tell him. Her gaze fell on the copper plaque: 'Purchasing Office'. François Tavernier's words came back to her.

'I was told that they bought precious metals here.'

'That is correct. Have you got some jewellery you want to sell?'

'That's right, some family heirlooms.'

'I understand, mademoiselle, these are hard times and one sometimes has to give up one's most treasured possessions. Come in and I'll see what I can do for you.'

He unlocked the door with his own key and stood aside to let her pass. There were a lot of people in the big hall: the respectable gentlemen she had seen earlier, men in jackets with guns bulging in their breast pockets, three women dressed in black sitting in a corner crying. Opposite them, a young man, his hands and feet in chains, was lying on the ground with a filthy dressing on his forehead, apparently asleep. A woman in a fur coat and a sort of gigolo whose hair was slicked down with Brylcreem were laughing loudly. A young girl, in tears, her clothes torn, was dragged out of one room and into another despite her protests. Everybody in the room pretended not to notice.

Léa wheeled round.

'What's going on here? Who are these people? What are they doing to that woman? First of all, who are you?'

'It's true, forgive me, I forgot to introduce myself. I'm Christian Masuy, director of the French Finance Department. Here's my card. As for the people who are here, they've got something to sell, like you. If you would like to follow me into my office, I'll call my secretary in.'

Masuy's office was a big light room. French windows opened out on to the garden lining the Avenue Henri-Martin. The woodwork was beautiful and so was the imposing marble fireplace. There was a huge long desk on which there was a portrait of a woman and two little girls and the other furniture consisted of two leather armchairs and a Chesterfield settee. The temperature was pleasant.

'Do sit down. Would you like a drink? A little champagne, it'll do you good . . . Make yourself comfortable. Take off your wet jacket, you'll catch cold. It's not very warm in here either. What can you expect, there's a war on! I'll have a fire lit.'

'Thank you, there's no need, I'm not cold.'

'Come on, be sensible, get that jacket off.'

His tone had changed. Léa obeyed. Just then, a man in his fifties, with a moustache and a bald forehead with very light eyes hiding under his bushy eyebrows, came into the room. 'Good morning, sir, you wanted me?'

'Come in, Humbert, let me introduce Mademoiselle . . . what is your name in fact?'

Caught off guard, Léa stammered:

'Delmas.'

'Mademoiselle Delmas. Good. Mademoiselle has come to discuss some jewellery she is selling. We'll see what she's got. Meanwhile, light a fire, we're freezing in here.'

'But the radiators are boiling hot, monsieur.'

'Don't argue, do as I tell you.'

While Humbert busied himself around the hearth, Masuy opened the French windows, leaned out and brought in a bottle of champagne.

'It's the best icebox I could think of in this weather,' he said triumphantly.

He took two champagne glasses out of a drawer in his desk.

'No, thank you, not for me,' said Léa.

'If you won't drink with me, I'll take it as a personal insult. The best business deals are clinched at the dinner table or over a good bottle of wine.'

Léa resigned herself and watched him pour out the sparkling liquid. Her hand was not shaking when she took the glass he offered.

'To your good health. May this new year of 1943 be a prosperous one for you. You'll see, we'll do lots of business together and we'll earn a lot of money.'

'To your health, monsieur. I don't wish to set up in business, I don't know anything about it. All I want to do is sell a few pieces of jewellery and silver to help out my family.'

'Have you got the items in question with you?'

'No, because I wasn't sure how to go about it nor whether this was the right address.'

'Talking of addresses, who gave you this one?'

Oh dear! That was the question she had been dreading since the beginning. She sipped her champagne trying to think of an answer.

'I heard one of my friends mention the office in the Avenue Henri-Martin. I don't remember the exact circumstances.'

'Humbert? Have you finished lighting the fire? You can leave us.'

'Very good, monsieur.'

As he went out, someone came rushing in, bumping into the secretary, who did not have time to get out of the way.

Masuy's reaction was faster than Humbert's. By the time the intruder was standing in front of the desk, he already had a pistol in his hand.

'Steady, Christian, don't you recognize your friends any more?'

'My friends don't usually barge into my office like that. You're lucky you didn't get a bullet through the brain. I'm a good shot, you know.'

'I'm sorry . . .'

'What's more, I thought I told you I didn't want to work with you any more.'

'But it's not for me, it's for my friend who's sitting here.'

'What are you talking about? This young lady is a friend of yours?'

Léa could not believe her ears. Raphaël Mahl, here! Had he been following her?

98

'I was supposed to be meeting her.'

'Is that true, Mademoiselle Delmas?'

'Yes, when I couldn't find him, I didn't know what to do.'

The grey-green eyes darted suspiciously from one to the other.

'I thought you were a respectable young girl and you're a friend of someone like Mahl! I can't get over it.'

In spite of the tension, Léa nearly burst out laughing. It was almost exactly what Richard Chapon had said to her about the writer. Her friend Raphaël certainly had a bad reputation, no matter what circles he moved in.

'We've known each other for a number of years, he advises me in business.'

'And you're still on good terms!'

The poor man was so astonished that Léa and Raphaël nearly burst out laughing. This mirth exasperated Masuy who banged his fist down on his desk. This did not have the desired effect. Léa was literally choking.

'Poor Raphaël, even here they don't trust you, it's too funny!'

'They have good reasons not to! They know me well, don't you, old chap? This is terrible, may I sit down?'

'Will you stop it, you're grotesque!'

'Don't I know it . . . This world disgusts me as much as I disgust myself. It's better to laugh about it than to cry, isn't it? Look at your face! A minute ago you were bright red, now you're green. You ought to laugh more often, it's good for the complexion. Look at our lovely friend, it's laughter that's given her that peaches and cream complexion. Come on, the joke's over, we came to talk about business. You know I'm being watched by the French police and your little friends in the Gestapo. That means I can't carry on my fruitful little business. But you know me, friendship is sacred, I don't hesitate to do a friend a favour. So when Mademoiselle Delmas asked me to sell a diamond tiara for her, I thought of you at once.'

Léa winced at the mention of the so-called diamonds.

'Diamonds,' said Masuy, sitting down again. 'I thought it was just a few trinkets. I would certainly have taken them to do

99

such a charming young lady a favour. But diamonds! When can I see them?'

'First of all I've got to persuade my family to entrust me with them.'

Masuy gave her a conspiratorial look.

'I do understand, mademoiselle. Come back and see me soon. But come alone, without this swindler.'

'My dear Christian, you're so vindictive! You're not going to sulk for ever over a little minor embezzlement, are you!'

'What you call "minor embezzlement" did cost me more than a million francs.'

'I was unlucky. I was taken advantage of. You'll see, after the deal you're going to do with Mademoiselle Delmas, you'll thank me.'

Léa was standing up ready to leave. Masuy gallantly helped her on with her jacket.

'Goodbye, mademoiselle, I'm looking forward to your visit. Farewell, Mahl. Remember, the less I see of you, the better for you.'

'Nobody understands me,' said Raphaël melodramatically as he left the room.

The hall was now full of people, most of them standing.

'Monsieur Masuy, we have an appointment!'

'I've thought about it, Monsieur Masuy, I'll let you have it for half-price.'

'I beg you, monsieur, have you any news of my husband?'

'What's going to become of me, they've arrested my son?'

'Monsieur, you told me to come back if I saw any of my neighbours acting suspiciously. I heard English being spoken, that's odd, isn't it?'

'Be patient, my friends, I'll see all of you.'

Léa gradually became filled with disgust and fear.

Why was Raphaël holding her hand so tightly? He was hurting her. Léa looked at him, about to protest. What was he staring at? No. That woman with a swollen face, with long, black, wet hair . . . it wasn't . . .

'Distract Masuy and his men's attention,' muttered Raphaël between gritted teeth.

Léa's handbag fell to the floor, scattering the contents.

'Don't worry,' said Masuy, bending down, 'we'll help you pick up all these bits and pieces.'

She would never have imagined there were so many odds and ends in her bag. When those polite gentlemen stood up again, they were crimson.

'Thank you very much, gentlemen, thank you.'

'Here, Léa, I've got your lipstick.'

'But . . .'

'I had a job, it was hidden behind the bench.'

Suddenly understanding, she put the lipstick, which she knew was not hers, in her bag.

It had stopped raining. Léa unlocked her bicycle, mounted it and rode off without bothering about Raphaël Mahl.

'Hey! Wait for me!'

He soon caught up with her, astride a racing bicycle. 'Don't run away like that. We've got a lot to talk about.'

'Leave me alone, I don't want anything to do with you.'

'You're making a mistake. First of all, you should thank me. If I hadn't intervened you'd doubtless have become familiar with my friend Masuy's methods.'

'I'm sure you know all about his methods: no doubt you give him a hand from time to time.'

'Think what you like. Anyway, you must be completely mad to throw yourself into the lion's jaws. What on earth were you doing there? Is that story about the jewels true?'

'No more so than the story about the diamonds. Whatever got into you, making up such a cock-and-bull story? Now he wants to see me again.'

'I know him very well. He has a passion for diamonds. It was the only way to stop him asking you any more questions. Léa, please, slow down, I'm not twenty any more, I can't keep up with you.'

'It's good for you, you eat too much, you're as fat as a pre-war pig.'

'You're cruel. But I need to talk to you in private.'

'On a bicycle, in the middle of the Avenue Henri-Martin, isn't that the ideal place to be out of earshot of nosy eavesdroppers?'

'You're right, but I'm too breathless. Before we stop, answer me: what were you doing in that place?'

'The same as you, I suppose, trying to get news of Sarah.'

They pedalled in silence for a few moments. They reached the Place du Trocadéro. It had begun to rain again.

'Come and shelter from the rain.'

They padlocked their bicycles together against a tree and ran into the nearest café. They seated themselves in the back room which was still virtually empty.

'I'm hungry,' said Léa.

'Have you got any ration tickets?'

'A few, why?'

'It's the only way of getting anything to eat. And don't complain, at least it's edible here. Waiter, please!'

An elderly waiter wearing a long white apron dragged his feet over to their table.

'What can I get you?'

'Mademoiselle is hungry, would you recommend today's speciality?'

'It depends!'

'We've got tickets.'

'I'm sure you have, because here, without tickets, you don't get anything to eat.'

'You mean that with tickets, and a little something or other, we can eat better?'

'Monsieur understands perfectly, and the bigger the little something or other, the more generous the portions.'

'That's absolutely shameful,' said Léa.

'Be quiet, you'll upset him,' murmured Raphaël. 'Have you got any money on you because at the moment my finances are pretty low.'

Léa fumbled in her jacket pocket and took out a few crumpled bills which she held out to him.

'Is that enough?'

'It should be with what I've got left.'

Raphaël slipped the waiter a bill which he quickly put in his inside pocket as he took their ration cards to the till. In the kitchen, they could hear him shout:

'Two specials, and make them big ones.'

Léa got up and went over to the iron stove in the middle of the room. She removed her damp jacket and put it over the back of a chair near the fire. For a moment she thought Raphaël was going to come over and join her but he remained at the table, smoking, lost in thought.

Léa was thinking: If Raphaël had nothing to do with Sarah's arrest, as François insisted, then what had he been doing there? I saw him go over and speak to her when he was picking up my things and she gave him something . . . the lipstick no doubt. She obviously did not imagine for one moment that he could have denounced her . . .

'It's on the table, mademoiselle!'

'Thank you.'

On the table was a steaming casserole dish half full of what looked like hare stew. It smelled good.

'It's black-market hare,' whispered the waiter as he served them.

Hare or not, it was extremely tasty and the house wine that accompanied it was extremely palatable.

'I might have a way of getting Sarah out of there.'

'What do you mean?'

Raphaël looked around, the room was gradually filling up with local office workers.

'There are too many people here. Hurry up and finish eating. I'll tell you when we're somewhere more private.'

Around them people jostled, laughing and joking. Four young girls came and sat near their table. They were wearing gaily coloured woollen hoods with matching mittens and socks which made them look like merry little pixies. They removed their coats and wet raincoats. Despite the restrictions on cloth, and their wages, which could not have been very high, their dresses were pretty and suited them. Léa glanced enviously in their direction, comparing her dull grey suit which had belonged to her mother. Raphaël was quick to notice.

'You're very elegant like that, it makes you look like a good little mouse, which is rather different from your usual image. With your hair, bright colours could easily make you look like a bad sort of girl.'

'I'd rather look like a bad sort, as you say, than look like a

nun in plain clothes. I should have worn my pink angora
pullover.'

'What I love about you women is that in the worst
situations, you worry about which colours match and choosing
the right shoes and bag. You're like children: you cry over the
fate of a friend and two minutes later you're talking about
clothes.'

They finished the meal in silence.

By then, the restaurant was full and the din was deafening.
Raphaël called over the waiter and paid the bill.

A feeble sun was trying to break through the cloud, catching
the raindrops which fell from the trees and making them
glisten. Léa walked towards the bicycles.

'No, leave them there, we don't need them for the
moment.'

'Why not?'

'I'm taking you somewhere we can talk in peace. This area's
infested with spies from the various German and French police
forces. How do we know we're not being followed? It will be
easier to tell in a cemetery.'

'In a cemetery?'

'Yes. Do you see that big wall over the road? It's the Passy
cemetery. At this time of day and in this weather, it's almost
deserted. Come on, let's not waste any time, Sarah's life
depends on it.'

It was this last argument that made Léa decide to follow him.

Raphaël stopped at the florist's shop opposite the entrance
to the cemetery and bought a bunch of violets.

'It's to make us look like genuine visitors,' he whispered.

'It's the first time I've been in a Paris cemetery,' thought
Léa, going under the arch.

She looked about her: the cobbled courtyard, with the white
mausoleums towering above them. A young caretaker with an
effeminate face came out of the lodge and looked them up and
down. Raphaël took Léa's arm.

'Don't worry, he's one of my young lovers. He's simply
surprised to see me with a woman.'

While they were talking, they walked up the little slope to

the right. Léa gazed at the necropolis in amazement.

'Aren't those little chapels pretentious! Look at that one, it's incredible. Who's buried there?'

'A strange girl, Marie Bashkirtseff, who died from tuberculosis at the age of twenty-four. She was an impressionist painter. After her death, her diary and intimate journal were published, you should read them . . .'

Skirting the puddles, they reached the end of the cemetery. Several times, as he pointed out a grave to Léa, Raphaël looked over his shoulder to make sure nobody was following them.

He dropped on to a stone bench by the side of the path, removed his hat and heaved a sigh of relief.

'Phew! Give me back that lipstick. It contains directions to where they keep Sarah locked up at night and the name of the person to bribe.'

'To bribe?' she queried as she fumbled in her bag.

'Of course, you don't think we'll get her out of Masuy's clutches without an ally on the inside.'

'I don't know, I thought we could storm his office with the people from her network.'

'They've all been arrested.'

'All?'

'All except two. Are you interested? Did you know them?'

'No, no!'

'That's better. I didn't denounce Sarah, she gave herself away through her own carelessness. On the other hand, the rest of the network was caught thanks to my information.'

Even though she was not really surprised by what Raphaël was telling her, it was still a shock to hear him confirm that he was an informer. She turned so white that he thought she was going to faint. He put out his hand to support her. She recoiled.

'Don't touch me or I'll scream. You disgust me, you . . .'

'Quick, pretend to be putting on your lipstick.'

'But . . .'

'Do as I tell you, for Christ's sake!'

A couple in mourning walked past, staring at them.

'I'm sorry, but you can't be too careful at the moment. Give me the lipstick.'

'How do I know you won't use it against Sarah?'

'Poor Léa. Give it to me. Keep a look out.'

He turned his back and, facing a tree, he removed the stick of red lipstick from the container. Then, with the help of a match, he pulled out a little scroll of paper which he smoothed nervously.

Her face buried in the bunch of violets, Léa was keeping a look out.

When he had finished reading, Raphaël seemed lost in thought.

'Well?'

'Well? If this succeeds, my life won't be worth much . . . it won't if it fails either. Well! Be a gambler to the end . . . In any case, the noose is tightening. They'll get me in the end, French or German . . .'

'If you've reached that point, why did you denounce the others?'

'Quick, let's walk. We mustn't just stand here. You know, my sweet friend, that those of my ilk and race are not supposed to be very brave, especially when they're being interrogated and shown very sharp, very shiny pointed instruments taken from a surgeon's instrument case one by one. The sight of a scalpel has always upset me, especially if I'm told everything that's going to be done to me. Believing they hadn't convinced me, they took me down to a cellar in the Boulevard Lannes where they showed me a miserable wretch whose eyelids they'd cut off . . . As he hadn't talked, they offered to cut off his nose, then his cheeks. As for the ears, I think they'd already been done . . .'

'Why are you telling me these horrible stories straight from the depraved imagination of a lousy writer . . .'

'My dear, you can insult me as much as you like, call me an old homo, a dirty Jew, a squealer, a collaborator, a thief, but never a lousy writer. My talent is the only good thing in me, don't spoil it.'

'I don't give a fig for your talent, it doesn't entitle you to tell about the so-called tortures inflicted by the Germans.'

'Who says they're only committed by the Germans?'

Astonished, Léa stopped and dropped the bunch of violets

106

in the mud. Raphaël picked it up and held it out to her murmuring:

'Poor kid! What on earth do you imagine? This country's been occupied for more than two years, Pétain, Laval and company advocate collaboration. Some of them truly do collaborate, not always of their own free will, it's true, but they're often the most savage ones . . .'

'What do you mean?'

'Earlier on, when we were leaving the Avenue Henri-Martin, didn't you notice a beautiful tall boy coming in?'

'No, I wasn't in the mood to notice beautiful boys.'

'That's a pity, it could have been useful. Think, he stood aside to allow you past.'

'Oh! Yes, perhaps . . . yes, I remember, he reminded me of Mathias, a childhood friend.'

'Good, you remember his face? Pleasant, nice eyes, a lovely mouth . . .'

'What are you getting at?'

'This pleasant young man was a Paris fireman. He wasn't in the Resistance but he was a sympathizer and was always voicing his opinions on the war, the occupation and even of London in the cafés. One day, in a bar, a man started up a conversation with him. The two of them soon began exchanging very anti-German sentiments. This man, who said his name was Lescalier, confided that he belonged to a Belgian Resistance network, that he was looking for arms and that he was prepared to pay a lot of money. The good-looking young man agreed to meet him the following week. He turned up punctually with five revolvers, not brand new but in perfect working order.'

'How did he get hold of them?'

'Through a friend in the Saint-Ouen fire-station. Lescalier gave him two hundred francs and asked him if he could get any more. He left him a phone number and asked him to telephone if he found any. A few days later, our fireman arranged to meet him at the Place de la Bastille together with two of his friends who were to hand over the guns. They had only just arrived when the three young men were arrested and taken to the Hotel Edouard VIII where one of the German Secret Service.

the *Abwehr*'s offices, is. In that office, he found himself face to face with Lescalier, or Masuy, if you prefer. Masuy had been an *Abwehr* agent since 1940. He has one great talent: he's a good judge of character. He quickly told our man what the deal was: either he agreed to work for the German secret service or he would be deported. The fireman did not hesitate: that same evening, he was released.'

'Did he warn his superiors?'

'No, he went back to his fire-station as if nothing had happened. His superiors were suspicious and interrogated him. He told them everything except why he had been released. That cost him a month's imprisonment during which Masuy brought him cigarettes. As soon as he was free, he went to visit him like the well brought-up young man that he was. He returned to his fire-station and worked for Masuy for a salary of two thousand francs a month. This went on for six months. Then, in July 1942, he deserted, not without allowing the arrest of an officer from the French special services for whom he had also "worked" and twenty or so others. Since then, he has been Masuy's right-hand man. In the interrogations, he actively backs him up. Remember his name: Bernard Fallot.'

'He's the man with the scalpel?'

'I didn't say that. But you're asking me too much. You already know too much for your own good. I'll add that he easily gave in to blackmail, without many threats.'

'How is it possible?'

'I think the fright he had made him lose, after a fall from a horse, as Jules Renard said, all sense of morality . . .'

'Aren't you ashamed of joking about things like that?'

'What do you expect, my dear, I'm not the only one who prefers to lose a friend than to miss a witticism.'

Léa gave up the argument.

'You still haven't told me what you intend to do to save Sarah.'

'Do you really want to know?'

'Yes.'

'I can't tell you. If you were arrested, you'd talk . . .'

'But . . .'

'Of course you'd talk, it's a matter of time, of means, of the dosage. All I can tell you is what I expect of you. Look, we've reached the tomb I bought these flowers for.'

'Who's buried there?'

'Pauline Tarn. The name wouldn't mean anything to you, of course. She was a lesbian poet whom Maurras called "Baudelaire's little sister". The great Colette spoke a lot about her in *Ces Plaisirs*[1]. She died, still young, ravaged by alcohol and drugs. Her works were published under the name of Renée Vivien, at her own expense more often than not. Some of her poems are beautiful and moving, as she was.

Give me your kisses, bitter as tears.
In the evening when the birds linger in their flight
Our long loveless copulation has the charms
of plunder, the savage attraction of rape.

Just as it is for me. This woman, who only loved women, talks about them the way I talk about boys. Listen to these lines:

I feel the emotion of the looter before rare spoils
During the feverish night when your gaze pales
The soul of conquerors, blazing and barbaric,
Sings in my triumph as I leave your bed!

Not bad, what do you think?'

Léa shook her head and said with a helpless smile:

'I'm sure you'll still be talking about literature when you're on your deathbed.'

'Please God. It's the only thing that's worth living for.'

He slipped the bunch of violets through the crisscross bars on which he rested his forehead.

'Pray for me, forgotten little sister . . .' then without moving, 'Léa, listen to me carefully. If all goes well, in two days time, Sarah will be free but in pretty bad shape. The day after tomorrow, at three-thirty, be at the florist's at the entrance to the cemetery. A cycle-taxi with a grey and yellow hood will pull up. Come out of the shop and help a lady in deep mourning to get out. That will be Sarah. Pay the taxi driver. Give her your arm and go into the cemetery. The young keeper you

[1] These Pleasures

109

saw earlier will come up to you and offer to help. Between you, you will help Sarah up the steps which lead straight to Renée Vivien's grave . . .'

'Why make her go up the steps?'

'It's quicker than going along the path and it's behind that grave that I discovered the door to an open chapel. I've already found out that nobody has come to visit it for years. The keeper will lead you to it and will leave you. On the pediment is written "The Maubuisson Family". Push open the door. I've oiled the hinges and had a key made, here it is. Give it to Sarah.'

Léa took the key and slipped it in her pocket.

'Under the tiny altar, there'll be food, medicines and a blanket. Settle Sarah in as comfortably as possible.'

'Is that the only hiding place you could find? Isn't there anywhere else?'

Raphaël shrugged helplessly.

'Of course I thought of a male brothel where I go, but it isn't safe, Germans go there in secret. For the time being, I haven't got anything better to suggest.'

Léa sighed with exasperation.

'At least, are your plans to get Sarah out of the Avenue Henri-Martin foolproof?'

'Not really.'

'What do you mean, not really?'

'The name she scribbled is that of a low-down underdog. I don't really see what he can do for us, even with money.'

'So why stage this macabre setup if you don't even know if it'll be needed?'

He pouted sadly.

'Don't hold it against me, I'm not at all practical. But I have got this hiding place well organized. I promise you I'll get her out of there. I've already got another idea. In any case, unless you hear from me to the contrary, she'll be in this tomb in two days' time . . .'

'Dead.'

'No, alive. When she's settled in, give her the key and tell her to lock the door behind you. Explain that we'll get her out of there when it's dark. Around midnight we'll scratch at the door and someone will say: "Be good, my sorrow, and be still . . ." She should reply: "The dead, the poor dead, have strange sorrows . . ."'

'Literature again!'

'Poetry, madame, poetry. Then she will open the door and follow that person.'

'But she'll die of fright, shut up in there half the night!'

'Sarah's not the sort of woman to be afraid, even in a tomb, even if there are ghosts.'

'Shut up, just the idea . . .'

'No doubt you'd prefer Masuy and his bathtub?'

'I think I'd choose the ghosts of the family Maubuisson.'

'I like to see you being sensible!'

'Stop laughing at me.'

'Is everything quite clear?'

'Yes, but there is one thing. If by some misfortune Sarah didn't get out, or, once she's out, gets arrested again, I'll hold you directly responsible and I'll kill you. Unless I denounce you . . .'

He gazed at her fondly.

'I don't doubt for a second that your revenge will be terrible.'

Chapter 8

When Léa returned to her aunts' apartment, there was an unusual atmosphere of excitement.

Without giving her time to take off her jacket, Françoise grabbed her hands and whirled her round laughing as they used to do when they were children.

At first, Léa tried to disengage herself but her sister was gripping her fast.

'Spin, please, spin.'

And so Léa let Françoise have her way: arms outstretched and feet together, they began to go faster and faster, squealing like little girls again. As they spun round, everything around them became blurred. Gone were the hall walls! The cold Paris winter! The greyness of the weather! Under their half-closed eyelids, the colours of summer in Langon burst out, the heat rising from the terrace, the countryside stretching out forever. It was their mother's laughing voice that shouted:

'Françoise, Léa, stop, you'll make yourselves giddy, you'll fall over!'

Oh! Yes, if only they could feel giddy, if only a great upheaval would banish the images and fears of these last few days! To no longer hear the syrupy voice of Tino Rossi on the Vichy wireless station, singing from dawn till dusk the merits of Work, Family and the Fatherland, to no longer see the lists of hostages who had been shot posted up in the metro, on trees and on the town hall doors. To no longer walk past children and old people wearing the yellow star. To no longer imagine the cries of Sarah being tortured and raped. To no longer feel so lost, so alone, alone . . . Laurent . . . If only she could go on whirling round for ever. If only their locked hands could stay like that. If only her mind could go blank . . . faster . . . still faster . . .

'Careful! You'll fall over!'

Françoise and Léa collapsed, laughing and crying, hurled towards opposite ends of the hall.

Lisa rushed over to Françoise while Albertine leaned over Léa.

'These children are mad, they could have hurt themselves,' fussed Lisa, contemplating her niece still convulsed with laughter as she tried to struggle to her feet.

'Oh! la! la! I feel so giddy . . . We've never been so fast. Léa, where are you? I can't see a thing, everything's blurred . . . it's still going round. Can you get up?'

Léa was not moving. She remained lying on her side, her face buried in her hair. Worried, Albertine seized her shoulder and turned her over. She was pale and her nostrils were pinched, her cheeks wet with tears and her eyes were closed. She seemed to have fainted.

'Quick, Lisa, go and get your smelling salts.'

'Why? I feel perfectly all right.'

'Not for yourself, silly, for Léa.'

The old lady painfully rose to her feet and rushed off as fast as she could. She fell to her knees beside the unconscious girl and carefully raised her head making her smell the salts. Very soon her nostrils quivered and it was not long before she wrinkled her nose in disgust.

In her corner, Françoise had managed to stand up but had to hold on to the chest of drawers to stop herself from falling over. Gradually the dizziness left her.

'Ah! I won for once, I got up before you. Come on, make an effort!'

But Léa was trying very hard not to make an effort. She wanted to remain in that whirling hazy state. Françoise crouched down beside her and took her hands.

'Léa, listen to me: Otto's coming tomorrow! We're going to be able to get married.'

Léa's stomach churned with deep disgust. But Françoise looked so radiant, so happy, that she stifled her repulsion and managed to say, almost naturally:

113

'I'm very happy for you.'

'Frederic told me. He was given leave for good conduct at the Front. He'll be so happy to see his son!'

Françoise was so absorbed in her own happiness that she did not notice the forced smiles of everyone around her.

'What a wonderful day!'

Léa bit her tongue.

'Oh! My goodness! I forgot, it's feeding time.' In a flurry of skirts, a radiant Françoise left the room.

'Are you feeling better?' asked Lisa.

'I feel so giddy!'

Léa sat up and leaned against the doorpost for a few moments.

'Your sister's so happy!'

Léa gave her a look that left her in no doubt as to her feelings about Françoise.

Her aunt changed the subject.

'Here, there's a letter for you. It's from Germany . . .'

'Why didn't you tell me before?'

Léa snatched the envelope and went to sit in 'her' armchair. She looked at the back of the envelope. Mathias! Mathias Fayard! The son of the manager of the Montillac estate, her old playmate who had suddenly become a man and wanted so badly to marry her . . . The memory of Mathias was accompanied by smells: that of the wood in autumn, of grapes in the barrels, of the water in the Garonne when the weather was very hot and it 'smelled of fish', of the dampness of the caves of Saint-Macaire, of the moss on the Verdelais shrine, of hay in the loft, of sweat after their games and lovemaking . . .

She tore open the envelope. He had small, fine irregular handwriting.

'Beautiful Léa,

I learned from my father that you were in Paris and I'm writing to you there to tell you I'm due for leave soon. I'd like you to be back at Montillac when I arrive.

I'm glad I chose to go to Germany against everyone's wishes. They are a brave race, united behind their leader, sure of victory. All the Germans are fighting, in the towns

114

and villages there are no men aged between eighteen and sixty, they are all scattered all over Europe and Africa. It is foreigners like me who are working in the factories and fields.

When it's spring, the Eastern Army will take over the leadership of operations and, before the summer, the German flag will fly over Moscow and all the big Russian cities. The Germans are the best soldiers in the world. Nothing can defeat them, they are our bulwark against communism. Without their sacrifice, it would be the end of our civilization. We've lost the war because we refused to see where the danger was coming from. We must join forces with them to quash this peril. I do what I have to do as well as I can because I know I'm working for world peace. The people here put up with hardships that you would find hard to imagine. Food and clothes are rationed but nobody complains. I'm dying to tell you all about it.

My father told me that the grape harvest wasn't very good. Apparently the vines aren't being properly looked after because there isn't enough labour. While I'm on leave, I'll help out. But it won't be for long . . . I don't want to find myself in a retaliation camp with the Russian prisoners. Tens of thousands of them die of starvation and illness.

I'd like to hold you in my arms, just wait till I get hold of you!

See you soon,
Mathias.'

'The fool,' thought Léa.

She angrily crumpled the letter into a ball and flung it across the hall.

How could Mathias be such a traitor? What force was driving him? Léa was more astonished than indignant. What had happened? She wished with all her might that she could understand . . .

The telephone had already been ringing for some time when Françoise, her baby under one arm, picked up the receiver.

'Hello . . . I can't hear you . . . who's calling? Who? Fayard? Fayard, it's you! I can't catch what you're saying . . . Hurry up, before we get cut off . . . What! It's not possible, say it again . . . Oh! no! Léa! Léa! Come quickly, don't just sit there in your armchair, come and help me!'

Albertine and Lisa came running out of their rooms.

'What's going on? What's all the shouting about?' asked Albertine.

'Mademoiselle, please, don't cut us off . . . Hello . . . hello . . . Fayard, are you still there? Hello . . . where have they been taken? To Bordeaux? Have you told Luc Delmas, the lawyer? Well, tell him. Hello . . . hello . . . don't cut us off.'

'Stop crying! What's happened?' cried Léa.

Françoise was sobbing so hard she could not reply.

Léa grabbed her by the hair and shook her mercilessly as she used to do when they were children.

'Tell me!'

'Laure . . .'

'What about Laure?'

'Laure . . . and . . . Camille . . . arrested . . .'

'Arrested? Why? Who by?'

'By the Gestapo. They came to Montillac, this morning, to arrest you and Camille. You weren't there so they took Camille and Laure . . .'

Albertine and Lisa's joint shriek rang in Léa's ears for a long time. In a rage, she threw off Françoise who was clutching her arm. She forced herself to control the volley of swearwords that rose to her lips. To do so, she turned her back, opened the door of the main parlour which they kept closed because of the cold, and in the half-darkness of that rainy late afternoon, she pressed her forehead against the icy pane of a tall window looking out on to the street. Gradually, she felt her anger subside and give way to a state of confusion that made her feel weak. Mechanically, she noticed that a man, lurking in the corner of a carriage entrance, was looking in her direction. With a feeling of indifference she thought: 'Perhaps it's my turn now.'

What did they have against little Laure who was so fond of Pétain that she had wanted to have his picture on the piano in the parlour! And quiet Camille? Camille? Had she been denounced by Fayard? Had she been caught handing out leaflets or clandestine newspapers? Unless they'd arrested Laurent. Laurent!

Without even realizing it, she curled up on the floor by the window, lying on the freezing wooden parquet. How long did she stay there?

Two arms lifted her and carried her towards the light.

Once again, her father had found her sleeping in a barn and, holding her tight, carried her back to her mother, grumbling:

'What a big baby!'

How happy the big baby felt. What bliss! She was back home at last. They were all there! She had been so afraid that she would not see them again! But why did everything seem so little . . . so little . . . Why were they gradually disappearing into the mist? No! They weren't going to vanish! Not now! There was Laure, Camille and Sarah! Sarah! . . .

Léa sat up with a start.

She was on her bed, surrounded by anxious faces.

'You gave us a fright!'

'Are you feeling better, darling?'

'Lie down, you need to rest.'

'We must call the doctor.'

'Aunt Lisa, I'm not ill, it's nothing. Françoise, what exactly did Fayard say?'

'I told you.'

'And they didn't do anything?'

'They all protested. Ruth didn't want to be separated from Laure. They took her away too.'

'What about little Charles?'

'Camille left him with Madame Fayard and Madame Bouchardeau.'

'Where were they taken?'

'To Bordeaux. Don't worry, perhaps it's a misunderstanding, they'll be released . . .'

'It's not a misunderstanding, as you well know. You've always known that Camille and I acted as a letter-box, that we carried letters across and distributed leaflets . . .'

'Nothing of any great importance.'

'People have been shot for less.'

'Is Uncle Luc still on good terms with the Germans?'

'I presume he is. Our cousin's married to one of them.'

'We'll have to go and see him. He'll get them out of it.'

'I'll go.'

'No,' cried Françoise, 'I don't want you to, it would be too dangerous for you.'

'How well you know them, little sister, to give me such advice.'

'Don't criticize me. Otto isn't like them. He'll be here tomorrow, he'll help us, I'm sure he will.'

Following an attack on a German car the previous evening that had killed one occupant and injured two others, the curfew had been brought forward by two hours. The evening was long and trying for all of them: Françoise and Léa tried in vain to telephone their uncle, Luc Delmas. The operator told them that the lines were down and nobody knew when they would be open again. On the wireless, it was impossible to tune into London, the interference was so bad that the announcer was inaudible. And to cap it all, just after midnight, there was an air-raid warning that sent the frightened and exhausted women rushing down to the cellars that served as an air-raid shelter. They found their neighbours, hurriedly dressed, huddled in blankets. Estelle had brought a Thermos flask filled with lime-blossom tea which never left her bedside table. She kept it in case anyone had a fit of hysterics, or suffered from the damp cold that was slowly permeating them. The good woman did not have to use it, everybody kept themselves to themselves in their own corner. Only Françoise's baby gave vent to his feelings. Luckily the air-raid warning did not last long.

Chapter 9

Early the next day, Léa rode off on her bicycle in search of François Tavernier. He was not at home. At the clandestine restaurant in the Rue Saint-Jacques, Marthe told her that she had not seen him since the last time he had eaten there with Léa. She thought Léa was looking under the weather and made her gulp down a bowl of soup and take a small sausage, saying she would be sure to like it. The kindly cook kissed her on both cheeks promising to tell Monsieur Tavernier, if she saw him, that his young friend was looking for him.

Feeling a little comforted by the soup and the hospitality, Léa set off again, riding at random up and down the streets which even the bright winter sun, the first after the endless days of rain, did not make any more cheerful.

After the air-raid warning the previous evening, she had not been able to sleep, going over and over the events of that day in her mind and trying to organize her thoughts. She had never felt so totally powerless to do anything. Unbearable images sprang to her mind: Laure being raped, Sarah being ducked in the bathtub, Camille being tortured, Laurent and Adrien shot, old Sidonie decapitated, Ruth strangled, little Charles murdered and Montillac in flames watched by Mathias and Fayard. She had tried to read, to no avail; the lines danced a macabre dance before her eyes. Unable to stand it any longer, she had got up and wandered barefoot through the freezing apartment until daybreak. Just before dawn, she had once more tried to get through to Bordeaux on the telephone with no more success than the previous evening.

Léa crossed the Alma Bridge and rode up the wide avenue

119

leading to Trocadéro standing on the pedals. On the other side of the square towered the massive high grey wall which imprisoned the dead in the Passy Cemetery. What was she doing there? Breathless from her exertions, she stopped outside the restaurant where she had eaten with Raphaël Mahl. A group of young people – grammar school boys judging by their briefcases – were jostling each other taking up the whole pavement. Unintentionally, they bumped into three German soldiers. One of them made a gesture of anger but was quickly calmed down by his friends. Behind their backs, the boys laughed and made the victory V-sign.

This derisory and forbidden gesture suddenly made Léa feel better. She walked into the café with a radiant smile.

At the bar, two workmen wolf-whistled at the entrance of this beautiful smiling girl with sparkling eyes and cheeks glowing from the cold. She swept off her tartan beret and freed her mass of hair.

'Wow!' said one of the schoolboys, 'me Tarzan, you Jane.'

Tarzan had an exaggerated opinion of himself, he was skinny with thick spectacles. Léa, on the other hand, with her hair dishevelled, really did look like a jungle creature.

'You're mad to be making such a spectacle of yourself. Get out!'

Where on earth had he popped up from? Why did he have to come and spoil things when she was having a bit of fun for once?

'But Raphaël . . .'

Taking no notice, he took her arm and piloted her towards the steps of the metro station. On the platform, after making sure that nobody was looking at them, he sat down, breathless.

'What's got into you? Will you explain?' asked Léa angrily.

'You nearly ruined everything . . . I've got an appointment for Sarah's escape. Fortunately he didn't see you.'

'Why, does he know me?'

'Slightly, he's even taken a fancy to you.'

'I don't understand, who is it?'

'Masuy.'

'Masuy?'

120

'Yes, on second thoughts, I came to the conclusion that he was the person to help us.'

'You've certainly got cheek.'

'There's no such word as impossible, my friend.'

'How did you manage it?'

'I talked to him about diamonds.'

'Mine?'

'No, someone else's, I didn't want to drag you into this business.'

Léa had difficulty in concealing a smile.

'And did it work?'

'I've got an appointment with him now to show him a sample and if he still agrees, to leave them with him as a deposit.'

'And if he doesn't agree?'

'I know him, he won't be able to resist an eight-carat diamond, especially if I promise him the other one after the escape.'

'How did you get hold of them?'

'It's a long story, I won't go into it now. But after this business, I'm going to have to disappear.'

'The arrangements for tomorrow are still the same?'

'Maybe. If there's a problem or a change of plan, the boy at the cemetery, do you remember him . . .?'

'Yes, of course.'

'. . . will come and give you this,' he said, tearing out a page from the latest novel by Montherlant and holding out the book to her, 'and he'll tell you what to do. I have to go now. Go home by metro.'

'What about my bicycle?'

'Give me the key to the padlock. I'll leave it outside the Gallimard bookshop later today.'

'If you think that's best.'

'I do. Here's your train. Don't forget to change at La Motte-Piquet-Grenelle.'

Léa did not like taking the metro which was always packed no matter what time of day it was. She was a country lass at heart and she hated the smells, the overcrowding and above all the feeling of being buried alive. In her carriage, a few German soldiers were trying to look inconspicuous, helped greatly by the Paris crowds who took absolutely no notice of them. At Sèvres-Babylone, a man handing out Communist Party leaflets had just been arrested by the French police. A German officer was shaking the superintendent's hand.

Outside, the sun was gently shining, children were playing in the square at Boucicaut, the flags outside the Hotel Lutétia were still there.

'You're never at home when you're needed. Where have you been?' said Françoise grumpily.

'Have you had any news of Laure and Camille?'

'Yes, Uncle Luc phoned. He managed to get Superintendent Poinsot to free Laure. He's responsible for her until further orders. Poinsot told him it would be better for you if you went back, he'd interrogate you for the sake of appearances.'

'What about Ruth and Camille?'

'There's no problem as far as Ruth's concerned. She's at Uncle Luc's too.'

'And Camille?'

Françoise hung her head, looking uncomfortable.

'They've taken her to Fort Hâ. The interrogation will take place this evening, or tomorrow, perhaps.'

'Camille will never resist their interrogation . . . No news of Laurent, or Uncle Adrien?'

'No. The Bordeaux police are looking for both of them.'

'I know.'

'What do you want to do? Go to Bordeaux?'

'I honestly don't know. Not for a few days, in any case. Still no news of François Tavernier?'

'No. There was a phone call for you. A woman, Marthe, I think.'

'Marthe!'

'Is she a friend of yours?'

'No, no she isn't, she's a shopkeeper . . . Look, I forgot, she gave me a sausage.'

'Gave!' exclaimed Françoise wide-eyed.

122

'I mean sold.'

'I was going to say. Let me see.'

Léa took the sausage wrapped up in newspaper out of her bag and gave it to her sister who unwrapped it enviously.

'What a beauty! It's a long time since I've seen such a fat sausage. Estelle, look what Léa's brought!'

'Gentle Jesus! It's magnificent. Mademoiselle Albertine, Mademoiselle Lisa, come and see!'

Léa's aunts came running and they too went into ecstasies over the sausage. Since the feast on New Year's Eve, they had only eaten beef twice and a rather tough chicken on one occasion.

'What did she say?'

'Who?'

'Marthe?'

'That she'd be at the market in the Rue Mouffetard at four o'clock this afternoon.'

'Where?'

'She says you know where, near the church of Saint-Médard.'

That was a good one! The church of Saint-Médard! Léa had never set foot in the place! She'd find it all right. The main thing was that François had received her message. He was the only person who could have given Marthe her telephone number.

'I'm pleased you seem happy,' said Françoise, 'and in a few minutes I'll be seeing Otto.'

It was only then that Léa noticed the elegant woollen dress her sister was wearing. She had almost got her figure back! Léa had completely forgotten about Otto.

'Is he coming here?'

'Of course,' said Françoise on her guard. 'He's got the right to come and see his son, hasn't he?'

'Yes, and I've got the right not to want to see him. I'm going out.'

'Léa, that's not nice of you. Otto's very fond of you, he'll be very hurt if you're not here.'

'Well, that's just too bad! Your lover's fellow-countrymen . . .'

'We're going to get married!'

'. . . have arrested Camille and are looking for Uncle Adrien and Laurent, they're also looking for me, they're torturing my friends and forcing others to betray, to do their dirty work for them! And all you can say to me is that your Jerry will be hurt! Do you not think you're a little lacking in the most basic decency?'

'You have no right to talk like that. Otto isn't like that, he disapproves what some of them are doing as much as you do . . .'

'Calm down, girls, don't shout so loudly, the neighbours will hear you!'

'I don't give a damn about the neighbours, Aunt Lisa, it makes me want to scream when I hear that her Otto isn't like that! He's just like the rest of them: capable of anything for his Führer . . .'

'That's not true . . .'

'Yes it is true, or you've never listened to him talk. But what I hold against your German friends is not that they've won the war, but that they've shown us that we're a nation of cowards who took to the roads in fear like a flock of sheep, who quietly return to the fold and submit after listening to the mumblings of a senile old man, who allow whole families to be deported, hostages, some of whom are no older than Laure, to be shot, who encourage informers, who make decent lads like Mathias lose their heads and men like Uncle Luc bring disgrace on themselves . . .'

'Léa, don't talk about your uncle like that!'

'Aunt Albertine, we accept too many things . . .'

Léa was interrupted by the sound of the doorbell ringing.

'My God, he's here! Because of you I look a sight,' cried Françoise, rushing to her room.

Léa locked herself in her room, leaving Albertine and Lisa on their own. Like cowards, they went to fetch Estelle from the kitchen so that she could open the door to Otto, who was becoming impatient.

'All right, all right, I'm coming . . .'

Estelle found herself face to face with a giant wearing a German motor cyclist's outfit:

'*Wohnt Madame Françoise Delmas hier?*'[1]

Wide-eyed and holding her head high, the old servant looked at him and shook her head.

'*Ich komme in Auftrag von Kommandant Kramer.*'[2]

'Mademoiselle Françoise, Mademoiselle Françoise,' cried Estelle, 'it must be for you.'

Françoise, having repaired her dishevelled appearance, deigned to come out with a radiant smile.

'Otto!'

She stood there dumbfounded before the giant who saluted her most civilly and clicked his heels.

'Madame Delmas?'

'Yes . . .'

'*Herr Kommandant Kramer hat eine Mitellung für Sie. Er schickt Ehnen einen Wagen um fünf Uhr. Er bitte Sie, ein Abendkleid anzuziehen. Am frühen Nachtmittag werden Ihnen ein paar Modelle Vorgeführt. Aufwiedersehen Madame Delmas.*'[3]

He clicked his heels once more.

Françoise stood rooted to the spot with a silly smile on her face. Estelle shut the door behind him.

---

[1] Does Madame Françoise Delmas live here?
[2] I have a message from Commander Kramer
[3] Commander Kramer has given me a message for you. He will send a car to pick you up at five o'clock. He requests that you wear evening dress. This afternoon, some dress designers will be coming to show you different models. Goodbye, Madame Delmas.

Chapter 10

Léa reached the church of Saint-Médard a little before four o'clock. She was numb with cold and in a bad mood. Although she was tired of riding up and down the streets of Paris in the freezing cold, she preferred that to the metro, which she had had to take to get there. Raphaël had not returned her bicycle as promised. She had got out at the metro station Monge and had walked to the church in the rain.

She looked around her; nothing resembling a familiar face. The frail shapes of little old ladies scurried towards the long queues outside the butchers' shops and the dairies. The grey crowd stood waiting with resignation, stamping their feet to keep warm, their ugly umbrellas not adequate to keep off the rain.

The clock struck four. A fat man came out of the church and locked the door behind him. Not knowing what to do, Léa followed him towards the Rue Mouffetard. On the corner of the Rue Arbalatte, two women were arguing outside a green-grocer's over the last kilo of potatoes. When she reached the Rue de l'Epée-de-bois, she turned round and almost bumped into a woman who was walking up the street.

'Excuse me, madame . . . Oh!'

Beneath the headscarf knotted under the woman's chin, she recognized Marthe Andrieu.

'I'll meet you a little further down in the café that sells wood and coal. It belongs to a cousin of mine. Tell him you're from Montcuq, he'll know you're a friend.'

It was warm inside the cousin's café. At the back of the little room, a cast iron stove roared away. On top of it there was a large copper kettle belching out steam. All the tables were taken by elderly men playing cards or dominoes. The damp sawdust lay in little heaps on the blue patterned tiles. Behind the bar, a man with an impressive pepper-and-salt moustache, wearing a beret and a black coal merchant's jacket, was wiping the bar in front of some young people. When he had finished serving them, he came over to Léa.

'Good afternoon, mademoiselle. What would you like?'

'I'm from Montcuq,' she said, sneezing.

A flash of suspicion showed in his face. However, he replied jovially:

'Anyone from my village is always welcome here. The Paris climate doesn't seem to suit you, you've caught a fine cold. I'll make you a nice hot grog, like in the old days.'

'Make that two, cousin.'

'Cousin Marthe! To what do I owe the pleasure of seeing you? Any news since yesterday?'

'Nothing much, Jules. I was standing there freezing in one of those wretched queues and I said to myself: "Let's go and warm ourselves up at Cousin Jules" and have a little tipple.'

'Good old Marthe! Always boozing!'

'Well, these days, we mustn't miss an opportunity to cheer ourselves up. Don't you agree, mademoiselle?'

'Yes, madame.'

Jules took an unlabelled bottle from under the bar, put three thick glasses on the counter and half-filled them with an amber liquid to which he surreptitiously added three lumps of sugar and a slice of lemon.

'This'll keep the colds away. Hey! Cousin, pass me the kettle. Mind you don't burn yourself,' he said, handing her a dishcloth.

Marthe came back holding the kettle at arm's length.

'Whew, it feels like a ton of bricks,' she exclaimed as she put it down.

'It's a sturdy kettle,' he answered, pouring out the boiling water.

They all stirred their drinks in silence.

'To your health, ladies,' said the proprietor.

'To yours, Jules.'

'To your health,' said Léa, putting her glass down quickly.
'It's hot! But that's the way to drink it.'
'I'll wait a bit, if you don't mind.'
At last the cousin moved away.
'Have you heard from François?'
'Yes, through my son. He said to tell you not to do anything foolish. For the moment, it's impossible for him to see you. If you have a message for him, I can pass it on. My boy, who is going to be seeing him, is waiting for me at home . . .'
'Don't do anything foolish . . . it's all very well saying that from a distance . . . Sarah's going to need me tomorrow if Raphaël hasn't betrayed both of us . . . what should I do? What should I tell him?' thought Léa.
'Could you get a letter to him?'
'Of course.'
'I haven't anything to write with.'
'I'll ask Jules. Drink your grog, otherwise he'll be offended.'
Léa obeyed. It was still very hot, but bearable. It was strong and good. By the time she had drunk half of it, a pleasant warmth surged through her body. When Marthe came back with a sheet of paper, an envelope, a pen and a bottle of ink, Léa was feeling almost euphoric. She opened the bottle of ink and dipped in the quartermaster's pen.

'Dear friend,
    Camille is in the same situation as S. My Uncle Luc, whom you know, advises me to come back. What should I do? My sister's fiancé is back and Raphaël is dealing with S. Can I trust him? Let me hear from you quickly, I feel lonely. Love and kisses,
                                        Léa.'

She folded the paper and slipped it into the envelope which she held out to Marthe.
'You've forgotten to seal it,' said the cook, running her tongue over the gummed flap. 'I'll be in touch with you as soon as I can.'
'Tell him that it's very important, I must see him.'

'I'll do everything I can, my dear child. Drink up your grog and leave otherwise you won't be home before curfew. Did you come by metro?'

'Yes.'

'You'd better go home on foot. At your age, it'll take less than an hour. Go down the Rue de l'Epée-de-bois: that'll take you into the Rue Monge, turn left and walk as far as the Seine. You'll be able to find your way from there. Goodbye.'

'Goodbye, Marthe, goodbye, Monsieur Jules, thank you for the tonic, I'm warm all over and I feel as if I've got wings.'

'Just what the doctor ordered. Goodbye. Hope to see you again.'

The rain had given way to the cold, but thanks to the grog, she did not feel it. It was almost dark, there was no light and the streets were almost deserted. It was eerie. Léa set off at a run.

Breathless, she stopped near the square of Saint-Julien-le-Pauvre. On the other side of the Seine, the dark mass of Notre-Dame rose up. After a few seconds, she set off again without running. The idea of finding herself in Françoise and Otto's company was unbearable.

The curfew had begun twenty-five minutes before she reached her aunts' apartment. Tied to the door was her bicycle. That was a good sign, Raphaël had kept his word in the end. She unlocked it, pushed open the door and wheeled in her bicycle. Under the porch, a hand grabbed her arm. Léa stifled a scream.

'Are you Mademoiselle Léa? Don't be afraid, I'm Monsieur Raphaël's friend. I have a message for you: don't go to the cemetery tomorrow.'

'Haven't you got something for me?'

'Oh! Yes, I forgot, the page torn out of the book. Here you are.'

He struck a match so that she could see.

'Don't leave your apartment, it's important. You will receive news of you know who. Have you a message for Monsieur Raphaël?'

'No, I don't think so. Is everything going well?'

'I don't know. I do this to please Monsieur Raphaël and

because it's more fun than being a cemetery keeper.'

'What's your name?'

'To you, I'm Violette. It's a pretty name, isn't it? It was Monsieur Raphaël's idea. Do you like it?'

'Very much,' said Léa, trying not to laugh.

The apartment was quiet. The Montpleynet sisters were listening to a classical music concert on the Paris wireless station. It was warm in the little parlour.

'No news of Camille?'

'No, nothing, but we did speak to Laure and Ruth on the telephone. They're going back to Montillac in two days' time.'

Léa went to her room to get changed. Shortly afterwards, she returned to the parlour wearing a thick white pullover and a long tartan skirt which had belonged to her mother. Her feet were snug in thick socks which were warm if not very elegant. Her freshly-brushed hair was her crowning glory.

'You look lovely, my darling,' exclaimed Lisa. 'Youth is such a wonderful thing. Make the most of it, my love, it's so short.'

'If you think being young's any fun at the moment!'

'It's true that your generation hasn't been very lucky,' said the old lady, taking up her knitting.

'Has Françoise gone out?'

'Yes, she's having dinner at *Maxim*'s where her fiancé is introducing her to his superiors,' said Albertine in a tone of forced casualness.

'Aren't you shocked by this situation?'

Lisa got up to put a shovelful of coal on the fire, leaving her sister to answer.

When Albertine, whose severe features were softened by her kind eyes, looked up, those eyes, once a deep blue, were full of tears. This was so unusual that Léa felt awkward. The old lady took off her spectacles and clumsily tried to dry her eyes.

'It more than shocks us. Apart from the terrible shame we obviously feel, when we think about the future that obviously lies in store for your poor sister . . .'

'She's brought it on herself!'

'That's a spiteful thing to say. It could have happened to you . . .'

'Never! Never would I have fallen in love with an enemy!'

'You talk like a romantic child. All this might not have happened if your mother had been there . . .'

'Please don't talk about mummy.'

'Why not talk about her? Losing her was like losing our child for your aunt and myself. We're constantly reproaching ourselves for not watching over Françoise properly. For having, perhaps through our own selfishness, made things worse. If we had stayed at Montillac . . .'

'It wouldn't have made any difference.'

'Perhaps, but if there had been a chance that things would have been different, it is unforgivable of us not to have protected our daughter's child from herself.'

Now, large tears were rolling down Albertine's wrinkled cheeks.

'Darling aunt, I'm sorry, it's my fault, I don't want you to cry. Lisa, come and help me comfort her.'

But Lisa, upset by her sister's grief, was not in a state to comfort anybody. No more was Léa who started crying too. That was how Estelle found them when she came in to lay the table.

'Mesdemoiselles! For the love of God, what's the matter? What's going on?'

'Nothing,' they chorused, blowing their noses loudly.

Thinking they were keeping something from her, the good Estelle grumbled as she set the table.

The frugal meal was miserable. The BBC was jammed. Léa went to bed early.

The following day seemed endless. She went from the telephone to the windows overlooking the street and from the windows to the front door. Nothing, nothing but silence occasionally punctuated by the cries of the baby left in Estelle's care. Françoise had not come back yet.

After dinner, Léa settled into her armchair in the hall, trying in vain to read the newspapers.

It had already been dark for several hours when there was a

131

ring at the door. Léa, who was sitting just by it, jumped out of her skin.

'Who is it?'

'It's Raphaël, open up, quick.'

Trembling with anxiety, she obeyed.

Raphaël was not alone. He was supporting a woman in mourning wearing a black veil.

'Are you on your own?'

'Yes, the curfew was prolonged; my aunts are at the theatre and Estelle is looking after the baby.'

'Perfect.'

Léa looked at the woman.

'Sarah?' she ventured.

'Yes. Quick,' replied Raphaël, 'let's go into the apartment at the back, she's going to faint.'

'But why bring her here, it's dangerous?'

'I was caught unawares. I'll explain. The main thing is, she's alive . . .'

Léa led them down the dark corridor by the light of a torch and showed them into a bedroom. Very gently, Raphaël laid Sarah on the bed and raised her veil.

'Oh! No!' groaned Léa, clapping her hand over her mouth.

A filthy dressing covered Sarah's forehead, one of her eyes was closed and her burst lips had doubled in size. But what horrified Léa most were the three purulent holes on each of her grey cheeks.

'Cigar burns,' said Raphaël in an expressionless voice.

Léa drew near, dry-eyed, and looked closely at her friend. Wordlessly, she removed the widow's hat and unbuttoned the coat which she took off aided by Raphaël.

'Light the wood which is in the fireplace and go and get the electric fire from the bathroom. Then go and heat up some water in the kitchen.'

The flames burned high and brightly. Léa paced up and down with her arms folded, followed by Sarah's gaze. They had not exchanged a single word. Raphaël returned with a pitcher of hot water and towels, which he placed beside the bed. They carefully undressed her completely in utter silence. She was shivering.

'There's hot water in the kitchen. Take the basin and the sponge from the bathroom.'

When Raphaël had filled the basin with water, he stood before Léa and held it for her.

Léa very gently sponged Sarah's tortured beautiful body, avoiding the burns on her breasts, and encountering the wound she had received in the Rue Guénégaud. She cleansed the dirt from her stomach, thighs and legs. When they turned her over on to her stomach, she was unable to suppress a groan. Her back was one continuous wound. They must have beaten her mercilessly for a long time to reach that point.

'Look in the medicine cupboard and see what there is for making dressings.'

In spite of the fire and the radiator, Sarah was shivering. Léa covered her with the red eiderdown.

'This is all I could find.'

Tincture of iodine and compresses: they would just have to manage with those.

After drinking herb tea and taking one of Lisa's tranquillizers, Sarah, dressed in a long nightdress of fine lawn belonging to Albertine and covered with three eiderdowns, fell asleep. Raphaël and Léa, sitting on the hearthrug, talked in low voices and smoked English cigarettes which Raphaël had brought.

'What happened?'

Mahl inhaled deeply before replying.

'As promised, in exchange for the matching diamond, Masuy released Sarah, but look at the state of her! The bastard must have tried to get her to talk right to the end. He wanted his money's worth. I had planned another hiding place, the one in the cemetery was complicated and dangerous . . .'

'I don't understand: why do you want to hide Sarah, at least for the moment, seeing as she's been released by Masuy himself?'

'Because it won't take him long before he finds out that the second diamond is a fake.'

'Obviously.'

'I left the widow's disguise in the cycle-taxi. I dressed her in it. Do you remember my apartment in the Rue de Rivoli?'

'Very well.'

'I haven't given the keys back to the owner. He's been sent to Germany for a holiday, so I thought I'd use it.'

'Then what?'

'Then? When we got there, a car was parked outside the door. It was Masuy's. I turned straight round, with Sarah unconscious. Given her condition, the cemetery was out of the question. I didn't know which way to turn. Then I thought of you.'

'We were very lucky. You could have come across Françoise or her fiancé. What would we have said to that brilliant officer if he'd bumped into us carrying a tortured woman?'

'I'd have thought up something. Is he coming back this evening?'

'I don't think so. Apparently my sister's moving to a big hotel with him and the child. But there's still the risk he'll turn up here at any time. What's more, Sarah's presence here is putting my aunts in danger.'

'I know, but for the time being, what choice have we? Sarah won't be in a fit state to walk for several days . . .'

'Several days! But you seem to forget that Masuy knows you're a friend of mine. It won't take him long to find out where I live. And if he comes here, we'll all be arrested.'

'I've thought of that. If he finds out your address, he'll also find out that your sister entertains German officers. I know him, he'll be careful.'

'I hope you're right, because I would not be able to bear what Sarah has endured, I wouldn't have her courage. Neither would you, would you?'

'As I've already told you, people like me are very cowardly when it comes to physical pain.'

'Hush! I can hear my aunts. When they're in their rooms, you can leave.'

'But I'm not leaving! Where would I go? I've got nowhere left to go. Let me spend the night here. Tomorrow, Violette will bring me a change of clothes.'

'How did he know you'd be coming here?'

'He was supposed to wait for me outside the block of flats in the Rue de Rivoli. He saw me turn round at the Place des

Pyramides and drive off in the direction of Pont-Royal. He ran after me. I stopped on the corner of the embankment and he caught up with me. I told him that I was going to the Rue de l'Université. He'll bring me some clothes tomorrow.'

'You were so sure that you'd be staying here?'

Raphaël Mahl stood up painfully.

'I wasn't sure of anything.'

For the first time that evening, Léa looked at him closely. He looked dreadful! His movements were sluggish, he was going bald on top, a nervous twitch made the corner of his mouth jerk up from time to time, and his hands, which were beautiful even though they were a little plump, shook more and more frequently.

He realized what she was thinking for he straightened up his slumped body and said:

'All right, I'm off.'

'Don't be stupid. Stay here for tonight. We'll see about tomorrow when it comes. Don't move, I'll get you a blanket.'

Léa had not had a wink of sleep. She kept going to look at Sarah. She was worried by her friend's restless sleep, her burning forehead and her incoherent words. Several times, she almost wakened Raphaël. But he was sleeping so soundly on the floor, wrapped in his blanket.

Unable to stand it any longer, at six o'clock, she got up, slipped on her ugly dressing gown and went into the kitchen to boil some water. There was still some coffee left from the packet Frederic Hanke had given them for New Year. Selfishly, Léa decided she would make herself some real coffee and that, after all, she deserved it. She poured the precious beans into the grinder, sat on the stool and wedging the grinder firmly between her thighs, began turning the handle. The rich aroma soon took her back to the kitchen at Montillac when the cook would ask her to grind the coffee in exchange for one of her famous toffees or no less famous quince jellies.

This nostalgic memory got the better of the calm façade she had maintained since the previous day. She felt a weight crushing her chest, nausea rose in her throat and tears began streaming down her face. Hunched over the coffee grinder,

135

she sobbed the way abandoned children had sobbed over their mothers who had been killed in the Orléans air-raids. Her whole body, racked with grief, hurt. She swayed backwards and forwards as children often do. The kitchen clock struck the hour, making her jump. She tried to sit up.

A dark shadow stood in the doorway. She stifled a cry. The coffee grinder clattered noisily to the floor, echoing through the silent apartment. The drawer and the grinder fell open, powder and beans scattered over the kitchen floor.

The shadow stepped into the kitchen.

'François!'

They stood rooted to the spot facing each other. Both were on their guard. Nothing moved.

François's hands gently brushed her hair from her face. He caressed her cheeks with his thumbs . . . She closed her eyes and gradually calmed down.

'Excuse me.'

Raphaël Mahl came in, wrapped in his blanket, his face puffy and his hair dishevelled. François instinctively let go of Léa and put his hand in his pocket.

'What are you doing here?'

Raphaël was about to reply but Léa forestalled him:

'I put him up for the night, he didn't have anywhere to go.'

'I suppose you had no choice. What about Sarah?'

'She's in the back bedroom.'

François shot her a look of admiration.

'How long has she been there?'

'Since last night. It was Raphaël who brought her here.'

'Thanks, old chap. How is she?'

'Bad,' answered Raphaël. 'We must call the doctor.'

'That's impossible!' exclaimed Léa. 'He'll denounce us.'

'That's a risk we'll have to run. I'm going to see her,' said François. 'Meanwhile, try and salvage a little coffee, I could do with a cup.'

'Just a minute, how did you get in?'

'You gave me the key!'

'Oh! So I did, I'm sorry.'

'I came as soon as I heard you were looking for me. It's to do with Sarah, no doubt?'

'Yes, and also . . .'

'Tell me the rest later. I'm going to have a look at Sarah. Don't forget the coffee.'

'Raphaël, help me clear all this up. Hurry up, Estelle will be up soon.'

They worked in silence for a few minutes, putting the beans back into the grinder.

'Have you got a broom so I can sweep up the rest?' asked Raphaël.

'In the cupboard over there, I think.'

As he walked past the cooker, Raphaël turned off the gas under the water which was boiling and found the broom while Léa splashed a little water on her face and went back to grinding the coffee. She watched the writer doing the housework with an impish grin.

'Anyone would think you'd been doing that all your life.'

'My dear, I'm a perfect housewife, ask my friends,' he simpered.

'Stop it. This is no time for clowning around.'

'It's always time for a laugh, especially during these troubled times. For neither of us knows what tomorrow holds in store for us, nor even if we will be alive.'

'Don't say things like that!'

'You're not afraid, are you, sweet child? And yet the valiant knight came running in answer to your cry of distress . . . How lovely you are when you smile like that. I've never seen such a gentle smile on your face. Ah! Love . . . youth, how I envy you.'

Still smiling, Léa shrugged, got up and poured the coffee she had ground into the filter of the coffee pot.

'There isn't enough, I'll grind some more.'

'Let me do that. I love doing it. Go and see how Sarah is, I'm worried.'

In the bedroom, François was sitting on the bed holding the young woman's hands in his.

'How is she?' murmured Léa, walking over to the bed.

He shook his head without answering.

She knelt down against him and looked at their friend.

137

Large beads of sweat stood out on her forehead and the holes in her cheeks were open sores on her ashen skin.

'François? Sarah isn't going to die, is she?'

Oh! The tears that welled up in his eyes! Why was she so surprised? She'd seen men cry before: her father, Laurent, Mathias – she had been moved, but not astonished. She stood up.

'I'm going to call Doctor Dubois.'

'Who is Doctor Dubois? Are you sure of him?'

'You know him, he's the doctor who treated Camille. He may still be in Paris.'

'I remember him, he's an excellent man. Call him.'

Léa was only out of the room for a few seconds.

'We're in luck. He'd just come in after spending all night at the hospital. I had great difficulty in getting him to understand what it was about without giving too much away. He's on his way. He remembered Camille and me very well. What time is it?'

'Half past six.'

'My God! Estelle must be up. If she finds Raphaël in her kitchen there'll be a terrible fuss.'

All the coffee was gone!

Estelle and Raphaël were sitting facing each other, drinking coffee and chatting like old friends.

'Ah! There you are, Mademoiselle Léa. I nearly died of fright when I saw Monsieur Raphaël wearing my apron and getting the breakfast ready. Lucky he quickly told me what it was all about.'

'I told Mademoiselle Estelle how I missed the last metro and that you kindly allowed me to sleep in the parlour.'

'Where you could have caught your death of cold,' grumbled the housekeeper.

'Estelle,' asked Léa smiling, 'do you know if Françoise is coming back here today?'

'Yes, she is. Mademoiselle Françoise's fiancé is coming to pay his respects to your aunts.'

Léa and Raphaël exchanged a worried look.

'You don't know when?'

138

'I think Mademoiselle Albertine mentioned this afternoon. Mademoiselle Léa, you should have used the coffee sparingly and mixed it with chicory. Firstly, it's more digestible . . . True, it's not as good,' she said, draining her cup appreciatively.

She gave a contented sigh and stood up.

'This won't do. I'm sitting here chatting when I should be queueing up at the butcher's in the Rue de Seine. Today, Monsieur Mulot's expecting some mutton in. I'm going to get dressed. Your aunts don't like me walking around in my dressing gown and curlers.'

When she finally left the room, Léa prepared a tray on which she placed the cups and the coffee pot. Raphaël ferreted out a packet of biscuits that had hardly been touched and proudly waved it around.

They went into Sarah's room noiselessly.

All three drank their coffee in silence without taking their eyes off the unfortunate woman who lay moaning and unconscious.

The front door bell made them jump. A revolver appeared in Tavernier's hand.

'Léa, go and open the door.'

She obeyed.

'Who is it?' she asked through the door.

'Doctor Dubois.'

How he had changed! Now he looked like a very old man.

'Good morning, Mademoiselle Delmas. You find it hard to recognize me? So do I. Every day, when I look at myself in the mirror, I ask "who is this old fellow?" You've changed as well. You're even more ravishing. Enough of this joking, why did you call me and why all the mystery? Are you sheltering an English pilot?'

'Come in, doctor. Please don't make too much noise, my aunts are still asleep.'

'How are they?'

'They're fine,' said Léa, opening her bedroom door.

'Good God!' cried the doctor on seeing Sarah. 'Who on earth did that?'

'People who neither you nor I are particularly fond of,

doctor,' said François Tavernier, coming forward.

'Monsieur? . . . Ah! I know who you are: the croissant man!'

While he talked, he examined the burns on Sarah's cheeks.

'How did they make these dreadful burns?'

'With a cigar,' said Raphaël.

'The swine! How long ago did she fall into their clutches?'

'About ten days.'

'Poor woman. Gentlemen, would you leave the room, please?'

'We'd rather stay. Léa's aunts don't know we're here. They haven't been told about our friend's presence in the apartment yet.'

'Very well. Turn round. Mademoiselle Delmas, help me sit her up . . . there, that's fine . . . Hold her in that position . . . They certainly don't do things by halves! Mademoiselle, my bag is by you, pass me the big metal box . . . Thank you.'

He took some cream which he applied to Sarah's back and then covered it with compresses. Then he proceeded with a more intimate examination. On the insides of her thighs, the scabs on the cigarette burns were already old ones.

'Was she able to speak to you?'

'No,' replied Léa. 'She recognized me but I couldn't make out what she was saying.'

'She has a high temperature caused by the emotional shock and the torture. I'm going to give her an injection now and another one this evening. That should bring her temperature down during the course of the afternoon. As for the rest, we must leave it to time.'

'Will it be long?' queried Léa.

'It all depends on her general condition. One or two weeks.'

'One or two weeks! But that's not possible! Not only are my aunts unaware that she's here, but also, it won't take the Gestapo long to find out.'

'My dear child, there's nothing I can do. She can't be moved for at least two or three days. You'd better inform your aunts.'

Stunned, Léa sank into a low armchair.

'And in three days' time?' asked François Tavernier.

'I could hide her at the hospital, in my department, until she's able to walk. Here's a painkiller. Ten drops every three hours. I'll drop by late this afternoon. Good luck,' he added stroking Léa's hair, 'everything will be all right. You've already had quite a lot of practice as a nurse. Just remember Madame d'Argilat.'

'That was different, the Gestapo hadn't arrived yet.'

'That's true, but like today, you were endangering your own life to save another's . . . I'll see you this evening. Goodbye, messieurs, goodbye, mademoiselle.'

Léa gently closed the front door and leaned against it, feeling distraught.

'Good morning, darling, I thought I heard the door close. Has somebody been here at this hour of the morning?'

Albertine de Montpleynet was there, in her dressing gown with a long pale blue shawl of Pyrenees wool wrapped round her. Her grey hair was concealed under a white silk headscarf. With her mittens and her thick lined slippers, she was the image of fragile France, trying to bear the coldness of the apartment by wearing layers and layers of clothes. Unlike her sister Lisa, Albertine never complained about the many hardships imposed on them by the Occupation. She would often say how lucky they were compared to a lot of people and that they should never forget that fact. Lisa had scolded her when she had taken some of the provisions they had been given for Pierre's christening to the refugees living on the top floor.

Although her aunt had never spoken to her about it, Léa sensed that her aunt was reluctant to accept the 'presents' they received thanks to Françoise's situation. She dreaded the visit from Otto Kramer that would make his engagement to Françoise official. She thought she would die of humiliation when, in the chemist's in the Rue du Bac, two women customers had talked of collaboration and looked meaningfully in her direction. She was so upset that she walked out without buying what she needed. Since then, that word had been going round and round in her head. She knew what they said about collaborators on the London broadcasting station. At the beginning of the war, she had been, like so many other French people, a great admirer of Marshal Pétain, but the measures the Vichy government had taken against the Jews, and above all, the arrest of her old friend, Madame Lévy, had turned her against Pétain once and for all. If Lisa and Estelle continued to believe in him, it was to be like all the other women at the bridge club which she and her sister went to twice a week in the Boulevard Saint-Germain. For some time, she had been feeling very isolated.

'Léa, I'm talking to you. Answer me. Has someone been here? What's the matter, darling? You look like a little bird that's fallen from its nest.'

'Aunt, I've got to talk to you. Let's go into your room, it's a long story.'

Twenty minutes later, Albertine de Montpleynet pushed open the door of Léa's room and walked over to the bed where Sarah was sleeping.

François Tavernier and Raphaël Mahl looked at her anxiously.

'Everything's settled,' murmured Léa. 'My aunt has agreed to let Sarah stay here until Doctor Dubois can take her away.'

The old lady gazed silently at what had been the face of a very beautiful woman. She stood rooted to the spot with horror and amazement, growing gradually paler. When she finally took her eyes off Sarah's tortured face, Albertine asked François Tavernier with the strange voice of a little girl:

'Monsieur Tavernier, how is such a thing possible?'

Without replying, he walked over to her, put his arm round her shoulders and drew her to the other side of the room.

'Thank you, Mademoiselle, for what you are doing for Madame Mulstein. However, I must remind you that this woman is wanted by the Gestapo and that everyone living in this apartment is in danger of being arrested.'

'I know, monsieur, but I would be failing in all my duties as a Christian and a Frenchwoman if I refused her shelter. For the time being, I shan't say anything to my sister or to Françoise and Estelle. Léa and I will take it in turns to watch over Madame Mulstein and keep this door locked. We must be particularly careful this afternoon when Captain Kramer comes to visit.'

'With your permission, I'd like to be here when he comes. My connections with certain of the German commanders in chief will distract his attention from anything which he might find suspicious . . .'

'You have connections with the German commanders in chief!'

'Yes, but I can't tell you anything more except that I'm acting on orders,' he said in a low voice.

'On orders? I don't understand.'

'So much the better. Just remember one thing: as far as you know, I'm a businessman who's wooing Léa. It is essential that Captain Kramer believes that this afternoon.'

Albertine de Montpleynet gazed at this man with his strong features, his unshaven chin, his mouth which was too big and his beautiful eyes which burned with strength and sincerity. With a sudden gesture, she held out her hand to him.

'I'll do as you say, monsieur. I trust you.'

With a conspiratorial smile, François bowed and respectfully kissed Mademoiselle de Montpleynet's hand.

'Come, come, monsieur, one kisses the hand of a married woman, not of an old maid!'

'Oh! Aunt, you're wonderful! You? An old maid! You must be joking. You're younger than the lot of us,' cried Léa, throwing herself round her aunt's neck.

'You'll knock me over, let go, I must go and get dressed.'

As she left the room, there was a ring at the door followed by one long knock and three short ones. They all froze except Raphaël who calmly announced:

'It's Violette with my clothes. That's the signal we agreed on. May I go and open the door?'

Albertine mopped her brow.

'Do as you think best, I haven't the foggiest idea what's going on. I'd rather leave you to it.'

Before opening the door, Raphaël asked Léa:

'Can I get changed in another room, I don't want him to see Sarah.'

'Use Françoise's room. It's the third door on your left. Watch out, here comes Estelle.'

Léa rushed up to her and dragged her into the kitchen in spite of her protests.

The door was finally opened to the boy whom Raphaël nicknamed Violette. He came in carrying a heavy suitcase.

'Good morning, everybody, good morning, Monsieur Raphaël, I've brought everything I could. Just in time, the Jerries arrived as I was going round the corner.'

'Have you got the make up?'

'Don't worry, it's all there.'

'Thank you, angel. You weren't followed?'

'You must be joking! Just let anyone try following Violette, she'll show 'em!'

'Have you found a hiding-place?'

'Yes, in the Rue . . .'

'You can tell me that later. Now, come and help me get dressed.'

'Monsieur Raphaël, that's the first time you've wanted me to dress you,' sniggered Violette.

Mahl prodded him into Françoise's room and carefully closed the door.

Léa and François found themselves alone; they both had the same eager look in their eyes.

'I want you . . .'

'So do I . . . but what can we do?'

'Let's go into the "cold rooms".'

'But it's *bitterly cold* in there.'

'I'll warm you up.'

'We can't leave Sarah alone.'

'She's asleep. Come on.'

They walked into the dark and freezing room with their arms entwined. Léa groped around and lit a little lamp on a coffee table by one of the settees covered in white dust sheets like all the other pieces of furniture in the room. The carpets had been rolled up and the icy room had a ghostly atmosphere.

François's arms closed round Léa. They swayed towards the settee, clinging to each other, and collapsed on to it, raising a little cloud of dust as they mingled kisses and words.

144

'I was so afraid when Marthe said you were looking for me . . .'

'I thought you'd never come.'

'I missed you, you little devil . . . I couldn't stop thinking about you, I couldn't work . . .'

'Shut up and kiss me.'

François's hands relentlessly explored Léa's body which was naked under the thick and rather unflattering nightdress. She shivered from a mixture of cold and pleasure. She impatiently forestalled her lover and thrust forward her hips to receive him. Fear, the Gestapo, torture, death, Sarah, Camille, Laurent no longer existed; the only thing that mattered was her vital desire for this man whose every caress was bliss.

When he slid inside her, her legs closed round him as if to hold him captive.

When their lovemaking was over, each felt like the other's prisoner, but they were too weary and too elated to attempt to escape.

The cold got the better of their happiness. They struggled into their clothes and left the room. The white dust cover bore the imprint of their bodies.

They crept noiselessly into Sarah's room. Her grey pallor had improved and she was breathing regularly: she was asleep. The two lovers stood hand in hand watching her affectionately.

'Has she ever been your mistress?' Léa asked softly.

'That's none of your business, sweetheart, and it is hardly relevant now. I consider her as my best friend. Her respect matters more to me than anyone else's.'

'What about me?'

'You? It's not the same, you're a child. Not even this war, or this,' he said, pointing to Sarah's ravaged face, 'will make an adult out of you.'

'I think you're mistaken. It suits you to think of me as just a child who's only semi-responsible, a pretty little animal to be used by the adult, the big man you think you are, when he needs a soft warm body. I'm a woman, I'm twenty years old

145

and you're not so old yourself. I don't even know your age, how old are you?'

He smiled at her.

'Even in that far from erotic outfit I want to leap on top of you.'

'Oh! My God! I'd forgotten I was wearing this awful dressing gown. I'm going to get dressed. It won't hurt you to wait for a little while!'

When Léa returned, wearing a dark red angora jumper and cardigan, knitted by Lisa, and a short black pleated skirt which emphasized her legs on which she wore her best black woollen stockings, François was sitting on the bed talking to Sarah. She stopped in the middle of the room, afraid she would be in the way.

'Come here, my love,' said Sarah in a voice which was barely audible.

Léa faltered.

'Come on, you're the first person she asked to see.'

Sarah held out her hand.

'Come and sit beside me.'

Léa obeyed and sat down by the sick woman.

'I'm so glad you're a little better. Are you in a lot of pain?'

'François has given me my drops. Thank you for all you've done.'

'It's nothing. Don't tire yourself out talking.'

'I must. François will make sure the Gestapo don't come here.'

'How?'

'It doesn't matter. Do everything he tells you.'

'But . . .'

'Promise me.'

Léa grudgingly gave her word.

'When will you trust me?' he asked.

'When you treat me like an adult.'

'Stop arguing. The only dangerous person here is Raphaël.'

'But it was he who saved you!'

Sarah could not answer, she had overexerted herself and had just lost consciousness.

146

François rushed into the bathroom and came back with a damp towel which he placed on her bruised forehead. This brought her round. She thanked him with a weary smile, murmuring:

'I'll keep quiet to save my strength.'

She fell asleep almost immediately.

'We've got to stop Raphaël doing any damage,' said François.

'Do you mean kill him?' asked Léa, wide-eyed.

'Without going that far, we've got to put him out of action for a few days to protect you and Sarah.'

'What do you intend to do?'

'I've got an idea. I'm going to suggest that he and Violette take a sybaritic little break.'

'What does that mean?'

'It means, you beautiful ignoramus, that for a short while he will live in decadent idleness with his pansy friend, which will prevent him playing the sycophant, or squealer if you prefer.'

'And if he won't agree?'

'He hasn't any choice. I've got some men outside waiting to drive him and his friend to an idyllic spot.'

There was a gentle knock on the bedroom door.

A tall fairly well-built woman, outrageously made-up, wearing a skilfully arranged turban on her head and a grey suit, a pink blouse and a rather fine fox-fur, came in tottering on her high-heeled platform shoes.

'Raphaël!'

'Not bad, eh? You were almost taken in. Unfortunately I've put on a bit of weight since I last wore this suit, I need a new corset. What do you think?'

Léa shrugged.

'Poor old Raphaël, you look ridiculous in that get-up.'

'It's the only thing I could think of to avoid being caught.'

François Tavernier made his way to the door.

'Excuse me for a moment. A fine disguise, old chap, very good.'

'Where's he going?' asked Mahl, suspiciously.

'I've no idea. Probably to see Aunt Albertine. Where's Violette?'

'He's waiting for me in your sister's room. I'll send for news of Sarah tomorrow. I'm going to see how I can get her out of Paris. I'll keep in touch . . .'

François Tavernier came back into the room.

'Goodbye, Léa. I'm leaving you and Sarah in good hands,' he said, waving in Tavernier's direction.

'Get in touch with us as soon as possible,' François responded.

'You can count on me. Take good care of our friend. Give her my love when she wakes up.'

Léa saw him to the front door where Violette was waiting with his huge suitcase.

Raphaël gave her a last kiss and said:

'Take good care of yourself, be careful and whatever you do, don't go back to the Avenue Henri-Martin.'

In the entrance hall downstairs, four men were waiting. When they saw the couple, they seized them, dragged them into the street and pushed them into a van parked outside the building.

Not a word was spoken. The two friends offered no resistance.

François Tavernier also left the apartment, promising to return at three o'clock for Lieutenant Kramer's visit. Just as he was leaving, he turned round with a grin.

'Here, Léa,' he said, holding out a brown envelope. 'In all the tumult I forgot that I was postman.'

Then, suddenly becoming serious again, he added:

'I advise you to read it and burn it at once. It arrived by a safe route, but now it's in your hands, you are in danger.'

He disappeared down the stairs with no further comment.

'Léa,

Be careful. I don't want anything to happen to you because of me. Camille's suffering is unbearable and my only comfort is knowing that you are free. Carefully weigh every move you make and don't take any decisions without consulting F.T.

I'm afraid. Not for my own life, I stopped being afraid

148

for that long ago, but I'm afraid of the disastrous consequences that each one of my actions may have. The idea
that Camille is being tortured, at this very moment, to
extract information from her that she doesn't have, is
driving me crazy. It is taking all the strength of my
comrades' conviction to stop me from falling into the trap
they've laid for me. I can't do anything for her: I'd have to
attack Fort Hâ! I'm trying to lose myself in action.
Camille's arrest has thrown me into a state of despair that
makes me a dangerous adversary. I've learned to kill. I
know how to deal blows where it hurts. I killed because I
had to, but today, I can't say that I didn't derive some
pleasure from it.

Each day our numbers grow. Many people fleeing
forced labour in Germany come and join us. We are
becoming increasingly efficient and increasingly mobile,
but each new recruit increases the risk of infiltration. Our
operations are multiplying. It's all so demanding and so
intense that we all wonder how we'll get back to a normal
life again. And yet, each one of our actions is aimed at
getting back to a normal, peaceful existence, even more
peaceful than before if that is possible . . .

Camille is showing the strength of her love for me by
remaining silent, prove your affection for me by being
careful.

Love and kisses,
Laurent

p.s. I decided not to enclose my diary with this letter, I'd
rather it wasn't burnt. You must get rid of anything
you've received from me.'

Léa screwed up the letter and set light to it in the fireplace. She
watched the flames devour the paper and only let go when she
could feel her fingertips burning. She was too overcome with
anguish to think or even remotely feel anything very clearly.
The only thing that might have comforted her at that moment
was to take refuge in François's arms.

Chapter 11

Otto Kramer did not notice that Léa and Albertine were never in the room at the same time. The Montpleynet sisters entertained their niece's fiancé with their usual politeness in the little parlour. Françoise, glowing with pleasure at being reunited with her lover, noticed nothing either. That was doubtless mainly due to the presence of François Tavernier who was both witty and provocative in turn and who had adopted his role of cosmopolitan businessman for the occasion. He spoke in German of this war that went on and on, the rationing and the black market that made it possible to survive. He discussed Aragon's latest novel, *Les Voyageurs de l'Impériale*,[1] he talked about Léa, with whom he was in love (alas with no success!) and especially about little Pierre, who was dozing in his mother's arms, and who he thought was the most beautiful baby in the world.

'*Das ist genau meine Meinung,*'[2] the baby's father declared. Françoise enthused over the wonderful luxuriously furnished apartment they had found near the Bois de Boulogne, and the nanny, cook and butler they had hired.

Irritated by her chatter, Léa hypocritically asked, with her most innocent voice:

'When's the wedding?'

Interrupted in her enumeration of her domestic pleasure, Françoise blushed and replied acidly:

'As soon as Otto's received permission from the Führer, which should be any day now since his father has given his consent.'

[1] Travellers on the Upper Deck
[2] I couldn't agree with you more

'I'm thrilled for you, darling, and for you too, Otto. But I thought it was forbidden for Germans to marry Frenchwomen.'

Everybody was aware of Major Kramer's embarrassment.

'Not always.'

'So much the better, in that case we'll all soon be invited to the wedding.'

Léa turned to the German officer.

'I hope that with your connections, your friends in Bordeaux will release Camille d'Argilat.'

'Françoise has already mentioned it to me. I telephoned the head of the Gestapo, he's going to call me back this evening.'

'What? Madame d'Argilat has been arrested and you didn't tell me,' cried François Tavernier, playing the innocent.

'My dear friend, I've seen so little of you recently.'

'How long ago?'

'We heard about it on the tenth of January.'

'What has she done?'

'They want to know where her husband is.'

At that moment, Albertine came into the room carrying a teapot and said brightly:

'I've brought you some more hot tea, the other must be cold by now.'

It was the agreed signal. It was Léa's turn now to keep watch at Sarah's bedside.

'François, will you come with me, I want to show you something?' she asked as she left the parlour.

When they were in her room, sitting beside Sarah, she told him what she knew of her uncle's intervention on Camille's behalf.

On seeing his anxious look, Léa murmured:

'Is it bad?'

'Very. Do you think that Madame d'Argilat knows where her husband is?'

'Of course she doesn't, otherwise she'd have told me.'

'I'd be very surprised.'

Léa was speechless with rage.

'How dare you! Do you think I'd be capable of denouncing Laurent?'

151

'What a hothead you are! No, of course I don't. But you never know how you will act under torture.'

'I'd rather die than say anything that will bring harm to Laurent.'

He continued, with a hint of malicious irony in his voice:

'I don't doubt your courage for one moment, but I know these gentlemen's methods. It's easier to accept death than some of their tortures. We all have a flaw in us which can make us capable of denouncing the person we love most. It's the executioner's job to discover it. For some it's rape, for others, castration, enucleation, being disembowelled, being deprived of sleep, snakes, insects or threats to a child. Of course, I'm not talking about genuine heroes who are able to stand all manner of cruelty . . .'

'I don't believe you. I'm sure there are people who don't talk.'

'It does happen, but it's very rare. The bravest prefer to kill themselves like your fellow citizen from Bordeaux, Professor Auriac, after his first interrogation led by Superintendent Poinsot whom you've already met.'

'Sarah didn't talk, did she?'

'How do you know?'

Once again Léa was speechless.

Her eyes went from Sarah to François. Brimming with tears she spat out:

'How can you say that about the person whose opinion matters more to you than anyone else's? You're disgusting!'

'No, realistic.'

'He's right,' said a feeble voice coming from the bed.

Léa and François both leapt to her side.

'He's right,' continued Sarah, 'if I'd had to put up with the vile touch of those swine one more day, I would have talked. You see, Léa, you can get used to suffering, but the humiliation of being tied up, torn apart by hands and penises covered with the blood of other victims, of having your mouth forced open by a male organ filthy with excrement . . . the threat of being handed over to a ferocious dog if you continue to keep silent . . . it's terrible . . . If Raphaël hadn't managed to get me out of the clutches of Masuy and his accomplices, I

152

would have told them everything they wanted to hear . . .'

'Don't talk about that any more, Sarah. I didn't doubt your courage for one second. It was stupid of me to have questioned it to give Léa a lesson. I have to go now. I'll come back when Doctor Dubois is here. Sarah, please don't cry, I didn't mean to hurt you.'

'You haven't hurt me . . . it's the memory of all that. Go now and come back quickly. When you return, you can bring me news of Raphaël.'

'Don't worry, he's in a safe place and he's being well-treated. See you later.'

After he had left, Sarah wanted to go to the bathroom supported by Léa. She let out a shriek when she caught sight of herself in the mirror over the washbasin. 'They've made me into a monster!'

Léa tried desperately to think of something to say. She felt ashamed of having been envious of Sarah's beauty before. It was awful watching these tears trickling down her face around the craters oozing with blood.

'Leave me alone for a minute,' she requested.

Léa obeyed. Just at that moment, there was a knock on the door. It was not Albertine's signal.

'We're leaving,' shouted Françoise. 'We wanted to say goodbye.'

Léa hastily smoothed the crumpled sheets and ran to unlock the door.

'Why did you lock yourself in?'

'I must have done it without thinking, I had such a headache.'

'Are you feeling better?' Françoise's fiancé kindly enquired.

'A little better, thank you. I lay down for a few minutes,' she said, closing the door as naturally as possible.

Luckily the goodbyes did not last too long but Léa had to promise to go and have lunch with them soon.

When she came back into the bedroom, Sarah was back in bed and seemed to be asleep. Léa too fell asleep in one of the armchairs.

*   *   *

153

She was wakened by the sound of Doctor Dubois, Albertine and Françoise Tavernier's voices. She sat up and rubbed her eyes, feeling ashamed of herself.

'I'm sorry, I fell asleep.'

'So we noticed,' said the doctor good-naturedly. 'A fine thing for someone who's supposed to be looking after the patient.'

'I'm very sorry. How does Madame Mulstein seem to you?'

'As well as can be expected. Luckily, she's got a sound constitution. She should be up and about in two days. I've arranged an ambulance for the day after tomorrow. Officially, it's for your aunt who has been taken ill and needs to be hospitalized. Everything will go smoothly. One of my friends, a member of the Resistance and a burns specialist, will take care of her.'

'Thank you, doctor. Then we'll take charge of smuggling Madame Mulstein out of Switzerland, or Spain. How long do you intend to keep her in hospital?' asked François Tavernier.

'For a maximum of five days, for her own safety and that of my colleagues.'

'That'll be the eighteenth of January?'

'Yes. On the morning of the eighteenth, an ambulance will take her to wherever you tell us. That's the best time, it's when most departures take place. Then, Mademoiselle Delmas can come and fetch her aunt.'

'Do I have to stay in hospital during those five days?' asked Albertine.

'The success of our whole plan depends on your doing so.'

At that moment, Sarah sat up and said:

'I'm sorry to have caused you so much trouble.'

She did not appear to understand why everyone burst out laughing.

'Don't worry about anything, child,' said Albertine, 'just concentrate on getting better. The most difficult thing will be lying to Lisa and causing her so much worry . . .'

'It is most important that your sister should be the first to believe in your illness,' replied the doctor.

'I know, doctor, but ever since we were children, we've never kept anything a secret from each other.'

154

Holding François's arm, Léa shivered from the damp gloomy cold that engulfed Paris. Housewives stood in endless queues outside the shops, stamping their feet as they tried in vain to keep warm.

Everything had gone according to plan. Sarah, who had regained her strength a little, had left for an unknown destination and Léa had had to look after Lisa, who became ill at the thought of her sister being in hospital. Mathias had written to say that he was in Bordeaux and Françoise had telephoned. The news was good: Camille was going to be released and Léa could return freely to Montillac. Major Kramer would act as guarantor. Léa was immediately almost her old self again, full of the joys of life, and, to celebrate, François had decided to take her out to lunch, to Chataîgner's, in the Rue du Cherche-Midi. As they walked past the Gallimard bookshop on the Boulevard Raspail, they automatically slowed down and glanced at the window display, where Rebatet's *Décombres*[1] seemed to want to crush all the other books.

'There's the most disgusting book published last year,' said François Tavernier, 'full, unfortunately, of talent and painful truths amid a torrent of hatred and filth against Jews and other groups . . .'

Bursting out of the shop like a jack-in-the-box Raphaël Mahl hailed them:

'Léa, François!'

'What are you doing in Paris?' asked Tavernier brusquely. 'I thought we'd agreed that you would leave for the south of France immediately after we last met.'

'Don't be cross with me, old chap, I've only postponed my trip for a few days.'

'But I thought you were wanted by Masuy?' said Léa.

'Not any more. Thanks to me he's got his hands on one of the biggest gold reserves. We're in business again.'

'After what he did to Sarah!'

'My dear Léa, he was quite happy to forget my part in Sarah's abduction and the way I swindled him. In exchange, I've forgotten about the tortures inflicted on our poor Sarah.'

[1] Debris

'You've forgotten!'

Raphaël seized the young girl's hand which was raised to strike him.

'I had no choice. It's that or a bullet through the brain,' he said grimly. 'It hurts, my pretty, a bullet through the brain,' he went on in a jocular voice. 'Don't worry, you have nothing to fear from him, he knows about your family's German connections now and he's much too careful to attack a friend of Monsieur Tavernier, who is often seen at the Hotel Lutétia and at the German Embassy!'

Léa, pale and frosty, was quick to recognize the veiled threats in the mention of those places. She was not mistaken.

'My dear François, if you had not treated Violette and me so well, I would never have forgiven you for kidnapping us and I have no doubts that your friends in the *Abwehr* and our charming ambassador, His Excellency Otto Abetz, would have been more than interested to know about your activities which are contradictory to say the least. But you acted wisely and carefully, showering my friend and me with the best food and the choicest wines in the most idyllic surroundings. We had all the literature and music we could have wanted. And so, as a token of my appreciation, I forgot to mention you . . .'

'I suppose you expect me to say thank you,' said Tavernier dryly.

'That would be exaggerating.'

'You know that before long you will be arrested and perhaps assassinated.'

'Perhaps. You know, you have to accept it; death is never accidental.'

'You're completely mad, it's ludicrous.'

Raphaël Mahl suddenly stopped bantering and his expression changed to one of suffering.

'If you think it's any fun being me! It's all right for you, you can laugh at my lunacy, but I have to live with it!'

Mahl gave a friendly wave to the young assistant who was arranging books in the window. Léa recognized him and waved too.

'What a charming young man! Have you heard Cocteau's latest? It was he who told me about it. The poet was having

156

dinner with Auric at Mademoiselle Valentin's bistrot. The latter was telling him that a Jew had complained about having to wear a yellow star. "Don't worry," said our friend, "after the war, you'll be making us wear false noses." As funny as ever, the great darling, don't you think?'

François Tavernier refrained from replying but found it hard to suppress his smile. Léa, on the other hand, burst out laughing but immediately felt ashamed of herself for doing so.

'Laugh, young lady, laugh, laughter suits you . . . It's better to laugh than to cry. Goodbye, my lovely, God protect you. Goodbye, Monsieur Tavernier, I hope I don't have to meet you again,' he said pushing open the door of the bookshop.

Before going inside, he turned round and said:

'Thank you for all you've done for Sarah.'

Léa and François did not exchange a single word until they reached the Rue du Cherche-Midi. Chataîgner's was packed. The head waiter led them to their table which was near a large table laid for twelve.

'I hope our neighbours won't be too noisy,' remarked Tavernier.

'I may be greedy, but I don't like these places,' said Léa, looking around her.

'Nor do I, but don't let that spoil your appetite. Today, I want you to forget about everything except us. I selfishly want to keep you all to myself.'

'Let's have a bottle of Bordeaux, I want to be reminded of the smells of home.'

A few moments later, the wine waiter served them a sublime bottle in the customary fashion.

The food was equal to the wine.

They faithfully kept to their promise that they would only talk about love and pleasant things: the shortening of hem-lines, the changing hairstyles, clandestine dance clubs, the jazz generation setting the fashion for all young people, journeys they'd make together when the war was over . . . Their legs were entwined under the table.

Several people walked past their table: men with relaxed expressions and sounding very high and mighty, pretty, gaudily dressed women with shrill laughs. They took their places at the big table and were joined by an athletic looking man with heavy features and a keen, intelligent eye behind thick spectacles.

'Who's that?' asked Léa.

'A remarkable man who has fallen by the wayside: Jacques Doriot, the founder of the *Parti Populaire Francais*.[1] We're a long way from the campaigns in the *Cri du Peuple*[2] against the black market and restaurants at five hundred francs a head!'

'These restaurants are such pleasant places to be in!'

'That's true.'

The atmosphere had been spoiled. They finished their meal in silence.

In the street, he took her arm although she was reluctant.

'Don't sulk, sweetheart, we've got so little time left to spend together.'

'What do you mean?'

'I'm leaving first thing tomorrow morning.'

'Where are you going?'

'I can't tell you.'

'How long for?'

'I don't know.'

'You can't leave me on my own!'

'I must, and you're big enough to look after yourself.'

'Sarah was big enough to look after herself and look what they did to her.'

Tavernier winced. He could hardly tell her that it was agonizing for him to have to leave her at the mercy of Masuy and the like! He cursed himself for being in love with the girl. In what he had to do, all feelings should have been banned. It meant taking unnecessary risks and what was worse, making her take risks too. Since their brief reunion at Montillac, he had been conscious of the danger and avoided thinking of her. To be honest, it had not been too difficult. Since the beginning of the war, girls, even the most demure of them, had been less timid. The urge to live was so strong that they threw propriety

[1] The French Popular Party
[2] Cry of the People

158

to the winds and gave themselves almost as spontaneously as Léa. But seeing her again both stronger and more fragile had revived that feeling in him for which he had little time and which only served, as far as he could see, to make life more complicated.

'Why don't you say something?'

'What can I say? Mahl's right: your sister's connections protect you, at least as long as Major Kramer is in Paris. If I were you, I'd go back to Montillac for at least three reasons. The first is that your Dominican uncle and your beloved d'Argilat aren't very far away . . .'

'How do you know?'

'I know . . . Secondly, Madame d'Argilat needs you and thirdly, you can't leave the estate in the sole hands of your manager.'

'If Laurent and Uncle Adrien are nearby, as you say, why haven't they done anything for Camille?'

'Because if they had, it would have made matters worse for her and you can't escape from Fort Hâ. But it is possible to escape from the camp at Mérignac.'

'But I thought they were going to release her.'

'It's been postponed.'

'Why?'

'I've no idea. No doubt to entice Laurent out of hiding. They often use those tactics to break their adversaries' resolve. It's obvious they've got nothing out of Camille. Either she knows nothing or she's shown extraordinary courage.'

'She's capable of it. Beneath her shy, gentle façade she's the most stubborn person I know.'

'Lucky for her husband.'

Irritated, Léa shrugged.

'I'm sure she doesn't know anything. I think I'll take your advice. I'm going back to Montillac.'

Talking all the while, they reached Léa's apartment.

'Are you coming up?' she asked.

'I can't, I've got an appointment. I'll try and drop by before curfew. If you don't see me, don't be angry with me.'

'Don't worry, I won't be angry with you.'

She had the impression she had hurt him and felt a malicious pleasure followed by a feeling of emptiness. She pushed him into the entrance hall and there, hidden from the eyes of the rare passers-by, she flung herself at him.

'François . . .'

He put his hand over her mouth.

'Don't say a word. Stay here, hold me tight, don't move. Kiss me.'

That night, Léa waited in vain.

Chapter 12

'Dear Léa,

I've just returned from Hell. After my last interrogation with Dohse in the Gestapo headquarters, at 197 Rue du Médoc, I was thrown into one of the dungeons. The ceiling was so low that I couldn't stand up. The ground was covered with damp earth and straw and everywhere was filthy with excrement and vomit: it was awful. Screams could be heard from the other cells. A man whose testicles had been ripped off was shrieking. A woman was groaning incessantly. I collapsed with exhaustion and terror. I don't even know how many days I spent there, half asleep, shivering with fever, without food and relieving myself on the floor, like an animal.

When Dohse realized that I could no longer talk even if I wanted to, he had me taken to Fort Hâ. I spent three days in the infirmary there with a high temperature and now I'm in a cell with three other women. It's almost luxurious. We can stand up, we can wash, we can use flea repellent powder. If we stand on one of the beds, we can even see the rooftops through the bars. A cup of "coffee" in the morning, two hundred grammes of bread, a bowl of soup at 10 o'clock, another at 4 o'clock and, from time to time, a snack from the Red Cross with biscuits that smell of rancid oil. Then there's prison life: the messages through the bars, the news we glean at Sunday mass, the joy of being given a pencil stump and a scrap of paper, the happiness at being able to find a way of sending a letter . . .

Amélie Lefèvre, Raoul and Jean's mother, came to visit me, so did Ruth who came to tell me how little Charles is. I think of him every single moment and that gives me the strength to keep going. I haven't heard from L. at all. I've no idea what will become of me, no idea how long I'll have to spend here. The only thing I can be certain of is that it won't be long before they come to fetch me for a fresh interrogation and I don't know how I'll be able to stand the blows, the harassment and solitary confinement. My companions are admirable. There's Odile, a nineteen-year-old youth hosteller who was arrested because she was distributing leaflets; Elisabeth, a communist, whose husband was shot on 21st September 1942; Hélène, whose husband has joined the Resistance and who was denounced for taking in English aviators. We give each other support when we're in low spirits.

If anything happens to me, look after little Charles, he's the most precious thing I have in the world. Forgive my small handwriting, but paper is like gold dust. Take care of yourself. I love you deeply. May the Lord protect you.

Camille'

Léa, wrapped up in a blanket, got up slowly and placed the pages of the letter on her bed. Her young face wore an expression of horror and disbelief.

'How did we get into this situation?' she said aloud.

It seemed as if the walls of her room were closing in on her to become those of a prison.

She rubbed her eyes with the back of her hand. She had just made a decision: she would return to Montillac. Once there, she would see if together with Mathias, the Debrays and Madame Lefèvre, she could obtain Camille's release. This decision made her feel a little calmer in her mind but, before she left, she would have to have a talk with Otto Kramer.

She could hear the distant ringing of the telephone. Someone answered. Shortly afterwards there was a knock on her door: it was Estelle who had come to tell her that Françoise was on the telephone. For once, Léa was pleased to hear from her.

Léa accepted her invitation to dinner the following evening.

After dinner, which they ate in the little parlour, Léa sat on the floor in front of the fire and read Camille's letter to her aunts and Estelle. Not one of the three elderly women interrupted her. When she had finished, Lisa wiped her reddened eyes, Albertine dabbed at hers with a trembling hand and Estelle blew her nose loudly. Their knitting, tapestry and mending lay untouched on their knees.

Léa stood up and switched on the wireless.

She twiddled the knobs and found the London broadcasting service. The interference was not too bad that evening and they could hear what was being said. It was 9.25 p.m. on the 15th January 1943.

'The son of a worker from the North who was assassinated by the Germans in 1917, a veteran of the French Campaign, a fellow prisoner of the twenty-seven martyrs of Chateaubriant who escaped in July 1941 after nine months of torture in German prisons, Fernand Grenier, the Member of Parliament for Saint-Denis speaks to you . . .

Men and women of France.

After experiencing the prisons of Fontevrault and Clairvaux, after living with Charles Michel, Guy Môquet and the Chateaubriant martyrs for nine months, after sharing the everyday danger of the Resistance fighters in Paris itself, after experiencing the same hardships, the same moral suffering and the same hopes as our enslaved but undaunted people, I have just arrived in London, as a delegate of the Central Committee of the French Communist Party to bring to General de Gaulle and the National French Committee the support of tens of thousands of our people who, in spite of the terror, in the factories as well as in the ranks of the Resistance and partisans, in the universities as well as in the German camps, from Nantes to Strasbourg, from Lille to Marseilles, carry on each day, risking their lives in the implacable struggle against the hated Nazi invasion.

I have come here to state that, in the mind of the farmer or the worker, in the mind of the patriotic industrialist or that of the civil servant, in the mind of the lay teacher or that of the priest, there is no ambiguity: you're either with the Vichy government or you're with the France which is resisting and struggling . . .'

The interference became worse for a few minutes making it impossible to hear the speaker.

Lisa rolled her eyes in horror.

'Did you hear that! General de Gaulle accepts the communists! The man's completely mad. Communists!'

'Be quiet,' snapped Albertine, 'you don't know what you're talking about. France needs all those who are prepared to fight. For the moment, they aren't too many . . .'

'That's no reason to take just anybody!'

'Be quiet, we can hear it a bit better.'

'. . . *The vast majority of French people, all those who fight, all those who resist, all those who hope – and they are many, in short, the whole of France – are with General de Gaulle, who has the now historic virtue of never giving up, even when everything was collapsing around him, and with all the members of the Resistance who have gradually formed into groups and who continue to meet in the very bosom of fighting France with the aim of the sacred struggle for the liberation of our fatherland . . .*'

Once again Fernand Grenier's voice was drowned by the interference. Léa started twiddling the knobs again. Estelle took the opportunity to fetch their bedtime herb tea; Albertine put another log on the fire.

'We're going to have to be careful with the wood, we've nearly run out.'

'*Friends of France, terrible is your suffering, magnificent your courage and great are your hopes. You salute each victory of the Red Army, each destructive raid of the R.A.F. and each tank and cannon that comes out of the American arsenal. Keep holding on! Show solidarity and mutual support! Step up your persistent and heroic action against the occupying forces! May you be inspired by the great breath of fraternity and constant courage!*' . . .

Interference drowned the speaker once more, this time for good.

The four women drank their hot tea in silence then went to their respective beds.

The following day, Léa took a lot of trouble dressing up for dinner with her sister. She put on a fine black woollen dress which fell in folds from the hips and had a low neckline. It was a present from François Tavernier. It was made by Jacques Fath and must have cost a fortune. It was the first time that Léa

164

had worn it. She put her hair up and perched a tiny round hat on top trimmed with a single violet. Her carefully made-up eyes sparkled. She wore the pearl necklace Camille had given her and borrowed Albertine's inevitable black fox-fur cape. A pair of stockings with impeccably straight seams, another present from François, clung to her legs which she knew were very shapely and which, emphasized by her high platform shoes, made her look 'stunning'. Lisa was of the same opinion and lent Léa her last pair of decent gloves.

She took the metro to Etoile.

As soon as she set foot inside, Léa hated the apartment in the Avenue Wagram. Otto Kramer and her sister had rented it furnished from a famous doctor who preferred the climate of the Riviera to that of Paris.

'A Jew, no doubt,' Françoise had said about her landlord.

That remark annoyed Léa.

'Of course, it's not like the apartments of Bordeaux high society who like to conceal their wealth. Here, it's the opposite, one shows it off. A bit too much perhaps.'

'That's what I think too,' laughed Otto Kramer, 'but we were in a hurry. How beautiful and elegant you look! Come and see the nursery, you'll see how nice and cosy your nephew is here.'

The nursery was a large airy room. Frederic Hanke was there rocking his screaming godson, a little too violently perhaps, in an effort to soothe him. 'Can't you see this child's hungry?' he cried as they entered the room.

'Léa, I'm delighted to see you again. How do you feel like seeing if he'll listen to his godmother.'

Léa gingerly picked up the baby and put him back in his cradle, saying:

'Now you're going to be a good boy and go to sleep.'

To everybody's amazement, the child stopped crying and closed his eyes.

'Well done! The voice of authority! You should come here more often because neither his mother nor I can stop him crying.'

165

'We'll see about that . . . when he starts to cry again! For the time being, I want to ask you a favour: I want to go back to Montillac as soon as possible and my pass for Bordeaux has expired.'

Léa showed him the card with the Nazi eagle stamped over part of her photograph.

'I'll have a new pass delivered to you tomorrow. Soon, you won't be needing it any more since the demarcation line is being abolished now that the south is occupied as well.'

'I know,' said Léa, sounding more morose than she had intended.

'Oh! Forgive me, I'm upsetting you. One day your country will be free again and our two united countries will be reconciled.'

She did not answer but the two German officers could clearly read the message in her eyes: never.

They moved into the dining-room where a lavishly laid table awaited them.

'Are there just the four of us?'

'Do you mind? We thought that you would have no desire to find yourself in the company of my fellow countrymen.'

'Thank you, this is fine.'

Léa had been so apprehensive at the idea of finding herself surrounded by uniformed German officers that she felt genuinely relieved and her good humour was restored. All the more so since Otto and Frederic were in civilian clothes.

'I told the cook to prepare all your favourite things,' said Françoise with a big grin.

'What? Tell me.'

'You'll see, greedy guts.'

The meal went off smoothly and, as each new dish was brought to the table, Léa showed her gratitude to her sister for all the trouble she had taken to please her: *oeufs en meurette*, *navarin* . . .

'I made it with only 15 grammes of butter from Edouard de Pomaine's recipe. You know, he's the one who wrote the cookery book that's essential these days, *Cooking and Rationing*,' said Françoise proudly.

166

As for the apricot clafoutis, it was delicious. Léa had three helpings.

At no time during the course of the dinner did they talk of the war. They discussed music, literature, the cinema and the theatre. They adjourned to the lounge for coffee. A fire was burning in the hearth. Françoise told the maid she would pour the coffee herself.

They sipped their coffee slowly, in silence, watching the flickering of the flames. Otto went over and seated himself at the piano which took up part of the room.

'It was mainly because of the piano that we rented it,' whispered Françoise in her sister's ear.

For an hour, time stood still. There were no longer French and Germans, winners and losers, the only thing that mattered was the music, uniting them in a common love that had no frontiers.

For a long time after the last note had died away, they remained silent, reluctant to step back into reality. It was Léa who broke the precarious silence first by saying, with genuine emotion:

'Thank you, Otto, for giving us those moments of real peace.'

Touched, Major Kramer stood up and kissed her hand.

'Thank you for coming.'

Now, Léa could bring up the subject of Camille and find out how much he knew.

Otto Kramer did not answer Léa's question at once. He seemed absorbed in gloomy thoughts. When he finally did decide to speak, he addressed his friend:

'*Soll ich ihr alles sagen?*'[1]

'Ya.'

'I shan't keep it a secret from you that Frederic and I are very worried about Madame d'Argilat. She was arrested, as you know, because she was denounced. She is accused of acting as messenger for her husband and your uncle, Father Delmas, who are both members of the Resistance and wanted

---

[1] Shall I tell her everything?

by both the French police and the Gestapo. Madame d'Argilat was found in possession of leaflets calling on young people to join the Resistance. That was sufficient for her to be arrested. What's more, Dohse suspects that she belongs to the same network as Laurent d'Argilat . . .'

'That's completely idiotic! All Camille is interested in is her baby and she understands nothing about all that. Besides, her health is poor and she hasn't heard from Laurent for months.'

'Léa, we're not stupid, you know. When I was in Langon, we received shoals of letters denouncing you and Madame d'Argilat. Frederic and I destroyed a lot of them even though the information they contained was quite specific. While it was a question of smuggling a few letters across the demarcation line, we could turn a blind eye, but now, things are more serious and the accusations against Madame d'Argilat are subject to the death penalty if proven. Your friend is a pawn in Dohse's hands: he wants to use her in the hope that Laurent d'Argilat and the others in his network will slip up in an attempt to release her. Fortunately, he doesn't seem to believe that she really knows anything about her husband's activities nor that she knows his whereabouts. That is why he is being careful during the interrogations. What is more, he is aware of the family ties that your Uncle Luc has with our country.'

Léa was haunted by the image of Sarah Mulstein's tortured face.

'I know what your Gestapo friends do to those they interrogate and how they treat their prisoners.'

'I am the first to agree that it is deplorable. But as for you, you'd better put it out of your mind. For your future safety, please forget it.'

Léa stood up, furious.

'Forget! You have the audacity to tell me to forget what your people inflict daily on men, women and children. Did you know that Guy Môquet was only seventeen when he was assassinated, and did you know that last September, when the Souges hostages were shot because there had been an attack in Paris, there were seventy of them? And that old Jewish lady who was a friend of my aunts, who was taken away to one of your camps and who said, crying: "Gentlemen, there must be some mistake, I'm French, my husband was killed in the Great War and my son is a prisoner because he fought for France."'

Françoise, her eyes filled with tears, took her arm.

'Please, be quiet.'

'Don't touch me! Let me go!'

'Léa, I understand how you feel, but this is war. Neither you nor I can do anything about it. I promise you I shall do everything I can for Madame d'Argilat that is not against my honour as a soldier. But for your own safety, and for that of your family, I beg you not to repeat in public what you have said here.'

'Can you swear to me that what I'm going to tell you about Camille's imprisonment in Fort Hâ won't be used against her?'

Otto Kramer thought hard for a few seconds before replying.

'You have my word.'

'May I speak to you alone?'

Françoise stood up:

'Come on, Frederic, can't you see we're in the way.'

How irritating she could be with her false airs and graces. Already as a little girl, her touchiness had exasperated Léa and even their father used to tease her about it.

'What I have to say is not about myself, that's why I think . . .'

'You don't have to justify yourself,' interrupted her sister as she left the room followed by Frederic.

'Poor you, I don't know how you put up with her.'

'Stop squabbling like children,' he scolded with a broad grin. 'Come and sit opposite me.'

'Well,' she said, 'I've had a letter from Camille. She was shut up in a dungeon where there wasn't even standing room for several days. She was interrogated three times by Dohse. Unable to get anything out of her, he had her thrown into a filthy cell where she became sick. What will he do next time? The Bouscat jailers haven't a good reputation. In Bordeaux, they say that sometimes the screams can be heard through the thick dungeon walls. I beg you, don't let Camille fall into the hands of those people.'

'I despise the behaviour of "those people" as much as you do. There's no love lost between the army and the Gestapo. Unfortunately the Gestapo is becoming increasingly powerful and its police powers cover us too. Believe me, France is one of the occupied countries that is suffering the least. As for Madame d'Argilat, I was not aware of the treatment she was receiving. So they lied to me when they assured me she was being well-treated. Dohse must be convinced that she is in possession of important information for him to have kept her in those conditions in spite of her connections. It's not going to be easy to get him to let go of his prey.'

'But I assure you he's mistaken: Camille knows nothing about Laurent's activities!'

'Has she told you so?'

'No, but we live together, if she had heard from Laurent, I'd have been the first to know about it.'

'I don't want to hurt you, Léa, but when someone is involved in underground activities, they don't shout it from the rooftops. Even though the members of the Resistance are sometimes so careless that we are the first to be astonished.'

'I don't believe a word of it. Camille knew very well that she could trust me and that I was willing . . .'

Léa stopped in mid-sentence.

'Don't be afraid, go on. I can't blame you. I know that if I were in their shoes, I would have done the same as your uncle and your friend's husband, I'd have continued the fight. Having said that, my duty, and that of German soldiers engaged in this war, is to stop them. You must understand that. When we arrest and shoot people who plant bombs, or we execute hostages and imprison people for distributing leaflets, hiding English aviators, communicating with London using secret transmitters, it is still war, in spite of the armistice. I cannot be ashamed of that. But when the Gestapo use violence in their interrogations of suspected members of the Resistance and of women, I am ashamed. Although most of the time that sinister task is left to the French Gestapo. Do you know that when I was in Langon, two hundred salaried French policemen swelled the ranks of the Gestapo and the auxiliary groups. Since the meeting between the head of the Bordeaux

Gestapo, Dohse and Poinsot's superintendents in April 1941, your fellow countrymen have done a good job to say the least.'

'Be quiet.'

'That's only part of the sad truth of the matter. Do you think we had to force the hand of the prefects of police, the mayors, the judges and the French police? They obeyed the orders of the head of the French government, Marshal Pétain, who asked them, and all French citizens, to collaborate with us. They are acting perfectly legitimately. Your marshal didn't come to power through a sudden coup, as far as I am aware.'

'The honourable thing is to carry on fighting.'

'With what? You're forgetting that the defeat of the French army was confirmed in a few days.'

Léa looked away. She saw the images along the road to Orléans, those groups of soldiers, dirty, bearded and bedraggled, who had thrown away their guns so as to be able to run faster, looting abandoned houses, throwing civilians out of their cars . . .

'To get back to Madame d'Argilat, I'm going to use the little influence I have in her favour. That's all I can promise you. If I manage to get her out of Fort Hâ, make sure that she behaves herself as she will be watched even more closely than she was before her arrest. If I don't succeed, not only will I have lost all credibility, but my intervention will probably result in my being sent back to the Eastern Front again. It's not for myself that I fear that possibility, but for Françoise and my son. I wouldn't like to leave them on their own here before legalizing their situation.'

Léa rose.

'Thank you.'

She went over to the door and cried:

'Françoise! Françoise! Frederic! You can come in.'

'You're mad to yell like that, you'll wake Pierre!'

The following day, Léa received not only her pass, but also a first class reservation on the train to Bordeaux that would be leaving in two days' time. She spent those two days going to the cinema and the theatre with Françoise and consoling her aunts who were saddened by her departure. She left a message

171

for François Tavernier with Albertine in case he dropped by to find out how she was.

She was not sorry to leave Paris.

Chapter 13

On her arrival at Bordeaux station, Léa was surprised to find Mathias waiting for her on the platform. She saw him at once, even before the train had come to a halt. He seemed taller and stronger and he had a crew cut. She felt a mixture of pleasure and an indescribable foreboding.

He rushed up to take her suitcase, kissed her on both cheeks, hovered for a second in front of her, not quite knowing where to begin, as if he were measuring how much time had passed, then he led her to the platform where the train for Langon was waiting. When they were settled in their carriage, he took Léa's hand but she withdrew it.

Why had his eyes lost their mischievous sparkle?

'I wanted to be the first to break the good news to you: Madame Camille has left Fort Hâ.'

'Is she at home?'

Mathias looked a little embarrassed.

'No, she's been transferred to the camp at Mérignac.'

'And you call that good news?'

'Yes, because there's more freedom of movement in Mérignac, the guards are French and I know the director.'

'I don't care whether you know the director or not. What I want is for Camille to be released.'

'Be patient, it's being dealt with. It's only a matter of days. Believe me, to rescue her from Dohse's clutches wasn't easy. I had to negotiate with him.'

'Negotiate? Who? You? Do you know that swine?'

'Swine's a bit strong. He's doing his job, keeping order in a town like Bordeaux which is swarming with English agents, communist terrorists and jokers who only want to make trouble!'

She shot him a look of contempt.

'Do you realize what you're saying?' she hissed between gritted teeth so as not to be overheard.

'I certainly realize that if you and Camille don't change your attitude and if you continue flirting with the Resistance, you will be executed. And I don't want you to be executed.'

Léa shrugged and huddled up on the seat. She was touched by Mathias's naïve and violent passion but terrified at the idea of what he might have done. As she was discovering now, he was capable of doing anything to please her and most definitely of betraying her. What was he up to with the Germans? She preferred to change the subject quickly, and talk about the vineyards and the estate. In the end she pretended to fall asleep.

At the station, she was thrilled to find her blue bicycle which Mathias had brought down with his own bicycle. Despite the bracing wind blowing up the hill by the estate of La Prioulette, Léa reached the white gates at the entrance of the Montillac estate before Mathias. For a split second, she strained her ears expecting to hear her father's voice.

Dinner was waiting for her in the big kitchen with its flagstone floor. In the soot-blackened hearth crackled a fire of dead vines. The copper pans shone against the whitewashed walls. The long table, with its blue oilcloth, was laid with all the best china as if for a special occasion. The first thing that struck Léa was that the armchairs from the parlour had been arranged round the fireplace. Following her gaze, Ruth said:

'We haven't got enough coal or wood to heat another room. Here we get the benefit of the heat from the stove when we cook and in the evening, we throw an armful of dead vines into the fire as a treat. With this cold weather, the kitchen is the only pleasant room in the house. There are days when we find it hard to go up to our rooms. The beds are stone cold, even with hot water bottles. It's not so bad for me: in Alsace, the cold is even worse than here and I was brought up to be tough, but your sister and aunt are suffering terribly. Their hands and feet are covered in chilblains. I've only got them on my hands but that's from doing the washing in freezing water that's just about thawed.'

Poor Ruth, who had once been a governess, teacher and companion, was now the maid of all work. She was as willing and conscientious in her new role as she had always been. As in the old days, Léa flung her arms round her.

Ruth was as loving as ever:

'My sunshine, my little one . . . my little tomboy . . . I'm so happy you're back. Montillac isn't the same without you. Do you remember what your poor father used to say?'

Léa shook her head.

'He said that you were the spirit of this house, and that without you it wouldn't be the same and that if ever you left for good, Montillac could well lose its soul.'

'That won't happen, Ruth, and papa knew it. This earth and these walls are part of me, like my arms, my head or my heart, I couldn't live without them. You know, each time I leave here, I'm afraid I shan't ever be able to come back, and each time I return, I feel a happiness and strength that always surprises me.'

'That's love, darling.'

Bernadette Bouchardeau had joined them. They sat down to eat dried beans and a chicken donated by Fayard. Léa told them what had been happening in Paris and Ruth described Camille, Laure and her arrest.

Léa was unable to dispel the feeling of unease that had been with her since she had set foot on the platform at Bordeaux station. Montillac was not quite the Montillac she knew and loved. This huge, vulnerable house was not really hers. She was tired of the cold and the hunger; she longed for summer, the sunshine, fruits . . . Laure had grown up a lot, she was a woman now. Charles toddled everywhere – he looked like his mother, the same mouth and the same eyes . . . Léa felt as though everything had happened without her, almost behind her back. In spite of the familiar rituals, the same old habits, Montillac was beyond her reach. Furniture had been moved, Ruth seemed less lively, more wrinkled . . .

Just as Ruth was picking up Charles to put him to bed, the door was flung wide open.

A man with a droopy moustache, a beret rammed down over

his eyebrows, a suitcase in his hand and wearing a fur-lined jacket was standing on the doorstep.

'Close the door, you're making the room cold,' cried Bernadette Bouchardeau.

The man did as he was told.

'Who are you? What do you want?' she asked. 'It's the middle of the night, you don't go calling on people at this hour.'

The man did not reply. He stood looking around him as if he were familiar with his surroundings.

Léa rose, her heart in her mouth.

'Really, monsieur, will you please tell us who you are.'

'Be quiet, aunt. Welcome, Laurent.'

There was a rush of panic. Everyone wanted to greet Laurent at once and hug him. Ruth was determined to give him his son to hold. The baby howled in terror at this tall whiskered man who was a total stranger . . .

Laurent calmed them down.

'Be careful, I'd rather Fayard and Mathias didn't come to see what all the noise is about.'

He sat down at the table to have a bite to eat. His eyes constantly went from Léa to Charles who was allowed to stay up late and was playing on the floor.

'Tavernier told me that Léa was arriving this evening. I imagine you're here with the blessing of the authorities and so will be able to visit Camille. I want to give you a message for her . . . I have an important appointment concerning her tomorrow in Bordeaux.'

Bernadette Bouchardeau rummaged in the cupboards to find a little food. Laurent had difficulty convincing her that he was not hungry any more. He got down on all fours and Charles accepted his new playmate without further ado. He even allowed himself to be carried to bed and was promised a game of hide-and-seek the following day.

When everybody had finally gone to bed, Léa and Laurent sat close together on the little stone fireside seat inside the enormous hearth. Léa was happy. She laughingly stroked Laurent's moustache, and ran her hand over his chest. His muscles had become as hard as steel. She ran her finger over

176

the crow's feet that now showed at the corners of his eyes.

'You've aged.'

'So have you. But you're even more beautiful. You look like a real lady now. Even Tavernier's noticed.'

They talked for hours of everything that had happened to them since they had last seen each other.

With Lécussan's men at their heels, Adrien and Laurent had been forced to leave Toulouse for the Limoges area, sleeping rough in barns or sheep folds, dependent on the hospitality of members of the Resistance and sympathizers. The zone was under the orders of a certain Raoul, a former communist primary school teacher, who had gone underground in 1941, hounded by Superintendent Combes's men and then by the Gestapo. After two months of being on the run, Adrien decided to go back to Bordeaux in secret where he felt he could do more useful work than in the woods. As for Laurent, he stayed to train young recruits in military tactics. Together they had broken into town halls and tax offices to obtain ration cards which were vital for their survival, official stamps, blank identity cards and money.

'The war has made me a highwayman!'

But he was not a communist, and very soon, deep rifts had developed between Laurent and the underground Party leaders. He was seriously considering the possibility of going back to Toulouse to try and get himself sent to London and then to North Africa to fight. That was the point he had reached when he learned of Camille's arrest and imprisonment in Fort Hâ. The same evening, he left the Limoges underground and contacted his old network in Toulouse. There a meeting had been arranged for him with Grand-Clément.

'Papa's insurance broker!' exclaimed Léa.

The very same man who had become *the* head of civilian and military operations in the Bordeaux region, which had not failed to astonish Laurent, particularly since, in 1940, Grand-Clément had made no secret of his support for the Vichy government. But he was not the only member of the Resistance to have trusted Marshal Pétain for a while. In Toulouse, Laurent was told to go to the Café Bertrand on the

177

Quai des Chartrons and to ask for David, who, in August 1942, had been parachuted from London to somewhere near the town of Châteauroux. Laurent was to introduce himself under the pseudonym of Lucius. David would receive a message from the London broadcasting service warning him of Laurent's visit. The appointment was for the following day.

Léa showed Laurent Camille's letter which he read with emotion. Léa was surprised to find that she did not feel at all jealous. She told him of her conversation with Otto Kramer and his promise. Strangely, she did not talk about Mathias's return nor what he had said about his new connections. She simply told him that Camille was at Mérignac.

'Tomorrow's visiting day and I'm going to see her. Write to her if you like and I'll find a way of slipping your letter to her.'

'No, I can't accept. It's too dangerous.'

'Write anyway and if I see we're being watched, I'll keep it. I'll get you some paper and ink.'

When she returned, he was sitting at the table.

She gently placed her hand on his shoulder.

'Don't worry.'

He looked up at her, put his arm round her and rested his head on her stomach. They remained quite still in that position for a long time.

Léa was the first to stir.

'I'm going to bed. Ruth has made up a bed for you in Papa's room. I hope you won't be too cold, she's given you two hot water bottles. What time do you want to get up tomorrow?'

'Not too early, my appointment isn't until three o'clock in the afternoon.'

'Sleep well, then. See you tomorrow,' she said giving him a sisterly kiss.

'Léa . . . Léa . . . it's nothing . . . don't be afraid, it's only a bad dream . . .'

Laurent awoke with a jump when he heard the screams and groans coming from Léa's room. He rushed in. In the grip of her usual nightmare, Léa was sitting up in bed in tears, she was warding off the attacks of the man she had killed in Orléans. By a twist of fate, the man now had a companion: Masuy,

178

Sarah's torturer, who was coming towards her dragging a bathtub full of disgusting filth with serpents rising from it.

Léa wakened drenched with perspiration and saw Laurent's face in the soft glow of the lamp.

'Please come close to me, I'm frightened.'

As soon as he held her in his arms, she fell asleep like a child.

Léa persuaded Laurent not to come downstairs until she had made certain that neither Fayard nor his wife was in the vicinity. In fact, she was afraid of Mathias's jealous perspicacity. Rightly so. The previous evening, the young man had disappeared after taking Léa's luggage up to her room and had not come back.

When she walked into the kitchen, he was there, chatting to Ruth who was finishing her breakfast. Léa kissed her old governess and her childhood friend.

'You're looking marvellous,' he said. 'You look as though you've had a good night's sleep even though you went to bed so late.'

She was on the defensive at once.

'I go to bed when I feel like it.'

'Don't get angry, I only mentioned it.'

Léa relaxed.

'I slept very badly, I had the most awful nightmares.'

'This evening I'll make you a lime herb-tea,' said Ruth, practical as ever.

'You know that lime makes me irritable, even when I was a little girl . . .'

'Yes, yes, it's true, I'm getting you mixed up with Françoise. You like orange blossom. Shall I put some toast under the grill for you?'

'No, thank you, I'll do it myself.'

'There's a little coffee on the stove.'

'Thank you, Ruth.'

While she had been talking, she had cut herself a slice of hard coarse bread, stuck a fork into it and was toasting it in front of the embers in the hearth.

'Do you want some?' she asked Mathias.

179

'No, thank you, I've already had breakfast. Here, I've brought you some butter.'

'But it's your ration for a whole month!'

'Don't worry, I know where I can get some more.'

Sitting opposite her, he watched her eat.

Suddenly, Léa's expression clouded over.

'What's the matter?'

'I was thinking of Camille, I've got nothing to take her other than some jam and clothes.'

'I've thought of that. I've got a hamper full of goodies for her.'

'With butter?'

'With butter, sugar, little cakes, sausage, noodles and even some soap.'

'You're wonderful!'

'I know,' he said, looking pleased with himself.

Léa burst out laughing.

'The camp opens at two o'clock. You have to get the eleven o'clock train. You haven't got long.'

She glanced at the clock on the mantelpiece.

'I'm going up to get dressed. Come and pick me up in half an hour.'

As soon as he had gone out, she prepared a breakfast tray for Laurent, who was in ecstasies over the butter.

They did not have time to arrange to meet in a safe place in Bordeaux, especially as Laurent did not know when he would be seeing Grand-Clément. They decided to say goodbye there and then. When Léa was ready to leave, she hugged him tightly.

'Be careful, Léa, and don't take any unnecessary risks.'

She gave a fatalistic shrug and left the room. The letter for Camille was hidden in her right shoe.

Chapter 14

She clasped the handle of the heavy basket in her small hand encased in its darned woollen glove. On her feet, she was wearing wooden-soled ankle boots as she tramped along the muddy path that led to Mérignac. The camp was surrounded by a barbed wire fence. A crowd of people, mainly women, were queueing, waiting for the gates to open. They were shivering in their thin clothing, hanging their heads as if they were ashamed of being there. Suddenly, they all came to life: one of the high wooden gates crowned with barbed wire swung open. People straightened up . . . hearts beat faster. Léa picked up the basket in her other hand. The column advanced slowly, everyone was fumbling for their identity cards. One old lady, laden with parcels, dropped her papers. Nobody went to her aid. Finally it was Léa's turn. She wished she had not asked Mathias to let her go in alone. After inspecting her identity card, the gendarme let her through and another indicated that she should go into the hut next to the gate. There, other gendarmes were examining the contents of people's suitcases, baskets, bags and parcels, making a note of the visitor's name and whom they had come to see. Behind a dirty curtain, a more intimate search was carried out: there was a female officer to search the women. Léa stiffened as hands felt her coat and her body through her dress.

'Take off your shoes.'

Léa closed her eyes to conceal the smug glint in them. What a good idea it had been to remove the letter from her shoe in the toilet on the train. She calmly held out her shoes to the woman who felt inside them.

'It's not my fault. You know, there are people who hide

letters in their shoes,' she said, handing them back. 'You can go.'

Léa picked up her basket. She was still wearing her gloves. The letter was hidden in the left one. She took a few steps forward along the muddy path, unaware of her surroundings, not daring to believe she had got away with it. Someone bumped into her and brought her down to earth again.

So this was the famous Mérignac camp where the hostages were taken from: ten wooden huts with corrugated iron roofs, surrounded by barbed wire and overlooked by watchtowers. A few prisoners were wandering around. A hut had been turned into a visiting room for the occasion: a little corner set aside for the women and the main part for the men. It was heated by a stove in the centre of the room. Léa stood on the threshold.

'Close the door, for Christ's sake!' yelled a man's voice.

Léa was pushed inside by a gendarme who closed the door behind her.

'Who are you looking for, dear?'

'Madame d'Argilat,' she stammered.

'She's coming, don't worry. They've gone to get her from the sick bay.'

From the sick bay! So Camille was still ill!

'Léa! . . . Oh! Léa!'

That frail body, that wan face which had become so terribly thin, that lank hair, those burning hands, those eyes . . . those eyes which were full of joy at seeing Léa again . . . those kisses all over her face. Those tears she could taste on her lips mingling with her own . . .

'How's Charles?'

'He's well,' replied Léa. 'I've heard from Laurent,' she whispered.

She felt the feeble body crumple. With the help of one of the women prisoners, she laid her on a seat.

'She's too ill to get up, she should have stayed in bed.'

'No,' murmured Camille, sitting up. 'It's nothing,' she said to the gendarme who was walking towards her.

The young woman hardly looked at the contents of the parcel but seemed delighted as she wrapped herself in the big woollen shawl Ruth had knitted for her. That was the moment

182

Léa chose to slip her Laurent's letter.

'It's from Laurent.'

Camille blushed and began to tremble as she clutched the crumpled letter.

'Oh! Thank you.'

She coughed. Léa felt her forehead: it was feverish.

'You've got a temperature, you're mad to have got out of bed.'

'Don't scold me. Visitors aren't allowed into the sick bay, I wouldn't have been able to see you. Whatever you do, don't tell Laurent I'm ill.'

'Have you seen the doctor?'

'Yes, yes, he came yesterday. He comes round once a week. Tell me about Paris, your aunts, Françoise and her baby. Is he sweet?'

Léa chatted nineteen to the dozen. Camille was radiant.

When visiting time was over, they felt as though they had not had time to talk about anything.

Camille made Léa promise to return, and burst into tears.

'I'm frightened I won't be able to hold on,' she said.

Relieved of the basket, her arms dangling by her sides, Léa walked away from the camp with only one thing in mind: 'I must get her out of there.'

Mathias drew level with her on his bicycle.

'Mademoiselle, can I give you a lift?'

He'd come back to fetch her! That was sweet of him, as the trams between Bordeaux and Mérignac were few and far between, but that did not really suit her: she wanted to slip discreetly into the café Bertrand on the Quai des Chartrons.

'Can you take me to my Uncle Luc's?'

'Of course. Will you be long?'

'I don't know, an hour or two, maybe. I'll meet you at six o'clock in the café next to the Grand Théâtre.'

'As you wish.'

Léa sat side-saddle on the crossbar and was almost comfortable leaning against Mathias.

While they rode, they talked about Camille and her health. The young man once more reassured her that Camille would not be staying there much longer and that Rousseau, the director of the camp, had promised that he would ensure that she was more comfortable. An inexplicable feeling of unease prevented Léa from coming out with the questions that she was dying to ask.

He dropped her off at the Allée de Chartres, outside her uncle's house. She went inside the building and waited in the huge white marble entrance hall for a few minutes and then went back out again. Mathias had disappeared. She started walking hurriedly towards the Quai des Chartrons which was not far away.

Apart from a few dark huddled figures scurrying about in the icy drizzle that had begun to fall, the embankment was deserted. Léa had slowed her pace for fear of walking past the café Bertrand without seeing it. The card players at one of the tables did not even look up when she went in. She walked towards the bar watched by a kindly-looking plumpish waiter wearing a blue apron. But for him and the card players, the café was empty. The little man went behind the bar.

'What would you like to drink, mademoiselle?'

'I'd like to see David,' she said in one breath.

His open smiling face hardened.

'You must be mistaken, there's nobody called David here.'

'I'm sure there is, one of my friends was supposed to be meeting him here this afternoon.'

'Perhaps he was, but I don't know anything about it.'

Léa suddenly felt weary as she realized she would get nothing out of this man. She sat down at one of the tables.

'A coffee, please.'

The concoction he brought her was vile, but at least it was hot. The proprietor had vanished into the back room.

A few seconds later, Laurent was standing in front of her.

'You're mad, what are you doing here?'

'I was waiting for you.'

'Come on, don't stay here.'

Without answering, she followed him into the room behind the bar. There was no window, only an unmade bed, a white

184

wooden table, a large wardrobe and a few café chairs. Two men were standing watching her come in.

'It's her, all right,' said Laurent, pushing her into the room in front of him. 'You can trust her, Fortunat and I have often used her.'

'But why has she come here? It's highly dangerous.'

Those two were beginning to get on her nerves with their inquisitiveness. And who was this Fortunat Laurent was talking about? She knew nobody of that name. The three of them were ridiculous with their conspiratorial expressions. Suddenly, the smallest of the strangers smiled at her.

'Leave her alone, can't you see you're frightening her.'

Frightening? Oh well, if it made them happy to think she was a feeble little woman . . .

The small dark-haired man who had spoken asked her:

'Why did you ask to see David?'

'I knew that Lau . . .'

'Don't mention any names.'

'I knew that . . . my friend was meeting him.'

'Who told you?'

Léa let out a sigh of annoyance.

'He did, of course.'

'Is that correct?' he asked brusquely, turning to Laurent.

'Yes.'

'Do you realize that you have been very careless? And I think you were right,' he said, bursting out laughing. 'Forgive me, mademoiselle, for interrogating you like this. Allow me to introduce myself: I'm Aristide and this is David. What about you, what should we call you?'

Léa heard herself answer without thinking:

'Exupérance.'

'Exupérance . . .' said Aristide, 'that's a funny name; it sounds like exuberance, it's a good choice.'

Laurent was looking at her with a knowing smile. He knew where that name came from: they had gazed together at the 'little saint' in her shrine in the basilica at Verdelais.

'I saw Camille. I managed to give her your letter.'

'How is she?'

Léa chose to forget her promise.

'She's ill, she must get out of there as soon as possible.'

Laurent leaned against the back of a chair without showing how worried he was.

'Aristide thinks it's very risky going to see Grand-Clément. He doesn't trust him.'

'But he's wrong,' exclaimed David, who had not said anything so far. 'I know Grand-Clément, we worked together finding new landing places for parachutists and fixing up new arms caches. He's reliable and is trusted by the leadership. I don't know what Aristide's got against him, he's never wanted to meet him.'

'Listen, David, we're not going to argue over your great man again. Perhaps he is "reliable" as you say, but he talks too much, he's too much in the public eye, is involved in too many deals. It's common knowledge that "Monsieur" Grand-Clément is "a high up official in the Resistance". I don't understand what got into them in Paris to appoint a clown like that as leader of the B2 area. The Bordeaux Gestapo are the only people who don't know who he is.'

'You're exaggerating! Everyone has their own way of fighting.'

'I know I'm perhaps being unfair, but something tells me that one of these days, that naval officer, that ex-royalist, that good friend of Colonel de la Roque, will play a dirty trick on us.'

'You and your ability to see the future.'

Léa had looked on with amusement as they exchanged opinions about 'papa's insurance broker'. She tried to remember what impression he had made on her on the one and only occasion she had met him. She recalled a tallish man, with a pleasant manner, the sort of businessman who was well-liked in Bordeaux, nothing very distinctive about him.

'Supposing I went to see him?'

Three pairs of eyes stared at her.

'I've already dealt with him.'

'What do you mean?' asked Aristide.

Léa told them how she had been entrusted with certain documents for Grand-Clément which she had pretended were her father's insurance policies.

186

Aristide listened without comment. Perhaps it was not such a bad idea after all. They would have to see.

'When is the meeting supposed to be?'

'Tomorrow, at his place, an hour before curfew.'

'We can cancel it,' said David. 'I'll take care of that if necessary.'

'All right,' said Aristide.

'I'm supposed to go back to Montillac this evening. I'll have to telephone, otherwise they'll worry about me. I must also meet a friend with whom I was going to go back to Langon.'

'You haven't got time. Someone will phone your family from the post-office. As for your friend, it's just too bad. One of our men will follow you from a distance until you reach the Cours de Verdun and will wait to assure your protection. You will ask Grand-Clément one question: "Will the leadership agree to help Madame d'Argilat escape?"'

It was obvious that Léa had not been listening for the last few moments: she was thinking at top speed.

'That's absurd. If I ask Grand-Clément that, and if he talks too much, as you say, everyone will know I'm working with you and I'll be suspected too. What's more, if Camille does escape, she'll have to go into hiding until the war is over. In her condition, and for her son's sake, that's not a good idea.'

'That's true,' said Aristide. 'What do you suggest?'

'That I go and see him on my own account and beg him to do something out of compassion.'

'But he knows you're involved in the Resistance, because you've already passed documents on to him,' contributed David.

'I thought of that. I'll play the featherbrain who has no idea of the enormous implications of what she is doing.'

Aristide did not need to think about Léa's suggestion for long. It made perfect sense.

'I think she's right. David, tell "Mule" to follow her discreetly as soon as she leaves. Exupérance, you mustn't come back here, it'd be too dangerous.'

David left the room.

'I'll manage.'

'I don't know if I ought to let you take such risks for me,' said Laurent.

'It's not for you, it's for Camille.'

The strange thing was, she meant it and she realized that since their dramatic flight across France in the general exodus, she had felt responsible for the young woman.

Laurent silently hugged her.

David came back.

'"Mule" is hiding outside waiting for you. If there's anything wrong when you come out of Grand-Clément's place, put this headscarf on instead of your hat. "Mule" will get the message and will be ready to intervene. He'll follow you until you signal to him that you're safe by putting your hands in your mouth like this. Is everything quite clear?'

'Yes, it's not that difficult.'

'I'll be waiting for you tomorrow at the Régent, in the Place Gambetta, from midday onwards.'

The proprietor came into the room.

'It's all clear, she can go.'

Léa gave a little wave of her hand and left the café. As she walked past the proprietor, he said:

'Sorry about that but I have my orders, love.'

In reply, Léa flashed him her most charming smile.

Outside, it was almost dark; dim lights shone under doors, no light at all was shed by windows or shops. The street lamps were unlit. It was cold and damp. Fortunately, the Cours de Verdun was not far away from the café.

Several cars were parked outside number 34 and elegantly dressed people were going inside. Léa hesitated. Perhaps this was not the best time to see Grand-Clément. Too bad. She was there, she had to get on with it. She rang the bell.

A maid opened the door and stood aside to let her in without asking any questions.

'Fancy you being here, my dear.'

Léa turned round and immediately identified the man she had been afraid she might not recognize.

'What do you want?'

'I've got to talk to you.'

'It's a bad time, I'm expecting guests, come back tomorrow.'

'No, it's a matter of life and death,' she said, making her voice sound melodramatic, 'you're the only person who can help me.'

Grand-Clément gave a smug little smile.

'Believe me, mademoiselle, I'd be delighted to help a lovely young lady like you, but it is most inconvenient right now.'

'Please, I'll tell you in a nutshell what it's about.'

'Very well, come into my office. Darling,' he said to a young woman who was coming towards them, 'I'll only be a few minutes, greet our guests for me.'

He showed her into the office which she knew from the previous visit. There, she set about charming, wheedling, stirring and convincing him.

At the end of their conversation, he promised that someone who was so warmly recommended would soon be released.

'Not soon, immediately.'

'Hold your horses! To listen to you, anyone would think that all it takes is an order from me for the Germans to release their prisoners.'

'I'm sure you can manage it.'

'Come back and see me tomorrow at four o'clock and I'll tell you what's happening,' he concluded, rising.

In the hall, a tallish man was removing his coat, helped by the maid.

'Uncle Luc!'

'Léa, what are you doing here? I thought you were staying with your aunts in Paris.'

'I came to ask Monsieur Grand-Clément to help me get Camille d'Argilat out of Mérignac.'

'Do you know this young lady?'

'She's the daughter of my brother Pierre who died last year. Madame d'Argilat is a friend of hers. They have been living together near Langon with one of my sisters since the young lady's husband disappeared. I know her well. She's a person of excellent character. If you were able to do something for her, I should be most grateful to you.'

'My dear sir, I've promised your niece I'll do all I can.'

'Thank you.'

'Goodbye, uncle.'

'Where are you going? You're not going back to Montillac this evening? There aren't any more trains and it's nearly curfew. You can stay with us if you like.'

'Thank you, Uncle Luc, but I'm meeting some friends.'

'As you wish. Is all well at Montillac?'

'Yes, thank you. Goodbye. Goodbye, Monsieur Grand-Clément.'

'Goodbye, mademoiselle. Until tomorrow. I hope I'll have some good news for you.'

It was pitch dark outside. Léa had not removed her hat. Now it was a question of finding out if Mathias was still at the café by the Grand Théâtre. He was.

He was seething.

'Where've you been? Why did you take me for a ride? You weren't at your uncle's and nobody there has seen you. Where were you?'

'I'll explain.'

'Hey! You lovebirds, I'm closing! It's curfew in ten minutes.'

'All right, all right, we're going. Just you wait till I lay my hands on you! I can't stand being made a fool of.'

'I'm sorry, sir, we're closed.'

The man who was waiting in the doorway with his hands thrust deep in the pockets of his raincoat did not take his eyes off Léa. It was 'Mule'. She had forgotten about him. She gave him the agreed signal. He left, saying:

'Goodnight all.'

'Where are we going?' asked Léa as soon as they were out in the cold and the rain.

'Tell me where you were while I was hanging about like an idiot waiting for you.'

'Later, if you don't mind. For the moment, I'm freezing and I'm starving.'

'Ruth and your sister will be frantic!'

'They've been told. Do you know where we can go?'

Her question went unanswered. They walked in silence for a while and crossed the Esplanade des Quinconces which looked

190

like a great black hole. The young man pulled a torch out of his pocket which he handed to Léa. They skirted the sandbags in the Allée de Tourny and reached a narrow street near a church.

A steep winding slippery staircase led to a stained glass door on which was written, in large enamel lettering: 'otel'. The 'h' was missing leaving only an outline. Mathias, who was still wheeling his bicycle, pushed open the door jangling the copper pipes of a bell which rang for ages. The dimly lit place reeked of cat's urine and onion soup and the sickly smell of cheap perfume hung in the air.

'It stinks here,' whispered Léa.

Mathias shrugged.

'What do you want?' croaked a hoarse voice.

The glow of a lighted cigarette could be distinguished in the far corner of the room.

'It's me, Madame Ginette. Have you kept my room for me?'

'Oh, it's you, kid. You're lucky, I could have let it ten times over, but I said to myself: "Can't leave a nice boy like that out in the streets." What the hell . . .? There's someone with you.'

The fattest woman Léa had ever set eyes on emerged from the shadows. Two bright, beady, malicious eyes, dripping with mascara, were embedded in her puffy, outrageously made-up face. Her shapeless body, wrapped in a threadbare velvet dressing gown, lumbered towards them, her feet dragging in their worn out slippers. Léa recoiled like a frightened child.

'Madame Ginette, this is the childhood friend I've been telling you about.'

Madame Ginette replied in a crude local dialect:

'Well, well, well, you bumpkin, you didn't tell me that the brat was such a beauty, and quite a girl too, by the looks of her. With a piece like that I bet you're getting your oats all right.'

'Madame Ginette!'

'Don't you "Madame Ginette" me! I'm allowed to say what I think in my own place, aren't I? My word, anyone would think you were in love. I'm not going to deflower your little virgin. Mind you, with those peepers, I wouldn't be surprised if she'd already lost her cherry. Isn't that right, sweetie? You can't pull the wool over the eyes of an old whore like me.'

Léa stood there wide-eyed at this torrent of words she did not understand spoken in a very strong accent.

'Please, Madame Ginette!'

'Please what, you dirty bugger. Getting all upset over a bit of pussy. I'm a good woman but you're starting to needle me. I'm complimenting you on your hussy, I haven't got the hump, quite the opposite. I don't know why I don't put you over my knee. Christ almighty! I'm itching to . . .'

'Mathias, I think we ought to leave,' said Léa, 'I don't think madame is very pleased to see us.'

'Well, doesn't she talk pretty, your little dove! "I don't think madame is very pleased to see us" . . . it's not that, sweetheart, but this lazy bugger who takes me for an idiot. He pisses off without a word, comes back with his bicycle and his "childhood friend". He wants to fool around but hasn't got the bread to pay for a room. If you want to hit the sack here, I want the dough on the table or else you're out.'

'Here you are, madame, this is all I have on me. Will that be sufficient?' asked Léa, icily taking a few bills from her bag.

The fat woman counted them and stuffed them into one of her dressing-gown pockets.

'You're a lucky bastard, you are. You know the way.'

'Yes, thank you.'

Mathias pressed a light switch. The dim light from a single bare bulb revealed a long corridor into which he pushed Léa.

'Hey! Young whipper-snapper, don't forget your bicycle!'

He retraced his footsteps to collect his bicycle, which he carried on his shoulder.

The room was just like the rest of the hotel: sinister and freezing cold. At the end of her tether, Léa stood in the middle of the room and began to cry helplessly. Mathias could stand anything except her tears. He put his arms round her. She pushed him away.

'Don't touch me.'

She lay down on the bed, removed her ankle boots and burrowed under the heavy blue eiderdown which seemed an incongruous luxury in this wretched place.

192

'I'll be back in a minute.'

She got up, worried. He wasn't going to leave her here, alone in this disgusting place with that fat woman who frightened the life out of her.

'Don't be afraid, I'm going to get something to eat. I won't be more than ten minutes.'

All the time he was gone, Léa stayed buried under the eiderdown.

'You'll suffocate under there,' he said, pulling the eiderdown off her. 'The soup won't wait for you, it's getting cold. If madame would care to take the trouble of getting out of bed, dinner is served.'

It was unbelievable! Where on earth had he got that trolley covered with a spotless white tablecloth. The cloth was freshly ironed and the silverware looked as if it had come from a first class hotel. A bottle of Château Margaux lay in a wicker holder beside a basket containing four little white rolls, a cold chicken, a salad, a chocolate dessert and a large tureen of soup.

Léa could not believe her eyes! This boy, whom she thought she knew inside out, was becoming more and more of a mystery. He must be the only person in Bordeaux to be able to get hold of a meal after curfew – a meal that an honest woman in pre-war days would not have turned down.

'Where on earth did this come from?'

'Not from here, in any case. I have a friend who's the cook in a restaurant not far from here. You needn't worry, it's the very best, all the Bordeaux high society eat there.'

'It must be terribly expensive. I thought you didn't have any money?'

'True, but I've got credit. Come on, it's on the table. Stop dithering and let's eat.'

Léa swallowed a mouthful and then pushed her plate away.

'Why did you go to Germany?'

'You don't like it, do you? You can't bear me being on the winning side. I know. Since you've been back from Paris, you've been avoiding me. You don't think it's the Laurent d'Argilats and the Adrien Delmases who are going to lay down the law, do you? Do you think we're going to let the communists take over without a word?'

'But neither Laurent nor Uncle Adrien is a communist.'

'Perhaps not, but they're terrorists just like the communists.'

'Poor Mathias, you're completely out of your mind. No doubt you think it's perfectly natural to torture people.'

'It's only the Jewish scum they torture.'

'Jewish scum! Camille?'

'She should have been more careful about who she married!'

'Swine!'

'You'll see what a swine I am . . . You haven't always said that.'

He held out his hand.

'If you touch me, you'd better not set foot in Montillac ever again. Ever.'

He turned pale. It was no longer his childhood friend speaking but the owner of the estate where his father was employed. It was the first time Léa had ever talked to him like that. An employee! A servant! That's what he was. She had screwed him the way marquesses and baronesses screwed their page-boys.

'You're forgetting, my dear young lady, that "your" Montillac is mortgaged, and that if my father and I left you to it, all you'd be able to do would be to sell it off cheaply.'

'That's disgusting of you to say that. I thought you loved Montillac as much as I do.'

'You don't love what doesn't belong to you for long.'

He grabbed both her wrists in one hand, pushed her backwards on to the bed and straddled her, pinning her down with his legs. With his free hand, he undid his flies and took out his penis.

'No, Mathias! Stop it.'

'You're not going to make me believe you don't like this any more!' He hitched up her dress and ripped off her underwear. Léa struggled, fought, spat in his face, pressed her legs together . . . he slapped her with all his strength. Her lip split and blood spurted out. She screamed . . . he opened her legs and thrust himself inside her.

194

Léa watched him, horrified. She was in pain as she had never been in pain before. A terrible fear overcame her. Her tears soaked into the pillow.

'Stop it, Mathias . . . Stop! You're hurting me.'

'Just you listen to me. Will you stop giving yourself airs and graces. I've got everything I need to have you locked up whenever I want: the letters you used to smuggle over, the little messages on the blue bicycle . . . I know everything. I have a lot of friends in the Gestapo. So you'd better be a good girl. I'm going back to Germany until we've finished wiping out the vermin and then I'll come back. You are going to marry me and we will be the masters of Montillac. I've got a lot of patience.'

He fell with his whole weight on top of her, seeking her mouth, his penis deep inside her. Léa gritted her teeth, trembling from head to foot.

'I love you, Léa, I love you.'

He climaxed inside her and collapsed on top of her.

After a long time he rolled off. There was blood on his penis.

Léa pulled the eiderdown over her battered body and lay there motionless.

He caressed her face; she brusquely pushed his hand away. He stared at her in silence for a long time. She was asleep, or pretending to be. He switched off the light.

Chapter 15

Léa wakened first with a terrible pain in her stomach. It looked like a fine day outside and the sun was trying to shine through the ugly, reddish curtains. Daylight revealed the torn and peeling wallpaper, with its oppressive pattern of big blue and red flowers. She caught sight of her reflection in the large mirror on the wall opposite the bed, and that of Mathias who was still asleep.

She sat up. Her watch showed eleven o'clock. Eleven o'clock! With an enormous effort, she managed to drag herself out of bed. Shivering in the freezing room, she slipped on her boots and her overcoat. Mathias rolled over in bed. She froze for a second and then rummaged under the bed for her bag, bumping into the table and rattling the plates and glasses. Mathias was still asleep.

At the end of the corridor, a sickly-looking man with a sallow complexion, a cigarette butt hanging from his lips, was nonchalantly sweeping the floor.

Outside, the drizzle of the previous day had given way to blue skies. There was a hint of spring in the air as Léa made her way through the joyless streets. The Notre-Dame clock struck twelve. Léa began to run down the Rue Montesquieu. Still running, she crossed the Cour de l'Intendance, had to stop to let a tram pass and arrived breathless outside the Régent café. The terrace was packed with people drinking apéritifs before lunch. Several tables were occupied by German officers.

David was mad to arrange to meet her here! He was not outside. Léa resolved to go into the café. Suddenly, she spotted him sitting on a bench reading *La Petite Gironde*. He looked younger and happy.

'Have you heard the news?'

She shook her head.

'Yesterday the London broadcasting service announced that Leningrad had been liberated. Aristide and I were nearly in tears when we heard Jacques Duchesne's hoarse voice break the news. Do you realize, they held out for sixteen months! You don't look too happy . . .'

'It's not that, I've got a dreadful migraine . . . That's wonderful news.'

He studied her carefully.

'It's true you don't look as well as you did yesterday. Nothing went wrong, did it?'

'No, everything went perfectly.'

'What about Grand-Clément?'

'He promised me he'd do all he could. I've got to go back and see him this afternoon at four o'clock.'

'Fine. I'll tell Mule to be there. Don't forget, if there's anything wrong, put your headscarf on.'

'What would mademoiselle like to drink?'

'Nothing . . . er . . . I don't know.'

'Have you had anything to eat this morning?'

'No, I'm not hungry. Give me a Vichy and strawberry cordial with an aspirin if you have any.'

'I'll have a look, mademoiselle.'

A group of young people came in laughing rowdily. Léa felt David become suddenly tense. And yet they seemed a harmless enough crowd of boys.

The waiter returned with Léa's drink and two aspirin tablets in a saucer.

'You're in luck, the proprietor's wife had some in her handbag.'

'Would you thank her for me?'

'How much is that?'

'One Vichy and strawberry and a glass of Sauternes . . . six francs, monsieur, service not included.'

'Here you are. Hurry up, we've got to move.'

Léa swallowed the aspirins and followed David. Once outside he took her arm and led her to the Rue Judaïque.

'Why did we leave in such a hurry? Because of those young people?'

'Yes.'

'Why?'

'I hope for your sake that you never see them again. They are Superintendent Poinsot's men.'

'Them? They look like a crowd of students!'

'A funny bunch of students. They wield the bludgeon more skilfully than they wield the French language. They are dangerous little bullies with no scruples. They torture and kill as much for love as for money.'

'Why did you arrange to meet me there?'

'Because the safest place is amidst the enemy. We'll go our separate ways from here. What are you going to do until it's time to go and see Grand-Clément?'

'I'm going to walk around for a while, the fresh air will do me good. Then I may go to the cinema.'

'That's a good idea. Carné's *Visiteurs du Soir* is on at the Olympia. It's not bad even though the ending's a bit weak.'

'I saw it in Paris. What should I do when I've seen Grand-Clément?'

'Go to the station and take the train home. In front of the newspaper stand a woman holding a guidebook of French wines will come up to you and say: "The Paris train is late today," and you will answer: "I don't think it is." Tell her the outcome of your conversation with Grand-Clément and take the train to Langon.'

'And if for any reason I can't get to the station?'

'Mule will have told us. He'll be following you all the time. But orders are that you go back home as soon as possible.'

'Orders?' said Léa, frowning.

'Yes, whether you like it or not, you belong to the network now and you have to obey for your own sake and for everyone else's. Aristide is a stickler for obedience.'

'Where's Lau . . . Lucius?'

'In a safe place, on the moors. You'll be hearing from him soon. Goodbye, Exupérance, good luck.'

'Goodbye, David.'

'Your friend will be released tomorrow.'

Léa could not believe her ears. He was laughing at her, it wasn't possible!

'How come?'

'The Gestapo have come to the conclusion that Madame d'Argilat knows nothing of her husband's activities nor of his whereabouts. You wouldn't know, by any chance, would you?'

The unexpectedness of the question nearly threw her. How on earth did she manage to control the panic that made her turn quite pale, and reply in a perfectly innocent voice:

'Me? No, I haven't seen him since my father's funeral.'

Whether he was taken in or not, Grand-Clément gave nothing away.

'There's a careful man if ever there was, just the sort of man we like.'

'We?'

'The Resistance.'

'But that's very dangerous,' she said with a mixture of fear and admiration sounding so genuine that Grand-Clément agreed, flattered:

'Very. But that's the price we have to pay for setting our country free.'

Léa was beginning to tire of acting the featherbrain and felt increasingly uncomfortable in the presence of this man whom she could not quite make out. She asked:

'What time will Madame d'Argilat be coming out?'

'Late morning. She'll need a car, she's very weak. I took the liberty of discussing it with your uncle, Luc Delmas, who offered to put his car at your disposal for driving Madame d'Argilat home.'

'You did the right thing. Thank you for everything. But how did you manage it?'

'To tell you the truth, I didn't do very much. When I talked to the director of Mérignac, he told me he'd just received orders to release Madame d'Argilat and ten or so other prisoners for family reasons.'

Was that the truth? In any case, it was plausible. Léa contented herself with that explanation and took her leave of Grand-Clément, who said:

'I hope to see you again in more pleasant circumstances.'

If the memory of the previous night had not been oppressing her like a heavy leaden weight in the pit of her stomach, Léa would have danced for joy along the Cours de Verdun. She felt the warm caress of the setting winter sun on her skin. She decided to go to her Uncle Luc's house and have a wash, and hopefully rid herself of the feeling that she had been defiled. For the first time that day, she began thinking about what had happened.

The Mathias of her childhood and adolescence had died in a sordid hotel run by a disgusting old prostitute. She would never forgive him. What she could not work out was how real Mathias's threats had been. She now knew he was capable of anything, but did not know the extent of his real power over her. There was no question of throwing him out of Montillac until she found out the true position regarding the estate and the revelations he could make to the Gestapo . . .

It was warm in Luc Delmas's dining room, and the meal, served by the faithful old cook, was as tasteless as her food had been before the war.

Léa was beginning to feel increasingly ill at ease in the company of her Uncle Luc and her cousin Philippe who had finally finished his law studies and had joined his father's practice.

'It's lucky papa's a friend of the local governor otherwise Madame d'Argilat would probably have spent several months in prison.'

'Do you think it's right, you, the lawyer, that someone should be put in prison when they haven't done anything?'

'She might not have done anything, but her husband is certainly wanted by the police.'

'Which, the French or the German police?'

'You know very well that the police here are collaborating.'

'It would be hard not to know.'

'Stop arguing, children. You're wrong to take that attitude, Léa. Here in Bordeaux we're only following the government's orders. Any other behaviour would be against the interest of our country. In making the choice he did, Marshal Pétain saved France from chaos and communist anarchy, not to mention the thousands of human lives that have been saved . . .'

'Uncle Luc, you're forgetting that here human lives, as you call them, don't count for much and that dozens of hostages have been executed.'

'That's the sad result of criminal acts committed by irresponsible people in the pay of Moscow or London.'

'Uncle, how dare you say that when people like Uncle Adrien and Laurent d'Argilat . . .'

Luc Delmas stood up so violently that his heavy chair was knocked over. He flung his napkin down on the table in fury.

'I don't want my brother's name mentioned in this house. I've already told you, as far as I'm concerned, he's dead. As for Laurent d'Argilat, I don't understand what happened to him, he used to be an excellent officer. Goodnight, you've ruined my appetite.'

Luc Delmas left the room, banging the door behind him. Léa finished her glass of wine.

'That's clever, getting him all worked up. Now he won't get a wink of sleep.'

'A little insomnia won't do him any harm. He can think about what he'll do after the war when the Germans have lost.'

'Poor Léa. That's not likely to happen just yet. You'd be better off worrying about your suitors than getting involved in men's business.'

'Poor Philippe! You're as stupid as ever. You're incapable of seeing the world other than through your father's eyes. Not like Pierrot, he understands, he preferred to get out.'

It was then her cousin's turn to rise, white with anger.

'Lucky you didn't talk about my brother in front of my father otherwise I'd have thrown you out.'

Léa shrugged and asked:

'Where is he? Have you heard from him?'

'He's in prison in Spain.'

'In prison?'

'Yes, and it serves him right. Papa nearly had a heart attack when he found the note in his room saying that he intended to head for North Africa and join up.'

'Of course, you'd never think of doing such a thing.'

'It's all very well for you to laugh. If it weren't for Uncle Adrien's bad example, my little brother would never have gone off like that. Luckily, he was arrested before he was able to get to Morocco . . .'

'Luckily! . . .'

'Yes, papa has some lawyer friends in Madrid who promised to have him repatriated.'

'He'll run away.'

'I'd be very surprised if he did. It's not easy to escape from a Jesuit college, especially if the father insists on the necessity of saving a young soul in danger.'

'You're not taking any chances, I see!'

'Can't afford to these days, my dear. You'd do better to follow the example of your estate manager's son.'

'Mathias?'

'Yes, Fayard's son who, in spite of his origins, is behaving more nobly than the young people in our circles.'

'Oh yes! He certainly is behaving well! You really are ridiculous, pathetic: you sound like Aunt Bernadette: "the young people in our circles"! Our world is done for, wiped out, finished for ever. You and your ilk are extinct, dodos . . .'

'Dodos or not, for the time being, it's thanks to people like us that the country is still on its feet.'

'Do you think that we're still on our feet when we're being crushed by German boots and licking those same boots?'

'I can see you've been listening to the broadcasts from London and swallowing every word. Those pathetic creatures who, from the safety of their island, exhort all the good-for-nothing communists in our unfortunate country to commit acts of subversion.'

'You seem to forget the daily air-raids over England.'

'Serves the English swine right.'

'You, a citizen of Bordeaux, how can you say that about our cousins!'

'You're so stupid, it's no joke.'

Once again there was the same lack of communication between them, they were arguing and insulting each other just as they always had been.

Léa nearly stalked out, but what he had said about Mathias had her worried.

'What did you mean about Mathias?'

'Simply that his stay in Germany has knocked some sense into him and instead of spending his time gazing at you with lovelorn eyes, he's become a man we can rely on.'

'What is that supposed to mean?'

'It's too complicated to explain to you now. You'll soon find out. It's late. I've got to be in court early in the morning. Good night. You're sleeping in Corinne's room. Don't forget to switch off the lights when you go upstairs.'

'Good night.'

Léa remained at the table propped up on her elbows, her chin cupped in her hands. She sat there thinking for a long time. She wondered with growing anxiety what Philippe had been hinting at concerning Mathias.

The following morning, Luc Delmas and Léa went to Mérignac to fetch Camille. The young woman was so weak that a gendarme had to carry her to the lawyer's car. Once all the administrative formalities were over, they finally left the camp accompanied by the blank stares of the few prisoners who were wandering around in the cold drizzle.

Camille, half lying on the back seat, watched the huge barbed-wire-crowned gate swing open before her but was too exhausted to feel any joy.

Chapter 16

Camille barely had the strength to embrace her son; her illness had exhausted her to the point where she was totally unaware of what was going on around her. Doctor Blanchard diagnosed congestion of the lungs and concussion. She remained poised between life and death for three weeks. Ruth, Laure and Léa took it in turns to sit at her bedside fearing that the fever which consumed her poor emaciated body would never subside. The doctor, who came every day, was tearing out what was left of his white hair and had even begun to wonder if Bernadette Bouchardeau's novena at the chapel of the Virgin of Verdelais might have more chance of success than his remedies, which showed how pessimistic the old atheist was feeling.

In mid-February, Camille's temperature suddenly dropped and in the days that followed, she gradually regained consciousness. But she was so weak that she was unable even to eat unaided. Ruth had to feed her as if she were a child. Talking was also a great effort for her. At last, at the end of March, Doctor Blanchard pronounced her out of danger and watched with feeling as she supped a spoonful of broth. She was finally able to read Laurent's letters and the extracts from his diary that he had managed to send her. That gave her renewed strength. She carefully stowed them in her workbasket which never left her side.

Léa did not leave Montillac once during Camille's long illness. She knew nothing of what Laurent had written and there was no sign of Mathias either. Had he returned to Germany? The Fayards were keeping their distance, carrying on their work without saying a word to the inhabitants of the 'castle' other than hello and goodbye on the few occasions when they met by chance.

At the end of March Camille was able to spend some time outside in the sunshine. She lay in a chaise-longue with a blanket over her. She had put on a little weight, but she was still dreadfully thin and frail. It was no effort for Ruth to pick her up and carry her into the garden.

Money was becoming increasingly scarce at Montillac. Léa and Laure went to see their father's solicitor in neighbouring Cadillac. He advised them to try and sell a little land while making no secret of the fact that it would not be easy as land was not being sold at the moment, or, if it was, it was going for next to nothing.

'Can't we mortgage the pine forest?' asked Laure.

'Your estate is already heavily mortgaged. I don't know if I can let you mortgage any more of your assets.'

'If there were another solution, we wouldn't be here asking your advice,' exclaimed Léa.

'I know, my dear, I know. In memory of the friendship I shared with your parents, I can lend you some money which you can pay back when your father's estate has been settled.'

Léa was about to refuse but Laure forestalled her.

'Thank you very much, Monsieur Rigaud, we gratefully accept your offer.'

'I'll bring the money to Montillac next Thursday with some documents that need signing. Don't forget that if you wish to sell or mortgage part of the estate, you need the consent of your elder sister and your Uncle Luc who is Laure's guardian.'

'Is it absolutely necessary?' asked Léa.

'Yes it is, Laure is still a minor.'

As they cycled home, Léa had the feeling that a cyclist whom she had vaguely noticed on the way to Cadillac was behind them. It was not the first time since Camille's release that she felt she was being watched.

'Stop,' she shouted to her sister.

Surprised, Laure obeyed and got off her bicycle.

'What's the matter?'

'Let's sit down for a minute, I'm tired.'

They sat on the grass verge beside the road. The cyclist sailed past without looking at them. He was young and well-dressed. His face looked vaguely familiar to Léa.

'Have you seen that boy anywhere before?' she asked her sister.

'Yes, at the post office in Langon when I sent Aunt Albertine a parcel. He was standing next to me.'

'Did he speak to you?'

'No, but he smiled at me. I bumped into him yesterday as well in Verdelais. But . . .'

Laure looked at her sister with an expression of indignant anxiety.

'. . . You don't think . . .?'

'Yes, I've seen his face somewhere before but I can't think where. This is the first time I've left Montillac since I brought Camille back from Bordeaux . . . That's it! I remember! It was at the Régent café, he was with a gang of boys of about the same age, they were very rowdy.'

'Maybe he's on holiday in the area.'

'On holiday? In March!'

'Why not, it's nearly Easter.'

'I somehow don't think so. We've got to be very careful. It's a nuisance, I was planning to go to La Réole tomorrow.'

'What for?'

'I can't tell you, but I'm going to need your help.'

Laure stared at her sister in silence. Since the day when the Gestapo had arrested her along with Ruth and Camille, and she had heard two French policemen say laughingly that they had ways of making people speak, her passionate support for Pétain had been shattered. She was ready to help Léa cross the demarcation line.

'I'll do whatever you tell me.'

The two sisters left their bicycles in the little courtyard adjacent to the butcher's at Saint-Macaire and went into the shop laughing. The butcher, whose eldest son was their mother's godson, gave them a hearty welcome.

'Well, well, the little Delmas girls! We don't often see you together, my beauties.'

Then, in a low voice, even though there was nobody else in the shop:

'I've put in a nice piece for Madame Camille, that'll help her get her strength back. Is she any better?'

'A little, thank you, Robert. If it weren't for you, we wouldn't often eat meat at Montillac. We're going to be able to pay you, the solicitor is going to lend us some money.'

'Don't you worry about that, Mademoiselle Léa, we'll see about that later, when this bloody war's over. I haven't got much, but I've got enough to make a good stew. But today, I need a few ration tickets.'

'Have you got the ration books, Laure?'

'Yes . . .'

Laure leaned over and whispered to Léa:

'I've just seen him! He's not alone, he's with another boy.'

'Robert, look outside, discreetly. Do you know those boys outside the herbalist's?'

The butcher went and stood in the doorway, wiping his hands on his apron.

'No, but I've seen them hanging around here before. There's something fishy about them, if you ask me, they're too well-dressed for these hard times.'

'Laure, you know what to do. Robert, may I go out the back way?'

'Right you are, Mademoiselle Léa. They can wait till the cows come home. From where they are, they can't see the courtyard.'

Léa pedalled at top speed down the narrow sloping street behind the church. She rode past the grotto, took the towpath along the Garonne and joined the road to La Réole at Gaillard, just before Saint-Pierre d'Aurillac.

When she reached the sentry post at the demarcation line, the barrier was up. All the same, she stopped and got off her bicycle. An old German soldier came out of the hut.

'Ah! The young lady with the blue bicycle. You haven't been here for a long time. No need to stop, you can cross the line freely now. Take care.'

'It's true,' she thought, as she climbed back on her bicycle, 'I'd forgotten that the demarcation line between the zones was abolished at the end of February.'

It was to appease Camille's and her own anxiety that Léa had decided to go to La Réole to ask the Debrays whether they had any news of Laurent and if they could get a message to him. Ruth, to whom she had confided her fears that the inhabitants of Montillac were being watched, had tried to dissuade her from going, saying it was dangerous, not only for her but also for the people she wanted to see. Léa had replied that she knew, only too well, that Ruth was right, but that she could not bear not knowing what had happened to Laurent any longer. The old governess watched resignedly as her two 'girls' set off, her heart heavy with apprehension.

Léa raced down the hill outside the town. On the bridge she met three black front-wheel drive vehicles and two military trucks full of German soldiers who wolf-whistled and waved at her. This encounter made her feel quite weak and she got off and pushed her bicycle up the hill with a growing feeling of foreboding. As she crossed the Place Gabriel-Chaigne, a group of people who seemed very agitated about something, fell silent when she walked past. She was only a few yards from them when a man caught up with her and said, without looking at her:

'Go to the Place Saint-Pierre and then to number one, Rue de la Glacière. Go in and wait for me there.'

There was such a note of authority in the voice of this stocky stranger who was dressed in overalls and a navy blue cap, that without thinking, Léa turned into the Rue Numa-Ducros. The gate was open at the address in the Rue de la Glacière. She went inside. Less than five minutes later, the man in the cap arrived.

'Are you from the Château Montillac near Saint-Maixant?'
'Yes.'
'What are you doing in La Réole?'
What business was it of his?
'It's none of your business.'
'Don't get all high and mighty. I'm trying to keep you out of trouble.'

'What trouble?'

'Being arrested by the Germans, for example.'

'Why would they want to arrest me?'

'They've just arrested two friends of mine whom you know.'

'The Debrays?'

'Yes. Hey! You're not going to faint, are you?'

He caught her arm and sat her down on a step.

'Simone,' he shouted, 'bring a glass of water, quickly.'

The door in front of which Léa was sitting swung open and a young woman in a blue gingham overall appeared holding a glass of water.

'What's going on, Jacques?'

'It's for the young lady, she doesn't feel very well. She's a friend of the Debrays.'

'Oh! Poor thing! Here, drink this.'

Léa took the glass with trembling hands. She had a lump in her throat and could only drink a drop.

'What happened?' she stammered.

'Don't stay out there,' said Simone, 'come inside.'

She helped Léa to her feet. They went into a large kitchen where a pot of cabbage soup was bubbling over the fire. They sat down on the benches round the table.

'What happened?' asked Léa in a steadier voice.

'They must have been denounced. This morning, at dawn, twenty or so German soldiers and French civilians surrounded the house. A friend, on his way to his vineyard, hid when he saw them. One of the civilians with a loudhailer ordered them to come out otherwise he'd give the order to shoot. There was a moment of silence, then, two shots came from inside the house. Then the Fritzes began to shoot like mad. When, at last, they stopped, there was a cloud of blue smoke. Two civilians, pistols in hand, went into the house. They soon came out again, dragging Madame Debray's body by the shoulders. The poor woman was in her nightdress, her long grey hair was matted with blood and dragging along the ground. They leaned her up against a tree and went back into the house. When they reappeared, they were holding Monsieur Debray under the armpits. He was still struggling.

'His face was covered in blood. They put him next to his wife. According to my friend, it wasn't a pretty sight. He must have shot himself in the mouth after shooting his wife. What's more, he missed.'

'How dreadful. Why?'

'Because messages to London were transmitted from their place. The previous week some sophisticated equipment was parachuted in. The operator arrived the following day by train.'

'Was he arrested too?'

'No, he wasn't staying there. As soon as we learned what had happened, he was taken to Duras and hidden in the woods.'

'And then what happened?'

'The civilians and a few soldiers searched the house. They threw the transmitter, books and furniture out of the window. One of the civilians came rushing out and seized Monsieur Debray who was lying on top of his wife's body. My friend told me that from where he was hiding, he could see the poor creature's shoulders shaking with sobs. The swine began to shake the wounded man violently shouting:

'"The list, where is it? You'd better talk, you old fool . . ."'

'Not a word issued from his shattered mouth. Then the brute flung him to the ground and began kicking the hell out of him. The worst thing apparently was that Monsieur Debray made no attempt to defend himself, as if he were hoping to receive a mortal kick and end the whole thing. When he raised his head, the Germans bundled both bodies into a truck.'

'They were in one of the trucks I saw earlier which was full of laughing soldiers,' thought Léa, feeling nauseated.

'There were orders in German and shortly afterwards, flames were leaping out of the windows. Taking advantage of the smoke which was blowing towards him and provided cover, my friend fled and came to tell me what had happened. Between us we went and told all the other comrades.'

There was a knock at the door which was flung open to reveal a gendarme.

Léa sat paralysed with fear as he came into the room.

'Don't be afraid, mademoiselle, he's one of us. Albert, this is the dominican's niece. She was going to visit the Debrays. Do you remember, they told us about her.'

'You've had a narrow escape. They've left some men there to stop anyone coming near. They're arresting anyone who looks suspicious. They even arrested Manuel, the Rosiers' shop assistant. Fortunately, the mayor, who had come to visit the scene of the fire, offered to be his guarantor, and as he knows nothing, he did it in perfectly good faith.'

'Are we sure that Monsieur Debray is dead?'

'According to my colleagues he is. In any case, he was bleeding so profusely that without medical care, he must have bled to death. But just in case, our friends should not sleep at home for a few days. Father Terrible, can I have a word with you?'

The two men left the room.

'You're lucky Terrible recognized you,' said Simone.

'Who is Terrible?'

'He's a carpenter. A wonderful man. It was he who took the transmitter to the Debrays.'

'Are you a member of the Resistance too?'

Simone burst out laughing.

'That's too grand a way of putting it. I and the other women in the area carry messages, sometimes arms, we hide aviators and little Jewish children. We make soup for those who come back from parachute missions in the middle of the night.'

'Aren't you frightened?'

'No, you don't think about it, and with men like Albert Rigoulet and Terrible around we feel safe.'

'But after what happened?'

'That's fate. All those who have transmitters in their houses are aware of the risks involved and the Debrays knew better than anyone. What amazes me is that religious people like them should want to commit suicide.'

'They had no choice,' said Jacques Terrible who had just come into the room. 'Monsieur Debray would not have talked under torture, I'm sure of that, but he could not have stood seeing his wife suffer. If there's a God, I'm sure He'll forgive him. I say, Simone, how about something to drink?'

'Goodness, this tragedy has made me forget my manners.'

211

She took an opened bottle of wine and four glasses from a cupboard.

'We only need three, Rigoulet had to get back to the police station.'

Simone poured out the wine and they clinked glasses and drank in silence.

Terrible set down his glass and clicked his tongue against the roof of his mouth.

'Is this still from your little corner of Pied-du-Bouc?'

'Yes, it's a good drop of wine.'

'Mademoiselle, now you know who we are, will you tell me why you were going to the Debrays' and if they knew you were coming?'

'No, they didn't know. I was coming to ask them if they had heard from a friend of mine and if they could get in touch with him.'

'Which friend?'

Léa hesitated. Which name should she give them?

'Laurent d'Argilat.'

'I know him.'

'Do you know where he is?'

'Yes.'

'Take me there.'

'I can't just take you there, but I can get a message to him.'

'Tell him that his wife is better but still very weak, that the house is being watched and to let me know how he is.'

'The message will be passed on to him. You say your house is being watched. Are you sure you weren't followed here?'

'Positive. But I must get back. I mustn't stay out too late.'

'Will you take a message for us?'

'What?'

'In Saint-Pierre d'Aurillac, not far from the church, you'll see a café with a very beautiful creeper outside. Ask for Lafourcade and someone will show you where to find him. When you meet him, say: "Hosten's dog is fine".'

'"Hosten's dog is fine"?'

'He'll know what that means. Tell him not to forget to tell the Barie group.'

'"Hosten's dog is fine", I've got it.'

212

'Thank you, mademoiselle, you're doing us a big favour. If I have a message for you, have you got a code name?'

'Exupérance.'

'Like the saint at Verdelais. The first time I heard that name, it was spoken by your uncle.'

'Uncle Adrien? How is he?'

'Very well. He's boosting the morale of the younger ones. He often accompanies those who wish to go over to Spain.'

'Do you know if my cousin Lucien is with him?'

'Lulu? The one who plants bombs? Of course he is.'

'Please, tell my uncle I need to see him. It's very important.'

'I'll tell him. Now you must leave. Simone will accompany you to the edge of town. Be careful. If there's anything wrong, send a card to me at my workshop saying, "The doors won't close properly". We'll see what we can do. Goodbye.'

The clock had just struck one when Léa went through the back door into Albert's kitchen in Saint-Macaire. The butcher, his wife Mireille, his assistant and Laure were at the table about to tuck into a shoulder of lamb that made Léa's mouth water.

'Well, I can see you haven't been wasting time in my absence.'

'We were waiting for you,' said Laure, pointing to the empty place that had been laid for Léa.

'Did the others notice I'd gone?'

'No, I went out with Mireille to buy some bread and as we walked past them, I thanked her loudly for inviting us to lunch. They followed us at a distance. Since then, they've been taking it in turns to keep an eye on us. Did you see your friends?'

The tears which she had managed to hold back until then ran down her cheeks. Mireille went over and hugged her to her breast. This maternal gesture only made Léa cry all the more. The butcher was moved, and in his clumsy way he fussed over the two women.

'Good God! What's going on? What have they done to you, child?'

'Nothing . . . but . . . this morning they came to arrest my friends . . . they're . . . dead . . .'

'Dead!'

'Both of them?'

A little calmer but still in tears, Léa told them what had happened. There was a long horrified silence when she finished. Robert blew his nose loudly. His usually ruddy face was ashen. His enormous fist banged on the table rattling the plates and glasses.

'One day those bastards will have to pay for this. Mademoiselle Léa, I beg you, don't get mixed up in all that. With your friends, it was different, their son had been killed, they had nothing left to lose. But you, Mademoiselle Laure and Madame Camille, you're young, let the old fools like me, who weren't able to stop them in '40, try and do something.'

'Boss, we've got something to say on the subject too, you know! What about Jeannot? He joined the Resistance, didn't he?'

'True, but you're men.'

'Always the same old story,' exclaimed Mireille. 'Just because we women don't carry guns it doesn't mean that we're not taking as many risks as you are. You give me a pain in the neck, you do!'

'Don't get upset, that's not what I meant.'

'But all the same you said it: that a woman isn't as important as a man, all she's good for is changing nappies, minding the shop, cooking, scrubbing and a cuddle from time to time! But when it's a question of hiding your weapons or your English aviators, you and your friends turn to us women.'

Thanks to this family argument Léa was now certain that Robert worked for the Resistance. She felt so reassured that her appetite returned.

'You're splendid, both of you, but the meat's getting cold, and that would be a pity.'

'Well said,' replied the butcher. 'Starving ourselves won't bring those poor people back to life. But I swear they'll be avenged.'

Three days later, Léa received a letter from François Tavernier. It looked as though the envelope had been opened by the police and then stuck down again. She went to read it in the study, relishing every word written in François's large sloping handwriting.

'Dear, beautiful Léa,

You can't complain I never think of you because I'm even wasting a few moments of my precious time to write to you. I simply wanted to congratulate you on your superb business sense. I was lucky enough to drink a bottle of your Montillac wine yesterday evening in Paris, at the table of Otto Abetz. A marvellous wine, simple and honest, with a lot of character and a crafty little hint of sweetness. This wine resembles you like a brother and I am grateful to you for having sold it. If you go on like this, you'll become a businesswoman bogged down with work and responsibilities, married to your vineyards for ever. I don't find this image of you so unattractive.

As soon as I tire of drinking you from a distance, I shall not miss an opportunity to come and taste you at Montillac. Be warned and take care. Hugs and kisses,

François

p.s. I heard about the Debrays.'

Léa sat rooted to the spot after reading his short letter. How on earth had Montillac wine got to Paris? How on earth could it have ended up being served at Otto Abetz's table? She immediately thought of Mathias and Fayard. How had they dared? She felt humiliated, she would be seen as a collaborator . . .

Panic-stricken at the thought of confronting Fayard, she decided to wait until she had written to François. She sat down at once and asked him for more details and to advise her. She covered five long pages in which she told him all her news and how everyone else was. She scolded him for being so brief . . .

The solicitor came on Thursday as promised, bringing a large sum of money out of which Léa paid Fayard what was owed to him. She made no comment about his business activities. He pocketed the money without a word.

Sitting at her father's desk, she contemplated the slopes covered with tender young vines, the meadow where she used to chase Mathias, screaming and shouting. In the hay season, she would hide among the fragrant bundles before clambering up on to the high cart, full of dried hay into which she would sink, lying on her back, her hands behind her head, and look up at the swallows flying backwards and forwards in the blue sky to the slow rhythm of the two oxen, Larouet and Caoubet. She could never recall those peaceful moments of her childhood, of which Mathias was such an important part, without feeling overwhelmingly sad and heartbroken for hours . . .

She had decided to go through the accounts and try and find out how Fayard had managed to divert bottles for his own gain. François had not answered her letter. The figures swam before her eyes. How could she stand up to Fayard who had probably been cheating them for years? How could she discover the flaw in his accounts? She wore herself out making calculations in vain and nobody in the house could help her as she had decided to keep François's revelation to herself.

Each time she found herself alone, she felt terrified at the idea that Mathias was keeping her prisoner. The longer he stayed silent, the more he frightened her.

It was a very dark April night. It had rained all day and a cold north wind shook the branches of the plane trees which lined the front drive. Laure and Léa were sitting in the kitchen in front of a fire made from dead vines, playing cards on a fireside table, Ruth was mending, Camille was knitting and Bernadette Bouchardeau had gone upstairs to bed. Only the glow of the flames lit the room making the women look like a group in a painting by Georges de La Tour. The howling of the gale, the crackling of the fire, the clicking of the knitting needles and the laughter of the card players heightened the impression of a calm happy family scene. The war seemed a long way off.

A draught made Camille shiver. She laid down her knitting and drew her shawl tighter round her. Her eyes wandered to the door; it was slightly ajar, the wind no doubt. Although she

216

was still weak, she rose to shut it. She had already reached out to grasp the handle when the door was flung open, banging her fingers. By the fireside, her companions froze.

A man whose clothing was soaked through, supporting a second man, had entered the room, kicking the door open with his boot.

'Quick . . . help me.'

'Camille, go and sit down, you're in the way. Ruth and Laure, give us a hand!'

With their assistance, the man laid his comrade on the table. Then, with the air of someone who was perfectly at home, he switched on the light.

'Lucien!' cried Léa and Laure in chorus.

'He's lost a lot of blood. Ruth, go and get some dressings.'

'Yes, father.'

'Uncle Adrien!'

'Darlings, we haven't got time for sentiment. Léa, go to Verdelais and fetch Doctor Blanchard.'

'Can't we phone him?'

'No, I'm wary of the telephone.'

'Very well, I'll go.'

'Go via Bellevue, I don't want the Fayards to suspect anything. I noticed their lights were on.'

An hour later, Léa returned with the doctor who cursed the 'God awful weather'.

'Félix, you can have it out with God later, for the time being, look after the kid.'

Doctor Blanchard removed his old raincoat and went over to Lucien whose hands were bound with bloodsoaked rags. He skilfully removed the makeshift bandages.

'My God! Who did that?'

'A bomb.'

'What was he doing with a bomb?'

'He was making it.'

That answer, which no doubt seemed a good one, put an end to the doctor's questions. He started to examine the injuries.

'He's got to go to hospital.'

'He can't. They'd tell the police and the police would tell the Gestapo.'

'His right hand's done for, it's got to be amputated.'

Under the mud and grime that covered his face, Adrien Delmas turned pale.

'Are you sure?'

'Look, it's crushed to a pulp.'

'Poor thing, I'll go and get his mother.'

'No, Ruth! Whatever you do, don't get my sister. She'll scream and cry and the neighbours will hear. Félix, we'll help you, tell us what we have to do.'

'But it's out of the question for me to amputate this boy's hand myself. The last time I carried out an amputation was in a makeshift hospital in '17. I'm a country doctor, not a surgeon.'

'I know, but we have no choice. If the Gestapo catch him, they'll torture him until he denounces his comrades and then they'll kill him.'

Blanchard looked round the room at the people who were his lifelong friends, then at the unconscious young man he had known as a child and who was bleeding to death.

'All right. Pray to that bloody God of yours not to let my old hands shake too much. Boil some water. Lucky I brought my big bag. I hope my lancet hasn't gone rusty. Ruth, Adrien and Léa, I'll need your help. Camille, go to bed before you collapse. Laure, help Camille.'

Léa would have given anything not to have to be there. And yet her hand was perfectly steady when she applied the chloroform pad under her cousin's nostrils.

She was never to forget the noise of the saw cutting through the bone.

During the operation, Lucien groaned a couple of times. When Doctor Blanchard secured the final dressing, the young man of twenty-two had lost his right hand and two fingers of his left hand.

The following day, he awoke at midday and saw the worried faces of his mother, his uncle and Doctor Blanchard leaning over him. He smiled and said:

'I'd forgotten what it felt like to sleep in a real bed.'

Bernadette Bouchardeau turned away to hide her tears. At dawn, she had surprised everybody by the calm with which she took the news of her son's amputation. Everybody had been expecting her to shriek and faint. Tears simply ran down her cheeks and she had merely said:

'Thank God he's alive.'

Lucien made a movement in his mother's direction.

'Mummy!'

'Don't move, son. You've lost a lot of blood. You need total rest,' said Doctor Blanchard.

'What about my hand, it's not too serious, is it, doctor?'

They all stared at their feet. His mother let out a groan.

'Why don't you answer me?'

How heavy his hand was when he tried to raise it. What a strange shape it was all bandaged up like that.

Standing outside the door, Léa felt Lucien's scream like a dagger through her heart. It was what had been hammering inside her head all night:

'NO! NO! NO! NO! NO! . . .'

Chapter 17

In the children's room, Adrien Delmas paced up and down in the grip of the greatest despair that a priest can experience: he no longer believed. He had been struggling against doubt since the beginning of the war. Before joining the underground, he had discussed it with his confessor who had told him to accept this ordeal that God had sent to test his faith. The Dominican was prepared to put up with a lot of suffering for the love of God, but today, he was weary of his fruitless prayers, the words of which had lost all their original meaning. All that now seemed to be astoundingly naïve, and men who had spent their lives in the service of an illusion seemed to be either fools or evil beings, spiritually dishonest. In his confusion, he forgot his masters, the great Catholic brains who had enabled his own thinking to develop. Pascal, the Abbé de Rancé, Augustin, Jean-de-la-Croix, Thérèse d'Avila, Chateaubriand, Bossuet and other servants of the Church, all were forgotten. They were all mistaken, they had all misled him. What use were their vain words against the distress of a mutilated child? What could he reply to the mute reproach of a mother? What had become of the gentle words of comfort that had come so easily to his lips and helped him console the wounded and the dying of the Spanish revolution? He was like the barren fig tree in the gospel; withered with no fruits. What was the use of existing if his existence brought no comfort? Lucien was crippled for life because of him. For it was his fault that the kid had joined the Resistance. If he had been content to stay in his monastery in the Rue Saint-Genès as ordered by his father superior, instead of playing at rebel priests in the underground, his nephew would never have come and joined him. He was aware that that was not necessarily true, that Lucien had perhaps not been influenced by him at all. They had talked about it endlessly during the interminable winter evenings spent on the farm which served as a hideout for the Resistance. At first there were less than ten of them, but gradually, they were joined by all those who did not want to go to Germany and do compulsory labour. Now, he was responsible for about thirty young people. Not only was he the undisputed military chief of the little group, but he also provided the moral support. The members of the group had not for one moment ever been aware of his spiritual dilemma. Very few of them, in fact, even knew he was a priest. They all admired his caution, his sense of underground organization and the relative comfort in which he made it possible for them to live. Thanks to his detailed knowledge of the area, of both the land and the people who lived on it, he always knew which doors to knock on to obtain help, money and food. One of his friends from the seminary, a freemason and notable of La Réole, had set up, with the help of other freemasons, a network which liaised regularly with the British freemason network and had organized the parachuting of provisions, arms and clothes. Daily duties, protection, raids on tax offices, and town halls, sabotaging electricity supplies, the distribution of leaflets and underground newspapers, the search for false identity cards, the smuggling of Jewish families over to Spain, were enough to occupy his mind all day and most of the evening. But at night, during the long, endless nights, he wore himself out reading the gospel, resuming the dialogue with this God who was slipping away from him. At dawn, he would fall asleep for a short while, his dreams haunted by demons straight out of the imagination of a mediaeval monk, or by sophisticated torture worthy of Octave Mirbeau's *Garden of Tortures* which had perturbed his pious adolescence. He would emerge from this short respite tired and overwhelmed with sadness. He soon became haggard and deep wrinkles appeared on his face. His hair had become white and his clothes were falling off his thin body. When Doctor Blanchard saw how he had changed, he was quite worried about his health. Adrien had laughingly brushed aside his concern. What was he going to do with Lucien now? It was out

221

of the question for him to stay at Montillac, it was too dangerous. Take him back to camp? Not for three or four months.
Send him to Spain? Possible but difficult. A lot of people had
been arrested recently for smuggling refugees over the border.
He'd have to discuss it with Father Bertrand from Toulouse
who was in contact with Swiss monks.

There was a knock at the door.

'It's me, Uncle Adrien.'

'Come in. Forgive me for invading your territory. Do you
still come here?'

Léa smiled.

'Less and less often. I've grown up a lot, you know.'

'I know.'

'What about you, Uncle Adrien, have you come here
because you're unhappy?'

He raised his hand in a gesture of denial but she reached out
and stopped him.

'Don't try and tell me you're not, I can see you're unhappy.
I know you. I've been watching you since I was a little girl.
You've lost that glimmer in your eye that used to draw us all to
you, that made us want to be like you . . .'

'You're being very hard on me!'

'Perhaps, but you wouldn't want me to speak to you any
other way. What has happened to Lucien is dreadful, but it's
not your fault. Lucien made the choice. Laurent, Camille and
I have also made a choice.'

'You're not going to tell me that I'm not at all responsible
for your decision? After all, it was I who sent you to Paris.'

'So what? Nothing's happened to me.'

'Don't tempt fate. I saw too many boys and girls of your age
die in Spain and now here. Give all that up.'

'No, it's too late. Do you know what my code name is?'

'Exupérance!'

'Yes, like the little saint you used to be so fond of, do you
remember? Thanks to you, I loved her too. With protection
like hers, I'm not in any danger.'

Adrien could not help smiling. The protection of a saint
whose existence was dubious even in the eyes of the Church
was not worth much.

'Are you planning to stay at Montillac long?'

'No, it would be too dangerous for you. Lucien's presence is enough to get you into trouble. As soon as he's a little better, he'll leave here.'

'But where will he go? What will he do? He's an invalid now.'

The priest looked up.

'I was thinking about that when you came in.'

'Aunt Bernadette says that wherever he goes, she'll follow.'

'That's all we need! My dear sister in the Resistance!'

'How do you find Camille?'

'Not too bad. She's a brave woman. I agree with Félix, she'll recover.'

'If Laurent came to see her, I'm sure she'd get better at once.'

Adrien looked at her with surprised amusement.

'Well, well, aren't you in love with him any more?'

Léa's face blazed.

'That's got nothing to do with it.'

'You mustn't think about him any more, he's married, a father and he loves his wife.'

His niece's gesture of irritation did not escape his notice.

'As impatient as ever with lessons in morality, I see. Don't worry, I shan't go on about it. I merely want to warn you against future disappointments. Someone who seems to show a great interest in you was talking to me about you recently.'

'Who?'

'Can't you think?'

She did not feel like playing guessing games.

'No.'

'François Tavernier.'

Why hadn't she thought of him? Once again she blushed.

'Tell me, uncle, when did you speak to him?'

'A couple of weeks ago, I spoke to him on the telephone from Bordeaux.'

'Where was he?'

'In Paris.'

'Why was he calling you? What did he say about me? He hasn't answered my letter.'

'You are impatient, aren't you? I thought you couldn't stand him.'

'Please.'

'Nothing much. He asked after you; after the rest of the family . . .'

'Is that all?'

'No. He's going to try and come to see you after Easter.'

'After Easter! But that's ages away!'

'What impatience! It's the tenth of April today and Easter's on the twenty-fifth.'

Léa felt so bewildered and so anxious that she decided not to talk to him about Mathias.

Suddenly there was the sound of a car drawing up on the gravel, the slamming of doors, men's voices. They froze.

'Quick, go and see. If it's the Gestapo, we're done for.'

Léa rushed out into the corridor and looked out of the window overlooking the drive. No! It wasn't true! What on earth was he doing here? She flung open the window and shouted with forced cheerfulness:

'Coming!'

She ran back into the children's room.

'It's not the Gestapo, but it could be just as bad.'

'I'm going into Lucien's room,' said Adrien rising.

Before going downstairs, Léa went into Camille's room and briefly told her what was going on.

Downstairs, Ruth had shown the visitors into the parlour.

'Léa, how wonderful to see you in these surroundings!'

'Raphaël, what a lovely surprise.'

'Darling! . . . I knew you'd be thrilled to see an old friend again.'

She was seething with rage but she forced a smile. Whatever happened she could not let him sense how afraid she was. One of the three young men with him was looking at Jacques-Emile Blanche's portrait of her mother. When he turned round again, Léa dug her nails into the palms of her hands. She tried to control her fear.

The young man who was now facing her was the one she had

224

noticed in Cadillac and in Saint-Macaire. She casually went up to him.

'Good day, monsieur, are you from round here? I think I've met you somewhere before.'

The boy was obviously disconcerted.

'It's very likely, mademoiselle, my grandparents are from Langon.'

'That must be where I've seen you, at the town hall or on a market day. What's your name?'

'Maurice Fiaux.'

Léa walked over to Raphaël and took his arm, leading him into the gardens.

'Come and let me show you Montillac. Meanwhile you can tell me what we owe the honour of your visit to.'

'You are aware that I'm having a few problems with certain people whom you know. I had no alternative but to leave Paris, the climate was becoming unhealthy for me. I recalled my pleasant stay in Bordeaux in June 1940, my contacts with the local press, the fact that Spain isn't far away. In short, I said to myself, why not go to Bordeaux? I must confess that until yesterday, I hadn't thought of you. I was with these delightful boys, having a drink in the Régent before going out to dinner when one of their companions arrived. Montillac was mentioned in the course of their conversation. I wondered if it was the same as the Montillac belonging to the Delmas family and I was told it was. That's how I learned that this young man was a childhood friend of yours and that you were at Montillac at the moment. I expressed a wish to see you and your friend offered to drive me here. That's why I'm here.'

'Have you come with Mathias?'

'Yes, he's gone to say hello to his parents. You don't mind my accepting his invitation, do you?'

'Not in the least. I insist on thanking him for giving me the pleasure of seeing you . . .'

'What a beautiful place this is, my dear! If I lived here, I would never want to leave it. How peaceful it is! What harmony between heaven and earth! I can feel that I would be able to write masterpieces here.'

Raphaël Mahl leaned on the terrace wall and looked out over

225

the vast landscape crisscrossed with the straight black lines of the vineyards.

'It looks as though it's been drawn with a pencil and ruler, it's so regular.'

'You've come too early. In two or three weeks time, the vines will be silvery, then they'll change to a fresh green, then they'll flower . . . Look, here's Laure. Raphaël, this is Laure, my little sister.'

'How do you do, mademoiselle. Now I've met the three graces of Montillac.'

Laure spluttered with laughter, which irritated Léa.

'Camille's with Mathias. I asked Fayard to open the cellars so our visitors can taste our wine.'

'That's a good idea. Come on, come and taste the famous Château-Montillac,' she said playfully, trying to disguise the distress she felt at the mention of Mathias's name.

So he had dared to come back.

The three young men followed them silently. In the cellar they joined Camille, Mathias and his father. Léa went over and kissed Mathias as if nothing had happened between them, pretending not to notice the way he brusquely tensed his jaw.

'You could have come and seen us sooner, what have you been up to?'

'Léa's right,' added Camille, 'I wanted to thank you for the part you played in securing my release.'

'It wasn't anything to do with me. I did very little.'

'Don't say that. If it weren't for you, I might still be there.'

'You left just as it was made more comfortable. Now, there are showers,' said one of Mathias's friends.

'How interesting,' snapped Léa. 'When will there be a hairdresser's and a cinema?'

The young man blushed and his companions sniggered. Raphaël changed the subject.

'Come on, everyone, let's taste this wine.'

Fayard turned over the glasses waiting on a plank of wood covered with a sheet of white paper and ceremoniously poured the wine.

'It's only two years old. I think you'll like it.'

'Its renown has spread as far as Paris!' Léa retorted.

Fayard did not bat an eyelid.

When everybody had been served, they raised their glasses in silence.

They were on their third glass when Léa went over to Mathias and said:

'Come outside. I'd like to have a word with you.'

After the coolness of the musty smelling cellar, the mildness of the air and the fragrance of the early lilac made Léa want to run.

She set off, Mathias at her heels. She stopped suddenly, spun round and panted:

'I thought you'd gone back to Germany.'

'I changed my mind, I've got more important things to do here.'

'Why did you bring Mahl and your friends here. I don't want to see you any more.'

'I thought you'd be pleased. He seemed to know you so well.'

Léa shrugged.

'What about the others, do they know me too?'

'The car belongs to them. It was they who offered to drive us here.'

'I don't like them very much.'

'Hard luck. I do. And you'd better be nice to them.'

'What do you do with them?'

'We work together.'

What did he mean? If what she feared were true, Mathias could not 'work' with them, as he called it. She must not let herself panic; she had to stay calm and carefree, Lucien and Adrien's lives depended on it. Perhaps Raphaël had made a deal with the Gestapo in Paris to try and find Sarah? She took Mathias's arm and said, in the most natural voice in the world and with a conspiratorial smile:

'Go on, tell me, what do you do?'

He stiffened as he felt the pressure of her body, the mere thought of which made him tremble. As he met her innocent eyes, he looked away, embarrassed.

'Business.'

'I hope for your sake it's not the same sort of business that

227

Raphaël's mixed up in. I'd hate to think you were wanted for dealing in black market goods,' she said, still smiling.

'Don't worry about me. I've got nothing in common with a pansy like your friend. I act as go-between for the Bordeaux wine growers and wine merchants in Munich, Berlin and Hamburg. You know how the Germans love our wines. What's more, most of the high up German officers who are in the Gironde area were in business with the major wine growers before the war. I put the smaller wine growers in touch with German wine merchants.'

'And is it going well?'

'Very well. Business is business, and people carry on drinking good wine, war or no war.'

'Mathias, I forbid you to sell a single bottle of Montillac wine. Ever!'

Léa was not able to contain herself. The words resounded loudly. Once again they stood facing each other in hostile confrontation. Both of them were pale as they stood watching each other like two felines about to pounce.

Good God! The bitch was so beautiful when she was angry: her nostrils flared and her breasts heaved. He was torn between the urge to hit her and the desire to take her in his arms.

'When we're married, I'll sell the wine to whoever I please.'

Raphaël had come out of the cellar. He came bounding towards them waving his arms and shouting:

'Léa, this wine is exquisite! I mustn't have any more, I'm already tipsy.'

Dear Raphaël! she could have hugged him. He came up to them.

'I don't believe you. It takes more than that to get you drunk.'

'Don't you believe it, my sweet friend. I'm not as young as I used to be! For instance: before the war, I could eat anything, just like that, no problem. Now, a slightly rich dish, a boozy lunch and I put on weight. Look at my waistline! I know it's supposed to be cuddly! But even so! . . . It's sad to lose one's youthful figure.'

Léa could not help laughing as he opened his jacket to show her the damage.

'Go on, laugh, just you wait . . . For the moment you can hold your head up high with your firm breasts, your flat stomach and your pretty little behind! But wait a few years, when you've had three or four kids . . . we'll see.'

'You don't expect any sympathy from me for putting on a few kilos when most French people are tightening their belts! Do what everyone else is doing: eat turnips.'

'Yuck! Are you trying to kill me?'

What a strange character! Léa even managed to forget Raphaël Mahl's true nature.

'You'd still be capable of joking and making me laugh in front of a firing squad.'

Raphaël's eyes became doleful again.

'You couldn't pay me a nicer compliment: laughing and making people laugh in the face of death. I promise I'll remember that, sweet friend.'

He added with artificial cheerfulness as he drew her to one side:

'Have you heard from our friend Tavernier? There's a man who intrigues me. Some people think he's hand in glove with the Germans and others think he's a London man. What do you think?'

'Don't be silly. François Tavernier was in Paris last time I saw him. Since then he seems to have vanished into thin air. I'm cut off from the world down here and I've far too much to do to take an interest in a rogue like him. But what on earth's got into you? Let me go!'

'Don't treat me like an idiot, my dear, you would be making a mistake. Do you think I didn't notice he was in love with you and that you were more than just good friends?'

'I really don't know what you mean.'

'Do you think I've forgotten the dirty trick he played on me?'

'And saved your life, perhaps.'

'Maybe, but I don't like being treated like that.'

'Come, come, Raphaël, don't be so touchy.'

Without realizing it, they had wandered quite a long way from the house and were walking along the path that led to Bellevue, through the vineyards. The others had not followed them.

229

Mahl stopped and looked about him. He suddenly seemed old.

'How good it must be to live here! How inspiring this place must be! I shall never own anything like this. I'll never experience the joy of writing in perfect peace, both within myself and with my surroundings. Why am I driven by evil forces which take me away from my deeper self, from my creative efforts? Making the effort is what counts, even if it comes to nothing. Everything is productive immediately and yet it is barren. That is not what matters. There's always joy in making the effort. Alas! I don't have enough enthusiasm to be a great writer. Most of the time, writers are enthusiasts who place themselves at the service of the indifferent. One can speak as one likes, but one can only write as one is . . .'

What despair in this man who was seemingly frivolous, dishonest and unscrupulous! As on every occasion when she glimpsed how much he suffered from not being the great writer he had always dreamed of being, Léa felt an uncontrollable rush of compassion.

'Look at these fields, these woods! Let man and his works be wiped from the face of the earth and let the world go on as if nothing had happened. Man's uselessness seems obvious compared to the Infinite. Useless and mediocre. One day I shall write *In Praise of Mediocrity* – perhaps I've already mentioned it to you. I spend my time talking about the books that I never write. It's a good idea, don't you think? Unless I make an anthology of the atrocities perpetrated by man. An inexhaustible subject. But the glory of man is to have been capable of making beauty out of horror . . . One of the main reasons why I was unable to believe in a God who was good, kind and who knew us inside out was my own example. I said to myself that if God was all those things, he would not have let me exist, especially as I am. Sometimes my entire body fills with tears, more than can flow from my eyes, and I don't know how to let them out.'

He cried as he spoke and it was an unbearable sight.

'You despise me, don't you? Quite rightly. You'll never despise me as much as I despise myself. I prefer your contempt to your pity. I hate the appalling feebleness of pity . . .

Let's go back, our friends will be wondering what we're plotting.'

'Why did you come, Raphaël?'

Before replying, he took out a handkerchief and wiped his eyes.

'I told you: I wanted to see you.'

'There's another reason.'

'Perhaps. Who knows? What's become of our friend Sarah?'

Léa stiffened.

'No! Don't get the wrong idea. I'm not here to find out about her, I was simply asking if you'd heard from her because she's someone I'm very fond of.'

'I've got no idea.'

'Let's hope she's all right. Are you completely sure of your friend Mathias Fayard?'

'Here we go,' she thought.

'No more than you are.'

'You're quite right to be wary of him,' he said without turning a hair. 'His friends are convinced you work for the Resistance. I told them that you most certainly did not. I don't think they believed me.'

'Why are you telling me this?'

'Because I'm very fond of you and I'd be most upset if anything happened to you.'

He said that with a spontaneity that made Léa think he was being sincere for once. She slipped her arm through his.

'Raphaël, everything's so complicated at the moment. I feel so alone here what with Camille who is ill, my aunt who's always moaning, my sister who's bored, the Fayards who can't wait to get their hands on Montillac. Ruth's the only one I feel I can rely on.'

'There's your family in Bordeaux.'

'I want to have as little to do with them as possible.'

'And your uncle the priest?'

Léa let go of his arm.

'Surely you know that he's disappeared and that he's wanted by the Gestapo?'

'It's true, I'd forgotten. Forgive me. I thought I glimpsed

231

him shortly after my arrival in Bordeaux. He had changed a great deal and without his robe . . .'

'When you spoke to me about him the first time, did you already know him?'

'I heard his Lenten sermon at Notre-Dame. I very much liked the way he spoke of mercy and of the devotion of the Virgin. At that time I wanted to be introduced to him, but I never was. I was very sorry.'

'So he doesn't know you?'

'No.'

'It's a pity, he would have been interested in someone like you.'

'Who knows, perhaps we'll meet one day . . . Life is so strange.'

'I'm enormously fond of him. I miss him very much. I haven't seen him since my father's funeral.'

'They were telling me about that funeral in Bordeaux. Odd, isn't it, that the Gestapo didn't arrest him along with your friend's husband?'

'That was thanks to my Uncle Luc.'

'It's true that the stand Luc Delmas has taken, the marriage of his daughter to a high up German officer, and the forthcoming marriage of your sister to Major Kramer, all create a bond with the occupying forces which they can't ignore.'

'I'm pretty ashamed of it.'

'That's something not to be repeated for all to hear.'

'Which you are doubtless in a hurry to do, I imagine.'

'My dear friend, you are always getting me wrong. You know that I only act in my own interest. Which of your sympathies would I go and denounce? Everybody knows them. If you were at least hiding Englishmen or members of the Resistance! But that's not the case. It isn't the case, is it?'

Léa burst out laughing.

'You know that you are the last person I'd tell if I was.'

'Quite right too.'

They arrived, arm in arm, laughing, in the courtyard in front of the house where Camille, Laure, Mathias and the three young men were standing.

'Ah! There you are,' said one of them. 'We were wondering

where on earth you had got to. We've got to leave, we've got an appointment.'

'It's true, whatever was I thinking of! It had completely slipped my mind . . . Léa, thank you for your warm welcome. If you come to Bordeaux, do come and see me. I'm staying at the *Majestic*, in the Rue Esprit-des-Lois. It's a very pleasant hotel and it's full of antique furniture.'

'Are you staying in Bordeaux long?'

'That depends on whether I can sell a few articles to the local press or not. Otherwise . . .'

'Otherwise?'

Raphaël Mahl did not reply. He pressed Camille's hand to his lips and kissed Laure on both cheeks. The young men said a polite goodbye. The three women kissed Mathias.

Adrien Delmas left Montillac in the middle of the night after telling Léa that there were guns hidden in one of the chapels of the Verdelais grotto, under the cracked flagstone to the right of the door in the seventh chapel.

'Only use them in an emergency. There are ten guns and twenty pistols which you must know how to use.'

'I hope so.'

'Perfect. There are also hand grenades and a machine gun. Don't touch those.'

'When will you be back?'

'As soon as Félix tells me it's safe to move Lucien. Meanwhile, take extra precautions. Today's visit was extremely worrying, all the more so because the enemy is within.'

'The enemy?'

'Yes, old Fayard. He knows every nook and cranny of the estate and moves around unnoticed, he's so much part of the place. As for the three boys who were with Mathias, we know them very well. One of them has even been sentenced to death and will be executed shortly.'

'What has he done?'

'Denunciations, theft, rape, torture and murder of all kinds. I know he assassinated a Jew, with his own hands, to rob him. He had known the poor fellow since his childhood.'

'You talk about him as if you knew him too . . .'

'His mother was the housekeeper for a friend of mine, the doctor at Le Bouscat. As the child had no father, my friend took a great interest in him. But the only thanks he got was heartbreak . . . When the Germans arrived, the boy immediately went to headquarters and offered his services in exchange for generous payment. At first he was a bodyguard and then he gradually rose in status. At present he works for Poinsot, Dohse and Luther . . . He proved to be particularly efficient on the night of the nineteenth October, during the operation that was "to purge the region of the presence of foreign Jews". With the help of the police, he took part in the arrest of seventy-three Jews, men, women and children, most of whom were deported. He took advantage of the situation to strip the old people for whom his mother had worked as housekeeper of their possessions. He did a good job . . . so good that Major Luther thanked him in person in the beautiful house at 224, Avenue du Médoc, which is now called Avenue du Maréchal Pétain, just opposite number 197, where Camille was familiarized with their methods. The creature had the audacity, when he came away from that meeting, to go and see his mother and laugh at the terror of the "yids" he had dragged out of bed . . . My friend wanted to kill the evil beast. Crazed with anger, he contented himself with throwing him out and kicking his behind. Once outside, the kid swore he'd kill him. I advised my friend to leave Bordeaux but he refused saying his place was here . . . It was at his house that I met the leader of the F.T.P. who, by a strange coincidence, lived six hundred yards away from the Gestapo headquarters. Le Bouscat is a sort of centre of repression as well as crawling with members of the Resistance . . .'

'Which one of the three are you talking about?'

'Maurice Fiaux.'

'It's not possible. To look at him, he doesn't seem like a bully.'

'That's what makes him so dangerous: he seems like a nice young man, quite an attractive boy.'

'Does Mathias know all that?'

'No. He's still a new recruit, they're wary of him. They won't trust him until he's been put to the test.'

234

'What do you mean?'

'When he's denounced, tortured or killed someone. He's already begun . . . A few more weeks and he'll be a complete swine. Beyond redemption.'

'How you've changed, Uncle Adrien! Before, you'd have told me to pray . . . that even the wickedest creatures had an innocent side that was dormant, and now . . . it sounds as though you no longer believe in anything, not even God.'

Every word Léa spoke was like a dagger in the priest's aching soul. He looked away from his niece, checked his gun, pulled his Basque beret down over his ears, picked up a little cardboard suitcase full of linen, books and a few provisions, and headed for the door.

Then Léa made a gesture that was completely unexpected for somebody who had lost his faith: she fell to her knees at her uncle's feet and said:

'Bless me.'

Adrien faltered for a second and then complied.

When he traced the sign of the cross on the head of the child he adored, a feeling of great peace came over him. He raised Léa to her feet and kissed her.

'Thank you,' he murmured and disappeared into the night.

Chapter 18

'I've invited Maurice Fiaux to dinner.'

Léa dropped the saucepan she was holding in astonishment.

'Oh! You're so clumsy,' exclaimed Laure. 'What a waste of good milk.'

A slap round the face sent her reeling. The blue eyes of the youngest Delmas daughter filled with tears. Sounding more surprised than angry, she said to her sister:

'What on earth's got into you? You're mad! You hurt me.'

'And I'll hurt you some more unless you cancel that invitation.'

'I have the right to invite whoever I like.'

'No you haven't!'

'And why not, may I ask? You're not the only owner of Montillac as far as I'm aware!'

'Do you know who Maurice Fiaux is?'

'I know we thought he was watching us because of the Resistance business. But that wasn't the reason at all.'

'What do you mean?'

Laure hung her head, wiped her eyes and simpered, her cheeks still burning with the red marks of Léa's hand.

'He was following me.'

'You?'

'Yes, me! You're not the only one round here the boys are after. I'm no longer the little girl I was before the war. I've grown up.'

'Let's be sensible about this. I've no doubt that boys find you attractive. But you didn't honestly believe what he told you, did you? Have you seen him again?'

'Yes, this morning in Langon. He's charming, witty and

236

polite. He's on holiday at his grandparents'. After Easter, he's going back to Bordeaux. He has to go out to work to help his mother.'

Léa rolled her eyes heavenwards.

'It's so touching! And what does this young man do?'

'I don't know . . . I didn't quite understand . . . He's in business.'

'Business! That's a nice way of describing just about anything. I'll tell you what line of business your sweetheart's in: he works for the Gestapo.'

'I don't believe you!'

'I didn't want to believe it either . . . It was Uncle Adrien who told me. He's tortured and killed several people. By inviting him here, you walked straight into the trap and you're putting us all in danger. Did you think of Lucien? Of what would happen if he were discovered?'

Laure turned so pale that the slap marks on her cheeks stood out even more. She stood leaning against the stove, rooted to the spot, her arms dangling by her sides, too stupefied to notice that her white blouse was wet with tears. Léa felt sorry for her and put her hand on Laure's shoulder. This gesture made Laure's tears turn into great childlike sobs.

'I didn't know!'

'Laure, Léa, what's happened? What's the matter?' asked Camille, coming into the kitchen.

'This little fool has invited Maurice Fiaux to lunch tomorrow.'

'Oh! My God!'

For a few moments the only sounds were Laure's hiccups and the ticking of the clock. Camille was the first to break the silence.

'Well, there's no point moaning about it, we have to think of a solution.'

'I told her to put him off.'

'No, that's the last thing she should do! He'd suspect that we didn't trust him. On the contrary, the invitation must stand. It's up to us to make him believe he's got the wrong idea about us.'

'You're forgetting Lucien!'

237

'No, I'm not, I'm thinking especially of him. He'll have to leave here.'

'But he's nowhere near better!'

'I know.'

'Well?'

'Come with me, I've got an idea. Laure, tomorrow you must act as though nothing's happened, as if you still thought he was a suitable young man,' said Camille, drawing Léa away.

'Yes,' the poor girl stammered.

The two young women left the house by the north entrance.

'Let's go for a little walk in the vineyards. There we're sure we can't be overheard.'

They walked in silence, Camille leaning on Léa's arm.

The April sun bathed the countryside in its sharp light, picking out the outlines of the vines, Sidonie's cottage and the budding trees around the grotto so clearly that it felt as if one only had to reach out to touch them.

'How is it that the peacefulness of the countryside doesn't affect mankind?' said Camille, slowing down.

'What's your idea?'

'To hide Lucien in Sidonie's attic.'

'In Sidonie's attic!'

'Yes. We can trust her, she loathes the Germans.'

'It's much too close to Montillac!'

'Precisely. They'll never think that we can hide somebody so close to the house.'

Léa thought.

'Perhaps you're right. If it were anyone other than Sidonie, I'd say that her hatred of the Germans was not sufficient reason to trust her. But as it's Sidonie . . .'

'Let's go and see her. She's at home, there's smoke coming from her chimney.'

Sidonie's cottage commanded an all round view of the surrounding countryside. The old lady claimed that on a clear day, you could see the coast.

As usual, she was thrilled to see her visitors and she welcomed them with a glass of her home-made blackcurrant liqueur which nobody dared refuse.

'Well! Madame Camille. It's a pleasure to see you up and about again. You, Léa, you look a little under the weather. Is it you who's been ill? I saw Doctor Blanchard come up to the house a couple of times.'

From her doorstep, she did not miss a single thing that went on at Montillac, where she had worked as cook for many years.

'No, Sidonie, he came to see Lucien.'

'Poor little thing! But I thought he was in the Resistance?'

'He's been seriously injured. He's much better now but he can't stay at Montillac because it's too dangerous for him. He's too weak to go back underground for a while. We've come to ask you if you'd agree to hide him in your attic for a few days.'

'As if you needed to ask!'

'But you could be in serious trouble if the Germans found out.'

'That's not the point. When will you be bringing him here?'

'Tonight.'

'Fine. Who will know he's here?'

'If we can avoid telling his mother, it'll be just the three of us.'

'Can he walk?'

'I think so but we'll have to go along by the cypress trees where the path is quite steep.'

'I'll come and meet you. I'll wait for you in the third row of vines from the kitchen garden.'

Léa finished her glass of liqueur and, kissing her, said:

'Thank you, Sidonie.'

'You're welcome, my love. You don't think I'd let those dirty Jerries lay hands on a child belonging to Monsieur Pierre's family, do you?'

On the way back, Léa and Camille spoke little. As they approached the house, Camille said:

'Not a word to Laure about our visit.'

'How can you think that Laure would give away Lucien's hiding place?'

'I'm wary of a lovesick young girl.'

Léa looked blankly at her.

239

'You don't think . . .?'

'We have to be prepared for anything. Laure is bored. Her friends are in Bordeaux, we don't have any visitors. It's perfectly natural that she should fall for this boy.'

'But he's using her!'

'He probably is. It's up to us to convince her of it. I'm going to talk to her.'

It was a very dark night and a warm wind was blowing off the moors. Three dark silhouettes were making their way along the cypress lined avenue.

'Are you all right? You're not suffering too much, darling?' whispered an anxious voice.

'No, mummy.'

'Shh! Shut up! I think someone's coming.'

They all froze.

They heard the sound of footsteps dislodging stones and twigs snapping underfoot coming from the path which went round the edge of the vineyard at the bottom of the cypress avenue.

'Quick, get down.'

The regular footsteps died away.

'Lucien, Léa who was it?'

'Fayard. He sometimes does his rounds to make sure all is well. But I don't like that.'

'Why isn't his dog with him?' asked Lucien in a low voice.

'True . . . that is odd. Perhaps he's afraid the dog will make too much noise chasing rabbits.'

'Be quiet. He'll hear us.'

They stood still for a few seconds then they headed into the vines.

'Ah! There you are! I was beginning to worry. Madame Bernadette! You should never have come out.'

'Don't worry, I'll hold my tongue.'

'I understand, Madame Bernadette, I understand . . .'

'Let's hurry, I'm getting tired,' said Lucien, who was walking with the support of his mother and his cousin.

They continued in silence for a moment.

'Sidonie, thank you for agreeing to hide my son.'

'It's only natural, Madame Bernadette. I've told Doctor Blanchard that Lucien's at Bellevue now. He'll come by in the morning to treat my rheumatism.'

'Oh! My God!' exclaimed Bernadette Bouchardeau. Lucien had almost fallen over.

'Did you hurt yourself, darling?'

'No, mummy, no. My hands hurt a little, that's all.'

'We're nearly there.'

On the table of the humble living room, Sidonie had laid out refreshments which they ate by the light of the fire and candles. Cheered a little by the wine, Lucien rose.

'Mummy, you must leave now and promise me you won't come back until Sidonie and Doctor Blanchard tell you it's all right.'

'But darling . . .!'

'Mummy, if they catch me, they'll torture me, I'll give away my comrades . . . I've suffered enough already, I couldn't stand any more pain. Do you understand?'

Bernadette Bouchardeau was crying with her head bent, twisting her damp handkerchief between her fingers.

'I'll do as you wish.'

'Thank you, I knew I could rely on you,' he said, hugging her, his hands swathed in huge white bandages.

'Don't worry, Madame Bernadette, I'll look after him as if he were my own child.'

'Do you need any help getting up to the attic?' asked Léa.

'No thank you. Goodbye, Léa, take good care of yourself.'

'Goodbye, Lucien,' she said, kissing him.

Outside, a fine drizzle had begun to fall. It was very dark and the two women kept twisting their ankles in the ruts. They did not exchange a single word until they reached Montillac. Still silent, they kissed each other at the foot of the staircase which led up to the bedrooms. Bernadette Bouchardeau clambered up the stairs as if she were labouring under a heavy burden.

Léa locked the door and drew the heavy bolt across. She checked that the windows in the parlour were properly closed. These familar gestures, which she carried out in the dark,

241

made her smile: 'Every night I do exactly what my father used to do: check that the doors and windows are shut properly.' There was no need to go into the office, she had done that before going to Bellevue. But: 'Drat! I forgot to switch the little lamp off,' she muttered to herself.

'Oh!'

Comfortably settled on either side of the fireplace, Camille and François Tavernier were quietly chatting. Léa stood in the doorway, paralysed.

François was by her side in a trice. He hugged her so tightly she could not breathe. He was there . . . He had come . . . She was no longer afraid, he would protect her . . .

'Well, I'll be going to bed. You see, Léa is happy to see you again,' said Camille rising.

Still holding Léa, François took Camille's hand and kissed it.

'Thank you, Madame d'Argilat, for keeping me company even though you are so tired.'

'Ruth's made up a bed for you in the bird room. Léa will show you where it is. Good night.'

They devoured each other incredulously with their eyes, unable to get over their delight in seeing each other. François's large hand traced the outline of her face, her neck, her lips. Léa submitted, alive to the pleasure his light touch kindled in her. At last, their lips met. Their passionate kiss made them both tremble. Slowly his beautiful, experienced hands removed her clothes . . . She stroked the nape of his neck while he rolled down her stockings. She leaned on his shoulder as he picked up her foot. Soon, she was naked, splendidly naked. Her body glowed in the light of the dying embers, giving the impression of a sort of wild strength, both fragile and indestructible, despite her slenderness. Kneeling at her feet, he was gazing up at her, fascinated. Léa raised him up and it was his turn to be undressed. But her impatient fingers were clumsy. Smiling, he gently pushed her away and was naked in next to no time, not in the least embarrassed by his erection. He picked her up and carried her over to the old couch where, so often when she was a little girl, her father had comforted her woes. In the space of a second, the smell and feel of the leather had taken her back to her childhood. Her father's image sprang up behind her closed eyelids. She suddenly opened her eyes. François was leaning over her, murmuring her name.

'Come,' she said.

They made love for a long time. They kept wanting each other again and again. At dawn, exhausted and sore, they dozed off.

They awoke as daylight flooded the room.

Teetering and giggling, they pulled on their clothes.

Léa pushed François into the bird room which was the guest room and closed the door behind them. They tore off their clothes and dived under the huge old gold coloured satin eiderdown. They fell asleep at once in each other's arms.

'Léa, Léa, wake up . . . Where on earth is she?'

Laure knocked on Camille's door.

'Good morning, Camille, I'm sorry to disturb you, but you haven't seen Léa, have you? It's nearly twelve o'clock and Maurice will be here soon.'

'No, Laure, I haven't seen her yet. I expect she's in the garden, or in the kitchen garden.'

'No, I've looked there. She can't be far away, her bicycle's here. Perhaps she's with her friend who arrived last night. Don't you think it's odd, these people who turn up in the middle of the night without warning?'

'Monsieur Tavernier's always been a bit eccentric . . .'

'Oh, excuse me! I've left my flan in the oven.'

As soon as she had left, Camille went and knocked on the door of the bird room.

'Monsieur Tavernier, it's time to get up, it's twelve o'clock.'

'Thank you, Madame d'Argilat, I'm getting up . . . Wake up my love . . .'

Léa half opened one eye and stretched.

'I'm sleepy . . .'

'Darling, we've got to get up, it's twelve o'clock.'

'Twelve!'

She leapt out of bed.

'Quick, quick, we haven't a moment to lose. Laure's guest will be here any minute.'

'He can wait a bit.'

'Oh! No, I'd rather not keep him waiting. But you! You can't stay here.'

'Why not? Are you ashamed of me?' he asked, pushing her back down on to the bed.

'Don't be so silly. It's very important. Where's my skirt? I can't find my other stocking. Where are my shoes? Help me.'

'Here, I've found this.'

She snatched her slip from him.

'Get dressed quickly. I'm going to get changed and I'll join you.'

He tried to grab her but she was too quick for him.

When she came back into the room, dressed in a short blue woollen dress, formerly her mother's, which Ruth had altered for her, and wearing her hair up, revealing the nape of her neck, a clean-shaven François was knotting his tie.

'How lovely you are!'

He slipped on his jacket.

'How elegant you are! Anyone would think you bought your clothes in London.'

'That would be going a bit too far. But there are a few first class tailors left in Paris, you just have to be able to afford them. Tell me about this guest you seem to be in such a state about.'

Léa briefly disclosed what her uncle had told her and what she had heard about Maurice Fiaux's gang. She also told him about Mathias and about Raphaël Mahl's visit.

'Is he still with us?' interrupted François.

'Very much so. But Maurice Fiaux, Laure's guest, is the worst of the whole bunch. That's why I think it's better if he doesn't meet you. Do you understand?'

There was the sound of someone galloping down the stairs. Léa was being called. She half opened the door.

'Coming.'

'Tell her to lay an extra place.'

'But . . .'

'Do as I say.'

'Laure?'

244

'Yes!'

'Have you remembered to lay a place for Monsieur Tavernier?'

'Of course I have!'

Léa shut the door.

'You're completely out of your mind. If ever he guessed . . .'

'Guessed what?'

'That you're a member of the Resistance.'

'Huh!'

Léa stamped her foot.

'You can be so irritating. How am I supposed to introduce you?'

'Say that I'm a businessman from Paris who is visiting a colleague in Bordeaux and I took the opportunity of coming to say hello.'

'But when he sees Raphaël . . .'

'Don't worry about Raphaël, he's more of a threat to himself than anyone else. Come my love, I can't wait to see what this Bordeaux member of the Gestapo is like.'

At the foot of the stairs, they bumped into Laure.

'He's just arrived! Léa, I can't bring myself to believe what you told me.'

'It's the truth, little sister. Don't forget, all our lives, including yours, depend on your behaviour.'

'Yes,' she sighed. 'Where's Lucien? Camille told me he left yesterday evening.'

'I don't know. Some friends of his came to fetch him. Let's go and join your guest. By the way, let me introduce a friend of mine from Paris: François Tavernier.'

'How do you do, mademoiselle.'

'How do you do, monsieur.'

They entered the parlour where Bernadette Bouchardeau and Camille were already entertaining the visitor and Ruth was pouring a bottle of sweet white Montillac wine.

'Here you are at last,' said Bernadette, trying too hard to sound relaxed, 'we were about to have a drink without you.'

'François, let me introduce one of Laure's friends, Monsieur Fiaux. Maurice . . . may I call you Maurice? . . . this is

Monsieur Tavernier, an old friend of ours from Paris who's giving us the pleasure of his company while he's on a visit to Bordeaux.'

'How do you do, monsieur. Is that your car I noticed outside?'

'Yes, you could say so. My associate in Bordeaux lent it to me so I could drive over here.'

'Are you in the wine business, monsieur?'

'I deal in anything that's for sale, from wine to metals, including cloth and foodstuffs.'

'You aren't finding it too difficult to stock up?'

'No, I have a few contacts in government circles. In Vichy, I sometimes have lunch with Pierre Laval and in Paris . . . with a few compromises . . . if you get my meaning, it's possible to pull off some good deals.'

Maurice Fiaux drained his glass looking thoughtful.

François remarked with a grim look that Montillac wine tasted better at Montillac than in Paris.

'Let's eat,' said Laure good-humouredly, 'or my soufflé will collapse.'

What a lunch! Greedy Léa would never have imagined that a meal could drag on for so long. She had great difficulty finishing her chicken, leaving a large piece untouched on her plate. But, on the other hand, she drank a lot. So did Maurice Fiaux.

Tavernier had skilfully made him talk about himself and what he did. At first he was cautious, but the wine loosened his tongue and the young man gradually disclosed more details about his work at police headquarters.

'I check that the addresses of Jews to be arrested are correct . . . that the members of the family are all there. It's a responsible job because some police officers entrusted with the task let a few slip through the net,' he said smugly.

Léa almost screamed when she felt a foot rub up against hers. It was François, who was saying with a smile:

'Your conscientiousness is a credit to you. Ah! If only all young people were like you . . . France, with Germany's help, would become a great nation again.'

'It's not numbers that matter. A handful of determined men will be enough to eliminate the Jewish scum.'

'Do you know where they're taken?' asked Laure gently.

'To Drancy, I think, then to labour camps in Germany, but they could just as equally send them to Hell for all I care.'

'What about the children, do they work there too?' murmured Camille.

'No, madame. They're allowed to stay with their mothers out of humanity.'

When he had been talking about 'Jewish scum', Léa had been thinking of Sarah's burned face and tortured body. She could hear her husky voice with its slight accent: 'The Nazis want to kill us all . . . including the women and children.'

What a relief it was when he rose to leave.

'Forgive me, I must leave. I have an appointment. Business,' he said with a little snigger.

They all clamoured round him to wish him goodbye. Laure walked him to his car. Nobody said a word until Laure returned. She rushed crying into Ruth's arms.

'I don't want to see him ever again . . . I don't want to see him ever again,' she hiccupped.

Camille, Léa and François wandered down to the terrace where, in silence, they tried to let the moist, fragrant April air drive out their gloomy thoughts.

In the afternoon, Doctor Blanchard dropped in to tell them how Lucien was. The boy was as well as could be expected. He drew Léa aside.

'Raoul and Jean Lefèvre gave me this letter for you.'

Her pretty face lit up with happiness.

'Raoul and Jean . . . did you see them?'

'Yes.'

'How are they?'

'Very well. If you want to see them, come to my house tomorrow during surgery hours.'

Léa opened the letter and read:

'Queen of our hearts, the thought of you helps us to stay alive. The knowledge that you are so close at hand is driving

247

us mad and we cannot resist the desire to see you. Come quickly, it is agony waiting. Your devoted slaves. J. and R.'

She smiled.

'Good news?' inquired François Tavernier.

'Do you remember the boy who was waiting for me outside the church of Saint-Eustache holding *la Petite Gironde*?'

'Jean Lefèvre.'

'Yes, this letter's from him and his brother. I'm so thrilled! I was so afraid Raoul had been killed or injured when he escaped.'

'Are you sure it's his writing?'

'Not only is it his writing, but Doctor Blanchard told me that they were at his house and that I could go and see them tomorrow.'

'Don't go!'

'Why not?'

'I don't know. There's something fishy about all this.'

'It's perfectly natural that they should want to see me . . . From mixing with the sort of people like your friends in Paris, you see traitors and swine everywhere you go.'

'Yes, I expect you're right. Let's go for a walk to this famous grotto where you used to play as a child.'

Léa blushed as she remembered the rather more grownup game she had played with Mathias in one of the chapels.

'Tell me, you rascal, did you play something more than just hide-and-seek there?'

'Let's go through the pine wood, that way we don't have to go past Bellevue.'

As soon as they were in the shelter of the trees, hidden from view, the two lovers embraced and went slowly down the slopes leading to the grotto, stopping at each of the stations of the Cross to look at the stone chapels. In front of the seventh station, Léa kept silent. They reached the steep path that led past the cemetery. The door was open, they went in. It was a long time since Léa had visited her parents' grave for which she felt guilty. But the grave did not seem to have suffered from her neglect. Beautiful white cyclamens, her mother's favourite flower, were lying on the slab. It could only have been the devoted Ruth who had put them there.

Her grief at their departure made her kneel down and search in vain for words of prayer.

A shot rang out.

'It came from the square,' cried Léa standing up.

She ran through the graves, slipping on the gravel of the steep uneven path. She had rushed off so fast that François had been left standing there.

'Léa, wait for me.'

Without looking round, she carried on running, reached the gate and raced down the steps which came out opposite the church of Verdelais. She stopped. Everything was peaceful. Too peaceful. The square was deserted, which was unusual for that time of day.

Just as Tavernier caught up with her and grabbed her arm, another shot echoed.

'The Gestapo,' she murmured, pointing to two black front-wheel drive vehicles parked outside Mademoiselle Blanchou's haberdashery.

A horse and carriage could be heard approaching. François pushed Léa against the wall.

'It's Doctor Blanchard's carriage . . .'

'Are you sure?'

'Everyone round here knows the doctor's carriage.'

'Good God!'

As he stood up, the horse went thundering past.

'Doctor! Doctor!'

The carriage continued on its way, turned round on the far side of the square and drew up outside the house next to the haberdashery. Simultaneously, the four doors of one of the vehicles were flung open. Three men in suits leapt out, machine guns first. A German officer then alighted, without hurrying, and walked over to Doctor Blanchard who was calmly tying his horse to the usual linden tree.

Slowly, François forced Léa to retreat. They went up the steps leading to the little square where the war memorial stood. There, they lay flat on their stomachs in the sand. From this vantage point they could see everything that was happening in the square. They could do nothing but look on helplessly. The young leaves of the linden tree did not yet block their view of the houses.

It was as if time stood still while the doctor knotted the leather reins around the tree. When he was certain they were tied fast, the elderly doctor turned round.

The German officer's bark reached their ears but they could not make out what he was saying. Doctor Blanchard's gestures seemed to indicate that he did not know. No doubt he had not replied correctly for two men jumped on him and hit him with the butt of their guns.

Léa wanted to leap up but François held her down.

Then everything happened at once. Shots rang out from the doctor's house. A young man came out, clutching his chest, took a few steps forward and then crumpled to the ground, doubled up, not far from Father Adrien's friend, whose white hair was matted with blood.

'Jean!' groaned Léa.

There was a woman's piercing scream: it was the doctor's housekeeper, who, seeing her master injured, ran to his aid. A man followed behind her, his hands up, wounded in the face.

'Raoul!'

Two armed civilians tried to push away the housekeeper. She hung on, shouting out to the man she had served and loved all her life. A violent kick made her lose her grip . . . She ran forward again. A shot rang out behind her. Her heavy body sank to the ground. The man who had fired was wearing a hat.

'No!'

Léa's cry was muffled by the sand.

Doctor Blanchard's terrible shout reached them:

'Marie!'

He rushed over to help her. He was stunned by a blow on the back of the head. Two men picked him up and put him in one of the cars. They did likewise with Jean. They pushed Raoul into the second car. The doors slammed, the cars revved up raising a cloud of dust. They drove off in the direction of Saint-Maixant. A truck full of German soldiers appeared and followed them. They had taken every precaution. The dust settled slowly over the servant's body. The horse had not so much as blinked.

Still lying in the sand in the war memorial square, Tavernier was supporting Léa while she vomited. The man from the medal shop just opposite the memorial came running in their direction, his eyes popping out of his head.

'Did you see that? Did you see that?'

The villagers began to come out.

'Is the young lady hurt?'

'No, would you fetch a little water?'

'Yes, of course.'

He came back with a bucket borrowed from the cemetery which he filled with water at the pump. Leaning up against a tree, Léa had stopped vomiting. Her face, covered with sand and tears, was unrecognizable.

'Did you see that? Did you see that?' the man kept on repeating as he put the bucket down beside them.

Then he ran off towards Doctor Blanchard's house.

François dipped his handkerchief in the water and washed Léa's poor face.

'I'm thirsty.'

He cupped his hands and scooped up some water which she drank thirstily, twice asking for more.

'Why didn't you do anything? We let them be arrested and killed in front of our very eyes . . .'

'There was nothing we could do. Calm yourself.'

'I don't want to calm myself. On the contrary, I want to shout, to fight.'

'For the time being, the best way to fight is to get a grip on yourself.'

'If only we'd been armed!'

'Well, we weren't and it would have been the two of us against ten, or perhaps even twenty men. Armed or not, we had no chance of saving them but what is certain is that we'd have started a massacre and been arrested.'

Léa, her face wet with tears, was banging her head with increasing force against the tree trunk.

'Maybe, but at least we'd have done something.'

'Enough! You'll hurt yourself. Think instead of warning those who might be arrested. Your friends are likely to talk. The golden rule in the underground is to move when members of the network are arrested.'

She straightened up as if she had been stung.

'Lucien! Quick.'

Without a glance at the square which had filled with people, Léa raced up the path to the grotto. Still running, she reached the seventh station and went into the chapel, François close on her heels.

'Help me! Lift up the broken flagstone.'

François did as she bade him. Under the cracked flagstone, there was a cache of guns, revolvers, submachine guns, a sten gun, grenades and ammunition, wrapped in a canvas cloth.

'What an arsenal!' he whistled admiringly and grabbed a submachine gun. 'They're Stens, very useful in close range fighting, but very dangerous in the hands of someone inexperienced. What are you doing?'

'You can see for yourself, I'm taking the guns.'

'Leave them where they are! You don't intend to take these to Montillac in broad daylight, do you?'

'But . . .'

'No buts, put a grenade in each pocket and I'll take two revolvers and three boxes of bullets. If necessary, I'll come back and get the rest tonight . . . Let's put the flagstone back.'

After carefully concealing the arms, they sealed up the cache again. François brushed away their footprints with a handful of twigs. When he had finished, he put his arms round Léa and kissed her.

'Not now, let me go.'

'Be quiet, I thought I heard something.'

Standing in the doorway of the chapel, they made a perfect target.

'Let's get out of here, I must have been mistaken.'

Around them, the hill studded with little chapels seemed deserted. But who could tell? Each one could be concealing a hidden observer.

They walked to the foot of the three huge crosses which dominated the surrounding countryside. As he looked at the two thieves, François muttered as if to himself:

'I've always wondered if it was better to be crucified with nails or tied . . .'

Irritated, Léa broke away from him.

'Would you mind saving those kind of comments for later?'

As they came out of the woods, past the disused mines, Montillac stretched out before them. They both stopped instinctively.

'Everything looks quite normal, what do you think?' asked Léa.

'How can one tell? Perhaps they're waiting for us inside the house. I'll go first.'

'No! I don't want you to! Come on,' she said, setting off again. 'I'm going to stop at Bellevue. If there's anything wrong, Sidonie will know.'

'Sidonie? Is that where your cousin Lucien is hiding?'

'Who told you that?'

'Madame d'Argilat.'

Belle, Sidonie's dog, came bounding out to meet them, barking. When they entered the house, Sidonie laid an old shotgun down on the table.

'I thought it was you from the way Belle was barking, but there was something in her voice that told me you weren't alone.'

'This is a friend of mine. Have you noticed anything unusual at Montillac?'

'No, nothing, other than your guest at lunchtime. Is this the gentleman?'

'No, he arrived in the night while we were all here.'

'Funny, I didn't hear anything. Let's have a look at you, you've been crying, haven't you?'

'Oh! Sidonie,' she cried, rushing over to the old woman.

'What's the matter, sweetheart?'

'They killed . . . Marie . . . and . . . arrested Doctor Blanchard . . .'

'My God!'

'. . . and Raoul and Jean . . .'

'Madame, we haven't a second to lose, Lucien must leave your house, he's no longer safe here.'

Sidonie gently disengaged herself from Léa and sank into an armchair, one hand clutching her chest, her nostrils pinched and her breath coming in short gasps. She pointed to the sideboard. François understood. He opened the cupboard and found a phial on which was written: ten drops when necessary.

'Get some water.'

Léa took an earthenware jug from the draining slab and poured some water into the glass François was holding out.

'Drink this,' he said, forcing the sick woman's lips apart.

Outside, Belle was scratching at the door and whining.

'She's not going to die, is she?'

'No, look, she's breathing more easily.'

A trap-door above them slid open.

'Lucien!' cried Léa.

'Go and get me the ladder that's outside.'

'Leave it,' said François Tavernier, 'I'll go.'

He was soon back with the ladder which he leaned against the opening. Lucien climbed down without using his hands.

'I overheard everything. You're a friend of my Uncle Adrien's, aren't you?'

'Yes. Are you feeling better, madame? You should lie down for a while.'

Sidonie allowed them to lead her to the bed which was in the same room. François gently helped her lie down.

'Thank you very much, monsieur, thank you . . . Now deal with the boy.'

Lucien went over and kissed her on the forehead.

'I won't forget, Sidonie. Thank you for everything.'

'Go on, go on, leave.'

'Not right away, we must wait until it's dark. Léa and I will go up to Montillac, fetch the car and call a doctor.'

'If it's for me, there's no need. Just ask Madame Ruth if she'd kindly come and spend the night here.'

'As you wish, madame.'

'Come back quickly, I feel as if I'm caught in a snare with no way of defending myself,' said Lucien, showing his arms.

They had been driving in silence for ten minutes searching the

254

unlit road. The headlights, coated with blue paint, were not much help.

'Where are you taking me?'

'To friends of mine at Saint-Pierre d'Aurillac,' replied Léa.

'Are they members of the Resistance?'

'Yes.'

'Who are they?'

'A retired sailor and his brother . . . Where are we? I can't see a thing . . . I think we're at Gaillard . . . Yes, we are. We're nearly there.'

They left the village and drove through the countryside for a few minutes. Very quickly there were houses again.

'Let's park in the little square behind the church. The café Lafourcade is on the other side of the road opposite the war memorial. Wait for me here, I'll be back.'

She returned a few moments later.

'Hurry up, they're waiting for us.'

They crossed the road and went up two steps into the café which was on the corner of a little side street. In the dimly lit room, they could make out wooden tables and chairs. A woman in her fifties, dressed in black, came over to them:

'Come in, children, and welcome. Oh! Poor thing . . . what happened to him?'

'My hand was blown off when I was handling explosives.'

'How dreadful! Come and sit down. Jeannot, pour us all a drink.'

They drank the rough red wine from thick glasses. It tasted like stone and left a stubborn ring round their mouths.

The two brothers, Jeannot and Maxime, stared at this beautiful girl sitting at one corner of the table, drinking their father's wine.

François Tavernier told them what had happened at Verdelais.

'We heard from a kid from the village who acts as postman. You knew them well, I believe, mademoiselle?'

Léa lowered her head, unable to repress her tears.

'Yes . . . I've known them all my life . . . Doctor Blanchard brought me into the world and . . . Raoul and Jean were my best friends before the war . . . I don't understand . . .'

'They were betrayed. As soon as Doctor Blanchard left to go on his rounds, a car arrived containing a German officer and three civilians. A truck full of soldiers was concealed nearby. No need to tell you that everyone barricaded themselves inside their homes. Then another car arrived driven by a young man. He rang the doctor's doorbell. The door was opened and then we don't know what happened. People heard two shots . . .'

'We heard them too.'

'. . . and you know the rest of the story.'

'Where have they been taken?' asked Léa.

Maxime looked away; it was his brother Jeannot who replied.

'To Le Bouscat, to the Gestapo headquarters.'

'All three of them?'

'Yes.'

'But they were wounded!'

'Those bastards don't give a damn. They leave the wounded to die in a corner.'

'Is there nothing we can do?'

'Not for the moment, no.'

'Oh!'

'Exupérance, don't lose heart. They'll pay for all this, one day,' said Maxime. 'Meanwhile, we'll hide your wounded comrade, we'll look after him and get him to North Africa.'

'It's going to be costly,' said Tavernier, 'take this money.'

'Monsieur,' said the woman, 'we don't do this for money.'

'I know, Madame Lafourcade, what you do has no price, but railway tickets and doctors cost money. Exupérance, it would be rash to stay here any longer.'

'He's right, leave before curfew.'

François bowed to Madame Lafourcade.

'Madame, may I have the honour of kissing you?'

'The honour is mine,' she said, laughing and giving him a resounding kiss.

'Look after him well,' said Léa, kissing her in turn.

'Don't worry about anything, he's in good hands.'

Jeannot made sure the coast was clear and walked them to their car.

*　　*　　*

Snuggled up to François, Léa could not get to sleep. She kept going over and over the bloody scene of that afternoon. She blamed herself for not thinking of the guns. Someone had betrayed them . . . Who could have known that the Lefèvre brothers were at Doctor Blanchard's house? She herself had only found out an hour previously. What was it Maurice Fiaux had said? 'I've got a business appointment'. Despite the hat, she was convinced it was he who had killed Marie and wounded Jean in the stomach. So that was the 'business' he had referred to so smugly. Adrien had said he was a murderer. It was a murderer who had taken a fancy to her little sister . . . She absolutely had to get Laure away from Montillac. She sensed that although Laure had been warned against Maurice Fiaux, she was fascinated by him. First a German, now a Gestapo supporter! Her father would turn in his grave. At last, she fell asleep.

'Léa . . . Léa . . . Don't be afraid . . . I'm here. Is it your nightmare again?'

'Yes, they're still chasing me through Orléans in flames . . . I cry out . . . nobody comes . . . there are more and more of them who want to kill me and this time . . . Maurice Fiaux is with them . . . It was him, wasn't it?'

'Yes, I think so.'

'How can anyone be so cold-blooded about murder? Don't you find it strange?'

'Strange? No, I've met a lot of men capable of it, in Spain and now in France.'

'What about you? Would you be capable of it?'

'If I had to.'

'Have you already done it?'

'Yes, when it was necessary.'

'With the same indifference?'

'Indifference? . . . No, determination, yes. Even you, when . . .'

'It wasn't the same thing! He was going to kill us . . . I had no choice!'

'Granted, but if you had to do it again, you'd do it, knowing now that killing, in some cases and for some people, is very easy.'

257

'What you're saying is terrible . . . You're comparing me to that murderer.'

'Admit that if you had the opportunity today of killing him, you'd do it.'

Léa thought.

'Yes.'

'And you'd be obeying a feeling of revenge while Fiaux acts with the purity of indifference.'

'That's absurd!'

'I agree. At this time of night I'm capable of saying anything, I'm so sleepy.'

'Charming, all you think about is going to sleep!'

'I'll show you if all I think about is sleeping!'

Camille had got up three times to fetch a drink for little Charles who had been running a temperature for the last two days.

'A nasty cold,' Doctor Blanchard had diagnosed the previous day. Now he was asleep. She did not weary of looking at him, he seemed so vulnerable. As a child, Laurent must have had the same pout, the same blond hair, the same frailty. When would she see him again? During her illness, each time she awoke, Camille had hoped to see him at her bedside.

She paced up and down, trying to dispel her anxiety by keeping moving, trying to think of other things . . . Tomorrow she would tell Bernadette Bouchardeau that her son had left. She was expecting screams and tears and was not looking forward to it. How she wished she could spare this rather silly woman any grief. Léa had asked her to tell her and Camille could not refuse Léa anything. 'I love her as much as I love Charles,' she would sometimes say to herself. A thinking woman, she found it hard to understand the passion she felt for Léa. 'I love watching her live, it's more intense than living myself. I'm so afraid for her, even more than I am for Laurent, perhaps because she's a woman and I am able to imagine the harm she can come to, especially since I was in the Gestapo's dungeons and the cell in Fort Hâ. As soon as she's away from Montillac, I fear the worst. François Tavernier's like me, he's afraid of losing her!'

The shock of a pebble hitting the shutters of the window on

which she was resting her forehead made her snap out of her reverie. She switched off the lamp by her son's bed and went back to the window, opened it and drew back the shutters a little way. Down there, in the courtyard, was the silhouette of a man.

'Camille,' whispered the stranger.

That voice? She reeled, feeling giddy, her heart thumping. Her thin fingers gripped the windowsill with all her strength.

'Camille,' repeated the stranger.

There was no longer any doubt, it was him! Recovering from the shock, she raced to the door, bounded down the stairs four at a time, crossed the dining room in the dark, opened the front door and drew back the heavy shutters. Laurent fell into her arms.

For the first time in nearly three years, Laurent d'Argilat and François Tavernier found themselves face to face. Léa was more distressed by this encounter than she would have imagined. Seeing the two men together seemed shocking all of a sudden. Laurent, with his beard, his long hair and his shapeless clothes, looked more like a tramp next to François who was too elegant in his well tailored suit. It was Laurent who looked like an adventurer now. 'That's the limit,' she thought.

They spoke in low voices in a corner of the children's room. Léa had locked the door. She and Camille had agreed not to tell Bernadette and Laure that Laurent was at Montillac.

The weather was cold and miserable. Typical Good Friday weather.

'Where's Charles?' asked Léa.

'Laure's playing with him,' replied Camille. 'You should have seen his face when his father picked him up! He recognized him this time.'

The two men came back.

'Tavernier and I have tried to take stock of the situation. I agree with him entirely: you must leave Montillac for a while and take Laure with you.'

'What about Charles?' cried Camille.

'Charles too, of course.'

259

'I think you're right, but where should we go?'

'To Paris.'

'To Paris!' they chorused.

'Yes, that's where you'll both be safest; on the one hand because of Françoise, and on the other because of Tavernier who will be able to arrange for someone to keep an eye on you.'

'But what about you, Laurent, where will you go?' asked Léa.

'I'm leaving tonight. A plane will pick me up to take me to London and then on to North Africa.'

Camille tottered.

'You'll get yourself killed,' she sobbed.

'I'm in more danger of getting myself killed if I stay here. I stand a better chance of survival if I leave.'

'Then . . . go.'

Léa had sat down amid a pile of cushions and was frowning.

'Give us a smile, my love, otherwise I'll think you're still in love with this romantic hero,' whispered François.

'Leave me alone!'

'Stop sulking, the others will notice if you don't.'

'I don't care!'

'Don't be so childish. This is no time for brooding. Are you listening to me? Now, you're to telephone your aunts . . .'

'Why?'

'To ask if you can go and stay with them for a while . . .'

'All three of us! With the baby!'

'Yes. Tomorrow, if the Gestapo haven't come and arrested the lot of us, we'll all leave for Bordeaux, and I'll get the train to Paris with you.'

'But Laure might not want to leave.'

'You've got to persuade her. She of all people has to get away from Montillac. She mustn't see Fiaux again.'

'I understand. I'll go and phone.'

'Tell your aunts that Camille has to see a specialist and that you are accompanying her given her poor health.'

'What about Laure?'

'Say that she's bored, that's perfectly true.'

'Will we see each other in Paris?'

'As often as possible, my love.'

260

'Well, I'm going to phone. Will you come with me?'

'No, there's still something I want to discuss with Laurent before I leave for Bordeaux.'

'Are you going to Bordeaux now?'

'Yes, I'm going to try and contact your friends and make the train reservations.'

For the rest of that day, Léa had to watch Laure. She sat huddled in an armchair in the parlour and did not stop crying.

'What are you crying about?'

Léa's question only made her cry all the more. She did not answer.

François Tavernier telephoned to say he would not be back until first thing the following morning and they should be ready to leave. Ruth, who had been told, thought it was a good idea for them to go and had convinced Laure that it was vital for her to leave too.

'Don't you worry about anything,' she had said to Léa, 'I'll look after everything for you. Sidonie will move in here until she's better. Promise me you'll write often and let me know everything that's happening.'

Bernadette Bouchardeau, still grieving at losing her son once again, made no comment.

At ten o'clock, Laurent had torn himself away from Camille and after planting a final kiss on his sleeping son's forehead, he went off into the night, his haversack full of clean laundry. Léa walked as far as the road with him. They went along the path at the end of the terrace to avoid going past the Fayards' house. A man jumped out of the ditch and shone his torch in their faces.

'It is you,' he said, switching it off. 'Hurry up, the plane won't wait.'

He pulled two bicycles out of the bushes.

Laurent kissed Léa on the forehead.

'Take good care of yourself and of them,' he said pushing away her arm as she tried to restrain him.

Chapter 19

A hundred and ninety five dead! The allied forces' air raids had killed a hundred and ninety five people in Bordeaux on the 17th May 1943.

What a delight Hérold Paquis of Radio-Paris took in repeating it over and over again. The area around the station had suffered again, trains were having difficulty getting through. 'Lucky we got out in time,' thought Léa selfishly.

What a crush there was that Easter Saturday: the crowds, struggling with parcels, baskets and children, stormed the trains leaving for Paris. How had François Tavernier managed to get a first class compartment just for them? It was a miracle because even the corridors of the first class compartments were packed. Camille had refused to go to the dining-car with them saying that it would be difficult with little Charles.

As they entered the dining-car, Léa wished they had stayed in their carriage and eaten the snack Ruth had prepared for them. The diners consisted mainly of German officers and soldiers, and men and women who looked a little too opulent. Several heads turned as the two pretty girls walked past. They gave their tickets to the head waiter and were served one of the worst meals they had eaten during the entire war. François laughed at Léa's disappointment. Laure had left her plate almost untouched under the ravenous gaze of a young soldier . . .

The pleasure of seeing Albertine, Lisa, Françoise and her baby again had partly restored Laure's good humour. Léa found her aunts and Estelle looking older and tired.

Since their arrival, François had only come to dinner once

and he had left immediately after the meal.

Ruth wrote to them about Doctor Blanchard's suicide. Like the Debrays, he had not hesitated to kill himself rather than talk. Jean and Raoul Lefèvre were in Fort Hâ. They had been tortured.

It was while they were driving to Bordeaux that François Tavernier had told them what he had found out about their fate. They had been taken to 197 Rue du Médoc and interrogated with increasing brutality, even Jean, who was already in great pain from the wound in his chest. They had refused to talk and were thrown into the cellar and thoroughly beaten. Their torturers had to stop for fear of killing them. Doctor Blanchard was authorized to treat Jean. He had managed to extract the bullet which did not appear to have done any serious damage. He committed suicide that night by swallowing a cyanide capsule, as Tavernier found out a few days later.

Laure never mentioned Maurice Fiaux again.

There were only a few tatty volumes left on the shelves of the Gallimard bookshop in the Boulevard Raspail. Léa was flicking through the yellowed pages of a book whose author she had never heard of. The same sales assistant who had been there at the beginning of the war came up to her. He was wearing plus-fours and shoes with thick crêpe soles.

'Don't buy that book, mademoiselle, it's no good.'

'I've run out of things to read, I don't know what to buy . . . Why are your shelves half empty?'

'At the moment, we're selling any old rubbish. We've sold nearly all the books we had in stock. We can't get in new stocks.'

'Why?'

'Because French people have started to read like mad. What else is there to do? One can't go to the cinema every day, so they read.'

'What do they read?'

'Whatever they can lay their hands on: Homer, Rabelais, Spinoza, the Church fathers, I don't know . . . But I've got just the book for you. We reserve new editions for our oldest and best customers. What do you say to Marcel Aymé's latest book?'

'You certainly do like him.'

'Very much. Here, I'll give it to you already wrapped up so that the others won't see it.'

'What's the title?'

'*Le Passe-Murailles*.'[1]

She set off home clutching the precious book. At last, the prospect of a pleasant evening! She had read and re-read the entire contents of her aunts' bookshelves. Léa had never been so bored in Paris, stuck between Camille who devoted all her time to her son, her aunts who only talked about provisions, Laure who spent her days and sometimes her nights at their sister Françoise's apartment, or doing the rounds of the bars and tea salons, and Estelle who was always grumbling about her poor old legs!

She missed Montillac. She feared that during her absence, Fayard would be up to his tricks, even though Ruth and Sidonie were keeping an eye open. July was drawing near and Léa had not the slightest intention of spending the summer in Paris. It was stifling. What must it be like in August? If only François Tavernier had been there to entertain her . . . But no, he had vanished into thin air. Where was he? With his friends from London, or the ones from Berlin? It was anybody's guess.

Men turned round to stare after this attractive girl prettily dressed in a navy blue dress with red spots which showed off a large expanse of leg, her feet encased in high white canvas sandals with platform heels, a present from Françoise. She was so engrossed in her gloomy thoughts that she did not notice.

Back at the Rue de l'Université, Léa put her book down on the hall table next to a hat. Her aunts had a visitor.

'Here you are at last! Monsieur Tavernier's been waiting for you for more than an hour!'

She fought against the urge to fling herself into his arms.

'Hello, I thought you were dead.'

[1] The man who could walk through walls

'Léa!'

'Don't worry, mademoiselle, she was only joking. Her sense of humour is part of her charm.'

'Monsieur Tavernier, you are too indulgent with the child.'

'Aunt Lisa, I'm not a child any more and I don't give a fig for Monsieur Tavernier's indulgence.'

'What a temper! Paris air doesn't suit you.'

'No, I'm bored.'

'That's what I feared. I'll take you for a walk in the country.'

'At this hour! It's almost five o'clock!'

'It's not far, a quarter of an hour's drive from here.'

'You call that the country? A quarter of an hour away from the centre of Paris!'

'You'll see, it's completely wild and beautiful and few people know about it.'

It took them a lot longer than a quarter of an hour to reach the spot François Tavernier wanted to visit. He cursed as they drove round and round the streets of Bagneux, Fontenay-aux-Roses, Sceaux and Bourg-la-Reine. He stopped by the sign that said Châtenay-Malabry and looked at a map.

'Rue Chateaubriand, Rue du Loup-pendu . . . ah! here we are, Rue de la Vallée-aux-loups, it's this way.'

'Will you please tell me where we're going.'

'To buy some trees.'

'To buy some trees!'

'Yes, I've been promised a cutting from a tree planted by Chateaubriand.'

'What do you want to do with it?'

'It's not for me. One of my German friends who has a passion for French literature and is a great admirer of Chateaubriand, asked me if I could obtain this cutting for him . . .'

'You're mad!'

'I telephoned Doctor Savoureux who lives in the house that used to belong to the writer. He said that I wasn't the first person to make such a request and that at the moment he had a very pretty little larch tree.'

'You've got nothing better to do than get hold of trees for

your German friends?' asked Léa with all the contempt she could muster.

'My friend isn't just anybody and this larch isn't just any old larch. Think of it . . . the child of a tree lovingly planted by Chateaubriand.'

'You sound like Raphaël Mahl. He talked to me about Chateaubriand as well with tears in his eyes. He even gave me a book by your great man . . .'

'*The Life of Rancé?*'

'How did you guess?'

'It wasn't too difficult, knowing Raphaël Mahl . . . Have you read it?'

'I tried. I found it so boring! The life of a dirty old seventeenth-century monk!'

'Be quiet, you wretched creature! We are entering the property of the author of *Martyrs* whose ghost might very well rise up from the rock of Saint-Malo to come and tweak your ears for having dared to take his name in vain.'

They drove up a wide driveway lined with tall trees which cut out the sky. The air coming in through the open windows was warm and clammy.

'This place is sinister. What's it called?'

'The valley of wolves.'

'Just as I said, it's a dangerous deathtrap straight out of a novel by Ann Radcliffe.'

'You've read Ann Radcliffe!' he said with such surprise that Léa was annoyed.

'I suppose you think you're the only person who knows how to read. My mother used to love English novels of that period, she'd read them all and so have I. No doubt you find that sort of horror story too sentimental, too feminine . . .'

'What passion! I didn't know you were so fond of thrillers. Do you know the German authors of the same period? Some of them are very interesting, I'll lend them to you if you like.'

'No thank you.'

They drew up outside a house covered with virginia creeper and ivy with a large adjoining building resembling a small barracks or a hospital. A smallish woman was waiting for them on the doorstep.

'Good evening, monsieur, it's Monsieur Tavernier, isn't it?'

'Yes, madame. Good evening, madame.'

'I'm Madame Le Savoureux. My husband is terribly sorry but he was called to Paris and asked me to receive you and hopes you will accept his apologies.'

'That's most annoying!'

'Believe me, he was very sorry, he had no choice. If you would like to come inside, mademoiselle? . . .'

'Oh, excuse me, Mademoiselle Delmas.'

'You're very pretty, mademoiselle. My husband will be even sorrier to have missed you.'

Léa smiled and stepped inside.

So this was the house of the great writer! The interior felt rather fragile. She had the impression that the walls could hardly support the pictures on them and that the floor might give way under the weight of the furniture.

'What were you expecting?' asked François, who had noticed the disappointment in her expression.

'I don't know . . . something more impressive . . . this parlour could be at Montillac. Oh! François! Look at those lawns . . . those trees!'

'It's beautiful, isn't it, mademoiselle? My husband and I put all our energy into keeping this place as he would have wished it . . . If you like, later on, I'll show you round the park and I'll show you the trees he himself planted. Monsieur Tavernier, would you come with me? Excuse us, mademoiselle, we shan't be long.'

On a table piled high with papers, a leather bound book full of white paper bookmarks attracted her attention. Léa picked it up: *Memories from Beyond the Grave*, and went and sat on one of the steps outside the parlour, looking out over the vast empty verdant space surrounded by very tall trees, and opened the book.

'The Valley-of-Wolves, near Aulnay, October 4th 1811 . . .' 'The earth would be starting to smell of autumn,' she thought before continuing, '. . . I like this spot, it has taken the place of my native fields, I paid for it with the fruit of my dreams and my sleepless nights: I owe the little desert of

Aulnay to the great desert of Atala, but to create this haven, unlike the American settler, I have not stripped the native Indians of their heritage. I have become very attached to my trees; I have written elegies, sonnets and odes to them. There is not one tree that I have not tended with my own hands, rescued from the worm nestling in its roots, from the caterpillar stuck to its leaves. I know them all by name, as if they were my children; the trees are my family, I have no other, I hope to die among them.'

'I could say the same about Montillac. My true family is that land, with its trees, its vines and its meadows. Like him, I know the names of all my trees and I know how to treat their diseases. When I return, I'll plant a cedar tree in memory of today.'

'Léa, where are you?'

'Here.'

'Excuse me, I hope I wasn't too long. What are you reading?'

She held out the book without replying.

'Now there's a book I wouldn't have dared to recommend after what you said about *The Life of Rancé*.'

'But it's not the same, here he talks about his childhood, he talks about this place with such love . . . Did he die here as he wished?'

'Alas he didn't! My sweet ignoramus, Chateaubriand didn't have time to shelter in the shadow of the trees he had planted. He had to sell The Valley-of-Wolves "bought under Napoleon and sold under the Bourbons", and his library, keeping nothing but a little edition of Homer. He suffered so terribly from losing this place that he swore he would never own a single tree again.'

It was a beautiful evening and they were making their way back to the house through the woods. The house looked lost amid so much greenery.

'Let's not go through there,' said Madame Le Savoureux to Léa who was walking ahead.

'Why not? The path is perfectly all right.'

'That's not the reason, it's because we're close to the hostages' spot.'

'The hostages' spot?' asked Léa stopping.

'Over that way, on the other side of the wall, in the woods, the Germans shot some hostages. I can still hear the shots . . . Since then, my husband and I never go to that part of the grounds.'

They walked back to the house in silence and, shortly afterwards, François Tavernier took his leave of Madame Le Savoureux, clutching his precious larch tree.

They drove for ages through the quiet suburban streets. Men were playing bowls, women sitting on their doorsteps knitting and children were chasing each other squealing. The air smelled of suet, soup and freshly mown grass. Bursts of laughter and the sound of voices coming from the open café doors reached their ears. For a second, they were accompanied by the voice of Edith Piaf. Washing was hanging out to dry in the gardens, dogs slept in the middle of the road, war had made them forget about the existence of cars. They got out of the way at the very last minute, staring at the car with disdain. It was after supper and everyone was relaxing doing nothing in particular, dreaming or staring up at the sky. Gradually, the houses gave way to apartment blocks, there were more and more cafés. Music blared from wireless sets and could be heard through the open windows, rebounding from the walls. Young people on bicycles crossed the road in front of them. Now, the almost bucolic peacefulness had disappeared as they approached the city. Porte D'Orléans and the white signs with their black gothic lettering were a brutal reminder of the Germans' presence. Since they had left the Valley-of-Wolves, they had not exchanged more than a few words.

'Where would you like to have dinner?' he asked.

The anguished look she gave him felt like a slap in the face. He pulled up by the kerb and put his arms round her. 'I know what you're thinking about, my love. Forget all that for a while. Your tears won't bring back the dead. Get those ideas of revenge out of your pretty little head, the moment is not yet ripe. Cry, my little girl, I prefer your tears to that mute pain which makes me feel completely helpless. You don't know what I'd give to see you gay and carefree . . . for you to be happy at last. Léa, you're so strong, so brave, you mustn't give in. Fight, you're tough enough to resist all that.'

Léa allowed his warm persuasive voice to soothe her. What did it matter if he was mistaken, if she was neither strong nor brave but just a weak little girl thrown into disarray, carried far away from her dreams, confronted by a whole new world that she could not understand and where such violent instincts were released that they swept away all weaknesses. Since the murder in the Orléans bombing, Léa had realized that the survival instinct was strong in her and she knew she would kill again if she had to. But now, crying in this man's arms, she wanted to be nothing but a little girl being comforted.

'Is that better? Here, blow your nose.'

Léa blew her nose noisily.

'How do you manage to look even more beautiful when you're red-eyed and dishevelled?'

She gave a wan smile and heaved a great sigh.

'I'm hungry.'

François Tavernier laughed his booming laugh.

'As long as you've still got your appetite, I shan't be at all worried about you. We'll have to hurry if we want to get back before curfew. Shall we have dinner at my friends' in the Rue Saint-Jacques?'

'Oh! Yes, I love Marthe as much as I love her cooking!'

The restaurant in the Rue Saint-Jacques was packed, but the bedroom, which had been made into an improvised dining room for close friends, was empty. Marthe and her daughter-in-law were thrilled to see them.

'Monsieur François! Mademoiselle Léa! What a pleasure to see you.'

'Have you heard from your son?'

Marthe looked furtively about her as if she were afraid someone was hiding behind the shiny saucepans hanging on the wall and whispered:

'He's in the Resistance in the Dordogne area. Apparently it's a tough life, but it's better than working in Germany.'

As usual, in spite of rationing, the food was excellent.

'Conserves have become as rare as gold dust.'

Léa had drunk a little too much and was rather giggly. To hear her laugh more often, Tavernier would have made a complete idiot of himself clowning around, or made the most awful puns. In her company he became a mischievous boy again. He started telling her the latest jokes, the witticisms attributed to Sacha Guitry, the master of French humour, who was greatly appreciated by the occupying troops. And Léa laughed and laughed . . .

'How wonderful to be young and carefree,' said Marthe Andrieu, serving their dessert. The smell of roses wafted in from the Luxembourg gardens. Léa threw her head back and closed her eyes to savour the fleeting fragrance. Her attitude was so unrestrained that Tavernier's hands strayed under her blouse and skirt. She let him do as he pleased. When he touched the moist place between her thighs, she closed her eyes.

François Tavernier had given Ruth a large sum of money, unbeknown to Léa, to enable her to pay Fayard and the five labourers who worked all the year round in the vineyards. The honest governess had at first refused, but François was so convincing as he assured her that it would enable Léa to relax as far as Montillac's immediate future was concerned. He had also lent Laurent some money telling him he could repay it after the war.

Every day, Camille took her little boy for a walk in the Luxembourg gardens or in the Tuileries, sometimes accompanied by Françoise and her baby. On two or three occasions, Otto Kramer joined them and each time, Camille had left, on the excuse that she had an errand or an appointment. The sight of a German uniform made her ill. In Major Kramer's case, it was even worse: she could not refuse to offer him her hand without hurting Françoise. Tactful as ever, he understood and did not join Françoise when he knew she was with Camille.

She had learned from a message on the London broadcasting service that Laurent had arrived safely in North Africa.

Since her visit to the Valley-of-Wolves, Léa was more cheerful and more relaxed. Buried in *Memories from Beyond the*

Grave, she now swore by Chateaubriand, much to the amusement of François Tavernier, who came to see her at her aunts' apartment nearly every day.

As for Laure, she had changed beyond all recognition. Dressed in the latest fashions of the jazz set, she openly smoked English cigarettes and regularly went to the Pam-Pam and the Colisée clubs, stomping away to the music of Alex Combelle and Django Reinhart at clandestine dances. Their records were very popular among the swinging young things who played them over and over again in the fashionable bars. For some time, thanks to Laure, daily life had improved a little. One day she brought butter, the next it was coffee, sugar or potatoes. Where did she get the money from? When black market butter cost 350 francs a kilo and coffee between 1,000 and 2,000 francs, how did she do it? In reply to her aunts' questions, she said:

'I'm doing business. I get in touch with the person who's looking for a pair of silk stockings, and can pay for them in butter, and the person who's looking for butter and has twenty pairs of silk stockings for sale. I get a commission, it's as simple as that.'

Laure had decided to carry on with her studies and asked her aunts if she could stay with them until she finished. Of course they agreed.

The young girl introduced her new friends to Léa. They were amusing, cynical, rude and . . . very young. The eldest was two years younger than Léa. Their parents were doctors, teachers, lawyers or well-off tradespeople. The little group had been friendly towards her, finding her very beautiful. With them, she felt carefree again. There was no question of discussing the war, it was a taboo subject. They did not want to know about Hitler, de Gaulle, the Gestapo and the Resistance, it was nothing to do with them. It was all their parents' fault, let them sort it out. They looked rather pathetic trying to moralize about their children's jackets which were too long, their trousers which were too short, their shoulder length hair, their drooping or exaggeratedly padded shoulders, their striped stockings, their clumpy unpolished shoes and the inevitable umbrella which they never opened, when the parents themselves were prepared to do anything for a carton of cigarettes or a pair of silk stockings. They had lost the war and they had lost face. All they could do was keep quiet and especially keep off the subject of France's or Germany's greatness depending which side they were on. Maurice Schumann's voice meant as little to these young people as did that of Philippe Henriot, the ex-minister of the liberal right from Libourne, all-time enemy of the Communist Party, and who had become, after the German invasion of the USSR, the spokesman for the defenders of Christian civilization in the face of bolshevism. Along the Champs-Elysées and in Saint Germain-des-Prés they were superbly unaware of the enemy's presence, they never stepped aside to let them past in the street: they simply did not exist. They were lucky that so far, because of their young years, the soldiers had been lenient towards them.

The war had made Lisa de Montpleynet's need to know everything that was going on even keener. She wanted to know every detail of the German soldiers' retreat in Russia, which metro stations were closed, the number of dead in the latest allied air-raid, how much the price of butter had risen, she wanted to know everything from the latest pop song to the French National Resistance Committee's nomination for the new governor-general of French West Africa, from Mussolini's resignation to the next landing of the allied forces, she wanted to hear the eye-witness account of a Pole read by Jacques Duchesne in the programme 'French people speak to the French' as well as accounts of the massacres of the Jews – accounts which preyed on her mind and which she refused to believe right until the end.

'The field is situated about ten miles south of the town of Belzec. It is surrounded by a fence which is about twelve yards from a railway track. A narrow gap, less than a yard wide, leads from the entrance to the camp to the railway line. At about ten o'clock in the morning, a goods train drew up alongside the camp. Simultaneously, the guards, who were at the other end of the camp, began to shoot in the air and ordered the Jews to get on to the train.

They made the prisoners panic in order to stop them wavering or offering any resistance. The Jews, who were pushed into the

273

narrow gap I described, scrambled pushing and shoving into the first goods wagon stationed at the end of the path. It was an ordinary wagon, one of those that has a sign saying '6 horses or 36 people'. The floor was covered with a two-inch thick layer of quicklime, but in their panic and haste, the Jews did not see it. A hundred or so of them climbed on to the train until it was physically impossible to squeeze any more in. They were packed inside the train like sardines. Then, the guards bodily seized the others and began throwing them in over the heads of those already inside. Their task was made easier by the terrified prisoners' confusion when they heard shooting behind them. The murderers threw another thirty or so men and women on to the train in this way. It was a dreadful sight. Several women had broken necks. It is not difficult to imagine the horrible scene. One hundred and thirty people were thus pushed or thrown into the first carriage. Then the sliding doors were closed and bolted. The train moved a few yards forward.

The next carriage was now in the place of the first and the same scenario was repeated. In all, I counted fifty one carriages into which they crammed the camp's six thousand prisoners. Once the camp was empty and the carriages full, the train pulled away.

The train stopped in a field, in the middle of the country, about twenty five miles from the camp. The carriages remained where they were, completely sealed, for six or seven days. When the team of gravediggers finally opened the doors, the occupants were all dead and often in an advanced state of decomposition. They died from suffocation. One of the properties of quicklime is that it gives off chlorine gas when it comes into contact with water. The people packed into the carriages naturally had to relieve themselves. A chemical reaction immediately ensued. The Jews were thus immediately suffocated by the chlorine gas which was released, while the quicklime ate away at their feet until they were nothing but bones.'

'It's horrible,' cried Lisa, covering her ears.

'How can the good Lord allow such things?' asked Estelle with such stupefaction that in any other circumstances the others would have laughed.

'How can a Polish Resistance fighter don the uniform of the assassins and be a passive spectator at these murders?' murmured Albertine to herself.

'He did that in order to present irrefutable evidence to the civilized world,' said Laure quietly.

'I don't quite understand why they used the quicklime,' Léa thought out loud. 'After six or seven days, they would have suffocated anyway.'

The radio announcer continued:

'*Some people perhaps believe that France is enjoying preferential treatment, others perhaps think that we've never witnessed the organization of massacres like that here in France.*

And yet it is sufficient to remind ourselves what the Jews who were crammed into the camps at Drancy, Compiègne or even the Vélodrome d'Hiver stadium suffered. It is sufficient to remember the heartbreaking scenes in Lyon in particular, when Jewish women were dragged away from their children and shut up in trains without being able to say goodbye to their families. It is sufficient to remember the silence which followed the arrest of vast numbers of Jews to understand that no country is being spared.

What has become of all these men, all these women, all these elderly people and sometimes these children? Have they too left 'to go east' as the Germans call it? It is essential that every French civil servant dealing with Jewish affairs understands that by carrying out orders, he is an accomplice to murder, and is helping the German assassins of Lvov and Warsaw.'

The silence which followed reflected their shame and confusion.

'It sounds like anti-German propaganda,' said Léa when she found her voice. 'No nation is capable of perpetrating such abominable acts.'

'Remember Doctor Blanchard, and Jean and Raoul,' retorted Laure.

'That's different. On the one hand, they arrest people who fight them, and on the other, men, women and children whose only crime is the fact that they exist . . . That's what I can't understand. Why?'

'Because they're Jews, of course.'

'And does that sound like a good enough reason to you for being sent to concentration camps and murdered?'

'No, of course not.'

'What's to stop them from killing redheads because they're

275

redheads, or hunchbacks because they're hunchbacks and old people because they're old?'

'Children, we're in God's hands,' said Lisa in a quavering voice.

'If there's a Jewish God, he can't be very popular at the moment,' sniggered Léa, much to her aunts' disgust.

Lisa and Estelle would not admit it but they took the reports on the French radio station much more seriously than those on the London station which was such an effort to listen to because of the interference.

Although the sale of wireless sets was banned, the Montpleynet sisters had given one to Estelle as a token of thanks for twenty five years of good and loyal service. She kept it in the kitchen and would not have missed Jean-Hérold Paquis's daily broadcast just before the eight o'clock news bulletin for anything in the world.

Although her mistresses had told her time and time again that he was in the pay of the Germans, and that his invectives against the communists, the Jews and the de Gaulle supporters were vile and false, she could not help being 'all churned up' by his stirring voice as he ended his programme with 'England, like Carthage, will be destroyed!' Everybody knew that his speeches were directly influenced by the occupying powers but many listeners were worried when he thundered against the 'bolshevik threat' or he skilfully turned the allied forces' bombings to his advantage.

If Estelle had a soft spot for Paquis, Lisa had one for Philippe Henriot who 'had such a nice turn of phrase' and who was 'so cultured'. Ah! That 'extraordinary, deep, rich, cultivated voice with such a gift for oratory, which swells and mocks with bursts of petit-bourgeois smugness, a true and talented literary scholar.' The ex-member of Parliament from Libourne had a gift for invective and evoking images which appealed to the imagination of town and country dwellers alike. How cynically, how skilfully, he rubbed salt into the wounds of the defeated! Many people held him up as an example. He made the following speech on 4th July 1943:

'Our fellow countrymen who support de Gaulle and their ilk remain a never-ending source of admiration and surprise to me.

Everyone knows that they are the only upholders of uncompromising patriotism. They have a monopoly on the French sense of dignity. [. . .]

Germany is occupying France as a result of their resounding victory. I am not forgetting that these gentlemen say they have never been defeated, that Marshal Pétain should never have signed the Armistice agreement. Let us leave these ridiculous words in the mouths of people who, in their panic in 1940, from the Garonne to the Pyrenees, trembled at the mere idea that Germany would not agree to the armistice that they are now repudiating. No more army, no more weapons, no more planes; the Germans in Angoulême and in Valence: the roads flooded with military and civilian refugees, chaos and confusion everywhere . . . That's when certain voices should have made themselves heard, but we haven't had a peep out of them since. Our delayed action blusterers are unwelcome as they start raising their voices only now. What is more, they show an astonishing lack of logic.

For, why is it that these people who find the occupation of their country by a victorious opponent intolerable, find it reassuring to have their Empire invaded by peoples who had promised to help them and who confine themselves to exploiting them? Why is it so repulsive, in their opinion, to see Germany, their enemy, take what she requires from our resources, and why do they rub their hands together when they see England and America, their allies, seizing our North-African supplies? [. . .]

So I no longer understand. I am suffering from my country's fate. I suffer as any person who has been defeated suffers. But at least, painful as it is, these trials and tribulations are, alas! perfectly natural. But those of you who accept things that the victors have never inflicted on us from someone who claims to be your ally, do you not feel a little uncomfortable? [. . .]

And so, it is an American who arbitrates in the conflicts between French leaders; it is the king of England who comes to take possession of the new Crown colony: Churchill and Roosevelt refuse to recognize French sovereignty over a French territory; on this July 4th, the anniversary of American Independence, a reminder of the help France gave America to help chase out the English, the two former rivals now find themselves in agreement in order to reduce us to slavery. The French are there, so deprived of

277

their freedom that not one voice was raised to protest against the assassinations of their fellow-countrymen in the metropolis from the air. [. . .]

Whereas these gentlemen declare we are unworthy, because, in our determination to restore our country to a position it deserves in the world, we are not beginning by denying that we have been defeated. But, gentlemen, you are suffering at the hands of your friends, a fate which is a hundred times more humiliating than the one imposed on us by the victors. We are treated as the losers, but you are treated as slaves. It is true that if the Germans have defeated us, the Anglo-Saxons have cheated you. That is what gives them rights over you. For to be beaten proves that we were the weaker side; to be cheated proves that you are the less intelligent side. One can feel sorry for the weak but not for the foolish.

So carry on being enamoured of your occupiers, kissing the hand of those who are making fools of you and chasing you from your posts, say thank you every time London or Washington kick out a general who should never have been in in the first place. But ask your masters to be so good as to keep the leading roles for a little while longer. For there is more to come. De Gaulle and Giraud are drinking Algerian wine at George VIth's table. They exchange telegrams of congratulations with Stalin. [. . .]

The military defeat was only a test, which, as the victors themselves confess, left our honour intact. Over there, these men who claim to be the guardians of our honour are trading it off.'

His weekly speeches made Lisa get all worked up and it took all her sister's powers of persuasion to convince her that if Philippe Henriot could talk with such apparent freedom about the 'temporary occupying forces', then it was with the agreement of and under the control of those same occupying forces and that it did not automatically make you a 'terrorist' or a Gaullist if you refused to believe what French people who were firm Nazi supporters said of their fellow countrymen who would not acknowledge their country's defeat. After hours of discussions, Lisa would agree, until Philippe Henriot's next speech. Fortunately, Albertine de Montpleynet's influence was stronger than that of the voice which preached submission over the wireless. 'Radio Paris is lying, Radio-Paris is lying, Radio-Paris is German' people sang under their breath.

278

Like most French people, Lisa was subject to the tyranny of the wireless which was still new and mysterious. Those voices that came from some unknown place, murmuring advice on recipes, giving various information and news from all over the world, or which scolded, hurled abuse, prophesied, and flattered, were able to mould people's minds like putty, filling them with hatred or with hope. The listeners, sitting in their armchairs, listened to those voices with the same devotion as Joan of Arc listened to hers.

Léa, Laure and Camille were not immune to this addiction. Despite the reproaches of Lisa and Estelle, who feared they would be denounced by malevolent neighbours, Léa and Camille listened to London nearly every day and Laure listened to the latest pop songs. But, like most girls and boys of their own age, none of them took what they heard on either station at face value.

Chapter 20

The genuine friendship François Tavernier and Camille d'Argilat felt for each other had turned into a conspiracy which irritated Léa. Not that she was jealous of Camille as she found her too unattractive to be considered as a rival, but she could not bear being excluded from certain conversations that stopped abruptly when she came into the room. What did all this secrecy mean? Léa thought she had found out the answer when, one day, as she was lifting Charles out of his pushchair after his afternoon walk, she noticed a scrap of paper clenched in his little hand. She gently took it from him and unfolded it: it was a piece of paper torn from *Libération*, the clandestine Gaullist newspaper. What was it doing in the child's hand? Charles, who wanted to get down, was wriggling in her arms. She was about to put him down when she noticed that his little pants made a funny sound. She immediately unbuttoned his rompers . . .

She hastily picked up the newspapers and, taking hold of Charles's arm, steered him into his bedroom. Breathless as if from running, Léa sank on to his bed. The child heaved himself up beside her and stroked her hair.

'Your mother's crazy, completely crazy! Supposing it had been Françoise who had found that scrap of newspaper . . . Do you realize! We'd have all been deported, including you,' she said, grabbing hold of him and kissing him.

'Ah! Charles is with you. I've caught you flirting together,' joked Camille, coming into the room.

'It certainly is a matter of flirting! Close the door. When I think you dared get mixed up in all that!'

'I don't understand, what do you mean?'

280

'You don't understand? Do you think this is the sort of nappy you normally put on a baby?' she said, brandishing the little bundle of newspapers.

'How did you find them? Don't you think it was a good hiding place?'

What a cheek! Léa would never have thought Camille capable of such audacity.

'A good hiding place! But you could have got him killed!'

The young mother turned pale.

'But he didn't have anything to do with it.'

'Of course he didn't, so what?'

Looking back, Camille was frightened. She sat down on the bed and hugged her son to her.

'You could have told me what you were up to. You want to act the heroine all by yourself. Have you thought how worried Laurent would be if he knew you were distributing illicit newspapers?'

'He knows.'

'What do you mean, he knows?'

'It was he who put me in touch with the network.'

Léa stared at her incredulously.

'I don't believe you.'

'Well, it's true. He needed someone he could count on. Naturally, he thought of me.'

'That's stupid, you've got a child. He should have come to me.'

'He thought that perhaps you had enough to do already.'

'Since I've been in Paris, I haven't had any contact with the people from Bordeaux and I'm glad. I don't want to be arrested like Raoul and Jean, or to die like Doctor Blanchard or in front of a firing squad. Please don't bring any more illicit newspapers here. Too many people come and go in this apartment.'

'What happened today was an exception. I usually deliver them straight away.'

'Why didn't you today?'

'My contact didn't turn up. I didn't dare throw them into a litter bin.'

'What about François?'

'What do you mean, what about François?'

Camille was a bad liar. Her reply sounded false, but Léa pretended to believe her. She was having dinner with Tavernier and promised herself she would get to the bottom of the matter. For the moment, the most important thing was choosing what to wear that evening.

Léa was caught up in a social whirl. She wanted to have a good time, not to have to think about her dead friends, or those who had disappeared, or were fighting, or those who collaborated. No particular event had influenced her decision, she was simply weary, she had an overwhelming desire to live, to be frivolous. Perhaps it was due to the example set by her sisters who only lived for the present. Françoise lived for her lover and her child, while Laure lived for American music, black market deals and romance.

François had been a little surprised to notice the change that had come over Léa but deep down, he felt relieved. Ever since he had met Léa, he had lived in fear. When he saw how deeply involved she was with the Resistance movement in her area, that Montillac and all its inhabitants were under surveillance, when he heard about Mathias's attitude, Raphaël Mahl's visit and the arrest of her friends, he was very much afraid. That was why he had hastened their departure for Paris. Unfortunately he had been obliged to go away for a whole month. Now, he was back for a few days and he would, at last, be able to look after her. Tavernier loved watching her live. Since their first meeting, her personality had asserted itself and she had grown more beautiful. 'The sort of woman to be avoided at all costs if you want to keep out of trouble.' But he obviously was not bothered as he seemed to go out of his way to look for trouble of that nature. That particular day, for example, he had agreed to take her to dinner at Maxim's, after initially refusing, his only excuse being:

'The food isn't so good and the place is full of Germans.'

'I don't care,' she had retorted, 'I want to go somewhere where people look as though they're having a good time.'

Nothing would make her change her mind. That was why Léa was no longer concerned about Camille's underground newspapers but was busy getting ready to go out to dinner. Thanks to Laure, she had bought a beautiful dark red chiffon dress with the label removed. Françoise and her aunts were of the opinion that it could only be by one of the top designers: Chanel or Fath, which, given the very reasonable price, seemed impossible. A long black scarf and a pair of evening shoes which had barely been worn completed her elegant outfit.

'You look ravishing!' cried Camille, who was helping her dress. 'You'll be the envy of every woman in the room.'

Léa picked up one of the underground newspapers.

'What are you going to do with that?' asked Camille.

'It's for a prank. I'm going to put *Libération* in among all the other newspapers. I'd like to see their faces when people discover them.'

Camille smiled.

'You're crazy!'

'Please, they've got to feel threatened even in the places where they feel safest. And Maxim's is one of those places.'

'I don't understand you. I didn't think you wanted anything more to do with any of this.'

'So, I can change my mind if I want.'

Léa was putting the paper into a little black suede handbag when François Tavernier arrived. He was elegantly dressed but looked anxious.

'Do you really insist on eating at Maxim's?'

'More than ever.'

'All right,' he sighed, 'let's go then . . .'

'Anyone would think we were going to our deaths.'

A curious expression of amusement flickered across his face.

'Death is to be found there as it is anywhere else. There are worse places to die.'

'That's not funny.'

'I wasn't trying to be funny. That's a lovely dress. The bloodstains won't show.'

'Stop it, François, you'll ruin her evening.'

'Don't worry, Camille, it takes more than our friend's black humour to spoil my evening.'

'Just as well! Don't take any notice of me. I'm sure we'll

have a wonderful evening. Good night, Camille. Give little Charles my love.'

'Goodbye, have a lovely time.'

Outside, a chauffeur driven car was waiting for them.

At the bar by the entrance of the famous restaurant, daily and weekly newspapers were on display attached to long bamboo canes hanging from a dark wooden table. A few gentlemen were comfortably settled, drink in hand, flicking through the day's papers. Léa took out her underground paper, carefully smoothed it out and nonchalantly slipped it into the latest edition of the right-wing paper *Je suis partout*[1] among articles by Robert Brasillach, François Vinneuil (Lucien Rebatet), Alain Laubreaux, Claude Jantet and George Blond. After a smug glance around the room, she joined François Tavernier who was waiting for her at their table. A German officer gallantly stood aside to let her pass while Albert showed her to her table.

'Are you happy with this table, Monsieur Tavernier?'

'It's perfect, Albert.'

Léa sat down, looking perfectly relaxed and happy with a little smile hovering on her lips.

'You look like the cat that's been at the cream or a mischievous child.'

'Me?' she said with a look of such innocence that he began to feel vaguely worried. 'I'm just delighted to be here. So are you, aren't you? There must be lots of your friends here. Am I mistaken?'

The wine waiter brought the champagne Tavernier had ordered.

'Let's drink to your beauty.'

'My dear friend, allow me to raise my glass to mademoiselle.'

Léa immediately recognized the man she had already met in a restaurant with François. Today, he was not wearing a shapeless tweed jacket but a dinner jacket flecked with ash from the fat cigar he was smoking. There was no way of getting

[1] I am everywhere

away from him. With a frosty smile, François raised his glass.

'Monsieur Tavernier, my wife is convinced that you're ignoring her.'

'How could Madame Szkolnikoff think such a thing?'

'You still haven't been to dinner with us.'

'I was waiting for an official invitation.'

Szkolnikoff let out a great guffaw.

'But these days, nobody bothers. I'll expect you tomorrow at seven o'clock. Mademoiselle is invited of course . . . She's charming.'

'I'm afraid I shan't be free tomorrow evening.'

The smile was immediately wiped off 'Monsieur Michel's' face.

'I'm sure you can manage to be free. I'm counting on you. Without fail . . . at seven o'clock, 19 Rue de Presbourg.'

Smiling again, he added:

'Hélène will be thrilled! See you tomorrow.'

Under the table, François Tavernier was clenching his fists.

'Your friend's wife is charming, look, she's waving at you.'

Hélène Szkolnikoff, dripping with jewels, was waving a ring-studded hand in their direction.

'Will you stop calling that pig my friend,' he said in a restrained voice as he waved back.

'Perhaps he isn't, but his wife is!'

'You're not going to start that again?'

'Who's that with them?'

'Captain Engelke and his mistress.'

'The lovely Hélène's friend? Come on, relax, you're not going to ruin my evening by sulking. It's not my fault if we bump into people you don't want to see.'

From the look on his face, Léa thought he had forgotten where they were and was about to slap her. She prudently moved out of his reach and said in her sweetest voice:

'Let's not argue. It's so nice here. Let's drink, shall we?'

He picked up his glass of champagne and drained it in one go. A waiter refilled it immediately. Many men and women were looking in their direction, struck as much by Léa's youth and beauty as by the simplicity of her dress. She was not wearing a single piece of jewellery. Her almost bare shoulders gleamed. A beautiful young girl wearing a gorgeous white evening dress with great elegance was staring harder at Léa than anyone else. Her expression was one of both complicity and disdain. Léa thought she recognized her face.

'Who is she?'

'Corinne Luchaire.'

'She's pretty and she looks nice. Who's she with?'

'With her father, Jean Luchaire, and some journalists.'

'Do you know her?'

'No.'

'Pity, I like the look of her.'

Léa casually looked away.

'Has mademoiselle chosen?' asked the head waiter.

'I'd like something very expensive.'

This childlike remark brought a smile to Tavernier's rugged face.

'Have some caviar. I don't know how they manage it, they've always got some in.'

'Fine, I'll have caviar.'

'At the moment, all we've got is *ocietre* or *sévruga*.'

'Which is the more expensive?'

The head waiter raised an eyebrow to show he was somewhat shocked by such a question. He replied with a hint of reproach in his voice:

'The *ocietre*, monsieur.'

'Then we'll have that. The same for me.'

'Very good, monsieur, and to follow?'

'I'd like fish,' said Léa.

'We have sole, bream or salmon poached in sorrel. It's excellent, if I may take the liberty of recommending it to mademoiselle.'

'I'll have sole.'

'Very good, mademoiselle. And you, monsieur?'

'The salmon sounds good, I'll try that.'

'You won't regret it, monsieur.'

'Tell the wine waiter we'll continue to drink champagne. Is that all right with you?'

'Fine.'

The sound of muffled outbursts could be heard coming from

near the entrance of the restaurant, then an elderly gentleman with a goatee beard who looked like Alphonse de Chateaubriand came in brandishing a sheet of newspaper. He went over and sat at Jean Luchaire's table. The journalist must have asked him what the matter was. The man replied angrily. Snatches of their conversation could be heard.

'. . . den of terrorists . . . they're everywhere . . . communists and Gaullists . . . it comes to the same thing . . . red scum . . . should all be shot . . . no mercy . . . this rag . . . decent newspapers . . . a disgrace . . .'

People tried to calm him down. The old man rose and handed the page to a very dignified fat man.

'Have a look for yourself if you don't believe me.'

The fat man stared blankly at the sheet of newspaper.

'What you have in your hands, monsieur, is a Gaullist newspaper, slipped by a criminal hand into an honest publication.'

'Jacques,' cried the fat man's companion hysterically, 'let go of that!'

In a state of panic, he dropped the paper which fluttered to the feet of Captain Engelke. A hush fell over the restaurant. The orchestra imperturbably continued playing a slow waltz. Léa found it hard not to laugh. She watched in scorn as these people who had been all smiles a minute before the scandal, conversing easily with German officers, now showed their true faces where cowardice vied with spinelessness. It was a repulsive sight. Slowly, no doubt relishing the nervous anxiety of the gathering, Engelke picked up the paper.

'*Libération*,' he said aloud.

He read a few lines, ignoring the tension in the room around him.

'Very interesting. Do you know it?' he asked, showing it to Michel Szkolnikoff.

From where she was sitting, Léa could see the businessman's hand shaking. The music stopped.

'Would you give me a drink,' she said gaily, shattering the silence.

They all turned to stare at her in horror. Corinne Luchaire looked at her with a twinkle of amusement in her eye. Bursting out laughing, she raised her glass in Léa's direction. Léa, looking triumphant, raised her glass in response and nodded.

The insolence of the two young women relieved the tension and other people began to laugh. Engelke good-humouredly laughed with the rest, much to the relief of Szkolnikoff.

'These young girls are delightful, they are the spirit of Paris,' said the SS Captain, screwing the paper into a ball.

François Tavernier had difficulty hiding his mirth.

'Was it you who played that trick on that poor old man?' he asked.

'I really don't know what you mean.'

'You're a little monster, but I like you the way you are. That was a wildly risky thing to do. You can be arrested for less. Here's your caviar.'

The head waiter himself, assisted by two waiters, respectfully presented the precious eggs on beds of ice served on silver platters.

Léa shamelessly tucked in with such relish that anyone other than Tavernier would have been embarrassed. But Tavernier was excited and amused by this assertion of the young girl's sensuality.

'Little devil,' he said affectionately, taking a large spoonful of caviar.

Léa was perfectly aware of what lay behind his good humoured insult. She liked the way he was aroused by every one of her movements. When she was with him, she felt both anxious and reassured, but above all, she felt free. It was no more than a feeling, but it was very powerful. In his company, she did not feel the limitations of her sex, but more a celebration of her femininity as a value in itself and not as an object of submission or calculation. She could tell him anything. He knew better than she did what was best for her. This indefinable man had his own particular code of honour that was, in fact, very strict. Léa sensed that he had great respect for the other person's choice, even if he did not share it and, in some cases, fought against it. 'There's no hatred in him,' she thought. That reminded her of conversations she had overheard between her father and her Uncle Adrien. The latter had said of the Spanish Civil War:

'I have seen so much how hatred has ravaged both sides, that I too almost became a victim and hated all men. Then I saw the mark of the devil in their crimes and I pitied them, executioners and victims alike.'

At the time, Léa, who was still a child, had been very upset by the 'mark of the devil', the indelible stamp which made men irretrievably bad. François had the same disillusioned tolerance as the priest. She did not share that tolerance. She felt towards some people a desire to destroy them with vindictive cruelty. But once again, radiant in the rosy glow from the pink lampshades, sated from the rich food and the champagne, she only wanted to live for the present, and for the moment, she wanted that man, sitting opposite her, to take her in his arms.

'Dance with me.'

'How can I resist such a tempting invitation?' he said rising.

As they walked past Captain Engelke's table, Tavernier greeted Hélène Szkolnikoff with a nod which she returned.

Léa abandoned herself in her lover's arms and several people watching them felt a thrill of pleasure.

Outside, it was absolutely silent. The moon shed a gentle light on the obelisk at the Place de la Concorde. Despite the curfew, Léa insisted on walking home. The air was balmy with the nocturnal fragrance of flowers and grass from the Tuileries gardens and the Champs Elysées. A night bird called out, another responded. They slowly crossed the huge empty square, their footsteps echoing in the stillness. They stopped on the bridge to look at the houses of parliament, the façade covered with German propaganda. They watched the river flowing past, a wide shiny ribbon almost still between the two stone embankments. The smell of the water rose up. Leaning against the parapet, their lips met, their intoxicated bodies abandoned themselves to the illusory cover of the night and they let themselves be swept away on the tide of their desire.

For a long time, they swayed above the celebrated river. The gods were on their side: there were no patrols, no enemy vehicles marred their happiness.

289

The following morning, Léa told Camille how she had slipped the underground newspaper between the pages of the right-wing newspaper at Maxim's. Camille had laughed so much at her description of the clientele's faces that she could not find it in her to scold Léa.

'Your Aunt Bernadette phoned yesterday to say that Lucien had arrived safely and he is as well as can be expected. The gendarmes brought Pierrot back home to Luc Delmas's. Apparently, he wants to send him to a very strict boarding school run by Jesuits.'

'I know, my cousin Philippe told me. Poor old Pierrot . . . Did Aunt Bernadette say anything about Raoul and Jean?'

'Yes, their mother has heard nothing at all. She's rented a little apartment in Bordeaux and goes to Fort Hâ every day. But she's always refused permission to visit. She's not even sure that they're in the fort. She's setting great store by her appeal to the local prefect. He promised her he would find out what he could about her sons' fate and approach the occupying authorities on their behalf.'

'She'd be better off going to the German officials themselves than a man who receives his orders from Vichy.'

'Yes, perhaps . . . it's so complicated . . . I'm sure the prefect thinks he's acting loyally . . .'

'Loyally? Towards whom?'

'I don't know, he's a civil servant.'

'A civil servant! . . . Who's carefully counting the numbers of Jews deported, not forgetting the children.'

'I know. When I was at Mérignac, that's all the women talked about. Where are they now?'

A sad silence came over them.

'But I'm telling you I don't want to go.'

'Léa, once again, I have no choice and I'm asking you to come with me as a favour.'

'Seeing the faces of those scoundrels, thieves and murderers makes me want to vomit. I won't be able to stand it.'

'Very well, if you won't do it for me, do it for yourself.'

'What do you mean?'

'That the activities of your uncle and some of your friends

290

are no secret as far as these men are concerned. The Gestapo would love to interrogate you . . .'

'But you said . . .!'

'That was a few months ago. The situation is changing every day and I wouldn't be surprised if one day I have to start worrying.'

'Why?'

'Because they suspect me of not being entirely honest with them.'

'François? You're not trying to tell me that you're going to be arrested!' exclaimed Léa, pale with anguish.

'Darling, would you be upset?'

'Stop playing around! You know very well . . .'

'I know very well what?'

'Nothing! You're exasperating . . . I'll come with you.'

He drew her towards him. She felt his hard muscular tense body. He was holding her so tight it was almost painful.

'Thank you. When they see you, my love, they'll think, or at least I hope they will, that you wouldn't walk into the lion's jaws if you had the slightest connection with the Resistance.'

'And if they think the opposite?'

'Then all you can do is pray and disappear very quickly.'

'How do you want me to dress?'

'Very simply. I don't want you to look like those high-class whores. Wear that simple long dress you were altering the other day. You must have finished it by now?'

'Yes, thanks to Camille who helped me do the hem. I'm not very good at sewing. I'm going to get changed, I shan't be long.'

'Here, wear these orchids.'

'They're beautiful! Thank you.'

'Wonderful! You look wonderful! Don't you think so, Hélène?'

'Mademoiselle looks ravishing despite the simplicity of her dress. Why don't you wear any jewellery, my dear?'

'Because I don't have any, madame.'

'What! A pretty girl like you! But what on earth can you be thinking of, my dear Tavernier? You're not usually stingy

291

when it comes to women. You should be ashamed of yourself.'

'You're right. I'll need your advice, you have such perfect taste.'

'That's true. Tomorrow I'm seeing a jeweller in the Rue de la Paix who wants to show me some designs. Come with me, you'll be most welcome,' she wheedled. 'But! What's the matter?'

'Nothing, a slight twinge in my arm. Nothing serious, an old wound.'

The arrival of some new guests claimed their hostess's attention.

'Oh! Fritz, I'm always so delighted to entertain you.'

'It's always a pleasure for me to visit you, dear Hélène. I took the liberty of inviting General Oberg who has happy memories of the admirable dinner you and Michel gave in the honour of my friend the Reichsführer SS Heinrich Himmler.'

Oberg bowed and clicked his heels.

'Madame.'

'Welcome, general.'

Léa looked about her without even trying to hide her amazement.

'Why did you pinch me earlier?'

'It's unbelievable! I must be dreaming . . . What did you say? Ah! Yes. You could refrain from doing your Casanova act with that woman in front of me.'

François Tavernier laughed heartily and took two glasses of champagne from a tray being proffered by a servant.

'To your health. You're irresistible.'

Léa dreamily twiddled the glass round between her fingers for a moment. Then she drained it in one gulp.

'Quick, give me another one.'

He gave it to her.

'Anybody who's anybody is here. The only one who's missing is Raphaël Mahl. Look who's over there.'

In the overwhelmingly luxurious drawing room full of valuable furniture, old masters, magnificent antique carpets on the floor and heavy silk hangings on the walls, an extraordinary mixture of people was gathered. Pretty, gaudily dressed over made-up women, sagging beneath the weight of their expensive jewellery, German officers, very dignified and stiff in their black or green uniforms, two or three handsome young men dressed in the style of the swinging jazz set who looked like either thugs or gigolos, prosperous looking businessmen, a few shady-looking men in dinner suits, with guns bulging in their inside pockets. Michel Szkolnikoff went from group to group talking volubly. He looked as though he had slept in his dinner suit, it was so crumpled. For the moment, he was chatting to a little man with dark hair that had been carefully plastered down with Brylcreem. They were both smoking fat cigars. The smaller man turned round and his gaze came to rest on Léa. She flinched.

'Who's that?' asked Tavernier.

'Masuy,' she breathed.

François's knuckles turned white.

But in a calm voice, he said:

'Ah! So that's him. We've never met. He looks more or less how I imagined him to be.'

'I'm frightened, he's coming over here.'

'Don't worry.'

'Dear Mademoiselle Delmas! What a surprise and pleasure it is to see you here! I thought you had left Paris? Have you seen our friend Mahl? You know he played a dirty trick on me?'

'No, I left very suddenly. I haven't seen him since.'

'I heard he was in the Bordeaux area. You're from those parts, unless I'm mistaken?'

'Yes . . .'

'When you see him, tell him I'm thinking of him. As for you, mademoiselle, if you need me, don't hesitate. You know my address. Unfortunately, if you have anything to sell, it will be difficult. As you are no doubt aware, the Purchasing Office has been closed down, well . . . almost . . .'

'Dinner is served, madame.'

This timely announcement spared Léa from having to introduce Tavernier.

The table sparkled with crystal glasses and silver cutlery. One delicacy succeeded another and the best vintage wines flowed freely. Most of the guests were not eating, they were bolting the food down. When the dessert was brought, the excitement reached fever pitch: a procession of waiters carried in baskets piled high with fruit, silver platters covered with the most varied arrays of pastries, ice-creams, sorbets and cream desserts to the applause of the company. Sitting in the place of honour, that is, next to Szkolnikoff's beloved poodle, Peggy, who, with a napkin tied round its neck, was partaking of all the dishes ceremoniously served by the head waiter, Léa was so bored that she forgot her fear. Every day, the animal dined at its master's table in the company of people who made a great fuss of her in order to please their extravagant host.

At first Léa was annoyed at the seating arrangement, but before long she was pleased to have Peggy for her neighbour: at least she did not have to make conversation with the dog. The same could not be said for the person seated on her right, a fashionable young man who could only talk about the cuts of suits, bars which were in vogue and the difficulties in obtaining English cigarettes.

François, who had been placed to the left of the hostess, did not take his eyes off Léa, giving monosyllabic replies to Hélène Szkolnikoff, who was not slow to notice.

'Well, my dear, I find you somewhat preoccupied. Has that little girl made you lose your head? She's not bad, but she has no class.'

Tavernier gave a furtive smile at that last comment.

'She's still very young.'

'Oh! She's not as young as all that,' she pouted and turned to her other neighbour, General Oberg.

The guests talked of nothing but buying and selling. It was a matter of who could offer the largest quantities of the widest variety of goods: copper, lead, corn, brandy, silks, gold, paintings, rare books . . . An industrialist from Brittany offered to supply a fifty thousand metre batch of worsted 'like they used to make it before the war', a Belgian was offering miles of tarpaulin . . . From Alsace, perfumes . . . A hosier from Troyes could provide his entire range of silk stockings 'as usual', a West Indian had two cartloads of gruyère cheese . . . Michel Szkolnikoff listed the hotels which he had acquired on

294

the Riviera: the Savoy, the Ruhl, and the Plazza in Nice, the Martinez, the Bristol and the Majestic in Cannes. He had lost count of the villas, companies and factories he had bought. He talked of his château d'Aisne at Azé in the Saône-et-Loire region which he had just finished lavishly fitting out. Of course his guests would all be welcome visitors.

Léa had hardly touched the food in spite of her greedy nature. She was becoming increasingly impatient for the meal to end and even her stylish neighbour noticed.

'I get the impression you're bored. If you like, I'll take you to a cabaret afterwards, something you've never seen the likes of before. All right?'

'No thank you, I've had enough for this evening.'

'Oh! I see! You're afraid that the people there will be like the people here. There's no danger of that, everybody's young. Anyone over twenty-three isn't allowed in. We listen to the latest American records.'

'I thought they were banned.'

'They are, but we manage. I supply the records and the cigarettes. At Szkolnikoff's I'm bound to meet someone who can supply the goods I need. What about you? What do you do? Whose bird are you?'

'Mine,' said a voice in his ear.

The boy jumped to his feet.

'I'm sorry, monsieur, I didn't know.'

'That's all right. Are you coming, sweetie-pie?'

Léa rose, red with fury.

'What's got into you, talking to me like that?'

'Why didn't you slap that nincompoop when he called you a bird?'

'I was so astonished that I didn't think of it.'

'It's my fault, I shouldn't have brought you to a place full of people like that. I'm sorry, it won't happen again.'

'I thought my presence was essential?'

'Not to the extent that you should have to put up with that sort of thing. I sometimes forget who they really are and only see them as products of the war.'

'But did my coming here turn out to be useful to you?'

'Yes, it reassures Szkolnikoff to see me with a pretty girl. It tallies with his idea of what I'm like. When you're "in business", a beautiful woman places a man . . . It's as simple as that.'

'Can we leave soon?'

'Yes, after coffee which is served in the drawing room; I'll say you have to be back before midnight.'

'Will they believe you?'

'I told them you were a young girl of good family who lived with her aunts, two highly respectable maiden ladies. They are flattered to associate with decent people.'

Shortly afterwards, they took their leave of their hosts.

'Don't forget, tomorrow morning at eleven o'clock,' said Hélène as she offered François her hand to kiss.

'Until tomorrow, my dear, and thank you for such a marvellous evening.'

'Are you seeing her tomorrow?' asked Léa as she got into the car.

'Yes, to buy you some jewellery.'

'But I don't want any jewellery.'

'After a while, they'll find it rather odd that a woman I love doesn't have any jewels.'

'I don't give a fig. Can you see me parading around like those old bags, covered in stones each one bigger than the last?'

'Don't exaggerate. A beautiful jewel has never done a pretty woman any harm.'

They were stopped by a patrol outside the houses of parliament. At the same time, the air-raid sirens went off. The officer glanced briefly at their passes and advised them to go to the nearest shelter. The Boulevard Saint-Germain, which had been deserted a few moments before, filled with dark shadows running towards the metro station which served as an air-raid shelter. Léa preferred to go back to her aunts' apartment. In the courtyard, they found the Montpleynet sisters, Camille and her little boy, Laure and Estelle in their dressing gowns. In the distance, the first bombs began to drop.

'They're over in the west,' said their third floor neighbour.

Half asleep, they sat on the ground, or on folding chairs,

waiting until the air-raid was over. Léa snuggled up to François and let him stroke her in the semi-darkness. The end of the air-raid interrupted her enjoyment.

Not for long. Albertine offered to put François up on the divan in the parlour and he gratefully accepted. When everybody was in bed, he joined Léa who threw herself into his arms with flattering eagerness. He responded as was appropriate.

The sun was already high in the sky when François went back to his divan and fell into a deep sleep.

That night, only twenty or so people were killed by the allies' bombs. On the 14th July, an air-raid in the suburbs of Paris killed over a hundred people. Jean-Hérold Paquis had a field day over the air.

Léa felt like a prisoner in the city, which was stifling in the summer heat. François Tavernier had been obliged to leave Paris again. She found his absences increasingly unbearable.

Two or three times a week, alone or with Camille, she took leaflets, underground newspapers or forged papers to addresses indicated by messengers who were constantly changing. To avoid being trailed, she soon became expert at melting into the crowd in department stores, disappearing among the throngs in the metro, using the underground to her advantage, getting into either the first or last compartment so as to be able to see at a glance if she was being followed, and if there was the slightest doubt, she would jump off at the last minute. But she preferred getting around by bicycle, in spite of the risk of being wolf-whistled by crude young men. One day, at the metro station Opéra, she was jostled by a young man behind whom the doors immediately closed. On the other side of the glass panel, two men were brandishing their fists. The train gathered speed and they disappeared from view. Inside the compartment, everybody acted as though nothing had happened. Léa looked at the boy and had to summon up all her strength to stop herself from crying out. Beside her, breathless, pale and trembling, reeking of sweat and fear, was Pierrot, her cousin Pierrot. The train was already pulling into the next station. That was where she had to get off. When the train stopped, she seized her cousin's hand and dragged him

297

off. Startled, he began to struggle and then recognized her.

'It's you!'

'Don't run. Give me your arm, we're going to the Galeries Lafayette. How long have they been following you?'

'I don't know. They already tried to get me at Châtelet.'

'You've already thrown them off twice! For someone who doesn't know the metro, that's not bad. How long have you been in Paris?'

'I arrived yesterday evening. I was trying to make my way to your aunts'.'

'I thought you were in a Jesuit seminary.'

'I was, but I ran away. I don't want to wait until the war ends without doing anything . . .'

'Careful, not so loud! Your father will be beside himself with rage.'

'I don't give a damn. He disgusts me, so does my brother, completely under the old man's thumb, the pair of them allowing the Nazis to trample all over them.'

'What do you intend to do?'

'I haven't the foggiest idea. As the seminary was near Paris, I thought of you. My father hinted that you had connections in the Resistance.'

'That's a bit of an exaggeration. You'd do better to talk to Uncle Adrien.'

'I thought of that, but nobody knows where he is, or if they do, they won't say.'

'What am I going to do with you? Wait, I've got an idea.'

By then, they had come out of the big store and were walking towards the metro station Havre-Caumartin. It was suffocatingly hot in the underground and it was a relief to get out at Etoile and walk down the Champs-Elysées.

'Luckily, you're decently dressed.'

'Papa insisted on buying me a new wardrobe.'

'Just as well. You'll make a good impression on Laure's friends.'

It was a fine summer's afternoon and both Parisians and Germans were sitting around enjoying the sunshine on the café terraces, pretending not to notice each other. Pierrot and Léa went into the Pam-Pam. In the basement of the bar, which had a live pianist, twenty or so dreamy-eyed young boys and girls were standing round the pianist tapping their hands and feet in time to the music. They patiently waited for the number to end. Léa approached the group.

'You! Here! That calls for celebration,' said a good-looking youth who did not look much more than a child, as he kissed her on the cheeks.

'Hello, Roger, how are you. Have you seen Laure?'

'What do you want?' asked a voice from the shadows where there was a seat nicknamed 'lovers' nook' by the young people.

Laure sat up, her face smeared with lipstick.

'Wipe your face,' said her sister, handing her a handkerchief.

'Thank you.'

'Look who's with me.'

'Pierrot!' she cried, rushing over to her cousin.

He stared with amazement, causing a great deal of mirth.

'Laure?'

'Yes, it's me all right.'

'I would never have recognized you,' said Pierrot kissing her.

Léa drew her sister aside and explained the situation.

'Uncle Luc must be furious,' she giggled.

'Are you quite clear about what you have to do: all of you are to come to the Rue de l'Université at about eight o'clock, making a commotion as usual. If they're watching the house, they won't pay any attention to you. I'm going home now to warn Aunt Albertine and make sure everything is all right. If anything's wrong, I'll open the parlour window wide and that'll mean that you must turn round and go away . . .'

'. . . and I'll go to Roger's place. Understood.'

All went well. Camille managed to obtain false papers in the name of Philippe Dorieux, a student from Libourne. Pierrot was to go to Poitiers and there he would be taken care of by a local network. An appointment was fixed outside the church of Notre-Dame-la-Grande on market day and the password was:

'Do you know the church of Sainte-Radegonde?' to which

Pierrot was to reply: 'No, but I know the church of Saint-Hilaire.'

It was the fourth time in a week that Paris had been wakened by air-raid sirens and the inhabitants had found themselves in their cellars or in the metro. Furious, Léa refused to leave her room, in spite of the repeated warnings on the wireless and in the newspapers. Every day, people were killed because they would not go down into the shelters.

The weather was very close; the storm which had been threatening all day had not broken. Léa stood at the window watching indifferently as the beams of light swept the sky trying to locate the planes whose dull throbbing could be heard above. Suddenly she felt a rush of hatred for the tall buildings which blocked out the sky, not because they prevented her from seeing the fireworks, but because they hemmed her in like the walls of a prison.

'I'm suffocating,' she murmured.

Then she pictured the wide open spaces around Montillac, the sea beyond the horizon, the vibrant silence of the nights, the powerful smell of the warm earth when large raindrops released all sorts of rich fragrances. Léa closed her eyes to savour the pleasure of these memories.

Three days later, she took the train to Bordeaux. A week later, she was joined by Camille and her son.

Chapter 21

It was very hot. Every day, in the coolness of the late afternoon, Camille and Léa would get on their bicycles, and, wearing huge protective straw hats, ride down to the river opposite Langon to bathe. Charles came with them feeling perfectly safe in his snug wicker basket behind his 'Aunt' Léa. Camille carried the tea hamper, a bottle of cool lemonade, the towels and books.

The two young women were both strong swimmers and loved racing each other to the other side of the river. Sometimes they made the game more complicated: they had to dive and pick up a pebble, stay under water as long as possible or swim where the current was strongest, around the pillars holding up the bridge. Léa always won when they raced and Camille could hold her breath for longest under water. Charles did doggy-paddle. Every day, he made a fuss at being dragged away from his games.

After their swim, they stretched out in the sun, exchanging few words, immersed in a feeling of well-being. It took the child's persistent cries to make them shake off their lethargy. Everything was so calm, apart from the seagulls' screeching, the swallows' cries and children's shouts which were sometimes drowned as a train rumbled over the nearby viaduct. It was a familiar, reassuring sound.

Since they had been back, they had tacitly avoided mentioning the Resistance and Pierrot's departure which the network had taken care of. Those long sunny days by the river were a welcome respite and both women wished it would go on for ever. There was good news from Laurent who had finally managed to join Colonel Leclerc and was following a demanding training programme in Sabratha. As for François, he had let them know that he would come down for a few days in September. Lucien had made it to Switzerland and said nothing of his dreadful injury. Adrien was going backwards and forwards between Toulouse and Bordeaux, helping wherever he was needed. Jean and Raoul Lefèvre were still imprisoned in Fort Hâ but their mother was allowed to visit them once a fortnight. Not once did they allow their morale to sink. They had not yet come across Mathias who, according to his parents, had become 'a somebody'. Léa was very apprehensive of meeting him. During her absence, Ruth, Sidonie and Bernadette had done a good job and made things difficult for Fayard who was back in charge. He was keener than ever to take over the estate. Ruth had told him that if he ever brought up the subject again, she would throw him out. It looked as if the grape harvest was going to be good and the war would soon be over.

Leaning on her elbows, Léa was absently watching a swimmer who had just dived in from the opposite bank. He swam a swift, graceful breast-stroke. He climbed out and stretched out on the grass not far from them. He lay there for a few moments, recovering his breath, and then he rolled over.

Suddenly, the sky clouded over and Léa was cold.

'Hello,' said Maurice Fiaux.

Camille shuddered. She looked up apprehensively.

'Hello,' they said flatly.

'What a lovely summer, isn't it? Do you often come to this spot? It's the first time I've been here this year. I've got so much work in Bordeaux, you've no idea . . . When did you return? I came to Montillac twice, but there was nobody there . . . the birds had flown . . .'

'We were in Paris, staying with my aunts.'

'I know,' he snapped.

Camille looked away.

'Didn't Laure come back with you?' he asked in a gentler voice.

'She preferred to stay in Paris. It's more fun for her. Laure never liked the country and she was bored at Montillac,' said Léa.

'I sympathize. Couldn't she have gone to Bordeaux and stayed with her uncle, Luc Delmas? A remarkable man who has many friends and contacts . . .'

'But he's rather strict and proper. He certainly would not have allowed her as much freedom as she has in Paris.'

'You know, Léa, things have been changing for quite a while, even in Bordeaux. It's become a town where you can have a good time. You ought to come and see for yourself. It would cheer up your friend Raphaël Mahl to see you.'

'Is he still here? Why does he need cheering up?'

'Oh, you know him . . . he's fallen in love with a little guttersnipe from Mériadec who's unfaithful to him, beats him and takes all his money. So he got into a bit of trouble . . .'

'What sort of trouble?'

'He went a bit too far with his shady deals. The police arrested him. Thanks to our connections, we were able to get him out, but the cops are keeping an eye on him. That wouldn't be so bad but he tried to swindle us.'

Léa could not help smiling. Good old Raphaël!

'You think that's funny? Well, it most definitely isn't. I don't give a damn, in his shoes I'd probably have done the same, I'd have given it a try, it was worth it, but that's not what my companions thought. They wanted to kill him. I had a hard job persuading them he could be useful to us and do us a few favours to save his skin.'

'But that's despicable!' cried Camille.

'What do you expect, madame, this is war. Mahl knows about the roles certain people play in the Resistance and the assistance they give terrorists and Jews. In the Terrible affair, he was very useful to us.'

'The Terrible affair?'

'Haven't you heard about it? Everyone's talking about it round here. The Gestapo pulled off a nice haul at La Réole. First, Captain Gaucher was arrested at the station carrying a transmitter in his suitcase, then, a few days later, Adois . . . does that name mean anything to you?'

'No.'

'It's the code name of a carpenter in La Réole . . .'

Léa dug her nails into the ground to stop herself from crying out. She forced herself to ask:

'What's the connection between Raphaël Mahl and a carpenter in La Réole? Our friend isn't interested in manual work!'

'No, but he's interested in freemasons.'

'I had no idea.'

'It was Beckman, assistant to Doctor Hans Luther who is chief of the Bordeaux Gestapo in charge of surveillance of the clergy and freemasons, who had the idea of using Mahl when he learned he was a member of a Paris lodge. He was thrown out before the war for embezzlement, but had kept in touch with some brothers. Hence his connections with the lodge in La Réole. That's how he found out about the activities of Jacques Terrible, the carpenter.'

'Did Raphaël denounce him?'

'It wasn't necessary, others had done so already.'

'Were any other people arrested?'

'Yes, but I don't remember their names. If you're interested, I can find out.'

'I was only asking out of curiosity.'

'Were they shot?' asked Camille.

'No, they can give us lots of useful information about the network, whose mission was to organize parachute drops, the acquisition of arms, false papers, the centralization of information, and the hiding of Jews and deserters from compulsory labour.'

'Where are they?'

'In the prison of Saint-Michel in Toulouse.'

The arrests had taken place two days earlier and it was only now they were hearing about it from the lips of that nasty little scoundrel. They looked away to hide their disgust.

The Langon clock struck seven.

'Good God! I'm going to be late. Goodbye, I'll drop in and see you one of these days.'

A few drops of water splashed them as he dived into the water. They did not move.

'Mummy . . . mummy . . . can I go for a swim like the man?'

304

Camille grabbed her little boy and hugged him tight. He protested:

'You're hurting me . . .'

She kissed his tanned cheeks.

'Yes, darling, you can go for a swim.'

Without consulting one another, neither Camille nor Léa left Montillac the day after their meeting with Maurice Fiaux. They stayed within the confines of the estate the following days as well. They were so stunned by what they had heard that they were unable to talk about it for a long time. They wore themselves out working in the kitchen garden: they had to harvest the potatoes, pick the beans and water and hoe the soil.

In the evenings, they came in exhausted, their hands ruined, but content from their physical exertions which gradually soothed their anxiety.

In the evening, after dinner, Léa would wander through the vineyards just as dusk made the countryside glow pink and gold. She loved this rich earth, where the hand of man was visible everywhere, with her heart and with her body. The peaceful harmony never ceased to thrill her. Since that wretched encounter, the spell had been broken. She wandered up and down the paths, looking for a spot that would calm this panic which surged through her tortured spirit in waves. But all her favourite haunts had lost their magic. Neither Verdelais nor the shack at la Gerbette, half buried in the ground, nor the Cross at Borde which overlooked the entire region, nor the church at Saint-Macaire with its seamen's Virgin could pacify her. She wore herself out by going for long cycle rides to places where nobody knew her, like Langoiran, Targon and on the other side of the river, Villandraut and Bazas. It made no difference. The voice of the Gestapo agent kept hammering away inside her head, his image blending with that of Mathias:

'In the Terrible affair, he was very useful to us . . . it's the name of a carpenter in La Réole . . .'

Although Maurice Fiaux implied that Raphaël Mahl had not denounced Jacques Terrible, Léa could not help thinking that he was not completely innocent as far as that arrest went, just as he had not been completely innocent where Sarah Mulstein was concerned. She could not control the chill fear she felt which brought her out in a sweat, made her feel sick and her legs go weak. Next time, he'd denounce her to the Gestapo. He knew or had guessed enough to have her sent into the dungeons of the Gestapo headquarters in the Rue du Médoc and the prison cells of Fort Hâ. Perhaps even before a firing squad. Léa could picture the guns taking aim . . . could hear herself pleading with the executioners.

That was the state she was in when François Tavernier found her. Even her tiredness after the grape harvest was not sufficient to dispel her terror.

Léa and François were standing with their arms entwined watching the sun rise over the golden countryside tinged with russet.

For the last five days, they had risen, happy and exhausted, to admire with the same incredulous elation the promise of happiness which the dawn brought. No more dreadful fear, the presence of a man and his caresses had banished her terror. In his arms, she could laugh about the Raphaël Mahls, the Maurice Fiauxs and the Gestapo. Léa derived renewed strength from physical pleasure.

The war had abolished all prejudice. Even Bernadette Bouchardeau was no longer surprised that Léa shared her room with a man who was not her husband. It was true that Léa's attitude did not leave her any choice. She made it quite clear that she would not tolerate any comment on the subject.

On such a beautiful autumn morning, Tavernier was putting off the moment when he would have to tell Léa that he would soon be going away again. He was worried about leaving her alone. He knew the Gestapo were on Father Adrien Delmas's trail. The priest had escaped his pursuers in Toulouse by the skin of his teeth. Sooner or later, Dohse would send his agents to arrest and interrogate her, as he did to the close relatives of those who were suspected of belonging to the Resistance. It had taken an extraordinary amount of luck and a network of subtle protection for that not to have already happened.

Besides, the presence of Camille d'Argilat, who had already been interrogated because of her husband's activities and the connection with Doctor Blanchard, would automatically make the head of the Gestapo in Bordeaux want to hear what she had to say.

The previous evening, he had given the two young women false identity papers which, he told them, they might find useful. He advised them to get in touch with Françoise at once saying he would contact her regularly. He insisted they kept away from the Resistance. They were probably already being watched. They had to be extremely cautious. He added that it might be a good idea if they were armed, as long as they had a safe hiding place . . .

That evening, he announced his departure.

Léa was too proud to tell François about the growing problems she was facing with the estate, or about Mathias's attitude or her conviction that to save Montillac, she would have no choice but to marry him. He interpreted her silence to mean that the money the solicitor had lent them and the money he himself had given to Ruth that spring was sufficient. So as not to hurt her, he had not brought up the subject again. They were going for a last walk, warmly dressed and sheltering under a huge umbrella. They wandered through the vineyards after dropping in to see Sidonie at Bellevue. As they made their way back to Montillac, they hastened their steps to get away from the gusts of wind and the cold drizzle that seemed to penetrate everywhere.

The house was crushed by heavy black clouds racing across the sky. They seemed so threatening that Léa's heart contracted. The bad weather had arrived early this year. There were all the signs that it would be a harsh, early winter.

A little red blob was bobbing about on the green lawn and then started moving towards them, gradually taking on the shape of a child running. It was Charles who had slipped away from his mother and was rushing towards them as fast as his little legs would carry him. He ran into Léa's arms laughing.

'You nearly knocked me over, you little monkey,' she exclaimed, twirling him round in the rain.

307

The laughs and shouts of the child sounded completely incongruous to François in that sinister setting, and at the same time seemed to say: look, life goes on. Yes, life had to go on. Today it was raining, but tomorrow . . . What a beautiful pair they made, even Léa was laughing like a child again!

It felt as though it had not stopped raining since François's departure. The weather was not cold but the entire country-side lay under a cloud of damp sticky mist which rotted the vines.

Léa was sitting at her father's desk, supposedly doing the accounts which were an ordeal for her. To take her mind off them, she was copying out the words of a song by Pierre Dac which had been broadcast from London on the evening of December 5th and which Mireille, the wife of Albert, the butcher in Saint-Macaire, had taken down in shorthand and then written out in longhand for her friend. When she had finished, Léa stood up and sang, to the tune of Lily Marlène:

> *I've heard this song so many times before*
> *That I decided I would like to go,*
> *One lonely evening, to the corner gate,*
> *And there to wait*
> *And learn the fate*
> *Of Lily Marlène,*
> *Of Lily Marlène.*

> *'Tell me, my pretty, where your thoughts have fled?*
> *Why do your eyes not shine as once they did?'*
> *'The sadness that's become my part*
> *Will tear apart*
> *My breaking heart,'*
> *Said Lily Marlène,*
> *Said Lily Marlène.*

> *'Do you no longer look with eager eyes*
> *To your lord and master and the glory of his prize?'*
> *'The victory that he promised all,*
> *I've waited for,*
> *Three years and more,'*

Said Lily Marlène,
Said Lily Marlène.

'Are you not proud that you still belong
To that noble Empire, a thousand years long?'
'I know that in the Fatherland,
From hill to strand,
No building stands,'
Said Lily Marlène,
Said Lily Marlène.

'Haven't you heard of Prussia's iron hand
Whose mighty power is felt in every land?'
'I know that on the Russian Steppes
The soil is red
With German dead,'
Said Lily Marlène,
Said Lily Marlène.

'But, come tomorrow, and you shall surely see
On the German cross the flag of victory.'
'I know that in my desperate soul
All hope has flown.
We stand alone,'
Said Lily Marlène,
Said Lily Marlène.

'Bravo!' said Camille applauding.

'I didn't hear you come in.'

'You were too absorbed in your song. You should go on the stage.'

'I'll think about it. What's new?'

'Nothing, it's still raining. Have you checked Fayard's accounts?'

'Yes, but there's either nothing wrong with them or I don't know what I'm doing.'

'Ask Monsieur Rabier.'

'Papa's accountant! But he's completely senile! Remember, last year, all the mistakes he made in the tax returns and the

309

time I wasted with the Langon tax inspector who didn't want to know.'

'Couldn't we hire a chartered accountant from Bordeaux for a while?'

'I haven't got any money! Look at this bundle of bills. I haven't got a cent to pay them with. The bank has already called twice this week.'

Overwhelmed, Léa sank down into the armchair behind the desk. Camille went over to her and stroked her hair.

'If only you knew how miserable it makes me not being able to help you.'

'Please, be quiet.'

The two young women were silent for a while.

'Have you thought about Christmas presents?' asked Léa looking up.

'Yes, but this Christmas will be the poorest one so far. Ruth found an old pedal car in the attic.'

'It's mine!' exclaimed Léa possessively.

Camille could not help laughing.

'Would you mind giving it to Charles?'

'Of course not,' she said, blushing slightly, and it was her turn to laugh.

'Ruth has bought some red paint so we can repaint it.'

There was a knock at the door. Albert, the butcher from Saint-Macaire, was standing there, breathless and dishevelled.

'What's the matter?' cried Camille and Léa in chorus.

He took some time to get his breath back and answer.

'Your son?' asked Camille.

He shook his head.

'What then? Tell us.'

'They've arrested Father Delmas.'

'Oh! My God!' said Camille leaning against the bookcase.

A great chill came over Léa.

'How did you find out?'

'Early this morning, a comrade of mine, a schoolteacher from La Réole, who belongs to the Buckmaster network, came to the shop to tell me and he asked me to let you know.'

'How did he know about it?'

'Through a gendarme in La Réole who had seen you with

310

Terrible. According to him, the Gestapo doesn't realize what a big fish they've caught. Your uncle was arrested by chance during a round-up in Bordeaux. He would probably have been released if he hadn't had blank identity cards on him. One of the gendarmes who arrested him told his colleague in La Réole. They're in the same network.'

'If one gendarme recognized him, then others might and denounce him.'

'He's greatly changed physically, but it is a risk. As soon as we find out where he is, we'll try and help him escape. Meanwhile, we'll have to pray that he doesn't talk. This evening we'll move the weapons hidden in the tobacco drying sheds in Barie and Belle-Assise; the Lafourcade brothers will come and give us a hand.'

'Can we help?'

'Yes, there are two English pilots who have to leave in two days' time. They're no longer safe near Viot. Can you hide them?'

'Will they be any safer here?' asked Camille. 'We have every reason to be wary of Fayard.'

'Madame Camille, that's a risk we'll have to take. They'll be brought here this evening via Bellevue. Meanwhile, I'll drop in for a drink with my old friend Fayard. How's that?'

'Fine, Albert. We'll put them in the little room by the study. Nobody ever goes in there, it's used as a storeroom. It's on the ground floor which is practical in case they have to leave in a hurry,' said Léa.

'Thank you. If you notice anything suspicious, call me at Saint-Macaire and say: "Your meat's tough today". I'll understand and we'll keep our Englishmen.'

'How will we know about Uncle Adrien?'

The butcher shrugged.

'Since the arrest of Grand-Clément in August, a lot of our people have been arrested. We've lost our informers in Mérignac and Fort Hâ. We must be very cautious with the new recruits. The only contact we have at the moment is the gendarme in Bordeaux. As soon as he finds something out, he calls La Réole.'

'Supposing I went to Bordeaux?' said Léa.

311

'Absolutely out of the question! It's bad enough having one person in the family arrested.'

'Perhaps Luc Delmas could intervene,' said Camille.

'He's a collaborator, he won't do anything for his brother. Remember what he told me: Adrien is dead as far as he is concerned.'

Chapter 22

'You see, we're being very generous . . . take your choice: common law criminals or political criminals . . . by that I mean communists, saboteurs and other terrorists.'

'I thought they were all mixed up together without distinction.'

'They were at first, because we realized that the little pimps from the port and the little black market dealers could be useful to us. But to stop them being contaminated by the reds and the Gaullists – that was Poinsot's idea – we keep a few of them separate and we inject them into the political prisoners' cells when we need some information. It's incredible the things that are said at night in a cell where six or seven men are locked up together . . . you have no idea . . .'

'I have a very good idea. None of that's particularly attractive. Haven't you got anything else for me?'

'We've got a convoy of Jews for Germany soon . . . if you want to join them, you should feel at home, among fellow Jews . . .'

'I'm not sold on that either, I don't like one way trips.'

'Come on, make up your mind.'

'Couldn't I have a private cell?'

'And what next! With fitted carpet, telephone and bathroom?'

'Oh! Yes, I'd love that.'

'Stop taking the mickey out of us. The boss is too kind . . . If it were up to me, I'd put a bullet through your brain . . . or your arse . . . a pervert like you would probably enjoy that . . .'

'My taste in large-bores doesn't go that far.'

A heavy right hook sent Raphaël Mahl reeling against the metal filing cabinets in the office where his old friends had been interrogating him since the morning. His lips were reduced to a pulp. The most relentless was Maurice Fiaux who punched as if he were settling a personal score. Oddly, Raphaël, who knew he was a coward, had borne this beating with amusement. And yet, his little Gestapo friends hadn't exactly handled him with kid gloves. Only Mathias Fayard had not taken part in this session. He was strange . . . For a while now, the handsome Mathias had been moody and bad-tempered. He kept finding good excuses for not joining in the arrests, and, in particular, the interrogations. Raphaël Mahl picked himself up with difficulty. This was no time to start worrying about the state of mind of Léa's childhood companion. Léa . . . it was partly because of her that he was getting beaten up.

'I think I prefer the common law criminals,' he said before losing consciousness.

The jolting of the car brought him round. A German soldier was driving and there was an officer at his side. In the back, he had Maurice Fiaux on one side and another soldier on the other. Just opposite the imposing Fort Hâ, the bookstall where he had been rummaging only the previous evening was just closing.

He was handed over to German guards. Maurice Fiaux left without so much as a glance over his shoulder. He was taken to the first floor to complete the prison formalities. In the room he was shown into, there was a barrier separating the new arrival from the officials whose job it was to do the paperwork. Notices in French, Spanish and German instructed the prisoner to take a seat opposite the wall and not to speak. Behind this enclosure, there were three huge tables and some cupboards by way of furniture.

From a neighbouring room came the clatter of typewriters. This monotonous sound aroused a great feeling of boredom in Raphaël Mahl. He had always hated the atmosphere of offices. He always avoided the office at Gallimard, his publisher's. 'Bureaucracy is pursuing me,' he thought. Behind the railing, military clerks were applying themselves to tracing Gothic lettering. Raphaël, who, in spite of the orders on the notice, was looking round, shuddered as he recalled the handwriting lessons in the Catholic school he had attended and the raps of the ruler that rained down on his knuckles. He had never been able to write his name and the title of the piece of homework in tidy round letters as his teachers demanded.

A clerk stood up and sleepily asked for his papers. He appeared not to notice the state of Raphaël's face.

'Have you got any money on you, monsieur?'

His guard, who had not left his side, pushed him towards the barrier. Raphaël nodded.

'You must hand it over to me, together with any jewellery, your watch and your tie. It will all be given back to you when you leave, monsieur.'

He carefully wrote the new prisoner's name on a form, counted the money in his wallet and noted the total.

'A gold watch with a gold strap. A gold signet ring with a diamond . . .'

'Put down: a *big* diamond.'

'. . . with a big diamond . . . a gold identity bracelet, a gold medallion and chain . . .'

Raphaël felt a pang as he removed the medallion. It was from his christening, and, funnily enough, he was very attached to it. He liked to remember certain scenes from his childhood when he was pampered by a slightly mad, doting grandmother and a somewhat wayward uncle who was full of charm.

'Tie.'

He had difficulty undoing the knot which was stiff with blood.

The clerk put everything into a large paper bag and handed him the signed form.

The door opened and three men who were in an even worse state than he was were roughly pushed into the room. One of them, with hands that were beaten to a pulp and eyes so swollen from blows that he could not see, was groping his way forwards.

'*Wir bringen Ihnen Terroristen. Sie haben das Auto eines Offi-*

*ziers gesprengt. Einer von den beiden muss wohl Engländer sein
. . . alles, was er beim Verhör sagte, war: "Piss off filthy huns, go
and get fucked."*[1]

Raphaël could not help smiling.

'*. . . dem Leutnant, der englisch versteht, hat dies absolut nicht
gefallen, und er hat ihn daraufhin selbst verhört.*'[2]

'*Hat er geantwortet?*'[3]

'*Nein, wenn er nicht schrie, machte er schlechte Witze.*'[4]

This Englishman sounded more and more likeable to Mahl.
He looked as though he was quite a handsome boy normally, in
spite of his closed eyes, his swollen face and lips.

'*Hat er Papiere?*'[5]

'*Nein. Alles, was er bei sich hatte, ist das.*'[6]

The German sergeant threw a photograph of a very pretty
young woman on to the floor. Raphaël heaved a deep sigh.
'Another heterosexual!' he thought, looking away.

The Englishman and one of the prisoners could not have
been much older than twenty. The other was a lot older. Salt
and pepper hair and a moustache matted with blood, deep
wrinkles on his forehead and sagging cheeks. If it were not for
the look in his eyes, one would have mistaken him for a local
farmer. One of his eyes was shut.

'They must have received orders to make us all one-eyed or
blind,' thought Raphaël.

'*Los, kommen Sie . . . beeilen Sie sich, es ist zu Ende.*'[7]

The guard, who had not left them for a second, pushed them
towards the door.

'Your name, monsieur?' the clerk asked the old man.

'Alain Dardenne.'

---

[1] We've brought you some terrorists. They blew up an officer's car. One of
them must be English. When he was interrogated, all he would say was: 'Piss
off filthy huns, go and get fucked.'

[2] The lieutenant, who understands English, didn't like that and insisted on
interrogating himself.

[3] Did he reply?

[4] No, when he wasn't shouting, he was laughing.

[5] Does he have any identity on him?

[6] No, this is all he had on him.

[7] Come along, hurry up . . . it's over.

Raphaël Mahl started. That voice reminded him of someone. The German soldier placed his hand on his shoulder.

'*Vorwärts.*'[1]

He was led into a neighbouring room, similar to the other, where he was asked if he was a communist, freemason, member of the Resistance or a Gaullist. To all these questions, he answered no. Was he Jewish? Yes, half Jewish. Through his mother? No, through his father. Apparently satisfied with his replies, the clerk, who looked so similar to the other one that it was amusing, handed back his completed form and said, in his dreadful accent:

'Goodbye, monsieur.'

Raphaël Mahl's guard hustled him down a spiral staircase with uneven steps. Still being pushed, until he was almost running, he crossed the guards' room and went down a narrow passage with a high ceiling. Twelve doors led off the corridor. These were the 'reception' cells. The guard opened door number 5 and kicked the prisoner into the cell with unnecessary brutality . . .

Mahl stood in the middle of the floor for a long time with his head down. When he looked up, he looked around him and burst out laughing. This soon turned into a howl of pain: he had forgotten his swollen jaw and his torn lips.

The narrowness of the room – it was about four feet across – made it seem very high. The height of the ceiling must have been just under nine feet. There were two wooden bunk beds, with filthy straw mattresses smelling of mould and vomit.

Raphaël lay down on the bottom bunk, rolled himself up in the smelly blanket and fell asleep thinking: 'So, they've managed to arrest him . . .'

For two days, the only sustenance Raphaël received was the rusty tasting water from the pitcher. 'At this rate, I'll soon get my figure back,' he thought.

On the third day, they came to fetch him at six o'clock in the morning.

'Out you get.'

[1] Move along.

The guard led him into a sort of guardroom where he had to strip naked. They emptied his pockets in front of him and then they handed back his shoes and clothes and ordered him to get dressed. Nothing . . . he had nothing left . . . neither his papers, nor any money, not a notebook nor even the tiniest pencil stub. He was given a torn blanket, one bowl for washing in and another for food, a dented beaker and a tin spoon, not forgetting the receipt for his confiscated belongings and a little card bearing his reference number, that of his cell and his profession. Now, he was number 9793.

Followed by his guard, Raphaël Mahl, carrying his meagre possessions, came into a vast oval hall. The first thing he noticed was an enormous stove sitting in the middle of it with the stovepipe going out of the glass fanlight. There were three floors of cells going all the way round the hall. They were about two yards apart and had heavy metal doors, each with a big black number and a small board on which the numbers of the prisoners inside were written on different coloured cards: red, green and yellow. They all had a wire-meshed spy-hole.

'Stop.'

The guard had come to a halt outside number 85. Another guard opened the door with an impressive looking key. It was fairly dark inside. On either side of the cell, men were standing to attention. There were six of them, Raphaël was to be the seventh. As soon as the door was shut, they rushed up to him.

'You poor thing, they've certainly made a mess of your face, the bastards . . .'

'I'm Loïc Kéradec, I'm from Brittany . . . from Pont-Aven . . . I'm a sailor. What about you?'

'I'm Spanish, my name's Fernando Rodriguez.'

'And I'm Dédé Desmotte from Bordeaux.'

'Georges Rigal, I'm from Bordeaux as well, I'm a student.'

'And I'm Marcel Rigaux . . . I'm a dock labourer down at the port.'

'I'm Doctor Lemaître, the G.P. at Libourne. Let me examine you. It doesn't look too serious.'

Everyone except the doctor, who must have been in his forties, was young, very young.

'Raphaël Mahl, novelist and journalist, from Paris.'

'What a treat, chaps, a writer . . . he can tell us stories,' said Dédé with a guttural accent.

'Delighted to meet you. Here, put down your belongings,' said the doctor, showing him a little recess near the door.

It turned out to be the toilet with the beakers, spoons, soap, toothpaste and a large tin of insecticide arranged on a shelf over the cracked washbasin.

Raphaël put his mug and spoon next to the others. He had no toothbrush or toothpaste.

The prisoners had sat down again on the two beds, idle, bored and silent. They moved up to make room for him. Mahl looked around him. The cell, whose vaulted ceiling was about eight feet from the uneven floor, must have measured about twelve feet by six. Eight square yards for seven people. At the back of the cell, there was a fanlight protected by bars and it had the same hood and wire mesh over it as the windows in the 'reception' cell.

'Are there only two beds?'

'Yes,' replied Rigaux, 'at night, we push them together and put the mattresses on the floor . . . it's already a squash with six of us . . . we'll squeeze up a bit closer.'

Raphaël smiled at him gratefully.

'So, tell us, what's the latest news?' asked young Loïc.

'What news?'

'From outside! Fathead!' said Dédé Desmotte.

'I'm sorry . . . I'm not used to this. What do you want to know?'

'Well . . . the war . . . what's happening?'

'Things aren't going too well for the Germans . . .'

'We already knew that,' said the Spaniard.

'Let him carry on.'

'Ciano, Mussolini's son-in-law, has been executed.'

'Hurray!'

'De Gaulle and Churchill met in Marrakesh . . .'

'Hurray!'

'The allies have landed at Anzio . . .'

'Hurray!'

'Berlin has been bombed more than a hundred times.'

'Hurray!'

'Members of the French Resistance were axed to death in Cologne.'

A heavy silence greeted this information.

'Do you mind if we tell the others?'

Raphaël stared at them in amazement.

'We have our own radio too, you know. We call it "Bar-Radio".'

'And how does it work?'

'You'll see tonight after lights-out. We take it in turns to stand by the open window and listen. Those on the ground floor call those on the first floor who call those on the second who call those on the third. The sound reverberates very well in the quadrangle. We get news, which isn't always very precise, from the new arrivals, from the rare visitors we're allowed and from comrades who go outside for interrogation. Then we have a concert.'

'Concert?'

'Yes, we've even got professional singers. It's better than the wireless. There are Portuguese, Spanish, Polish, Czech and British singers, and even a Russian.'

'And the Germans allow it?'

'You know, they're as bored as we are and they find the music entertaining. One day, through a crack in the door, I even saw the N.C.O. on duty crying as he listened to a Portuguese song. We stop when the sentry starts kicking the doors.'

'Are there many of them at night?'

'No, three sentries, one on each floor, who do the rounds all night, and an N.C.O. who sits at his desk opposite our cell.'

'You mentioned visitors . . . is everybody allowed visitors?'

'In theory yes, ten minutes, once a month on a Thursday. Have you already been sentenced?' asked the doctor.

'No.'

'Then you're not entitled to have visitors. Only those who have been sentenced are allowed to, not those who have just been charged.'

'And what about mail?'

'It's censored of course. We can receive letters but we can rarely send any out. I haven't been able to get word to my wife, for example, she doesn't know if I'm dead or alive.'

320

'Aufstehen! Aufstehen!'[1]

The night sentry's order was accompanied by a violent kick on the door. As he went past, he pressed the switch outside each cell. The light, set in the ceiling, gave out a wan glimmer and the men began to stir, groaning.

Raphaël sat up, shivering, his sparse hair tousled.

'What's going on?'

'It's time to get up. Hurry up, the light doesn't stay on for long.'

'Why,' asked Raphaël, scratching himself.

'For the hell of it, to get up our noses. Come on, get a move on.'

Mahl rose with aching limbs, groaning. The straw pallet on the floor was not very thick.

'Out of the way so we can put the beds back.'

He was shooed into a corner with the others while Loïc and Dédé pushed the beds back against the walls and flung the mattresses on top neatly covered with the blankets. They piled overcoats, jackets and blankets brought by their families in a corner and covered them with an old floral bedspread. The floral material looked rather incongruous in this setting.

In the corridor, they could hear the 'coffee' being wheeled round. Loïc, whose turn it was to be orderly that day, placed two bowls in the doorway. They all stood to attention as they heard the N.C.O. draw back the three bolts and turn the key in the lock. The German glanced round swiftly to check that everyone was there while the sentry pointed his gun at them. Reassured, he stepped back and made room for a gigantic cauldron dragged by two prisoners. One of them dipped a ladle into the mixture and poured the contents into one of the bowls. His companion put a loaf of bread which had already been divided up into portions in the other. As soon as the door was shut, they held out their beakers to Loïc who filled them up. As usual, there was some left over. The orderly shared out the bread; about five ounces each. It was the day's ration. Raphaël's cell-mates crumbled a little bread into the brew before eagerly drinking it. Its only merit was that it was hot. It tasted and smelled revolting.

[1] Get up! Get up!

'At first, it takes a bit of getting used to . . . but you'll see . . . you'll get accustomed to it,' said the doctor to Raphaël Mahl who could not swallow it despite the hunger pangs in his stomach.

'No doubt I'll get used to it. I'll have to. But today, I can't . . . If any of you want mine . . .'

'Give it to Loïc, he's the youngest and he's always hungry,' said Doctor Lemaître.

'He always gets the leftovers, it's not fair,' cried Dédé.

'Stop yelling, we'll share it,' said Loïc.

Raphaël Mahl had never imagined that prison life would be so hard. And yet he had landed in what the prisoners called a 'good' cell. He could no longer stand the overcrowding, the vermin, the cold, the quarrels that broke out at the slightest provocation and the vile turnip soup. But the worst thing was not being able to read or write. He grew furious and was increasingly bad-tempered and irritable. If he could only converse with his cell-mates, but since the departure of the doctor and the student, who had been sent to Germany, apparently, three days after his arrival and been replaced by two young communist workers, the level of conversation had dropped considerably. He was astonished by these people's naïvety. Most of them had the most unrealistic view of the war. After a fortnight, he asked to speak to the director of the prison who agreed, much to everyone's surprise, to see him.

After being taken for a shower and a shave, he was shown into the director's office. Maurice Fiaux and one of his friends were there.

'I'll do anything you want but get me out of here.'

'Is monsieur not satisfied with the service? Isn't it comfortable enough?'

'No, I'm very disappointed, I shall complain to the manager.'

'Complain away, we're here to listen, aren't we, Raymond?'

'Yes, of course.'

'You know the little pansies in Quinconces are missing you a lot. One of them was asking me only yesterday . . .'

'Stop messing me around. Are you going to let me out of here or not?'

'It's not only up to me. The director must have his say too, isn't that so, monsieur?'

'Naturally. No doubt Monsieur Mahl has heard a lot of interesting things during his stay here.'

'Do tell us, I bet it's ever so exciting.'

'All right, but first promise you'll get me out of here before you use the information I give you.'

Maurice Fiaux nodded to the director.

'You have my word, Monsieur Mahl. We're listening.'

During the two weeks he had been there, Raphaël Mahl had gleaned a certain amount of information about other prisoners, in particular about members of the Resistance and English pilots whom the German authorities had been unable to identify. He coldly gave the names under which they were registered in the prison.

'You wouldn't have come across your friend the beautiful Léa Delmas's uncle by any chance, would you?'

'I only caught a glimpse of him once, and that was before the war, in Paris when he was preaching in Notre-Dame. I was a long way from the pulpit and he must have changed since then.'

'Pity . . . there's a big reward for whoever enables us to arrest him.'

'Yes, that is a pity.'

The director rubbed his hands together with satisfaction.

'Good work, Monsieur Mahl, I'm sorry you're leaving us. We could have done a fine job together.'

Raphaël said goodbye and rose. Fiaux showed him to the door and put his hand on the knob.

'All things considered, our friend isn't leaving us straight away . . .'

'What? But you promised me . . .'

Raphaël tried to push his way past. Maurice Fiaux thrust him roughly into the middle of the room.

'I didn't promise you anything. It was the director who made that promise . . .'

'You agreed! You nodded to him . . . I saw you.'

'Your eyes deceived you.'

Raphaël leapt at Maurice Fiaux, grabbing him by the throat and trying to strangle him.

'Bastard!'

The fellow called Raymond took out his revolver and hit Raphaël with the butt, knocking him out. Raphaël's large frame which was now much thinner lay on the floor where they rained blows on him.

'That's enough,' said Fiaux breathless. 'Let's not rough him up too much, the boss needs him.'

They sat smoking and chatting with the director, patiently waiting until the prisoner came round.

After about ten minutes, he sat up and rubbed the back of his head. Something warm and wet was running down between his fingers. He looked at his hand in horror.

'Raymond got a bit carried away, but it was the only way to make you let go. You nearly strangled me, you bastard . . . you didn't even wait to hear my suggestion.'

'Get stuffed!'

'Would you mind your manners? Stop trying to be clever. Either you do as I say or you'll end up in the depths of Poland . . . unless . . . I spread the rumour that it was you who denounced the pilots . . .'

'You wouldn't dare?'

'What's there to stop me? . . . with a bugger who tried to strangle me!'

Raphaël Mahl painfully rose and collapsed on a chair.

'What do you want me to do?'

'About time too! That's how I like you, docile and under-standing. Give him a cigarette . . . Good . . . Now, listen. Dohse thinks we could have caught a big shot in the Resistance, someone like Father Delmas, by accident. Both the Toulouse and the Bordeaux Gestapo would give anything to get their hands on him. This is what I suggest, you go back to your cell . . .'

'No! Please . . .'

'Wait. As I was saying, you go back to your cell for three or four days. We let all the prisoners out in turn for their walk. You and your cell mates will be on all the walks.'

'They'll wonder why.'

'We don't give a damn . . . the important thing is that you study each prisoner carefully. Here are the photos of the people we're interested in.'

Maurice Fiaux placed twenty or so portraits on the director's desk. Some were clearer than others and some were more recent. Raphaël Mahl recognized two faces including Loïc Kéradec's. He said nothing. The last photograph was that of Adrien Delmas, clean shaven and wearing the long robes of the Dominican order. 'How he has changed,' thought Raphaël.

'Look at them carefully. The boss is certain that some of them are here. What better hiding place than a prison, don't you think?'

Mahl did not reply but pretended to be absorbed in the photographs.

'Will you recognize them?'

'If they're here there'll be no difficulty.'

'I knew we could rely on you.'

'What about me, can I rely on you? How do I know that afterwards you won't leave me to rot here?'

'I understand. You'll only tell us once we let you out.'

'That would suit me. Where will you take me afterwards?'

'First we'd take you to Mérignac where you'd be allowed to have visitors, receive letters, parcels and all the books you could wish for. Then, it's up to you. Either you carry on working for us or you go and work in Germany as a volunteer.'

'Is it essential for me to stay at Mérignac?'

'Yes, because it's logical. Let me explain: we haven't got enough evidence against you to keep you at Fort Hâ, but as we can't really trust you, we're keeping you under observation at Mérignac. That's something your cell-mates and the others will be able to grasp. If they find out you're a grass, your life won't be worth much. Do you understand?'

Raphaël shrugged without replying.

'We'll come back and get you in four days' time. The director will sign your release.'

'Can I be taken to the infirmary?'

'Most certainly not! Those bruises are your best protection.'

The guard gave him such a violent push that he landed in a heap at the feet of his cell-mates who were standing to attention. When the door was closed, they crowded round him.

'The bastards! They've made a right mess of you.'

With the help of a wet towel, Loïc cleaned his face and the wound on his head.

'He should be sent to the infirmary. Fernando, call the guard.'

'There's no point, they wouldn't let me . . .'

'The bastards!'

'It's a pity the doc's not here any more.'

'You said it! Give me one of your clean towels.'

Loïc made a sort of turban compressing the wound and laid Raphaël on one of the beds.

'Thank you,' he said before falling into a comatose sleep.

The banging on the door announcing the soup roused him from his lethargy. A dreadful migraine prevented him rising from the filthy straw pallet.

'Get up!' yelled the N.C.O. 'You are forbidden to lie down during the day.'

Raphaël tried to obey and managed to sit up. The room swam.

'It's perfectly obvious that he's ill.'

'Him not ill . . . him lazy . . . get up!'

With an effort he would not have believed himself capable of, he stood up.

'You see . . . you not ill.'

As soon as the door had shut, the wounded Raphaël lost consciousness.

The following day, Raphaël Mahl was feeling a little better. He was taken to the infirmary where they bandaged his head. 'Like this, I probably resemble Apollinaire,' he thought as he made his way back to his cell. That afternoon, the whole of his floor went outside for a walk.

It was a fine but cold day. The prisoners jumped and squealed like children, anyone would have thought they were in a school playground. It was so rare that they were allowed out for a walk. After a few shouted orders from the guards, they became relatively quiet. They went back inside after ten minutes. Raphaël had not recognized anybody.

The following day, early in the afternoon, they heard shouting in the corridor:

'Smock . . . smock . . .'

That meant that all the prisoners who did not have red or yellow labels were to be allowed into the hall and out into the quadrangle in single file for a smoke. They stood in a semicircle, hands outstretched, while an N.C.O. threw them each a cigarette donated by the Red Cross. Then one prisoner was given a light which he passed on. That was when messages and news were exchanged.

Leaning against the wall, Raphaël Mahl dragged on his cigarette with delight. The bitter smoke of dark tobacco made his eyes smart but, funnily enough, soothed his headache. Savouring this brief moment of respite, he felt himself become light-hearted.

He saw him the minute he came into the quadrangle. 'That's strange,' he thought, 'I'd have thought they'd have given him a red label.'

Like Mahl, the old farmer was smoking a little apart from the others. His furrowed face was back to normal again and he did not seem to be suffering any after effects from his injuries. Raphaël went up to him. Their eyes met.

'Finished . . . finished . . .' yelled the N.C.O.

The smokers took one last drag, threw their butts into a beaker of water and lined up obediently. The smoking session had lasted six minutes. Mahl stood aside to let the bogus farmer pass.

'After you, father,' he whispered.

The other could not suppress a shudder.

And so, what he feared most had happened: he had been recognized. When he had seen Raphaël Mahl in the 'reception' office, Adrien Delmas had expected the worst. As nothing had happened, he said to himself that the writer had not realized who he was. That was not so . . . He did not understand, why hadn't he denounced him when he had

327

denounced so many others, in Paris as well as in Bordeaux? Like those two communist members of the Resistance and those two English pilots who had been dragged from their cells and taken to 197 Rue du Médoc to be interrogated by Dohse and his henchmen. Why had he made it obvious that he knew who he was? Was he being friendly? Was it to warn him he was in danger? Or simply to make him give himself away? This last explanation seemed the most plausible. During the smoking session, he had received a message telling him that he was going to be transferred to Mérignac and that his escape would be organized from there. Father Delmas did not get a wink of sleep all night.

Raphaël Mahl did not sleep either. In addition to his headache, he was being eaten alive by fleas and lice and had scratched himself until he bled. In spite of that, he was in good spirits: he was going to be released soon. So, there was the camp at Mérignac for a while but that did not worry him too much, he knew the place and he knew the director, he'd manage.

Loïc groaned in his sleep.

Raphaël was sorry for the kid, all the more so because he had always been kind to him, even affectionate. But he had no choice. Besides, he was convinced that it was no accident that the young sailor's photograph had been slipped in among the others.

Two days later, they came to fetch him. That very evening, Loïc Kéradec was taken to Le Bouscat on the Rue du Médoc. As the others had been surprised at such a poor catch, Raphaël Mahl told them he had given them all the names that were likely to interest them the first time. Apart from the Breton, he had not recognized any of the others. He did not say a word about Father Delmas.

At Mérignac, Rousseau, the director, made him work as a clerk. He had to register all the arrivals and departures. The French gendarme whose duty this was had more work than he could cope with. As a special favour, he was allowed to stay there until the evening.

The reception hut was one of the only parts of the camp that was more or less adequately heated. When Raphaël Mahl's work was over, he would drag a chair into the corner which was furthest away from the noisy, talkative gendarmes and would bury himself in one of the books Maurice Fiaux had given him. By some extraordinary coincidence, the little swine had managed to get hold of some of his favourite authors: Pepys's *Diary*, which had always been one of his bedside books. What a joy to have it beside him again! Dear old Stendhal was there with *Lucien Leuwen*, and Balzac, with *Lost Illusions*, and there was Rousseau's *Confessions*; and old Victor Hugo's *The Sea Workers* and *Ninety-three*. It only needed Chateaubriand and his happiness would be complete. But he was ever present in Raphaël's heart and mind! He was anxiously looking forward to receiving the pocket atlas and Bible he had requested from Fiaux, as well as a notebook to draft a novel which was beginning to take shape. As soon as he was out of there, he would do portraits, in the style of La Bruyère. He could picture himself classifying them according to their type: society people, followers of fashion, actors, writers, politicians, businessmen, and why not criminals, the police, pleasure seekers and the clergy. It was a good idea; as soon as he had a notebook, he would be able to develop it. To be a great writer! Recognized and loved by everybody! He could picture himself receiving the Nobel prize for literature, a member of the French Academy, looking elegant and distinguished in his robes. He would ask Jean Cocteau to design the handle and sheath of his sword: it would be an opportunity to make up his quarrel with dear old Jeannot. No more night clubs, alcohol and loose young boys.

His love life was extremely strange. Nobody could ever resist him, he had never been rejected, but they did not fall in love with him or love him. Whenever he wanted somebody, he was always able to charm the object of his desires into bed with him. He stole kisses and took bodies, he sometimes provoked sighs of pleasure, but he had never heard the childlike, naïve song of blind love. He fascinated people, but he was not loved. When he left, the spell was broken. Someone he had loved passionately had left him after sleeping with him for six months saying dreamily: 'Deep down, you're irreplaceable.'

It was the greatest compliment he had ever received. All that was over and done with now, he was going to devote himself to his book. As soon as he got out, he would find a beautiful, peaceful spot that was conducive to creativity. He immediately thought of Montillac . . . He pictured himself walking through the vineyards deep in thought, or sitting on the terrace . . . why not write to Léa? The dear girl was generous enough not to refuse him hospitality. Anyway, he certainly deserved it. One word from him and her beloved uncle and Resistance fighter would be arrested . . . Raphaël did not really understand why he had not denounced that man, after all, he did not know him. In fact, it was the others' fault . . . he hadn't liked Maurice Fiaux and his little friends' methods at all . . . let them manage without him. He was holding a trump card that he intended to play when the right moment came. He knew certain details of the priest's activities which Superintendent Poinsot and the Gestapo were not aware of. He'd see when the time came. Meanwhile, he'd write to Léa to ask her for books and food and to come and visit him if she could.

His reverie was interrupted by the arrival of some new prisoners. He rose to fetch the register. The gendarme on duty handed him the prisoners' identity cards one at a time. Pierre Moreau, from Langon . . . Jacques Lagarde, from Bordeaux . . . Alain Dardenne, from Dax . . . Raphaël Mahl looked up. The two men's eyes met. Neither batted an eyelid.

'Next.'

Raphaël carried on with his work.

A few days later, Maurice Fiaux came to visit him with the Bible and atlas he had requested.

'Here, I've brought you a pipe and some tobacco. Cigarettes are hard to come by at the moment.'

'Thank you.'

'How's it going?'

'Not too bad. I'm beginning to get a little weary of rubbing shoulders with the riff-raff: they have all our vices and none of our virtues.'

'You forget that my mother was a cleaning woman.'

'Maybe, but it was her boss who brought you up. You have

expensive taste and you're damned right. The French people disgust me, their lack of curiosity, their stupidity and their demanding nature flourish here like certain flowers which thrive on dung heaps. The people are attributed those virtues which we lack. That is absurd, they possess neither those virtues nor our qualities. On the other hand, they have practically all our vices. Believe me, there's little difference between a farm-hand and the calf he looks after.'

'Well said. Have you come across anything of interest since you've been here?'

'Not much that you don't know already. There's a lot of smuggling, illicit parcels and letters arrive every day thanks to the cooperation of the gendarmes. Certain prisoners even leave the camp for a few hours during the day to go and see their wives or girlfriends.'

'We know all that . . . you haven't discovered any contacts with Resistance networks or whether there are any members actually here?'

'It's a big camp. I haven't had a chance to go into all the huts yet. To make it easier for me, you should bring me more books. I'll rent them out and that will give me a better reason to go round all the barracks.'

'That's not a bad idea . . . I'll see if Poinsot agrees, and if he does, I'll send you a box of books every week.'

'Nothing too difficult, the level of intelligence isn't exactly high. While you're about it, send a couple of woollen sweaters and a pair of decent shoes, I'm freezing to death. Some sausage, biscuits and brandy wouldn't go amiss either.'

'Ha! You'll have to earn all that. For each piece of information you give us, you'll get a little treat or a woolly. That's only fair, isn't it?'

'All right, all right, you're such a stingy lot.'

'We're not stingy, just cautious. Keep your eyes and ears open, there are rumours going round the cafés and the salons in Bordeaux that we've picked up a big shot in the Resistance . . .'

'Who?'

'Who knows? We've put all sorts of squealers all over the place but none of them has come back with the right information.'

331

'Would it be a clergyman?'

'The boss doesn't know, but he doesn't think so. If it were someone well known like Father Delmas, someone would've denounced him long ago.'

'There's no doubt about that.'

'Well, this won't do, we're sitting here chatting and chatting. Meanwhile, the work's piling up. Cheerio, see you soon. Ah! I forgot: I don't know what's the matter with me at the moment, I keep forgetting things . . . exhaustion no doubt . . . You know the sailor who was in your cell?'

'Loïc?'

'Yes . . . poor thing, he didn't survive the interrogation . . . a weak nature . . . after three days the little fool died without talking, mind you, if you want my opinion, I don't think he had much to say . . . You can't imagine the row they kicked up at Fort Hâ! They yelled the place down. They made such a racket that the director had to call in reinforcements. The ringleaders were put in the cooler, there weren't enough cells. Just think, if they knew it was you who turned him in . . . I wouldn't like to be in your shoes.'

Raphaël Mahl did not move a muscle while Maurice Fiaux was talking. Despite the cold, he broke out in a sweat from the effort of restraining himself from beating the living daylights out of the little swine. He could sense that he was waiting for him to do just that.

'I wouldn't like to be in your shoes either.'

Mahl took to his heels and fled to his hut.

During the daytime, it was forbidden to lie down on the beds on pain of punishment. Under the disapproving gaze of his companions, who were sitting round the stove or playing cards on a blanket on the floor, he lay down and closed his eyes.

Adrien Delmas slowly closed the book he was reading, removed his glasses, rose from his chair and went over to the man lying on the bed, prompted by a sudden impulse.

Raphaël's legs were twitching and he clutched the sides of the bed. His chest heaved and his pale face was blotchy. The priest drew near.

A sour smell came from the bed, the same smell that he had

noticed on the breath of certain prisoners in Spain on the eve of their execution: the smell of fear. What had they said to him? What had they threatened him with? In the eight days that they had been sharing a hut, Father Adrien had never seen him in such a state.

'Are you ill? Do you need anything?'

He shook his head and opened his eyes, but shut them again at once.

If only he would go away! Another word and he would call the gendarme on duty and ask him to fetch the director and denounce him. It was up to him whether he lived or died. This thought gave him a slight erection. He had noticed that every time he held a destructive power over somebody, his penis stiffened. Oddly, although he was a deeply perverse character, he had never thought of exploiting that fantasy and had always considered the tension in his penis with amused detachment.

He had only taken advantage on five or six occasions of the fear he aroused in young boys who were just beginning their careers as male prostitutes in Montmartre clubs, to force them to humour whims which seemed fairly banal to him. Once, in the seminary where he had spent several years, he had forced a younger boy to suck him in exchange for his keeping quiet about the boy's reading forbidden literature. At that time he had felt a mixture of attraction and repulsion for clergymen: he wanted to be one of them and at the same time, he tried to lead them astray with words and deeds that were so sly that it took years for the abbot to discover what he was up to and expel him. That abbot was rather like Adrien Delmas at the time when he used to preach at Notre-Dame: he was the same height, tall and strong, that same look that seems to see right into your soul, a beautiful voice and large hands . . . Raphaël could sense the presence of the priest. For God's sake! If only he'd go away!

'Can I help you?'

'Leave me alone!' he shouted.

The room fell silent. Taking no notice, Adrien continued in a low voice:

'I think I know what's troubling you . . . I shall say nothing of what could be said in such a situation . . . I shan't say a word

333

except that, whatever you do, I'll forgive you and that, overwhelmed by doubts as I am, I shall pray for you.'

Raphaël sat up and grabbed the collar of the bogus farmer's
shirt, hissing in his face:

'Shup up, you filthy monk . . . you can shove your for-
giveness and your prayers up your arse.'

'Control yourself, everyone is looking at us.'

'Let the miserable buggers look at us!'

'Be quiet, otherwise you're going to have a rough time of it.'

'Let them come . . . come on, come on my beauties, come
and see the old queen . . . I'll fuck the lot of you . . .'

Two of them rose.

Raphaël did not see the blow coming as it crushed his nose,
nor did he see the blow that knocked him out.

When he came to, the priest was cleaning up his face.

'Not you again,' he said wearily.

'Get some rest. You're going to be taken to the infirmary.'

'Is it really necessary? I'm sorry, I was ridiculous earlier.
I'd just had some bad news.'

In the fight, Raphaël Mahl's nose had been broken and one of
his shoulders dislocated. He was in the infirmary when Maurice Fiaux, accompanied by Mathias Fayard, came to see him.
They were each carrying a box of books.

'Here are your books.'

'Thank you.'

'Rousseau tells me you got beaten up and if it weren't for
some tough peasant chap, you'd have been a goner.'

'Don't exaggerate.'

'Found out anything new?'

'Not much. They've smuggled in a wireless set into
barracks 3, and they listen to London every evening. The
communists in the camp have got together and are passing a
clandestine newspaper around.'

'Have you managed to get hold of a copy?'

'Yes, there, in my jacket pocket.'

Fiaux took a stencilled sheet out of the pocket and ran his
eye over it.

'Still the same rubbish! Nothing else?'

'No. I haven't come across any members of the Resistance yet, only a few minor characters. You ought to be looking in Fort Hâ.'

'You're quite sure you're not keeping anything from us? The boss thinks you're not coming clean with us.'

'What would be the point of keeping things back if I've agreed to collaborate with you? I can't invent a Resistance leader for you.'

'And yet the rumours continue. You're going to have some company: Marcel Rigaux and Fernando Rodriguez . . . Those names don't ring a bell? You shared the same cell in Fort Hâ.'

Raphaël shuddered.

'Don't leave me here, chaps.'

Fiaux pretended not to hear. The visitors soon left. Mathias Fayard had not opened his mouth. It was supper time, and already dark outside.

Mahl went back to his barracks.

The first two people he set eyes on were Rigaux and Rodriguez. Rigaux was coming towards him.

'Hello Mahl, we didn't think we'd bump into you here.'

The door suddenly opened. The director of the camp came in with Dohse and a dozen soldiers who aimed their guns at the prisoners.

'Gentlemen, Lieutenant Dohse wants to speak to you.'

'Thank you, director. Gentlemen, I shall be brief. We know that a dangerous terrorist is hiding in your midst. It is your duty to unmask him, is it not? Otherwise, we shall have no alternative but to take hostages. I hope I have made myself clear. You have got three days. After that, we shall shoot five hostages every two days. Goodnight and . . . enjoy your dinner, gentlemen.'

A heavy silence fell over the room after the Germans and Rousseau had left. It was broken by the arrival of the soup trolley. For once, there was no jostling around the orderlies whose job it was to dish out the broth. Nobody complained about the quality or joked about the ingredients. Everyone sat in their own corner and ate in silence. At the end of the meal, Marcel Rigaux and Fernando Rodrigeuz gathered a small group of prisoners around them.

Raphaël did not take his eyes off Adrien. He knew a terrible conflict was taking place in the priest's heart: should he give himself up to prevent the execution of innocent hostages? Open himself to the risk of talking under torture? Mahl knew that in his shoes, he would not move; his own skin was more important than that of those wretches locked up with him. Let them die. Besides, what use were they? One wondered.

The two men's eyes met. 'Don't say anything,' was the message in Raphaël's. 'Denounce me,' begged Adrien's.

The writer rose and went over to him. He tripped over a foot that someone stuck out in his path. A kick in the chin righted him again and another kick in the behind made him fall flat on his stomach in the centre aisle. His head caught the rough partition and his forehead was scratched. Rodriguez seized his arm . . . Raphaël yelled . . . the pain in his dislocated shoulder was like a red hot poker . . .

'Shut up, you poofter!'

'You're as soft as a woman!'

A blow in the stomach made him double up . . .

'Gentlemen . . . gentlemen . . . stop it . . .'

'You keep out of this, old man.'

'Why are you beating him? I have a right to know.'

'All right,' said Marcel Rigaux, 'we'll tell you why we're going to slaughter him like a pig. We were in the same cell in Fort Hâ . . . we had a good mate, a sailor, from Brittany, Loïc his name was. Ask this swine what little Loïc was like . . . Thanks to him, prison didn't seem so bad . . . always trying to make us laugh, a song to cheer us up, and as well as that . . .'

Rigaux's eyes were full of tears. His fist shot out and smashed Mahl's injured nose . . . blood spurted over the priest.

Rigaux went on:

'. . . he had a heart of gold . . . shared everything he had . . . comforted us . . . cared for us . . . As for this one here, whom you're trying to protect . . . the kid looked after him . . . watched over him . . . and he . . . he squealed on him, he squealed to the Gestapo.'

Everyone in the room groaned.

'Three days, three days he was tortured in Le Bouscat . . .'

Adrien Delmas looked at the crumpled body in horror.

'In prison he'd learned a lot, but he didn't talk . . . they drove red not needles under his nails . . . ripped the skin off his thighs and put salt on the raw flesh . . . broke his legs with blows . . .'

'Stop it!' screamed Raphaël.

Rodriguez pulled him up by his pullover and banged his head against a partition.

'Why? Why did you do that?'

'How did you find out?' he stammered.

'We'll tell you, just so you know there are some who are as base as you. It was one of your chums, a tall handsome fellow, who told us you were a grass when he was driving us here. And he told us it was you who squealed on Loïc and other lads, and that you were carrying on your dirty work here.'

'But why?'

'He doesn't think you're any use to them any more, now that you've denounced everyone you could.'

Raphaël Mahl suddenly felt a great weariness. He wished he could end it all. Poor fools, like him they were being screwed, manipulated by a little bastard like Maurice Fiaux. He was sure it was his idea: throw him to the prisoners and let them finish him off. Good old Maurice! He was pretty smart as bastards went. He wasn't so bad himself: he had managed to convince him that there were no Resistance leaders in the camp. Nice work. That made him smile.

'What's more, he's taking the piss out of us!'

'Swine!'

'Bastard!'

Blows rained on him from all sides.

Soon, there was nothing left of his face. Several times, Adrien Delmas tried to intervene. But hatred made the mob deaf. Someone knocked him out . . . when he came to, there was a smell of burning flesh. Above the guffaws and shouts, a long scream could be heard . . . the priest rose . . . sitting on the stove, held down by dozens of hands, Raphaël Mahl was being grilled . . . while they tortured him, some provided a lewd running commentary.

'Look how he's wriggling . . . he's enjoying it!'

'He's coming, the bastard, listen to him yell!'

'It would have been better if we'd stuck a red hot poker up his arse.'

'What an end for a pansy! Paradise!'

'Yes, but doesn't the flesh of a homo stink!'

'It's not his flesh that stinks, it's his shit, he's shitted all over the place.'

'Don't worry, now he's finished shitting and he's finished getting up everyone's arse.'

The horror of what he saw unleashed Father Delmas's strength. He pushed past the torturers and dragged Mahl from the stove. A piece of flesh remained stuck to the burning hotplate. They rolled at the feet of the crowd which parted. There was a moment of silence. Raphaël, lying in Adrien's arms, opened one eye and what was left of his mouth tried to form a smile that turned into a grimace. His massacred face was a dreadful sight. He tried to speak and a clot of blood dribbled down his chin.

'Don't say anything.'

'It's too bad . . . I had a good idea . . . for a novel,' he managed to utter.

There was admiration in Adrien's astonished expression as he looked at the man who had dreamed of becoming a great writer and who, on the brink of an atrocious death, found the strength to joke.

'Tell . . . Léa . . . that I . . . was . . . very fond of her.'

'I will.'

'Get out of the way and let us finish the bastard off.'

'Please! Leave him alone! Haven't you done enough damage already?'

'No,' said Fernando Rodriguez, snatching him out of the arms of his protector.

'No,' went on Fernando, 'let this be a lesson to all the squealers, to all those who collaborate, both here in the camp and outside. Come on lads, let's finish him off . . .'

All the men jumped on him . . . hands swarmed all over his body . . . faces pressed close to his . . . he could only make them out through a haze of blood . . . it was like a sort of mist . . . It reminded him of Amel's steam baths, the Mecca of

338

illicit pornography, where people sought each other out, touched and embraced. A terrific place where arms and hands were as moist as octopi . . . a descent into hell among these clusters of men . . . a single spasm shakes them, a single deep sigh which seems to rise from the very bowels of the earth to their trembling chests pressed so close together . . . There, loathsome unknown hands expertly pummelled his flesh trying to inflict pain . . . to kill him . . . Soon the images faded from his memory . . . only violent colours like electric shocks remained . . . a beautiful green, a lovely blue . . . red . . . black . . . silver stars quivered in the blackness . . . blackness . . . black.

In a corner of the barracks, a hand traced the sign of the cross.

The men were soon weary of beating the limp shapeless form that was still spattering them with blood. The body was a nuisance.

'Shall we put the pig's remains in the dustbins?'

'Good idea.'

During the night, Raphaël Mahl's body was thrown on to the rubbish tip and covered with refuse. At dawn, some prisoners were appointed to collect the body which was placed in a cheap coffin.

Neither the guards nor the gendarmes had budged.

Chapter 23

Two days after the murder of Raphaël Mahl, Adrien Delmas escaped thanks to his perfect knowledge of the camp and the guards' habits.

He slipped under the tarpaulin of the truck which came to deliver the week's supply of bread. The driver had been paid a fat sum to stop close to the spot where Adrien was hiding and pretend he had broken down. Once outside the camp, he was taken to Bègles, a suburb of Bordeaux, where Albert and Léa were waiting for him with three young Resistance fighters armed with submachine guns. They all squeezed into the butcher's old van.

'Father, a plane is coming to pick you up this evening,' said Albert.

'I don't want to leave. I must stay, I can be of more use here.'

'That's not what they think in London. If I were you, I'd go. At the moment you're in terrible danger and your presence in the area is a danger to all of us. Father, you must obey orders.'

Adrien held his tongue and closed his eyes. They all remained respectfully silent: he looked so weary. Léa, squashed beside him in the front of the van, laid her head on his shoulder and was soon asleep.

She awoke when they were driving across the strangely sloping square in Bazas. They drove past the cathedral of Saint-Jean and down to the old wash-house. They followed the road to Casteljalloux for a few hundred yards and then turned off to the right and stopped just before the little hamlet of Sauviac. An elderly couple came out of a low house with hens pecking about in front of it. Albert said a few words to them, they nodded agreement and went back into their house after signalling to the others to follow them.

'You'll be safe with the Laforgues, father. The plane will come to fetch you at eight o'clock this evening. The old man will take you to the landing strip near Beuve,' said Albert.

'I know the one.'

'Meanwhile, have a rest. I'll come back to fetch Léa this afternoon.'

'Thank you for everything, Albert. How is Mireille?'

'Well, thank you, father. She's a good woman, you know.'

'I know. Have you heard from your son?'

'He's in the Cantal region with the Revanche branch of the Resistance, near Chaudes-Aigues. The lads are hiding in the woods along the Tuyère. It's a good spot, difficult to attack. It's unlikely that the Jerries would venture there . . . I've got to go. Don't worry, father, you'll be back within a couple of months. Farewell.'

'Farewell, Albert. Will you take good care of Léa?'

'No need to ask. Madame Isabelle's daughter is sacred.'

Uncle and niece spent the day together, chatting by the fireside. They shared their silent hosts' humble meal. Carefully choosing his words, Adrien told Léa about Raphaël Mahl's horrible end. When he told Léa that his last words had been for her, she burst into tears.

'I was fond of him too,' she said.

The priest let her cry. When her grief had quietened down a little, she asked:

'But why didn't he denounce you?'

'I have no idea. I've been asking myself the same question ever since that dreadful night. Why didn't he denounce me? You knew him better than I, do you have any idea?'

'No . . . unless? . . . It's the sort of thing he'd do . . . He knew they were looking for you, perhaps they'd even asked him to identify you among the prisoners, and he refused just to be contrary.'

'But people don't allow themselves to be massacred just to be contrary!'

341

'Raphaël? Yes, he would.'

'Perhaps you're right after all. People's reasons for accepting death are sometimes so strange. But the look in his eye while they were beating him up! When his gaze met mine, he seemed to be saying: "You weren't expecting that, were you! I had you fooled all right."'

Léa found it hard to drag herself away from her uncle's embrace. She felt as if she were losing her father for the second time.

'Have a good Christmas, my darling. Go to midnight mass and say hello to Sainte-Exupérance for me. Give my love to everyone at Montillac and tell them I'm praying for them. God be with you . . . Take good care of yourself.'

How sad that Christmas was despite Charles's shouts of delight and laughter when he saw his new red car! As for New Year's Eve, it seemed to drag on interminably. Everyone was wondering if 1944 would see the end of the war at last.

On the 2nd January, Léa had a surprise when François Tavernier turned up out of the blue. His front-wheel drive was covered in mud and he looked as if he had been driving all night.

He hastily wished the household a happy new year, gave Charles a kiss and found a notebook in his pocket which he gave him. Charles was in seventh heaven. Then he led Léa into the study.

'I came as soon as I received your uncle's message. Why didn't you say anything about Mathias and his father?'

'I didn't want to bore you with all that.'

'You never bore me, and you know it. Come here, I haven't got much time and I have to leave this evening . . .'

'So soon! You're mad!'

'My time is not my own. I shouldn't be here.'

Léa locked the door of her father's study and threw herself into François's arms. They made love with their clothes on, in silence. Léa's moan broke into a sob.

They clung to each other for a long time.

Sleep was beginning to get the better of François and he was the first to speak.

'Go and make me some coffee.'

Léa went into the kitchen to heat up some coffee and cook some eggs. For two hours, François went through the accounts, the mortgage papers and the bank statements. He then explained to Léa in detail how all that could be falsified and fixed. He knew that the estate was virtually in Fayard's hands but said nothing to Léa.

'The situation isn't exactly rosy. First, you need a good accountant to sort all this out. I'll find you one.'

'But I haven't got any money!'

'Please, don't worry about that. I'll take care of it. Here's a cheque. That'll pacify your bank manager for a while. We must keep Mathias away at all costs. He's absorbed in his work, but he'll soon go into action. Now, my love, I have to go. Please, I beg you, no tears. It's the memory of your smile I want to take away with me.'

He rose and she gave him one last kiss, caressing his rough, unshaven cheek.

Léa and François went outside. His car was parked in front of the house in the drive lined with plane trees. Dusk was gathering and the vineyards and pine woods were fading into the darkness.

He was going to drive all night to reach Paris. The weather was mild for the time of year, but Léa shivered. The idea of being alone with Camille frightened her. He had been so light-hearted, so gentle as he juggled the figures that she had not realized how painful it would be to see him go.

Little Charles was glued to the glass hall door, his nose squashed against the pane; he waved eagerly to François. Tavernier turned round one last time and gave him a military salute. Laughing, Charles jumped for joy. They could not hear his laugh through the glass.

Léa drew her shawl tighter round her. The vines needed clearing.

François took her hand and gave it a quick kiss, as if he would be returning in a few moments. He had not stopped smiling. He slid behind the wheel and slammed the door. The noise resounded in the evening silence. He revved up the engine without taking his eyes off Léa.

As he left, he wound down the window and shouted:

'I think it would be advisable for you to come and live with me.'

The car drove down the gravel drive, paused when it reached the road and disappeared into the night.

Léa stood rooted to the spot.